THE LOST STARS

PERILOUS SHIELD

THE LOST STARS

PERILOUS SHIELD

JACK CAMPBELL

ACE BOOKS, NEW YORK

THE BERKLEY PUBLISHING GROUP
Published by the Penguin Group
Penguin Group (USA) LLC
375 Hudson Street, New York, New York 10014

USA I Canada I UK I Ireland I Australia I New Zealand I India I South Africa I China

penguin.com

A Penguin Random House Company

This book is an original publication of The Berkley Publishing Group.

Ace Books are published by The Berkley Publishing Group.
ACE and the "A" design are trademarks of Penguin Group (USA) LLC.

Library of Congress Cataloging-in-Publication Data

Campbell, Jack (Naval officer)
The Lost stars : perilous shield / Jack Campbell. — First Edition.
pages cm. — (The Lost stars ; Book 2)
ISBN 978-0-425-25631-2 (hardcover)
1. Space warfare—Fiction. 2. Imaginary wars and battles—Fiction. 3. Science fiction. I. Title.
PS3553.A4637L67 2013
813'.54—dc23
2013010872

FIRST EDITION: October 2013

PRINTED IN THE UNITED STATES OF AMERICA

10 9 8 7 6 5 4 3 2 1

Cover illustration © Craig White.
Cover photographs © Mr Twister / Shutterstock; © Eky Studio / Shutterstock.
Cover design by Judith Lagerman.
Interior text design by Laura K. Corless.

To Mary Hughes Gaudreau,
for all the good you strive to do in the world,
and for being such a long-standing
and excellent friend to the Indomitable S.

For S., as always.

ACKNOWLEDGMENTS

I remain indebted to my agent, Joshua Bilmes, for his ever-inspired suggestions and assistance, and to my editor, Anne Sowards, for her support and editing. Thanks also to Catherine Asaro, Robert Chase, J. G. (Huck) Huckenpohler, Simcha Kuritzky, Michael LaViolette, Aly Parsons, Bud Sparhawk, and Constance A. Warner for their suggestions, comments, and recommendations. Thanks also to Charles Petit for his suggestions about space engagements.

THE MIDWAY FLOTILLA

Kommodor Asima Marphissa, commanding
(all ships are former Syndicate Worlds mobile forces units)

ONE BATTLESHIP
Midway (not yet operational)

FOUR HEAVY CRUISERS
Manticore, Gryphon, Basilisk, and *Kraken*

SIX LIGHT CRUISERS
Falcon, Osprey, Hawk, Harrier, Kite, and *Eagle*

TWELVE HUNTER-KILLERS
Sentry, Sentinel, Scout, Defender, Guardian, Pathfinder, Protector, Patrol, Guide, Vanguard, Picket, and *Watch*

Ranks in the Midway Flotilla (in descending order), as established by President Iceni

Kommodor
Kapitan First Rank
Kapitan Second Rank
Kapitan Third Rank
Kapitan-Leytenant
Leytenant
Leytenant Second Rank
Ships Officer

THIS day hadn't started out badly, but now it looked very much as if one of the next few days would end with him dead. The most important questions General Artur Drakon still faced were exactly who would pull the trigger, exactly when it would happen, and how many other people would die along with him.

"Two hundred twenty-two alien warships," Colonel Bran Malin reported with an impressive show of calm. Above and behind Malin, the planetary command center's main display portrayed the entire Midway Star System and every ship within it in depressingly accurate detail. The warships of the alien enigma race were four and a half light-hours distant, having arrived at the jump point from the star Pele, which had been occupied by the aliens decades ago. "We face overwhelming odds even if the Syndicate flotilla commanded by CEO Boyens joins with our forces."

Our forces. Drakon focused on the depictions of those for a moment, trying not to let his gloom show outwardly. Many workers were at their control consoles in the command center, all of them supposedly focused on their work, but all of them certainly watching him for the first sign of panic or even uncertainty.

Near this planet orbited the main body of the grandly named "Midway Flotilla." Two heavy cruisers, four light cruisers, and twelve small Hunter-Killers. A pitiful force by the standards of the recent war between the Syndicate Worlds and the Alliance, but Syndicate losses had been so heavy in the last part of the war that this now ranked as a decent-sized flotilla within the territory where the authority of the Syndicate Worlds once ran unchallenged. About a light-hour distant, at the space dock orbiting a gas-giant planet, were a battleship and two more heavy cruisers. That looked more impressive, except for the fact that the recently constructed and recently named battleship *Midway* (recently stolen from a Syndicate-controlled dockyard at the star Kane, where it was being outfitted) did not yet have any working weapons.

"They're not really *our* forces," Drakon said to Malin. "The Kommodor in charge of the Midway Flotilla answers to President Iceni." She might call herself President now, but a few months ago Gwen Iceni had been a Syndicate CEO, just as Drakon had also once been. "We banded together out of necessity to overthrow the authority of the Syndicate Worlds in this star system before the Syndicate could order our deaths, but you know how little we can afford to trust each other."

"President Iceni has not double-crossed you," Colonel Malin pointed out.

"Yet. You know the words used in the Syndicate for CEOs who trust other CEOs. Stupid. Betrayed. Dead. Are you sure she hasn't tried to call Boyens and make a deal for herself?" The Syndicate flotilla controlled by CEO Boyens consisted of a battleship, six heavy cruisers, four light cruisers, and ten HuKs. The Midway Flotilla had faced a desperate and probably hopeless fight against that force until the aliens called enigmas had shown up in overwhelming numbers to menace all humans in this star system.

"Absolutely certain, General. If you and President Iceni can barely trust each other, neither of you is likely to trust CEO Boyens to honor any deal he agreed to," Malin insisted. "Even if Boyens wanted to play it straight, the snakes with his flotilla would demand that both you and Iceni die for your leadership roles in the revolt."

He could see the humor in that. "I have the Syndicate Internal Security Service to thank for being certain that Iceni won't betray me to Boyens. That's the first time the snakes ever made me feel more secure."

"Yes, sir. But Boyens and his flotilla are a relatively minor problem at the moment. It is possible that he will agree to a proposal from you and President Iceni that he join forces with us against the enigmas."

Drakon shook his head. "No, he won't. There's no percentage for Boyens in joining with us. He came here under Syndicate orders to defeat us and retake this star system, but now that the enigmas have shown up, every human at Midway is very likely doomed. Why should he die fighting a hopeless battle trying to save us?"

"He won't," President Gwen Iceni answered as she walked up to Drakon, her every movement and tone of voice carefully controlled to portray a calm confidence that in a lesser person would have seemed ridiculous under these circumstances.

But, Drakon admitted to himself, Iceni could carry it off.

"CEO Boyens," Iceni continued, "is a practical man. There is no hope for us there," she added in a matter-of-fact way at odds with her words.

Drakon turned to Iceni. "You've talked to the enigmas in the past. Is there any chance of a deal with them?"

Iceni shook her head, her own expression calculating rather than fearful. Like Drakon, she knew that it was critically important for leaders not to show fear. A display of fear communicated weakness, and in the Syndicate system, weak CEOs became targets for those under them. Workers might panic if they saw their leaders openly afraid, or senior subordinates might decide an assassination-driven change in leaders might improve their own chances of survival, or believing the situation to be hopeless, the workers themselves might rise up and wreak last-ditch revenge on their leaders for past suffering.

"The enigmas," Iceni continued, "don't talk *with* us, they talk *to* us. When they deign to speak to us, they make demands and never respond to anything except agreement. I would be very surprised if they even bother communicating with us this time before they kill us."

"Is this Black Jack's fault? Did he stir up the enigmas like we feared?"

"It's possible." Her gaze went to the main display floating in the middle of the command center. "Black Jack did promise to defend this star system against the enigmas."

"I don't see Black Jack's fleet," Drakon replied, his voice harsh, "and I don't think the enigmas will be impressed by our telling them that we've got that promise. Black Jack took the Alliance fleet into enigma territory, raised hell, very likely got blown to pieces, and now the enigmas are here to finish the job they wanted to do several months ago."

He didn't bother adding that, unlike that previous time, on this occasion the Alliance fleet under the command of the legendary Admiral John "Black Jack" Geary wasn't here to stop the enigmas. Until about a year ago, Geary had been thought dead for the last century, but he had reappeared to wreak havoc on the forces of the Syndicate Worlds and compel an end to the war everyone had resigned themselves to believing to be unending. In the process, Geary had also shattered any claim by the Syndicate government to be representing a superior system and annihilated the great majority of the Syndicate warships that had been a major factor in ensuring Syndicate control of the planets under their rule.

But Geary had taken his fleet into enigma territory to try to learn more about the first alien intelligent race encountered by humanity. No Syndicate incursion into enigma space had ever returned.

"The situation . . ." Iceni paused before continuing in a thoughtful tone "is difficult."

"Very difficult," Drakon agreed, surprised that he could let a trace of dry humor into his own voice at such a time. *Damn, she's impressive.* "All of my ground forces in this star system are coming to full combat status, but none of them stand a chance against the enigmas if the aliens bombard us from orbit."

"All of my mobile forces are also being brought to full combat alert," Iceni informed him. "Those at the gas giant saw the arrival of the enigmas an hour before we did, and we just received the status update from them. They are as ready as they can be."

"Too bad we didn't have time to get that battleship operational."

"Yes," Iceni said. "It would have been useful," she added in a masterpiece of understatement. "There's only one thing left to do besides trying to bluff the enigmas, and that is trying to arrange a truce with the Syndicate force."

"You just agreed with me that Boyens wouldn't fight alongside us," Drakon said bluntly.

"I said truce, not merger. Our very slim chance of bluffing the enigmas into leaving will be improved slightly if Boyens appears to be part of the defensive force instead of another invader. And Boyens has reason to assist us in that bluff. His masters on Prime want this star system back. If the enigmas take it, or destroy it, Boyens will not have succeeded in his mission." One side of her mouth curved in a humorless half smile. "As you and I both know from painful experience, the Syndicate government won't let the fact that it is impossible for Boyens to succeed in the face of the enigmas influence their decision that he failed, nor will it mitigate the punishment they mete out for that failure."

Colonel Roh Morgan had arrived while Iceni and Drakon spoke, and now saluted Drakon. Morgan's eyes glinted with a strange light, as if the prospect of a desperate fight excited her. "Colonels Rogero, Gaiene, and Kai report their brigades are ready for action and are stiffening the locals."

Drakon nodded, his mouth twisting in annoyance. "The locals are nervous, I suppose."

"It's not like there's anywhere to run," Morgan said. She stepped close to Drakon, so close they almost touched. Her voice came out whisper-soft yet still clear despite the background noise in the command center. "Nowhere for *them* to run. I have a special forces shuttle standing by. Full stealth configuration. We can lift without being spotted and be boarding one of the heavy cruisers in orbit within half an hour while decoy comms make everyone think you're in the ground forces headquarters."

He frowned, thrown off momentarily by her nearness and the memories Morgan's body aroused of a drunken night he wished had never happened. But it only took a moment to shake that and focus on her words. "Leave the rest?" he asked in the same quiet tones. A glance at the readouts on his wrist confirmed what he had suspected, that Morgan had personal jammers active that were blocking anyone else, even those nearby, from hearing what they were saying.

"Sorry about leaving Gaiene and Kai," Morgan said in tones that held no trace of actual regret. "But we can't take anyone else without tipping off what we're doing."

She hadn't mentioned Rogero or Malin, of course, neither of whom ranked high in Morgan's opinion. Drakon eyed her, knowing the rest of Morgan's plan without its having to be spelled out. He had, after all, made his own way up the ranks of the Syndicate hierarchy and learned the lessons that had to be picked up along the way. He and Morgan would hijack the heavy cruiser and head for a jump point, leaving everyone else here to fight against impossible odds. With that heavy cruiser's firepower, they might be able to establish control of some other, weaker, star system.

And everyone else at Midway would die, or whatever the fate was of those the enigmas captured. No one had ever learned what happened to humans who had fallen into the hands of the aliens.

"No," Drakon said, his eyes returning to the situation display and the enemy forces arrayed there.

Morgan sighed with exasperation. "All right. We can take Malin, too."

She probably thought that was a major concession given the level of mutual hatred between Malin and Morgan. But Drakon shook his head. "That's not the point." How to explain it in a way that Morgan would accept, when even he didn't fully understand his own reluctance to do what Syndicate CEOs were taught to do in a crisis? "I know the rule in a situation like this is to throw as many subordinates to the wolves as necessary. But I don't abandon people. You know that. That's how I ended up exiled to Midway." *And I guess that may be why I die here.*

Morgan leaned a little closer, her face almost touching his now, eyes blazing. "It is important that you and I survive. We can set up business elsewhere and come back here someday with enough fire-power to retake this star system and avenge—"

"I'm not interested in avenging people I left to their fates."

"You didn't get to be a Syndicate CEO by making looking out for other people your first priority, General. We *both* know that."

Drakon shook his head stubbornly. "I also know that if I leave here first, before President Iceni does, I'll look weaker than her. I'll also leave her in control of this planet and this star system." That was the sort of logic even Morgan could accept.

Morgan paused, her eyes going to Iceni. "Maybe you won't leave first. Maybe she's halfway out the door."

Drakon glanced that way, seeing Iceni locked in close conversation with her personal assistant/bodyguard/assassin Mehmet Togo. Both Iceni and Togo had moved a few steps away. Drakon didn't need a scanner to be certain that their conversation was also being protected by personal jammers.

"Iceni is planning her own escape," Morgan whispered. "Watch. She'll bolt out of here with some lame excuse and head for a shuttle. I've got snipers posted. We can nail her before she reaches the launch area."

Drakon frowned though he kept facing toward the display and not Iceni. *"No."*

The force of that reply earned him a searching glance from Morgan. "Why not? Is there some . . . personal reason?"

"Of course not," Drakon snapped back at her. He had gotten to know Iceni a lot better, had been able to learn more about the person behind the once-CEO and now-President, and he had found himself both having more (probably irrational) faith in her and enjoying their meetings. But none of those things were influencing him now. He was certain of that. "We need Iceni. If we get through this somehow, we need her control of the warships."

"Once the enigmas are done here, there won't be any warships," Morgan pointed out. "Except theirs."

"Stand down the snipers immediately. I don't want any accidents."

"You need to—"

"I need to have my orders obeyed, Colonel Morgan!"

That might have been too loud for even the personal jammers to completely mask. No one actually looked toward Drakon and Morgan, because everyone in this command center knew better than to appear as if they were aware of any arguments among superiors, but he could sense a stiffening among those nearest, as if they were trying very hard to overcome the natural impulse to glance at the sound of rising voices.

Colonel Malin, normally very sensitive to Drakon's moods, now seemed totally absorbed in his own work. As much as he disliked Morgan, he also knew better than to let Drakon see him taking any interest or pleasure in her being chewed out.

Drakon took a long, slow breath before speaking again, not looking at Morgan's furious eyes, gazing out of a face gone stone-cold. "I have my reasons. I always have my reasons for taking a chance on someone."

He knew she would catch the reference. Morgan herself, judged barely stable enough for duty after a disastrous mission into enigma space, had been turned down by every other commanding officer until Drakon gave her an opportunity.

The fury in Morgan flickered, and her mouth twitched, then she abruptly went back into projecting jaded amusement. "Sometimes that might work out. But I'm one of a kind, General."

Fortunately, Drakon thought. *Could the universe handle more than one Roh Morgan?* "Get the snipers stood down and work with Rogero, Kai, and Gaiene to get forces deployed to defend against a landing. We've got plenty of time to get people dispersed and dug in. Maybe the enigmas will sit in orbit and bombard us to hell, but if the enigmas want this planet in any shape for them to use, they'll have to come down here and take it from us. I intend making sure the price they pay will be one they remember."

Morgan grinned wolfishly and tapped the sidearm holstered at her hip. "If they do come down here, I can look one in the eyes as I nail it."

"And as it nails you," Malin said.

"It's been tried," Morgan replied, her tone teasing now. "Unsuccessfully."

Malin didn't flinch at the reference to an incident on an orbital platform in which his shot had narrowly missed Morgan before nailing an enemy. That incident had looked to Drakon all too much like an attempt to kill Morgan under cover of a firefight, but Malin had insisted otherwise, and the shot had killed a dangerous opponent.

Malin looked back at Morgan for a moment, his expression unreadable. "Perhaps you will die in enigma-controlled space after all."

"You sound unhappy at the idea."

"You're imagining things," Malin said, then turned to his display.

Drakon studied the display grimly as Morgan left to carry out his orders. Hopefully all of his orders. "Colonel Malin, ensure that none of our personnel are on any kind of alert status near this installation."

"I'll check on it, General. If there are any nearby, what am I to do?"

"Ensure that they're stood down and returned to their units." If only Morgan weren't so valuable as an assistant. But then, the more valuable people were, the more difficult they seemed to be to live with. Drakon had seen a number of CEOs who got rid of anyone who was hard to live with and instead surrounded themselves with people who caused no drama or problems at all. No problems at all, except for letting the CEOs in question go down in flames through sheer ineptitude, lack of initiative, lack of imagination, and/or lack of brains. Neither Malin nor Morgan was an easy subordinate, but they had bailed him out more than once in situations where kowtowing, compliant assistants would have been overmatched. "How is internal security going? Have the citizens figured out what's happening?"

"Word is spreading rapidly," Malin said, "but so far the citizens are not panicking." He looked thoughtful. "This may seem an inopportune time to mention the upcoming elections that you and President Iceni have allowed to go forward for low-level political positions—"

"It's a damned inopportune time," Drakon broke in roughly.

"But, General, you should be aware that a substantial number of the candidates for office have contacted local appointed authorities and asked if they can assist in keeping the citizens calm."

Drakon frowned in surprise. "They're taking responsibility for that? Even though they haven't been elected yet and may not be elected?"

"Apparently," Malin said, "many of the individuals running for office have already been playing leadership roles among the citizens though in underground, unauthorized ways. The opportunity to participate in real elections has convinced the people who are unofficial leaders to come out into the open."

"I should have expected that," Drakon said. Just how "real" the elections would actually be was a matter he and Iceni were still debating, but even the maximum level of vote manipulation being considered by them was a pale shadow of the total farce that Syndicate elections had been.

But it seemed that offering the citizens a real buy-in to the government, even if a low-level one, had already produced some benefits.

Drakon bent his head, thinking. "Make sure we keep track of everyone who offers to help and check back after this is over to see how successful they were." Odds were that after this was over, they would all be dead, but it never hurt to plan for the future even when that seemed insanely optimistic.

Out of the corner of his eye, Drakon could see Togo backing away from Iceni, an uncharacteristic amount of unhappiness visible on Togo's normally impassive face. But, unhappy or not, Togo nodded in acknowledgment of some instruction and left the command center.

Iceni looked around, focused on Drakon and walked briskly back over to him. He admired the walk, and not just because Iceni had the sort of walk any man would enjoy watching. She also knew exactly how to pace it. Just fast enough to communicate urgency and control but not so fast as to give the impression of fear or worry about being able to handle whatever happened.

She stopped near him, still radiating apparent confidence but her eyes questioning. "Will you be staying at the command center, General?"

"Yes. Are you going to stay, too, or are you planning on restructuring your business model?" It was an old joke, perhaps as old as the Syndicate Worlds, a semipolite way of asking if someone was preparing to abandon former partners and cut their losses.

Iceni's gaze on him didn't waver. "I think I will stay. Restructuring doesn't seem like the most profitable option at the moment."

"But staying does?" Drakon asked. "That's an odd business plan."

"I'm not running a business," Iceni said, her voice growing harder. "I'm responsible for . . . many other things. This is the best place to monitor events and pass on orders to Kommodor Marphissa as our warships defend this star system." Iceni looked toward the display as if the situation shown there were, if not favorable, at least survivable.

Drakon took one step closer and spoke quietly. "Careful. You're very good, but if you look too confident in the face of this, the workers might think you're insane."

"I want them to think I have a secret weapon in reserve," Iceni replied in the same low tones.

"Do you?"

"No. How about you, General?"

Was she telling the truth? "None that I know of. The only rational thing to do is something neither of us seems to be doing."

Iceni glanced his way. "I have my reasons. What's your reason?"

He paused. "We made a deal."

That actually brought a brief, mocking smile to her lips. "Even you can't believe that's your rationale for staying. But, feel free to claim that if you want. Isn't that what you told me just before we overthrew Syndicate authority here?"

"Something like that," Drakon conceded. "Even if I bolted right now, getting away wouldn't be easy or guaranteed. I'd rather not die running away."

"Having learned what I have about you, that's a reason I can believe," Iceni said. "I assume that you have been urged to try to escape anyway?"

"You assume correctly. I think you and I have disappointed some of our subordinates, Gwen." He let down his guard with that statement, but what the hell. If she was going to betray him, she already had plenty of knowledge of him to use as ammunition.

She smiled again for a moment. "It's just as well the people who work for us don't start thinking that they can call the shots, isn't it?" The smile faded as Iceni pointed at the display with one forefinger. "Where do you think the enigmas will go first?"

"If it were me, I'd head for the hypernet gate. They have to be worried about that now that we know how much damage one of those gates can do when it collapses." Drakon nodded again, this time slowly. "You know, we do have a secret weapon. Maybe not so secret, but it's nasty enough that even though we may lose here, we can make sure they don't win."

"Collapse the hypernet gate?" Iceni asked as casually as if Drakon had commented on the weather. She raised her hand, tapping one of the bracelets about her wrist. "I can send the command any time I want to."

"I know."

"Of course you did. I know that you're thorough, and finding out whether I could do that would have been an obvious thing to check on before we even started our rebellion." Iceni lowered her arm. "The command will disable the safe-collapse system and cause a collapse of the gate that generates the maximum-level burst of energy. About point seven nova-scale, I was told by the technicians who did the work."

There wouldn't be very much left at Midway if a point seven nova-scale burst of energy rampaged through the star system. The planets might remain, but scoured of their atmospheres and with ravaged surfaces. The star would be badly disrupted. Asteroids and comets would be vaporized or hurled into the darkness between stars.

Nothing human would survive.

But nothing belonging to the enigmas would survive, either.

"Do you think they'd believe us if we threatened them with that?" Drakon asked. "Get out now, or we destroy everything?"

"I'm sure they would believe us capable of carrying out such a threat," Iceni said. "We are human, after all, and humans do things like that when our backs are to the wall. But the enigmas may be able to stop us from carrying out that threat. The information the Alliance gave us, which implied the gates were originally enigma technology deliberately leaked to us, would mean the enigmas know more about the gates than we do. We've learned how to stop the enigmas from collapsing the gates and destroying human-occupied star systems, but they may still have a backdoor means to halt us from doing the same thing."

It felt odd, Drakon thought. This was a crisis situation. He could see the enigma attack fleet and the Syndicate flotilla as well as the mobile forces under the command of Iceni. Yet the opposing forces were light-hours distant. What he was seeing of the enigmas was what they had been doing four and a half hours ago. And no matter what they were doing now, it would take days for any forces to come into contact. "It can't hurt to try to bluff the enigmas." If Iceni *was* talking about a bluff rather than a cold-blooded plan to ensure mutual destruction if the enigmas were on the verge of wiping out the humans here.

"How far do you think can we trust CEO Boyens?" she asked.

"We both know Boyens." Drakon held up one hand, the forefinger and thumb barely a centimeter apart. "We can trust him about that far, in my opinion."

"He does some have some good qualities."

"And right now those qualities are focused on riding the waves of change rolling across Syndicate-controlled space so that he ends up alive, afloat, and adorned with high rank."

Iceni cocked her head slightly to one side as she thought. "That leaves room to appeal to his self-interest."

"It does," Drakon agreed. "What do we offer him?"

"We will submit this star system to his control without resistance or damage to any facilities as long as he works with us against the enigmas."

"He'll never believe it. Boyens knows we'd never keep such an agreement." Drakon frowned. "But it might be the best offer he can hope for with the enigmas here. Give it a try."

She made an exasperated sound. "We need more leverage. If only our battleship were operational. If only the battleship we captured at Taroa had been almost completed instead of being under construction."

"The Free Taroans weren't happy that we kept it," Drakon remarked. "Or that we kept the main orbiting docks at Taroa after we took them from the Syndicate."

"They'll have to live with it, though they're dragging their heels on getting us the supplies and workers we need to complete that ship."

Colonel Malin spoke with careful deference. "Madam President, if I may, what if we gave the battleship and ownership of a significant portion of those orbiting docks to the Free Taroans?"

Iceni had the look of someone who had heard something impossible to understand. "Why would we do that?"

"We need allies. We have Black Jack," Malin pointed out, "but he is distant, and so his help cannot be counted upon in a crisis. Taroa is close."

"Do you," Iceni asked, "have any conception of how much firepower a battleship carries? Of how much military capacity you are suggesting we offer to *give away*?"

Malin smiled thinly. "I have been on the receiving end of bombardments from Alliance battleships, Madam President. However, the battleship at Taroa has no military capacity and will not for some time. Its hull isn't complete. It is still not even able to leave the construction dock. Nor am I suggesting that we not ask for anything in return. The Free Taroans are already grateful for the military assistance our ground forces provided in defeating the Syndicate there. They are quibbling over the wording of mutual-defense agreements, though."

Drakon narrowed his eyes at Malin. "I imagine the Taroans would agree to just about any wording, to just about anything, in order to get their hands on that battleship."

"And then, rather than drag their heels, they would bend every effort to get the battleship completed and ready to fight as soon as possible," Malin agreed.

Iceni eyed them both, her eyes now hooded. "An interesting suggestion. We tie Taroa closer to us by playing on Taroa's desire for that battleship. Taroa invests the necessary resources into getting the battleship operational, thereby saving us the costs and effort. We gain a nearby ally who is even more grateful to us and committed to providing substantial support with a battleship that will be ready far sooner than if we try to do it all ourselves. A *very* interesting suggestion, Colonel. What if Taroa decides to betray us?"

Malin smiled. "We have complete access to the ship and will retain some access while it is being finished. There are many safeguards that can be covertly installed in the ship and its systems to ensure that any attempt to use it against us fails."

Their quiet discussion was interrupted by the subdued chime of an alert from the system display. "There's a shuttle lifting from this planet," one of the console operators reported. On the display, a symbol appeared with a graceful arc showing its projected path up into orbit. "It's not a scheduled lift, and all facilities were informed that lifts are not to occur during this alert period unless authorized from here."

Iceni's eyes hardened. "Who is aboard this shuttle?"

"They are reporting a routine cargo lift, normal crew, no passengers," another operator replied.

"A routine lift? When routine lifts have been ordered suspended?" Before Iceni could ask anything else, Togo had appeared again by her side.

"A regional governor cannot be accounted for," Togo said dispassionately. "Neither can his mistress. An industrial executive and her boyfriend are also not able to be located using planetary surveillance systems."

"Governor Beadal?" Iceni asked in a voice grown cold.

"Yes, Madam President. Perhaps he became aware of the investigations closing in on him, or perhaps he simply seeks to flee the enigmas despite orders for all executives to remain in place. The industrial executive is Magira Fillis, heavy construction office."

"She won't be missed." Iceni had her eyes on the track of the shuttle as it strained to clear atmosphere. "And Regional Governor Beadal's failures as an administrator leave me no reason to overlook his petty corruption and violation of a directive from me. But I hate to lose a shuttle."

Colonel Malin spoke up. "It's not ours. The shuttle is from one of the merchant ships in orbit. The ship is flagged to the Xavandi Group, but the executive in command of the freighter claims that it has gone rogue and is operating independently."

Iceni's gaze sharpened into that of a predator eyeing prey. "I never liked the CEOs heading up the Xavandi Group. It would be just like them to have a ship trading in violation of Syndicate government restrictions but pretending to be no longer answering to their control so they could pull in the profits but deny breaking government rules. I won't regret losing *their* shuttle. General?"

Drakon gave her a glance, wondering for a moment at the question. Assuming Iceni was right about that freighter, Xavandi Group wasn't that different from a lot of other Syndicate conglomerates. And the two executives riding on that shuttle weren't all that different from the worst of the Syndicate corporate weasels that Drakon had encountered in his time. "If you want to destroy the shuttle, you don't have to ask me."

"We reached an agreement a few hours ago," Iceni said, her voice brisk and businesslike as she discussed destroying the shuttle and the people on it. She had cut in the privacy field again to keep her words from being heard by anyone but Drakon. "No more assassinations of any kind unless we both agree. Arguably, this could be considered an assassination since the governor and executive involved will get neither chances to surrender nor trials."

Trials in the Syndicate system were just formalities to give a veneer of legitimacy to predetermined outcomes, but sometimes deals would be offered. Not this time. "Colonel Malin has already reported to me about Regional Governor Beadal's activities," Drakon said. "Some of his games caused supply trouble for one of my units." He hadn't heard anything about the industrial executive sharing Beadal's shuttle and wouldn't admit to that lack of knowledge, but Fallis's choice of companion was a pretty clear sign that she would have also been firing-squad bait at some point even if she hadn't tried to run. "We won't miss the shuttle."

"I'm glad we are in agreement," Iceni said, cutting off the privacy field. "Do I need to order one of the warships in orbit to deal with that shuttle?"

"No. Ground forces can handle it easily. Colonel Malin, order orbital defenses to eliminate that shuttle."

"Yes, sir." Malin entered three commands. *Target. Confirm. Fire.*

Somewhere else on the planet, a ground-based battery of particle beams locked onto the shuttle. Ground-based weapons could be very potent because of the amount of power they could draw on, but their range was still limited by the realities of space. The distances in space were so huge that the beams of the weapons spread over distance, the power being spread out as well, so that warships more than a few light-minutes distant could take the hits on their shields without much worry. But if anyone wanted to try landing on a planet, or wanted to conduct a precise bombardment from orbit, they would have to confront some nasty defenses. Since Midway had been facing the enigma threat for nearly a century now, its orbital defenses were substantially better than those of an average world.

The cargo shuttle still clawing its way toward orbit had weak shields, no armor, and was still inside atmosphere when the particle-beam battery fired. Multiple spears of charged particles tore the shuttle into pieces which flowered outward from the point of impact to fall back toward the vast oceans of the planet below. Those inside the shuttle never knew what had killed them.

But everyone on the planet would have been watching the shuttle lift and would know its fate.

"That should be the last attempt to flee positions of responsibility," Iceni said in a voice that carried through the command center. "I want every ship in this star system to be informed that if they change orbits or trajectories without specific approval from this command center or Kommodor Marphissa, that will be the last action they take."

"Yes, Madam President," the senior operations specialist in the command center replied, turning to immediately pass on that warning.

Iceni spoke to Togo in a quieter voice. "Ensure the investigation of Governor Beadal is continued. He is dead, but I want to know who else was working with him on his little schemes."

Drakon watched Togo leave again. He wondered if the mistress and the boyfriend had been aware of the risks they were running. Most likely, since there would have had to be a wild scramble to get to the shuttle. No one who had worked and lived under the Syndicate system could have been oblivious to the danger of disobeying a directive for executives to remain in place. The bribe offered to the shuttle pilot and crew must have been substantial to get them to risk a lift, but no one would be cashing any of those checks.

"Now that the distraction is dealt with, let's deal with the larger issues," Iceni said. "Communications. Give me a tight beam aimed at the path of the enigma force. I don't want CEO Boyens to also pick up the transmission and learn what we're saying to the enigmas."

"Madam CEO—" one of the specialists began out of long habit, then hastily checked himself. "Madam *President*. The beam will have to be directed to the point where the enigmas will be hours from now. But if the enigmas change their vectors significantly in the meantime, they will not be in the path of a tight beam. We can use a wider beam, which will offer a much higher chance that the enigma force will receive it, but keep it narrow enough that it will have no chance of being intercepted by the flotilla near the hypernet gate."

Iceni bent a stern look on the specialist while Drakon watched to see how she would handle this. For many CEOs, the only thing that counted was obedience. Suggestions for improvements on CEO orders could also be seen as criticisms of the original order. From what Drakon had seen of Kommodor Marphissa, promoted to her current position by Iceni, the President was willing to accept a rather high degree of independent thought in her subordinates. But was that simply because Marphissa had come from executive ranks or because she was a favorite of Iceni's?

"Your suggestion," Iceni began while specialists waited tensely throughout the command center, "is a good one. I appreciate such support when it is properly offered. Use the wider beam."

Moments later, the transmission ready to begin, Iceni activated the command and spoke to the alien invaders with clipped precision. "To those who have entered this star system without the authorization or approval of those who control this space, this is President Iceni. You are to leave. This is not your star. Go now. If you do not go, we will take any action needed to destroy you. The hypernet gate is here. We can make it destroy everything here. You cannot stop this. Go now. If we cannot defeat you by other means, we will destroy you along with ourselves. Go now. For the people, Iceni, out."

"I know they communicate with us in our own language, but how much do they really understand of statements like that?" Drakon asked.

"I don't know. No one does. But that's the sort of talking they do when communicating with us over video links using human-appearing avatars." Iceni breathed a small laugh. "Maybe Black Jack has learned how much the enigmas really understand human concepts. If he's not dead. Now, let's make our offer to CEO Boyens."

This time the beam was directed toward the flotilla hovering near the hypernet gate. "CEO Boyens, you have seen that we face a mutual enemy. You must stand with us. Together, we have a chance to turn away this attack on a human-occupied star system. If you assist in this matter, if you avoid offensive action against our forces while the enigmas are here and act as if coordinating your forces with ours, we will agree to surrender to you this star system and everything in it intact after the enigmas are convinced to leave. If you do not assist, your own mission here is certain to fail. Work with us against a mutual enemy for our mutual benefit. For the people, Iceni, out."

She shrugged as that transmission ended. "I doubt that he will agree, but asking can't make things any worse."

The atmosphere in the command center had changed, taking on a new level of tension. Drakon glanced at Colonel Malin, who subtly tilted his head toward the nearest specialists. *Of course. They just heard*

Iceni offering a deal to hand this star system back to the Syndicate Worlds. That couldn't be helped, but we can reassure our workers, who would all probably rather face total destruction to bring down the enigmas than accept having the snakes return.

"If Boyens does fall for it," Drakon said, speaking loudly enough that the nearest specialists who were listening-without-seeming-to could just hear, "we'll arrange things so the enigmas hit Boyens instead of our own forces. Once we've eliminated the enigmas we'll turn on whatever's left of the Syndicate flotilla and crush it."

Iceni kept her puzzlement at his open admission of their probable (if so unlikely to succeed as to be delusional) course of action from showing on her face, but her eyes questioned him before going to the nearby workers and lighting with understanding. "Yes, of course," Iceni agreed. "If CEO Boyens is desperate enough to accept our offer, we'll destroy him as soon as he lets his guard down. The snakes of the Syndicate Internal Security Service will not ever again control the fates of the people of this star system."

Their performance must have quelled some of the anxiety inside the command center. Drakon heard a low buzz of conversation that held none of the rising fears that could have touched off riot or revolt among the workers.

"I have the awful feeling that they might trust us," Iceni remarked in a very low voice which held amusement mingled with disbelief as she looked at the workers.

"You'd think they'd know better," Drakon commented, hearing a bitterness in his own voice that he had not anticipated.

Malin edged closer to speak quietly. "They know what they have seen of your actions. Do not assume they are stupid. Assume that, like all other people, they are often ruled by self-interest. You got rid of the snakes. You have granted them more freedom. You have shown concern for them."

"Have we?" Iceni asked. "Your officer is prone to odd notions, General."

"He's often right," Drakon said.

"Which is why you instinctively leap to his defense?" Iceni eyed Drakon, her look challenging. "You have a habit of doing that with your executives and your workers, don't you, General?"

"It's what works for me," Drakon growled in reply, wondering if Iceni was now going to issue even more pointed criticism of his un-Syndicate-like behavior. *Of course she won't approve of my methods. Just about every other CEO I've met feels the same. And it still ticks me off. I get better results than they do. How dare they criticize my way of getting the job done?*

But whatever Iceni's opinions might be remained hidden behind her eyes. She was good at that, too. Instead, Iceni simply nodded. "It's what got you sent to Midway and nearly got you executed by the snakes, General. Some might wonder at that sort of management record."

"I'm not a manager," Drakon said with more heat than he had intended. "I am a leader."

"And his troops will follow his lead," Malin said.

Iceni's eyes flickered toward Malin, a humorless smile barely bending her lips, her gaze appraising. It was the sort of look anyone below CEO rank in the Syndicate Worlds feared, the sort of assessment of an individual's worth and attitude that could result in promotion but more often in demotion or even a sentence to a labor camp. "I am not your General, Colonel Malin. I am not nearly as forgiving of unruliness in my subordinates, even those who offer valuable suggestions. Keep that in mind when you speak to me."

Malin stiffened. "I understand and will comply, Madam President."

"Good." Iceni walked off, raising her comm unit in one hand and speaking in a low voice, her personal privacy field once again blocking her words from being heard by anyone nearby.

Drakon watched her go. *Selling me down the river is the only card Gwen Iceni has to offer Boyens. But without me, she can't hold on to this planet and this star system. She knows that. Maybe she doesn't like that. Like me, she was trained by the Syndicate system not to depend on anyone else. Even if she doesn't want to betray me, Iceni has to be considering her survival options right now. What if it comes down to her or me?*

Whatever Iceni might be planning could take hours to materialize, if she was planning anything, and his defensive measures against her had to take into account that he needed Gwen Iceni just as much as she needed him, and that she was very good at whatever she turned her mind to. The external threats that might trigger a desperate internal fight to survive between him and Iceni loomed large on the main display behind Malin. But it would be hours before either the powerful enigma fleet or the Syndicate flotilla commanded by CEO Boyens received Iceni's messages as they crawled across the vast distances of space at the speed of light. Reactions or replies, if any, would take at least as long to be seen or heard. Time to make plans, time to prepare for action, time to worry about the plans your partner might be making and actions your partner might be preparing for. Time for the citizens to realize just how bad things were, and react with the panic or fury the Syndicate system expected of the mob, or with the resolve and reliability that he and Iceni hoped to create by offering more individual responsibility for the workers. Time for missteps and misunderstandings among supposed friends and allies to cause as much or more damage than deliberate malice.

Friends and allies. Drakon saw Iceni watching the display, revealing for a brief, unguarded moment a grim anxiety as she stared not at the enigma fleet nor the Syndicate flotilla but at the depiction of the Midway Flotilla. The warships upon which Iceni's power rested. "Colonel Malin, can you come up with any possible scenarios where the warships of the Midway Flotilla will survive even if the rest of us somehow manage to pull through?"

Malin paused for only a moment, then shook his head. "Barring a miracle, there's only one, sir. If they flee for an unguarded jump point. No one, ourselves included, could stop them."

"And the officers and workers on those ships surely know that."

"Yes, sir. As does Kommodor Marphissa. She is too capable not to be aware of her certain fate if her ships do not run for safety."

"So, even if we somehow survive, those warships will not, unless they run for it. They're doomed if they stay." Iceni would lose her shield against the hammer of Drakon's ground forces, would lose her power to bargain with him and Boyens.

"Yes, but if the warships flee," Malin said, "*our* fates will become certain. Any chance of bluffing the enigmas into leaving, any chance of dealing with CEO Boyens, will disappear with them. Either they commit to die fighting a hopeless battle or they run to save themselves and ensure that we die."

If Marphissa had been a Syndicate CEO, Drakon knew what he would have expected her to do. There wasn't any profit in hopeless battles. But, if they stayed, and with Marphissa knowing how vital her choices had become to Iceni's survival, what price might someone trained in the Syndicate system demand in exchange for the warships' almost certain sacrifice?

No wonder Iceni was watching the depiction of her warships with dour intensity, as if anticipating the worst.

A sharp tone announced a high-priority call arriving. "Kommodor Marphissa wishes to speak with you, Madam President," the comm specialist announced.

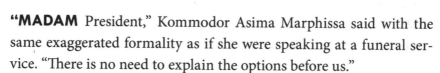

CHAPTER TWO

"MADAM President," Kommodor Asima Marphissa said with the same exaggerated formality as if she were speaking at a funeral service. "There is no need to explain the options before us."

"No," Iceni replied, trying not to reveal in her words or expression the icy ball in the pit of her stomach as she waited for Marphissa to either openly betray her or demand a huge price for continued loyalty. She had not left the command center and knew that Drakon was also watching from a slight distance even though he could not hear her conversation. "What is that you want?"

Since Marphissa's flagship (former Syndicate Worlds heavy cruiser C-448 now renamed *Manticore*) was in orbit near this planet, there was no noticeable delay time in the transmission. However, Marphissa paused as if reluctant to speak.

The first giant betrayal is the hardest, Iceni thought bitterly. *Don't worry, girl. They get easier as time goes on.* But the Kommodor's next words were not those Iceni had expected.

"I request permission to proceed with the flotilla to join up with the two heavy cruisers at the mobile forces facility orbiting the gas giant."

"What purpose would that serve?" Iceni asked, now trying to hide her surprise. Moving toward the gas giant at the current point in its orbit would take Marphissa and her ships considerably closer to the enigmas but only marginally closer to Boyens and his flotilla.

"To defend the star system," Marphissa explained. "To defend the people."

Iceni shook her head, as much in puzzlement as in disagreement. *That woman rose to executive rank in the Syndicate system. She must have learned how to negotiate better than that.* "Let me put it more plainly, Kommodor. I ask again, what do you want?"

"To combine my forces, Madam President."

"Even combined, your forces are inadequate to deal with the threat from either opponent in this star system!" *If she wanted to acquire the other two heavy cruisers, she could just order them to join her en route to one of the jump points. Why won't she lay out her demands?*

But Kommodor Marphissa just nodded in agreement. "Yes, Madam President. That is correct. We cannot hope to defeat either the enigma armada nor the Syndicate flotilla. But, if my forces are combined, I will have a better chance of striking some damaging blows at them before my warships are destroyed. We will fight as long as we can."

Iceni felt herself hesitating this time, thrown off-balance by the completely unexpected. *Not demands, and not a kiss of death, but an offer to sacrifice yourself? It's not just words with you? You truly believe in what you are doing?* "Kommodor," Iceni said, determined to bring everything out into the open, "you are aware that I cannot force you to take such an action. You are also aware that other options exist."

Marphissa's image nodded again. "Of course they do, Madam President."

"Then why would you stay to fight, Kommodor?" Iceni demanded.

"For the people, Madam President."

"What did you say?" Iceni asked, thinking she must have missed Marphissa's actual reply and only caught the end of the transmission.

"I am staying, this flotilla is staying, to fight for the people, Madam President."

Once again, Iceni took a few moments to answer as she tried to find the right words. "For the people? You intend waging a hopeless fight for people who are certain to die anyway? For an ideal?"

"Death is a certainty for us all sooner or later, Madam President. I would rather die for an ideal than for profit, or live knowing that I would not do all that I could to defend those who cannot defend themselves. I know you only ask me because you want to be certain that I believe as you do, that I am also willing to die for those who depend upon me."

Iceni barely avoided betraying her shock this time. *Die for the people? Does she think I'm that naïve?*

I did reject Togo's advice to flee immediately. But I did that because . . .

Why the hell did I do that?

Not to look weak compared to Artur Drakon. That must have been the reason.

And now she had to worry about how she looked next to Kommodor Marphissa, who was one of the few people in this star system who might have a chance to escape but instead was choosing to stay and fight a hopeless battle.

For the people.

Marphissa's workers also knew what choices she had, the crews, now designated specialists by Iceni's orders to give them pride in their particular jobs. Those words would inspire the crews, help them fight when the fight was without hope. But Marphissa's attitude, as useful as it was in this extreme case, could also create problems in the future.

If there were other days or a future for them all, which seemed extremely unlikely at the moment. "Very well, Kommodor. Take your flotilla to the gas giant, unite your forces, and defend this star system."

She issued the death sentence for those warships and their crews with the sort of pang she had long since learned to bury away inside when ordering the executions of individuals.

"Yes, Madam President." The Kommodor paused. "One question, Madam President. The entire flotilla? I can leave one Hunter-Killer in orbit in case it is needed after the rest of the flotilla has been destroyed."

In case it was needed for Iceni to flee this planet, this star system.

Do you want me to die "for the people" or not, you young fool? Iceni silently demanded of Marphissa's image. Nonetheless, faced with the final decision, she knew the answer. She would stay. Sending off all the warships, every fast means of escaping, meant the commitment was real. *Maybe I've gone crazy. But I have started to build something here, dammit! It may be flawed and it may be foolish but it is mine! I will not leave it to the enigmas or to Boyens. I won't even leave it to Drakon. It is mine. Including my insane Kommodor and her crews rushing off to fight a battle in the name of ideals the Syndicate Worlds gave lip service to but tried in every way to eradicate.*

Rushing off to die by my order, in my name, because they believe I also accept such ideals. Am I to be proud of that or shamed by it? All of my training and experiences in the Syndicate tell me that only a fool would feel either emotion.

I suppose I am a fool.

Iceni shook her head. "No. All warships are to go with you. General Drakon and I will remain in charge here."

"We knew that would be your answer," Marphissa said, smiling. She brought her right fist over to rest above her left breast in the Syndicate salute, but gave the routine gesture a ceremonious solemnity. "For the people, Marphissa, out."

You knew? How could you have known when I didn't know until this moment? During her long and distasteful climb to CEO rank, almost every mentor of Iceni's had warned her against subordinates who assumed too much or who acted in inexplicable ways.

But it was done. The decision had been made. And Marphissa had provided excellent service in the past. She would no doubt continue to be invaluable for however many hours she and her warships continued to exist.

Iceni dropped her privacy field and looked toward General Drakon. "I have ordered Kommodor Marphissa to take all warships out of orbit. They will meet up with the other heavy cruisers at the gas giant, and the unified flotilla will engage . . ." Iceni swallowed, wondering why her throat had suddenly tightened. "Will engage the enemy, fighting until they are destroyed," she finished.

A prolonged silence was broken by the respectful voice of Colonel Malin. "*All* warships, Madam President?"

"Yes, that is what I said," Iceni snapped, not certain why she felt so angry at the question. She pretended not to be aware of the subdued reaction sweeping through the command center, of the workers looking at her with amazement and gratitude. *You are happy because I'm not leaving you to your deaths? Is it so easy to buy your loyalty?*

Drakon walked toward her, moving with reassuring solidity. She hadn't realized how much she liked that, to see him stride forward, all stubbornness and strength. An anchor in a world where all certainties had given way. "Good," he said, as if Iceni's words reflected some prior consultation and agreement. "Let's talk about our plans for defending this planet."

"Certainly," she said. *A man who publicly backs my decisions without hesitation and yet maintains his own authority! If only you weren't a CEO, Artur Drakon. I could love a man like you if I could trust you.*

She let her gaze flit across Colonel Malin, looking for any indication of warning in his eyes or posture. Drakon had no idea that Malin had been for years secretly providing her with inside information, and he would have included one of his most trusted aides in any plans to betray her. But Malin gave no sign of warning as Iceni turned to walk beside Drakon toward one of the secure conference rooms opening onto the command center.

"What exactly did your Kommodor say?" Drakon asked, as the door sealed, and the small security lights over it turned green to confirm the room's countermeasures were active.

Iceni told him.

"Damn," Drakon said. "She really is an idealist. I didn't think there were any of them left in the Syndicate Worlds. Or anywhere else."

"There probably won't be any of them left in this star system much longer. She worries me," Iceni said.

"I can see why. But you need someone like that in a fight like this."

"And after the fight is over?" Iceni asked.

"The strongest horse is the hardest to handle," Drakon said.

"What the hell does that mean?

"It means that the best subordinates need to be led rather than coerced, but they usually turn out to be worth it in a crisis." He looked around, his hands moving, as if seeking something else to do. "I'll keep my troops digging in. Most of that activity will be in the cities and towns, which might upset the citizens. But if it comes to a fight to the death, my soldiers can hold out the longest in an urban environment even if it's been pounded to rubble by the enigmas."

Iceni leaned both hands on the table in the center of the room, gazing at the synthetic coral surface but seeing in her mind's eye the multitude of islands that dotted the planet. "The aliens are four and a half light-hours away. If their ships perform like ours do, we have three or four days before they can get here, depending on exactly where the enigmas go. Would it make sense to evacuate the citizens? Disperse them among the islands?"

"Can they get food and water?"

"From the oceans, yes. Fishing boats can deliver their catches to the islands instead of port cities, and there are many portable desalinization units."

Drakon shrugged, looking unhappy. "It's your call, but if you send citizens out to the islands, they'll be easily spotted by the enigmas when the alien ships get close enough."

"And then every island will be a target for bombardment," Iceni said. "And the small islands will be more concentrated targets than the cities are." She knew how it worked. She had participated in some planetary bombardments during the war with the Alliance, giving her memories that she shied away from, as well as the occasional nightmare despite every treatment modern medical science could offer to cope with what someone might have seen. Or done. "There's not enough land area on this planet to disperse everyone."

"No," Drakon agreed. "There isn't."

"And any large bombardment projectiles that hit the water will generate tidal waves that swamp the low islands. I'll do what I can to keep the citizens calm and work out a limited evacuation. Maybe the enigmas won't slaughter civilian families if they're unarmed and obviously no threat." She knew that was wishful thinking. Drakon was trying to hide his skepticism and not quite succeeding, but she couldn't blame him for that.

"We don't *know* what has happened to citizens in star systems taken over by the enigmas," Drakon pointed out.

"We know we've never heard any trace of them afterward." Iceni took a deep breath, stood straight, and met Drakon's eyes. "I'll do what I can and keep sending occasional messages to the enigmas and Boyens. If either of them reply, I'll negotiate."

"And I'll make sure my troops are ready when the enigmas get here." He offered her a half mocking salute. "Did you ever watch those old drama vids? The ones about that ancient empire and its arena fights to the death?"

"Yes. The gladiators. We who are about to die salute you." She returned Drakon's salute, smiling sardonically. "Are you going to betray me, Artur?"

He looked back at her, no answering smile appearing. "No. Do you believe me?"

I want to. "I think we both have no chance of survival, no matter what we do. It's annoying, actually. I always hoped that I'd be able to choose my own death."

Drakon glowered at the floor, then raised his gaze to her. "It won't be a stab in the back. Not from me."

He sounded like he really meant it.

"WHAT the hell are they doing?" In her frustration, Iceni spoke her thoughts out loud. "It's been twelve hours, and they're just *sitting* there!"

The only other person in the office off the command center was Mehmet Togo, who seemed momentarily uncertain as to whether he was expected to reply.

Iceni glared at the much smaller version of the star-system display floating above the conference table in this office. "I know what Boyens is doing. He hasn't answered me, and his flotilla hasn't moved because he's minimizing the risks to himself. He's going to do nothing, pretending to be ready to charge to the rescue of the humans here while actually preparing to run back to the hypernet gate and escape."

"If he does flee," Togo pointed out impassively, "then CEO Boyens will have to provide justifications for his superiors back on Prime explaining why he could not save this star system from the enigmas."

"He's doubtless working on those excuses right now," Iceni said scathingly. "Prime won't accept the impossible odds as a justification, especially since it looks like Boyens will have to claim he did all that he could but didn't suffer a single scratch fighting either us or the enigmas. But his excuses don't have to be valid. They just have to sound good. I understand Boyens and what he is doing well enough. But the enigmas. What are *they* doing?"

She glared at the display again as if it could be intimidated into providing the answer that Togo could not. The enigmas had proceeded in-system only thirty light-minutes from the jump point from Pele where they had arrived. The alien attack force had braked there, all two hundred twenty-two ships, and since that time had hung in orbit, unmoving relative to that jump point.

"What possible reason would they have for sitting there?" Iceni demanded. "We're at their mercy. They must know that."

She shot to her feet and walked out of the office, ready to demand that someone in the command center provide an explanation for the inexplicable.

The first person Iceni's eyes locked on was General Drakon, standing talking in a small group that consisted of him, Colonel Malin, and Colonel Morgan. *Note to self,* Iceni thought as she concealed her reaction to seeing Morgan again. *If we survive this, have a long talk with Drakon about why he keeps that murderous bitch around. Loyalty to subordinates is one thing, and Togo has told me enough about how capable and deadly Morgan is to make it clear why Drakon values her, but the woman is borderline psychotic. I don't care if she got that way because of what the Syndicate did to her on that mission into enigma space. That's not my fault or my problem.*

And she slept with that idiot male Drakon when he got too drunk to know better. I have no doubt that she knew what she was doing, though. What was her goal? That encounter has only ensured that Drakon won't risk any similar outcome again. What was Morgan after?

And why does it bother me so much to know that Drakon slept with her? Because it proves that even Drakon is just a foolish man at his core? Or because . . . ?

No. I know better. Mixing business and pleasure is a recipe for disaster.

Colonel Malin still wasn't giving any subtle warnings of danger for Iceni, and in the last day he had not used any of the available convoluted means of passing information to her. Either Drakon wasn't planning anything against her or he had kept Malin in the dark. Had he been doubled against her, passing information with Drakon's knowledge so that in a case such as this he could keep Iceni in the dark and lull her into complacency? Or were Malin's priorities his own? *What is your game, Colonel Malin?*

She could never tell whether such worries were legitimate or a product of the Syndicate system in which she had grown up and been promoted. Paranoia made sense when lots of people were almost always out to get you. But it crippled you as well, which Iceni had realized was the intent. An environment built on distrust had hindered attempts to band together against the Syndicate leadership.

Drakon looked over at Iceni as she approached, a very brief smile flickering into existence before he extinguished it.

Did the man actually *like* her? That was an intriguing thought.

"The enigmas are not going anywhere," Iceni said without preamble, outwardly ignoring the presence of both Colonels Malin and Morgan, just as Drakon ignored Togo where he stood to the left and slightly behind Iceni. Togo had shifted position a bit as they came to a stop, ensuring that he had a clear shot at Morgan if she twitched in a threatening manner. Neither Drakon nor Iceni made any sign they had noticed that, either.

Drakon nodded in response to Iceni's statement, displaying frustration that matched her own. "I noticed. What's your guess?"

"I have none."

"All I have is a wild estimate based on human behavior." Drakon swung an angry hand toward the main display, where the images of the far-distant enigma ships were shown clearly. "If this were a human force, the only reason they wouldn't attack was if they had orders to wait for someone or something."

"Waiting? For what?"

"I don't know. But if these guys were human, I'd assume they had orders not to attack until some exact time, or to wait until some CEO who wanted credit for the victory showed up, or until reinforcements they didn't need arrived."

Iceni frowned as she looked at the display. "Those reasons would make sense. If the enigmas were human."

"And I know they're not." Drakon shrugged. "Maybe they're like us in that way, though."

"It would be nice to think we're not the only intelligent species capable of such mindless behavior. There's nothing we can do even if they are being stupid, though," Iceni said.

"We could attack," Drakon replied with a sardonic grin.

"If they're waiting for that, they'll be waiting awhile. Kommodor Marphissa is still on her way toward the gas giant."

"Where will she go after she picks up the other two cruisers?"

"I've ordered her to await further developments, to see someone else do something, so we know who to react to."

"Fair enough. What's going on with the battleship?"

It was Iceni's turn to shrug. "It stays where it is. For now."

"Why not get it out of the star system? It doesn't have any military use for us."

She sighed wearily. How long had it been since she had slept? "That battleship is, to the eyes of everyone watching, the strongest defensive asset this star system has. It still *looks* like a mighty warship even to those with access to sensors that tell them its weapons don't work. What happens if everyone watches it run away?"

Colonel Morgan gave her an appraising glance, as if surprised that Iceni had been astute enough to think of that. That condescending look gave Iceni one more reason to contemplate having Morgan murdered despite her agreement with Drakon not to carry out any unilateral assassinations. But a hit on an assistant that close to Drakon would create massive problems even if it could be carried out successfully. From all Iceni had heard, Morgan would not be easily eliminated even if Iceni chose to send Togo after her.

"So we wait, too," Drakon said. He didn't sound any happier about that than Iceni felt. "I've been wondering something about the enigmas."

"If you're planning on asking me, I hope you don't expect me to know more than anyone else does."

"It's a mobile forces question," Drakon said, using the old Syndicate term for warships and pointing to the images of the enigma invaders. The alien craft were shaped much like turtles or tortoises, curved carapaces forming flattened hulls, the dark enigma armor glinting dully in the distant light of Midway's star. "I understand the curved armor. It deflects anything that hits it much better than a flat surface would, and it lacks stress junctions like corners and edges."

His hand moved to indicate the shapes of the human warships shown elsewhere on the display, sharklike hulls varying from the slim Hunter-Killers and light cruisers to the beefier heavy cruisers. At the gas giant, the battleship *Midway* rested at the space dock like a much more massive, chunkier version of the heavy cruisers. "Why don't the enigmas have battleships?" Drakon continued. "Their largest ships aren't much bigger than our heavy cruisers."

"Their ships are more maneuverable than ours," Iceni replied. "And our least maneuverable ships are the battleships because of all the armor, shield generators, and weapons they carry. They're slow to accelerate and slow to brake and take a very wide radius to change vectors. That sort of sluggish ship may be incompatible with how the enigmas fight."

"But what about battle cruisers?" Drakon asked. "Aren't those pretty maneuverable?"

"Yes. Very swift because they have the propulsion of a battleship but not nearly as much armor and significantly less weaponry and shield strength." Iceni shook her head, looking at the enigma ships. "I don't know why the enigmas don't have anything as large as one of our battle cruisers. Maybe Black Jack found out the answer to that."

Drakon's expression hardened. "While he was getting his fleet blown away and stirring up the enigmas to attack us again, you mean?"

She found herself defending the Alliance admiral despite how absurd the idea would have been less than a year ago. "We don't know if the enigmas would have come back anyway. And we don't know that Black Jack's fleet was destroyed."

Malin frowned as he received a report over his link, then faced Drakon. "General, one of our satellites brushed against the edge of a tight-beam communication from this planet aimed toward the Syndicate flotilla."

She should pretend to be focusing her suspicions elsewhere, but Iceni couldn't help herself. Her eyes went to Drakon, and found him looking at her. *Did you send that transmission?* their eyes challenged each other.

Drakon shook his head in answer to the unspoken question. "The snakes must still have agents active on this planet," he said.

"Yes," Iceni agreed. "The transmission did not originate from any source known to me. Did we get the origin of the beam localized?"

"No, Madam President," Malin replied. "The contact was too fleeting, then the beam cut off. It was a burst transmission, so whoever it was could have sent an encyclopedia of information in the brief time it was active."

"We should still be able to get some indication of where it came from," Morgan insisted.

Malin gave her a bland look. "Initial analysis narrowed it down to this half of this hemisphere of this planet."

"And I suppose you're happy with that level of incompetence?" Morgan said, her tone growing fiercer.

"I'm willing to accept real-world limitations but have no intention of being satisfied with this level of analysis," Malin replied, maintaining that indifferent expression, doubtless knowing it would further provoke Morgan.

Drakon made a small gesture, and both colonels fell silent even though Morgan had clearly been ready to fire another verbal volley. "I want you two to check the data the satellite picked up. Do it independently and see if either of you can get a better idea of the signal's location of origin."

Both officers saluted, Malin returning to a nearby terminal and Morgan walking quickly out of the command center.

"What?" Drakon asked, having noticed how Iceni was regarding him.

"I watched how you handled that," Iceni said. "I admit I wonder why you keep those two as assistants despite their unquestioned individual skills. But then I saw how you can use their rivalry. If anyone can narrow down the place where that signal originated, it will be one of those two because they're very good at what they do, and neither one wants the other to succeed where they have failed."

"That's pretty much the idea," Drakon agreed. "They also backstop me and each other. If there's a flaw in my plans or thinking, one of them will spot it and tell me before the other does. If one of them is missing something, the other will catch it. It makes for some drama, but they both know when to knock it off."

"Do they?" Iceni asked.

Perhaps something about her tone made it clear she was referring to Morgan because Drakon reddened slightly. "No one is perfect," he muttered, before turning to study the main display intently.

Iceni wondered if he was talking about Morgan, himself, or her. Had Drakon's words been an oblique apology, a criticism of her, or a defiant defense of himself?

Why do I care? It's not like there aren't much more important things to worry about.

On the display, the Syndicate flotilla and the enigma attack force remained passive, giving no clues as to their intentions. It was very odd how hard it could be to deal with a lack of action.

TWENTY-ONE hours after the arrival of the enigma force, new alerts sounded in the command center. On this part of the planet, it was nearly midnight, but Iceni took only moments to reach the main room, finding Drakon already there.

"What is it?" she asked, trying to reconcile the symbols appearing on the display with her own expectations. But those symbols stubbornly refused to make sense until Drakon suddenly laughed harshly.

"Your hero Black Jack is back."

She blinked, the symbols abruptly reordering themselves in her mind and finally becoming clear. "The Alliance fleet. The enigmas didn't destroy it after all."

"They took out a big chunk of it," Drakon growled, one hand waving toward the display. "All I'm seeing is battle cruisers, light cruisers, and destroyers, and those numbers are down from what Black Jack left here with."

Iceni stared, her eyes running from totals to individual ship symbols. "None of the battleships? None of the heavy cruisers? The enigmas hurt that fleet badly."

Drakon frowned. "How could a mobile force lose just the battleships and heavy cruisers in total?"

"If they needed to escape," Iceni explained in a voice she could tell had gone cold, her memory conjuring up dark recollections of some events she had witnessed during her time serving with the Syndicate mobile forces. "The battleships are slower, but massive. They form a rear guard, holding off pursuit. In the worst case, they sacrifice themselves so swifter ships can escape to fight another day. I suppose the heavy cruisers stayed with the battleships."

"Damn." The one word from Drakon fell heavily, carrying a weight of meaning. "I know how that works in the ground forces. It's a very hard thing to demand of people, to tell them to fight to the death so others can get away."

Iceni shook her head, her eyes still on the display. "Their auxiliaries aren't here, either."

"Auxiliaries?"

"The repair ships the Alliance uses to accompany their fleets. And the troop transports they had aren't here, either. The enigmas must have gotten them, too, because they weren't swift enough to escape."

"Is it possible," Drakon asked, "that we're interpreting this wrong?"

"There's a way to check." Iceni took a few steps toward the primary control console. "Give us close-up views of those Alliance ships," she ordered the operator.

Large virtual windows appeared before her and Drakon, in which every detail of the far-distant ships could be plainly seen. Those ships were four and a half light-hours away, having arrived at the same jump point from which the enigmas had come. Each light-hour was a bit more than a billion kilometers, making the distance to those ships over four and a half billion kilometers. But optics in orbit around this world could see across space with crystal-clear precision. Every detail on the Alliance warships stood out cleanly; so sharp were the images that it was difficult to remember that what they were seeing was light from such distant objects.

"Look at the damage visible on many of those ships," Iceni pointed out. "They've seen hard fighting." She paused. "Let's see where they go. Where they went," she amended. They were seeing the Alliance ships as they had been four and a half hours before now. What had they done afterward? Had Black Jack taken the remnants of his fleet on a swift course for the hypernet gate and a swift journey home? Or would the Alliance warships aim for one of the other jump points that Midway boasted? If they headed for the hypernet gate, they would have to get past the enigmas—"That's what they've been waiting for."

"What's that?" Drakon asked.

"The enigmas," Iceni explained. "You were right. They were waiting for Black Jack. They're sitting between the jump point for Pele and our hypernet gate. In order for the Alliance fleet to reach the gate, they'll have to fight their way past the enigmas."

"The enigmas knew Black Jack's ships were coming." Drakon nodded slowly. "They want to finish him off before they engage us. But according to the vectors that display is showing, the Alliance ships are heading straight for the enigmas. They want to fight."

"If they're running for home, that doesn't make much sense, does it? No one ever accused the Alliance fleet of being crewed by cowards, though."

"No." Drakon's eyes had taken on that distant look he acquired when seeing memories rather than what was happening now. "Their ground forces weren't cowards, either, no matter what Syndicate propaganda claimed. This fleet may have been cut to pieces, but it's not beaten." He looked directly at her, eyes now focused intently. "Do we help them?"

"We don't have much to help them with." Iceni knew she was dodging the real issue.

Colonel Malin had shown up and now stated that issue directly. "If we choose to assist Black Jack's fleet in its fight, the gesture will have immense symbolic value. Black Jack will know we stood with him even when the odds were poor. If we stay out of the fight, if we wait to see what happens, that will have immense symbolic value as well, but in a very negative way in the eyes of Black Jack."

She knew Malin was right, yet she hesitated. *I have so few warships to call on. Committing them to this battle might lose them all, and my few cruisers and Hunter-Killers will not tilt the balance in the fight between Black Jack and the enigmas. Moreover, the last twenty-one hours, spent waiting impotently for the enigmas to strike and destroy the human presence at this star, emphasized in the clearest possible way that I cannot afford to depend upon the Alliance to save the day.*

Even if we pursue the idea of working with Taroa to get that second battleship finished, it will be several months before it could be available. We need our own ships. But if I don't risk them, I may lose the most important ally in human-occupied space.

Drakon most likely understood her dilemma because after a few moments, he spoke with measured emphasis. "If we move to aid Black Jack, we might win. If we do nothing, we lose no matter who wins when Black Jack fights the enigmas."

She didn't answer, looking down, fighting her own battle against the need to make a decision that could decide everything after it. The safer course would be to wait. Wait like CEO Boyens was doing. There was no doubt of that.

Safer in the very short run.

She could have waited before launching her plans to rebel against the Syndicate government. She could have rebuffed Drakon's feelers as premature and avoided doing anything that could have condemned her in the eyes of the ISS snakes. And when the snakes got the orders to haul in system CEOs for loyalty checks, as they did, she would have been helpless.

There were times when even an insane risk formed the best option.

"You're right," she told Drakon. "Black Jack will not forgive us if we sit out this fight." Iceni gestured to the command center supervisor. "I need communications to Kommodor Marphissa on the cruiser *Manticore*."

It took only a couple of seconds before the supervisor saluted Iceni. "We are ready to transmit, Madam President."

In her mind's eye, Iceni could see Marphissa on the bridge of *Manticore*, the Kommodor doing her best to project determination and courage to a crew that had doubtless grown unhappier with every minute spent evaluating the odds against them. How had they reacted at the sight of the Alliance fleet, a force the habits of their entire lifetimes told them was just as much an enemy as the enigmas? "Kommodor," Iceni said, "you are to change course as necessary to proceed with your flotilla on a vector to join with and assist the forces of . . ." She had been about to say *the forces of the Alliance*. But that wouldn't do. Not even now, when those Alliance forces were fighting a mutual enemy. A century of war, a century of hate, could not be so easily cast aside. "Assist the forces commanded by Black Jack, which are acting in defense of this star system. You are to respond to any commands given by Black Jack as long as they do not conflict with your responsibilities to me.

"For the people. This is President Iceni, out."

It was only after the words were out of her mouth that Iceni realized she had emphasized the phrase "for the people" rather than mouthing it like the meaningless phrase it had long been. Since the rebellion led by Iceni and Drakon, there had been a change in the way many at Midway spoke those words. People who actually took the words "for the people" seriously were well motivated, but they also might decide that "the people" would benefit best from different leaders. *And yet I also just said them as if the words had meaning. Was Marphissa right? Are the attitudes of my workers rubbing off on me?*

Drakon was eyeing her but saying nothing. She could tell what he was thinking, though. "I was just motivating Kommodor Marphissa in the most effective manner," she muttered in a voice so low only Drakon could hear. "That strong-horse thing you talked about."

He was wise enough simply to nod in reply.

Iceni stood looking across the command center, trying to assess an alteration in the feeling of the place. Something had changed here. The fear, the anxiety which since the arrival of Boyens's flotilla and the enigmas had ruled under the surface of the workers' stoic façades, had given way to something else. Worry was still there, but also a strange sort of resolve that Iceni was not used to sensing in the workers around her.

Colonel Malin spoke softly. "The Alliance is here. They don't want to look bad in front of the Alliance. Those in the ground forces and the mobile forces have often felt that way, but the average citizen, the average worker, has not. You have given them much more pride in themselves and in what they do, Madam President. With the Alliance watching, they will not falter."

"Too bad I didn't think of such motivational factors before," Iceni replied dryly in the same low tones. *Actually, I did. But the Syndicate system wouldn't let me try such experiments. Better the universe crumble than anyone do anything that might compromise the subservience of the workers.*

"We should send a message to Black Jack," Drakon broke in. "You and I."

"Both of us, this time?" Iceni asked.

"Yes."

"All right. Let's send this one from the private office."

Drakon walked with her to the office, waiting until the door closed behind the two of them before speaking again. "You gave in on that pretty easily."

"Did I? It made sense for me alone to speak to the enigmas because I've done that before, and you haven't. But you have a right to demand to speak with Geary alongside me." *And even though I would never say so, for all of my independence I don't mind at all sharing my current burdens a little with someone who has yet to openly betray me.*

"I almost demanded to speak with Boyens the same way. But Boyens is used to you as top CEO in this star system," Drakon said, "so I didn't object to your speaking to him alone, either."

Iceni faced Drakon, her eyes on his. "General Drakon, it has been clear to me from the first time we met that you think of yourself as military. You wore your mandatory CEO suit as if it were an instrument of humiliation and punishment."

"I didn't think it was that obvious," Drakon said.

"No more so than the average pulsar blanketing the surrounding light-years with radiation. I understand that when dealing with another military leader, you wish to present yourself as coequal with me. It matters to you that Black Jack understands you have as large a role as I do." She smiled crookedly. "That is what you're thinking, isn't it? Because if you want to present yourself as being in charge, we're going to have to debate that."

Drakon shrugged. "Coequal is fine. It has been from the first. You're right. I want Black Jack to know more of who I am. If half of what we've heard about him is true, he's someone I would like to meet in person."

"You'll have to settle for long-range communications," Iceni said, gesturing to the desk. "We'll sit side by side to emphasize—"

Malin burst into the room. Iceni could see Togo just beyond him, ready to act if Malin threatened her. But the colonel just spoke with unusual rapidity. "General, there's been another arrival in this star system."

Drakon frowned as Malin hesitated. "Who?" he demanded. "More Syndicate forces? More enigmas? More Alliance ships?"

"No, sir."

"No, sir, *what*?"

Malin shook his head, looking bewildered. "The new arrivals are not Alliance or enigma or Syndicate. They do not match anything we've ever seen." He moved to the desk's display controls and brought up the images. "There are six of them. Whatever they are."

Iceni stared, aware of Drakon watching her for some sign of recognition. "What's the scale?" she demanded of Malin, who made the adjustment while Togo stood nearby, glowering at the colonel who was usurping Togo's rightful role as Iceni's assistant.

"You don't recognize them, either?" Drakon asked.

"No." Iceni bit her lip, then drew in a deep breath. "Featureless ovoids. Almost perfectly smooth. Are they following Black Jack's fleet or pursuing it?"

"Why would Black Jack run from six ships that size?" Drakon wondered. "They're about the size of our light cruisers."

"We have no idea what armament those ships carry," Malin pointed out. "Or who or what is inside them."

Drakon didn't reply. Iceni was aware out of the corner of her eyes that he was watching her. "You see something," he finally said to her.

"Yes," Iceni agreed. "The formation of the Alliance warships. It is oriented forward, facing the enigmas. Those new ships had to have come from Pele also, so the Alliance ships must have seen them before they jumped for here. But Black Jack's fleet isn't worried about what's behind them. Are they allies?" Iceni wondered aloud. "Did Black Jack find someone else out there? Someone besides the enigmas?"

"He has led them here," Togo said, his voice accusing. "Whatever they are, they know where Midway is now."

"Let's hope they are allies, then," Iceni replied, wondering how she should spin this for public consumption. No one should be talking about those new ships to anyone outside of here. The workers in the command center should be watching, learning what they could, awaiting instructions. But she knew workers. They had doubtless already spread the word to friends and acquaintances across half the planet. And anyone else with access to information about that region of space, anyone simply looking in that direction with the right equipment, would have seen the six new ships as well. "They are allies," she said confidently.

Drakon eyed her, then nodded. "Yes. Allies. Of course." He understood as well as she did the need to keep this news from rattling the defenders of Midway.

Getting up from the desk, Iceni walked back into the command center. "Find out everything you can about those six new ships," she ordered in a firm, self-assured voice. "Black Jack has brought allies to assist him and us against the enigmas. We need to know what those allies can do."

She turned with measured assurance and strode back into the office, where Drakon, Malin, and Togo waited.

DRAKON watched Iceni walking back into the office, her movements broadcasting a sort of serene confidence. *President Iceni is even better at lying than I had realized.*

"We'd better make that call to Black Jack," Drakon said. "Colonel Malin, while the specialists outside see what they can learn by observing those six new ships, I want you to dive into every record we've got for any indication that ships like that have ever been sighted. Maybe the snake files we captured will have something that was kept secret from everyone else."

"Yes, sir," Malin said, saluting and departing in a single, swift motion.

Iceni took a seat behind the desk, indicating the chair to her right. For a second, Drakon pondered the idea of sitting on her left just to emphasize that Iceni didn't tell him what to do, but his common sense very quickly quashed the notion. *Save it for something important, so you don't seem insecure and petty.*

He sat down to Iceni's right while her assistant Togo adjusted the field of view for the transmission. "What do you want to say?" Iceni asked.

What do I want to say? This is primarily a space engagement until someone tries to land troops somewhere, and space is Iceni's playing field. Besides, this is Black Jack. I don't want to sound stupid the first time I talk to him. "I'll just introduce myself this time. You can handle the rest."

"Really?" Iceni leaned close. "Are you really beginning to trust me, General Drakon?" she teased.

But he knew there was a world of meaning behind that apparently amused comment. And, with at least two groups of powerful enemies vying to kill him right now, Drakon suddenly decided to stop playing the games he had been forced into for many years. "Yes . . . Gwen."

Iceni just looked at him in reply, skeptical, her own defenses still up, before finally smiling slightly. "Thank you . . . Artur." Settling in her chair again, she nodded to Togo. "Start."

"This is President Iceni of the independent star system of Midway." She stopped speaking.

Drakon kept his own voice professionally sharp. "This is General Drakon, commanding officer of Midway's ground forces." *There. He knows who I am. That's good enough for now.*

"We are happy to welcome your fleet back into our star system," Iceni continued when she was certain that Drakon was done. "Especially considering current circumstances and previous agreements between us. We will do our utmost to defend our star system against invaders and ask only that you assist us in that task until the people of Midway are once again secure. Kommodor Marphissa, our senior warship commander, has been sent orders to follow your directions unless they conflict with her obligations to defend this star system.

"Be aware that the battleship located at our main military dockyards has functional propulsion but not working shields or weapons at this time, so it cannot be counted upon to assist in the defense of this star system.

"This is President Iceni, for the people, out."

The transmission ended. Drakon relaxed. "By the time we get a reply, there'll have been a lot of fighting."

"Yes," Iceni agreed. "Perhaps that will let us see what those six new ships can do."

"We've committed our mobile forces, so Black Jack won't have any reason to doubt our resolve. I wonder how Boyens will react to Black Jack and those new players with him?"

Before she could answer, Colonel Malin returned almost as swiftly as before. "General . . . Madam President, my research on those six new ships was interrupted by the results of my attempts to localize the tight-beam burst transmission sent earlier from this planet to the Syndicate flotilla. That transmission came from within two kilometers of this command center."

Drakon looked steadily at Malin as he considered what that implied, what it might mean in terms of the woman he still sat beside. Had she been dealing under the table with him the entire time? "Or from within this command center?"

"I can't rule that out, sir."

CHAPTER THREE

ICENI turned a gaze on Togo, which must have communicated a message, because he nodded once and slipped out of the room.

"Find Morgan," Drakon said to Malin, not willing to trust in whatever Iceni's lackey aimed to accomplish. "Tell her, from me, that there may be a . . . snake agent in the command center. I want her to find that person."

Malin hesitated. "Sir, Morgan's methods—"

"She can be as subtle and sneaky as a demon when she wants to be. You know that. I want her on this. The odds against us are bad enough. I don't want a snake, or anyone else, feeding Boyens information on what we're doing before we do it."

"Yes, sir."

"And tell Morgan I want the agent identified, then notify me so a decision can be made on what to do."

"Sir," Malin said with careful formality, "I feel compelled to remind you that if you target Morgan on someone, she may not act in a restrained manner. I also feel obligated to point out one other thing. The tight-beam transmission was sent toward CEO Boyens's flotilla. That does not mean the transmission was intended for CEO Boyens."

Iceni picked up on that immediately. "The Syndicate flotilla surely has ISS representatives on board. Or are you implying there may be other players as well?"

"I am saying there are other possibilities, Madam President."

Malin's statement was clearly aimed at Drakon as well. He regarded Malin, wondering why he was bringing this up in front of Iceni. If she had been contacting the snakes aboard Boyens's ships . . .

But why would she do that? Iceni wasn't a fool. She knew the snakes wanted her blood. Iceni, the senior CEO in the star system, hadn't only revolted against the Syndicate Worlds. She had also, along with Drakon, ensured the slaughter of the snakes in this star system. The families had been sent back to Prime, but the ISS surely wanted to make a memorable example of Iceni to avenge their dead comrades and make anyone else think twice before massacring snakes.

There's no one who wants me dead as much as they want her dead. She knows that. She probably sent her man Togo to make sure I didn't send that message.

Whatever else Malin might have said was interrupted by a call from the command center's main room. "The enigmas are moving!"

Iceni walked quickly out of the office, but Drakon held up a restraining hand to Malin when he moved to follow. It felt silly to rush to see something that had happened over four hours ago, especially when this offered a good opportunity for private conversation with Malin without attracting anyone's notice. "There's a possibility that you didn't mention," Drakon told Malin. "The chance that the President herself sent that tight-beam message, a prerecorded offer for a secret deal that cuts me out in every sense of the word."

Malin spoke carefully as he replied. "General, I have no information indicating that President Iceni has undertaken such a move. Nor would such a move make sense."

"I know, and I have too much respect for Iceni to think she doesn't know that as well. But old habits die hard. How good is your information on what she's doing now?"

"I feel confident that I would know if she was planning to move against you, sir."

"Hmmm." Drakon glanced toward the doorway leading into the command center. "That's your assessment, or you have solid information?"

"Both, sir." Malin sounded confident, assured, as if he knew all the angles.

He sounded, in fact, like Morgan did at such times. Despite their immense dislike for each other, and despite being different in many ways, Malin and Morgan sometimes seemed disturbingly similar. "Keep your eyes open, anyway, and make sure you question everything you think you already know."

"Yes, sir." Malin smiled. "You have taught me that. It's a good rule to follow in planning any operation."

"I learned it the hard way, Bran. Get going."

After Malin left, Drakon walked into the command center to join Iceni where she was watching the display. Even a ground forces soldier like him had no trouble seeing what was playing out. "The enigmas are moving to intercept Black Jack."

The two forces, Alliance and enigma, were hurtling together at velocities a ground forces officer had trouble grasping. More than point two light speed. Drakon did the math. *About sixty thousand kilometers every second. How can any human get their mind around that kind of speed? I'm used to dealing with an environment on the surface of planets, where a kilometer is a significant distance.*

Nor did ground forces rush together as these warships did. He knew the reasons for the ways that spacecraft fought. The ships could see each other across huge distances, yet the warship weapons had such short ranges relative to the vast reaches of space and the tremendous speed at which the spacecraft moved that warships had to get close to each other in order to fight. They could waltz around forever, avoiding contact, if one side didn't want to fight and didn't have to go to some specific objective such as a hypernet gate. "Forever" wasn't all that long in this case, of course, being limited by the fuel and food supplies on the ships.

I don't like it. Drakon felt his jaw tightening as he watched the two forces rushing into contact. *Space warfare is too mechanical. You never see the enemy as people, just as ships. They can fly all over space, across distances so great it takes hours for light itself to make the journey, but in the end they have to bash head to head. How can you really use tactics when the other side can see everything you do no matter how far away you are? When there's nothing to hide behind and no way to conceal yourself? It all comes down to two groups of people running up to each other and hitting the other guys as hard as they can.*

But then how did Black Jack blow away the mobile forces of the Syndicate Worlds in battle after battle? There's got to be something else here, something different from what I know.

He looked around the display at the rest of the star system: the planets swinging in leisurely, nearly circular orbits; comets and asteroids following their own orbits along paths in any shape from circular to huge, narrow ellipses running from the cold dark near the edge of the star system to the bright heat near the star itself; the hypernet gate looming off to one side; the occasional group of warships; and a gratifying number of commercial ships, mostly transports passing through on their way to somewhere else and currently doing their clumsy, lumbering best to stay out of the way of the warships. It all made for a very different battlefield than those he was accustomed to.

Though as battlefields went, Midway was also different than the average star system. Drakon knew that jump points had roughly the same influence on space battles as passes through mountain ranges or bridges across major rivers had on surface fights. Anyone coming or going had to use them. Whereas the average star had two or three jump points, and an exceptional star might have five or even six, Midway boasted a remarkable eight jump points that led to eight other stars—Kahiki, Lono, Kane, Taroa, Laka, Maui, Pele, and Iwa. That alone had earned Midway its name.

Then, about forty years ago, the Syndicate Worlds had constructed the hypernet gate here as well, a massive structure orbiting slowly about five light-hours from the star. The gate gave direct access to any other star in Syndicate space with a gate of its own. All of this made Midway the junction for a lot of trade, for ships carrying cargo and people to any number of other stars, and for defense of this region of space. But it had also made Midway a target, even though officially there had been no enemy here, on the far side of Syndicate space from the Alliance.

The large Reserve Flotilla guarding this region of Syndicate space had lacked any admitted purpose because only a very few of the most high-ranking Syndicate officials were advised of the existence of an intelligent nonhuman species beyond Midway. So little was known of this race that they were called the enigmas, but they had pushed the once-expanding boundaries of the Syndicate Worlds back to Midway. Syndicate ships in the border regions would sometimes disappear without a trace, but enigma ships were never seen, even during the long-distance negotiations that consisted mainly of enigma demands.

Then the Reserve Flotilla had been called away, ordered by the government at Prime to confront the Alliance that under Black Jack Geary had shattered the other mobile forces of the Syndicate Worlds. The Reserve Flotilla had gone, had met Geary, and had not returned. Months later, as the enigmas pressed to take over this star system as well, Black Jack had showed up here, unthinkably far from Alliance space, with the news that the war was over. After expending countless lives and uncountable resources, the Syndicate Worlds had lost the war it had begun.

Already tottering from the human and material costs of the war, the Syndicate Worlds began coming apart in the aftermath. Drakon and Iceni had led the revolt here, destroying the hated Internal Security Service presence in this star system. The crumbling of the

Syndicate Worlds had also impacted neighboring stars. Kane had descended into anarchy as the Syndicate rulers fled and workers' committees feuded. Taroa had experienced a three-way civil war, which only a military intervention led by Drakon had resolved in favor of the Free Taroa faction.

Now the Syndicate Worlds was back with a flotilla to reconquer Midway, the enigmas were back with the intention of taking this star system for themselves, Black Jack's fleet had returned battered and apparently still fighting the enigmas but maybe or maybe not the Syndicate flotilla, the Midway Flotilla was going to help Black Jack's fleet unless it found Black Jack doing something it shouldn't assist, and the intentions of those six new ships were a mystery.

In some ways, space combat could be pretty complicated.

"Another front-row seat as we watch how Black Jack leads his forces," Drakon commented.

"That is no small thing," Iceni replied.

But he found it hard to stay engaged while watching depictions of two forces "rushing" toward each other at what seemed to be a snail's pace because of the scale of the battlefield. Especially since whatever happened when they met had already happened. Eventually, the light from that event would reach here, hours after the actual clash.

Drakon's thoughts strayed to the problem of finding out who had sent a message to the Syndicate flotilla from this command center. The software governing the many functions of the systems here was riddled with subprograms, worms, and sentries, many inserted by official actors in the name of monitoring activity, security, safety, and reliability. *Or, as the workers call it, Aim the Blame. They know if anything happens, the people in charge want to have enough data to be able to pin the fault on whichever scapegoat they choose.*

But Drakon knew there was also a welter of unapproved, unofficial, and outright illegal subprograms, worms, and Trojan horses woven through software that had become too complex to ever be purged of invaders. He had made use of such things himself at times in order to learn things he wasn't supposed to know, or to accomplish things he wasn't supposed to do. Another CEO had once speculated to him that half of whatever the Syndicate Worlds got done was the result of working around the system. *And I told him I thought half was way too low a figure. There's irony for you. For all that we disliked, or hated, the Syndicate system, we're the ones who kept it going by finding ways to get the job done even when that system tried to make it impossible.*

Right now, Malin and Morgan were both using their own methods to dig through the morass of software to spot the signs of their quarry. If someone had sent a message to the Syndicate flotilla using the comm systems in this command center, then there would be some trace of that activity somewhere. Like hunters nosing through the underbrush in search of a bent twig or a twisted stem, Malin and Morgan would find some sign. Once they had one hint of their quarry, one or both of them would use that to find other tracks. The tracks would form a trail, and the quarry would be run to earth. The only unknowns were how long it would take and whether both Malin and Morgan would nail the prey, or if one of them would manage to run it down first.

Iceni's right-hand man Togo had come back, leaning close to Iceni and whispering some report to her. It must have been something sensitive that he wouldn't want to risk being intercepted or overheard on even a supposedly secure comm circuit, but Drakon was certain Togo hadn't yet found the source of the transmission.

I don't doubt that Togo is good. Iceni wouldn't have him around, and so close to her, if he wasn't very capable. But Togo isn't driven by the intense rivalry between Malin and Morgan. That rivalry can be a real pain to deal with, but it's also invaluable a lot of the time.

I wonder what does drive Togo? That could be important to know.

"General," Malin said in a way that immediately brought Drakon out of his contemplation of Togo and Iceni's relationship.

Had Malin won the race already?

But as Drakon looked at Malin, he saw that the colonel wasn't displaying triumph. Instead, Malin was looking toward the entrance to the command center.

Morgan had come strolling in. She didn't appear to be in any hurry, moving with the leisurely certainty of a panther closing in on trapped prey. One of her hands had reached down and was in the process of drawing the hand weapon holstered on one hip.

And Morgan was walking straight toward President Iceni.

Drakon moved forward, but not as fast as Togo. Iceni's bodyguard/assistant swung about with startling speed, coming between Morgan and Iceni. A series of moves and countermoves occurred almost too fast to follow, ending with Morgan and Togo pointing weapons directly at each other's faces at point-blank range, while their free hands were locked together off to one side, each straining for advantage.

"Hold it!" Drakon said, the volume of his words low but the intensity strong enough to freeze everyone within earshot, which included Morgan and Togo. Under other circumstances, it might have been comical to see all of the workers sitting completely rigid at their consoles, afraid to even breathe. But, right now, Drakon could see no humor in anything. "Stand down, Colonel Morgan."

She took a deep breath, her eyes not leaving Togo's face, then Morgan stepped back, breaking contact with a graceful motion as if executing a ballet move. Her weapon's barrel lowered in a smooth arc, ending with it pointing at the floor.

President Iceni, her face impassive but her eyes revealing surprise, worry, and anger, spoke in a quiet voice carrying the same power as Drakon's had. "Back away."

Togo, his expression showing nothing, took one pace backward, his weapon disappearing into concealment in his clothing as rapidly as it had appeared.

"What the hell's going on?" Drakon asked Morgan.

Her eyes went to him, measuring his anger. Morgan didn't try to push things when she knew he was not in any mood for that. She answered with professional detachment, putting no feeling into her words, her expression similarly betraying no emotions. "Sir, you asked me to find the source of that message to the snakes. I found it."

"And then you were to notify me."

"The source is right here, General. Notification and arrest would have to be simultaneous."

Iceni had recovered enough from shock that she reddened in rage. "Is this officer implying that I am—"

But before she had finished speaking Morgan had stepped to one side, walking no longer straight at Iceni but toward one of the operator consoles close by her. Togo, his eyes never leaving Morgan, moved sideways to remain between her and Iceni.

Morgan stopped beside a specialist hunched forward over her console as if intently focused on nothing but the information her instruments were reporting. But Drakon spotted the sheen of sweat on the back of the operator's neck as Morgan's sidearm rose again, the barrel coming to rest against the head of the worker. "Don't worry," Morgan said to the operator in soothing tones of mock-reassurance. "I won't splatter your brains all over that equipment unless you try to hurt someone. No bombs nearby? No bombs on you? No bombs *in* you?" The specialist made vague sounds of denial. "That's good. Maybe you'll live. But I think some people want to talk to you before they make up their minds about that."

"P-please," the operator stuttered, visibly shaking with fear now. "I had to. M-my family—"

As two security guards ran up to stand by the unfortunate worker, Iceni gazed at the operator with an expression that could not have been harder had it been carved from granite. "Togo. Accompany the guards and this prisoner to a full-spectrum security cell. I want everything she knows, especially her contacts." As Togo began to move, Iceni added one more directive. "I want the facts, whatever they are. Nothing more."

The other workers nearby were gradually recovering from their own frozen shock, staring at their unfortunate former companion with faces in which growing anger and hate could be easily seen. "Snake." The word could barely be heard as it was murmured first by those closest to the caught agent, then repeated by those farther off, until the entire command center was filled with a low hiss of recognition and rage.

Drakon could see the despair on the face of the snake agent as she heard that, as the single, repeated word made it clear that she might still breathe and think but was effectively already dead to those who had once been her friends.

Morgan saluted Drakon with a self-satisfied expression. "You wanted the snake. You got the snake."

"Could you tell if she was working alone?"

"No, sir. I couldn't get past the cutouts her contacts were using, but there are all kinds of footprints."

"We couldn't have expected to clean out the snakes," Malin said, "just by getting the overt agents. If the snake files hadn't been partially destroyed, we might have tracked every mole and hidden asset the snakes had in this star system."

"Are you blaming me for that, *Colonel*?" Morgan asked.

"Of course not, *Colonel*."

Drakon gestured to break up the argument. "You both did well. Colonel Malin localized the signal, and Colonel Morgan found the one who sent it. However, I want less drama next time, Colonel Morgan. A *lot* less drama. You should have known the President's bodyguard would have seen you as a threat."

She smiled, baring her canines. "I am a threat."

"Not unless I tell you to engage someone, understood?"

"Yes, sir, yes, sir." Morgan slid a sly glance at Malin. "You must be getting old. I could have nailed half the command center while you hesitated."

Malin smiled back. "I may be a year older biologically, but in terms of maturity, I freely admit to being much older than you."

"Knock it off," Drakon ordered. "Morgan, don't do anything like that again. Now, get on that operator's console and see what you can find. Malin, scan systems planetwide for any indications that something might have been triggered from this console."

As they went to work, Drakon walked over to Iceni, who did not seem to be in a very good mood despite finding the source of the message to the Syndicate flotilla.

"If," Iceni said in the subzero tone of a CEO pronouncing a sentence on a subordinate, "that woman ever makes such a move in my presence again, I will treat her as an immediate and direct threat to me."

Drakon paused, knowing exactly what that meant. Loyalty to Morgan warred within him against his developing relationship with Iceni and the grudging admission that Iceni had every right to be angry. "I thought we had an agreement. No more executions or assassinations unless we both sign off on it."

"That agreement does not bind bodyguards, General Drakon. Don't try to split hairs on this. She will be dead if she does anything like that again."

He felt anger and stubbornness building, fighting to keep both emotions under control. "It won't happen again. But if your assistant goes after Morgan, you might end up losing him instead of me losing her."

Was that disappointment briefly apparent in Iceni's eyes, swiftly covered by imperial wrath? "You're threatening me? Threatening my closest associates? Now?"

"No." His own antagonism was rising and made his next words less well-thought-out. "The matter was handled clumsily, but there was no intent to target you. You must be aware of that."

"Do not use the word *must* to me, General. I am not required to act or think in ways that someone else finds appropriate."

She was getting angrier. So was he. *Break it off, you idiot. Keep pounding against this wall, and all you'll accomplish is cracking your skull.* "Perhaps we should discuss this later."

"Perhaps we should." Iceni's glare swept the command center. "I will be in my private office monitoring everything from there."

She stormed off, leaving Drakon fuming and feeling like he had lost even though she had been the one to leave this tiny field of battle. He cast a dark look across the command center, seeking anything to focus his ire upon, but everyone was at least pretending to be totally immersed in their duties. *Dammit, Morgan. Can't you use a little sense every once in a while? And why the hell didn't Iceni accept that it was just a mistake?*

Morgan must have known that acting like that would make Iceni mad as hell at her and at me—

She did know. Damn. You and I are going to have a long and clear talk, Colonel Morgan.

IT took a strong effort of will to keep from slamming the door behind her as Iceni went back into the office. She managed to seal the door firmly but without the sort of force that would have drawn comments.

That stupid man! He must realize how that looked! That woman threatened me. If it had been anyone else, they would be dead.

I thought she was smart. Malin told me she was smart. Why would anyone who was smart do something so incredibly . . .

Because they meant to?

Iceni forced herself to calm down, carefully seating herself and staring at nothing as she tried to order her thoughts. Above the desk, the display showed the enigmas and Black Jack's fleet slowly converging for an encounter that would not happen for some time yet. With that time to spare, Iceni focused on nearer events.

What if the whole thing was deliberate? The snake agent offered a cover for Morgan's actions. Those actions could have been fully intended to provoke me into attacking her.

Morgan knows Drakon. He's loyal to a fault. He got exiled to Mid-

way because, when the snakes suspected one of his subordinates, he helped her get away. The snakes couldn't prove it, but they could still retaliate against him.

She knew if I attacked one of Drakon's subordinates, he would reflexively defend that subordinate. But why would Morgan want that? To drive a wedge between Drakon and myself. She can see that we're working together. Maybe the brainless man has actually told Morgan that we have a relationship. A working relationship, I mean.

Morgan laid a trap, and an experienced CEO like myself stepped right into it. Malin was right about one thing at least, I can't underestimate Morgan.

Malin . . . He had said something that had caught her interest. What was it? Age? Something about . . . *"I may be a year older biologically."*

That was it. Why would Malin specify his age biologically relative to Morgan unless he knew her history? Malin must be aware that Morgan was actually about twenty years older than she appeared to be, having been frozen in survival sleep for that period in a suicide mission against the enigmas. The mission had been canceled, and Morgan had been one of only two of the volunteers recovered. But that mission, and Morgan's role in it, was still classified at a level that Malin should never have gained access to. And Drakon was not the sort to have shared that kind of personal information about one subordinate with another subordinate.

Yet Malin knew about it. Perhaps he had been tipped off by the medical waiver that had allowed Morgan to return to the service despite mental impacts from the mission that left her borderline stable. Had he been able to find out why that waiver had been granted and by whom? That was a question well worth asking. *Malin's mother was in the medical service. That might be where he got the connections to learn that, and maybe to learn how someone like Morgan got that waiver in the first place.*

Questions. Togo was off questioning the snake agent. There had been something bothering her about that. But what? The agent? The message?

No. Togo himself.

Iceni sat down, resting her elbows on the desk in front of her. She put her weight on her arms for a moment, relaxing her body and trying to think.

The shuttle. It had been too convenient, too easy.

Iceni checked the display again, seeing that Black Jack and the enigmas were still a good time away from contact. She tapped her comm tablet to put out a call. "Togo."

"Yes, Madam President." His response was almost immediate. Togo's eyes, his face, his voice, all as usual revealed nothing, carrying only the soft tones of respect that she always heard from him.

"How did you so quickly determine who was on the shuttle that tried to flee this planet?" Iceni asked.

"It was a simple matter of checking location readouts for important individuals, Madam President."

"And neither Governor Beadal nor Executive Fillis attempted to deceive the location-monitoring systems?" Iceni studied Togo closely, watching for any revealing reaction, but he maintained his poker face as he nodded.

"They did. Both attempts were easily spotted. Governor Beadal was using an older version of deception software and Executive Fillis employed a redirection mechanism that can be identified when searched for using the right parameters."

It sounded right. A reasonable explanation. *Am I simply being paranoid?*

An old bit of CEO humor came back to her. *What is the difference between a sane CEO and a paranoid CEO? The paranoid CEO is still alive.*

"What have you learned from the snake agent?" Iceni asked.

"Nothing so far, Madam President. She never directly communicated with her snake handler. Cutouts were employed, single-use points of contact who disappeared after each set of instructions were given to her. She knows nothing of her handler except the code phrases used to verify that an order came from that handler."

"Have you searched the back files for messages containing those code phrases?" Iceni demanded.

"Yes, Madam President. None are showing up even though the agent reveals no deception to the sensors in the interrogation room. Those messages may have contained coded instructions to wipe themselves a short time after receipt. The file names might still exist, but with no contents, those files would not appear in response to our search."

Another dead end. Damn the snakes and damn Colonel Morgan and damn stubborn General Drakon and damn the enigmas—

"We have very likely learned all we can from the snake agent," Togo said coolly. "Do you wish her retained for further questioning or disposed of?"

Iceni, angry at just about the entire universe at the moment, almost snapped a dismissive order to eliminate the agent. But she caught herself just before uttering that word. *I know what he's asking. Keep her locked up, or get rid of her? She's a snake agent. Her life is already forfeit. If in a moment of insanity we let her go free, then her own former coworkers would kill her.*

And yet . . .

"Retain her. I want her alive for now. Ensure she is not abused." Some instinct told her that was the right answer. Why? She didn't know. All the more reason to give that answer. She needed time to figure out why something was telling her to keep the snake agent alive. "Keep me informed of anything else you learn."

After Togo's image vanished, Iceni glared at the top of the desk, then looked carefully at the display above it again. The light from the first clash of the Alliance and enigma warships would be visible here soon. She levered herself to her feet and walked out of the office, trying to project every ounce of confidence and command that she possessed.

Mess with me, will you, Colonel Morgan? Killing you might not be fea-sible now, but that doesn't mean I can't lay plans. And the next time you try to use Drakon's loyalty to his subordinates against me, I'll be ready.

Assuming Drakon had been motivated to defend Morgan by that loyalty and not by some other feeling toward Morgan.

Why that thought made Iceni bloom with renewed anger she didn't know, but the anger just strengthened her resolve to reveal nothing of her feelings at this moment, to act as if she and Drakon were co-rulers without a hint of friction between them. She walked up to Drakon and smiled politely, using the posture Syndicate rules laid out for interac-tions between equals. "It won't be long now before we see Black Jack and the enigmas cross swords."

Drakon, who had been standing stiffly, looking across the com-mand center with a thundercloud on his brow, turned a startled glance her way, the surprise quickly shading into relief, then suspicion. "Yes."

At least he's smart enough to say as little as possible so as to minimize the chance of saying the wrong thing. "The snake agent can't identify any handlers."

"I'm not surprised," Drakon said. "The snakes know their business. Maybe if someone else questions her?" He left the question hanging, waiting to see how she would respond and whether she would an-nounce that particular agent had been disposed of and wouldn't be answering any more questions for anyone.

"Feel free," Iceni replied.

"I will."

"Good."

"All right."

The meaningless exchange of words ground to a halt as the level of tension in the command center rose in a perceptible fashion. Iceni looked at the display, her eyes on the distant warships. "Let's see what Black Jack does. Or, rather, what he did."

Hours ago, Black Jack's diminished fleet had raced into contact with the enigmas and—"Huh?" Iceni said without thinking.

"Why did he swing so wide?" Drakon demanded. "He avoided an encounter."

"I'm not certain." Iceni studied the display, frowning, as the two forces began curving back up and around toward each other. Black Jack was known for last-second vector changes that allowed him to hit portions of his foe's formation, but this time the vector change had been so large that the two forces had avoided contact. She couldn't recall seeing any record of Black Jack misjudging an intercept that badly.

"General," Colonel Malin called. "Those six ships."

Everyone's attention had been on Black Jack and the enigmas, the six mystery ships momentarily forgotten. At Malin's prompt, eyes shifted that way.

One of the watch-standers was the first to grasp what was happening. "The enigmas aren't continuing back around to attack the Alliance force. They're aiming to intercept the six unknown ships."

In response, the strange ships had fled straight up, though of course "up" and "down" meant nothing in space. But humans designated a plane in every star system, one side being up and the other down, to enable them to view things in a context they could understand. Iceni let out an involuntary gasp at the way the six ships maneuvered. "Magnificent."

Drakon gave her a searching look. "They seem to be moving very . . . gracefully."

"Yes. Graceful, controlled, smooth . . ." Iceni shook her head. "Whoever or whatever they are, they know how to drive ships."

Far away and hours ago, Black Jack's fleet tore across the bottom portion of the enigmas single-mindedly pursuing the six unknown ships, ripping away a large portion of the enigma armada. "Well done," Iceni murmured. She noticed Drakon watching intently, trying to understand the tactics being employed, and felt pleased that he was smart enough not to dismiss a way of fighting alien to what he knew.

An alert flashed, drawing everyone's attention back toward the jump point for Pele. Iceni stared at the data flashing into existence as automated systems evaluated what they were seeing. Alliance battleships, heavy cruisers, destroyers, auxiliaries, assault transports. "It's the rest of Black Jack's fleet," she exclaimed as understanding struck. "He was chasing the enigmas here and came on with his swiftest ships."

"All right," Drakon said, "I can buy that. He wasn't hurt nearly as badly as we thought. But what the hell is *that*?"

That was a huge ship whose identity was giving the automated systems the fits. Or was it a ship? "Madam President, it looks like something immense with four Alliance battleships attached to it."

"It's that big?" She stared at the data pouring in. "Towing it. Those battleships are providing propulsion for that thing."

"It looks like a ship of some kind," a specialist suggested. "But it doesn't match anything in our files. It doesn't look like anything ever built."

"Anything ever built by humans," Malin said.

"That's not an enigma ship," Iceni protested.

"I did not say it was, Madam President. But, whatever it is, I do not think that humans created it."

Her eyes went back to the battle, seeing vectors bending about as Black Jack's fleet and the enigma armada swung again.

"The enigmas are heading for the jump exit!" another specialist announced, sparking a ragged cheer from the workers.

But Iceni shook her head, dampening the celebration. "Look at that vector. They're headed in that direction, but the enigmas are steadying out, aiming to intercept the second Alliance formation."

Minutes crawled by, the automated systems confirming Iceni's assessment, Black Jack's battle cruisers coming around and steadying onto a stern chase after the enigmas, the six mystery ships continuing up a little ways but then heading in toward the star at a high rate of speed, away from all of the combatants. Whatever they were, they didn't seem to be interested in fighting. Their vectors were bringing them rapidly closer to the planet where Iceni was, but they were still very far off, and she didn't feel any sense of threat.

Drakon stepped closer to her to speak in a low voice. "What's going to happen? Is that second Alliance force going to dodge like Black Jack did the first time?"

"They can't," Iceni replied. "Those battleships at their best can't outmaneuver enigma ships, and they're burdened with the support ships and that giant whatever-it-is."

"So what happens?"

"Look. The Alliance formation is compressing down. Battleships don't depend on maneuvering in battle, General Drakon. They depend on armor, shields, and firepower."

He nodded once, expression bleak. "A wall of death. Whoever is in charge of that formation is going to try to smash whatever comes at them. What will the enigmas do?"

They were once again talking without hindrance, the discomfort created by the earlier incident almost gone thanks to the requirements of dealing with new events. Iceni shook her head. "I don't know what the enigmas will do. What they *did*, since it's already happened. We don't know enough about them."

"Let's hope Black Jack does."

It took a while for the enigma armada to come into contact with the second Alliance formation, but this time no one took their eyes off of the main display. There was an awful inevitability to the clash this time, the sense of watching two objects coming into a collision from which little might survive.

"Madam President," the senior supervisor said. "I have taken a close look at the enigma track. They are aiming for the dead center of the Alliance formation."

"Meaning?" Iceni asked.

"They have highly maneuverable ships, Madam President. We

know that much. Yet they are making an attack that seems to take no advantage of that, and they abandoned their attacks on the faster Alliance formation to assault the slower one."

"Give me an assessment," Iceni said, knowing her voice sounded harsh this time. "I can read data as well as anyone else. Tell me what it means."

The supervisor swallowed nervously before speaking again. "Madam President, it argues that there is something in the new Alliance formation that the enigmas particularly want to destroy, and that something is in the center of their formation."

Drakon pointed. "Their support ships are around the center of their formation, and that huge thing they brought with them is right in the middle."

"They want it," Iceni said. "You're right. That's the target. Whatever it is, they want to destroy it so badly that they've abandoned other targets."

"The enigma formation is also closing down, tightening," Malin pointed out.

"Yes, sir," the supervisor agreed. "They intend to smash right into the middle of the Alliance formation."

"This is going to be ugly," Drakon growled. "I hate head-on attacks."

In fact, as the two sides charged together, the main display lit with a kaleidoscope of flashes, alerts, and flares that would have looked pretty to someone who didn't know those things represented massive destruction confined to a very small section of space. Silence fell in the command center as everyone watched the event.

"Never charge battleships head-on," Iceni finally said, as the command center systems sorted out what could be seen. "Not unless you have battleships of your own that you don't mind losing." The Alliance force had taken some damage, but the enigma armada had been gutted, the entire closely packed center annihilated.

Drakon nodded heavily. "I'll remember that."

"General, if we get to the point where you're commanding mobile forces, we'll really be in trouble," Iceni replied, feeling almost giddy with relief. Most of the enigma ships had been destroyed. Surely the others would—

"The enigma formation has broken into smaller pieces," a watch specialist reported worriedly. "They are all coming around back toward . . . toward . . ."

Iceni watched, feeling tension rise once more. One group of enigma ships looked very much like it would be heading for the hypernet gate, where CEO Boyens and the Syndicate flotilla still waited, having sat out the battle so far. She wasn't worried about what happened to Boyens, but if the enigmas attacked the gate—

"We have intercept vectors identified for enigma ship groupings. One is aimed at the hypernet gate, one is aimed at the gas giant, and the last at . . . at . . . this planet," the specialist finally managed to say.

Everyone looked at her. Iceni, not knowing what to say or do, simply tried not to look as worried as she was. Kommodor Marphissa and her flotilla might be able to do something to protect the mobile forces facility orbiting the gas giant. That and the battleship had to be the targets of the group of enigma ships headed for the gas giant. There wasn't anything she could do about the group heading for the hypernet gate except hope that Boyens would display more skill as a mobile forces commander than he had shown before.

But there wasn't anything to stop the enigma ships coming toward this planet. Marphissa's flotilla was too far out of position to manage an intercept. The Alliance warships, the battle cruisers and light cruisers and destroyers, had dissolved their formation and torn after the enigmas, but now were in a hopeless stern chase. If the enigmas came close enough to the planet, the surface defenses could engage them, but she felt a sick certainty that the aliens would not bother coming close to do what they wanted to do.

A strident alarm flashed red on the display, overriding everything else.

Drakon clenched one fist and looked at Iceni. "I know that alarm."

"Yes," Iceni said in a voice whose steadiness surprised her. The display was mechanically and unfeelingly providing the details of the death sentence she thought she might have miraculously avoided. "The enigmas have launched bombardment projectiles aimed at this planet. Seventy-two of them, many with substantial mass. That is enough to devastate the limited land area on this world and wipe out the human population."

"What can we do?"

"Nothing, General Drakon. Absolutely nothing."

CHAPTER FOUR

"GENERAL," Malin said urgently. He had come up close to Drakon without being noticed while everyone gaped in despair at the display with its deadly message for everyone on this world. "There are still a few freighters in orbit. We can get you up to one of them."

"I thought you wanted me to stay," Drakon said, feeling intense bitterness at the end of his hopes for this star system.

"When it meant something, General. It doesn't mean anything now. That bombardment cannot be stopped. You can save yourself, and as long as you live, you can still try to make something from the ruins. With the flotilla commanded by Kommodor Marphissa, you will have substantial influence someplace like Taroa."

"And my troops, Colonel Malin? What about my soldiers?"

"We'll lift as many as we can up to the freighters, General."

As many as we can? A few hundred, maybe. Out of thousands. Colonel Rogero would probably stay with his unit until the end, watching the enigma bombardment come down through the atmosphere in streaks of fire that would end in mushroom clouds. Colonel Kai, too. Colonel Gaiene? Drakon imagined Gaiene greeting the bombardment with a sense of relief that his long grief was ending. Gaiene would probably raise a defiant toast to the projectile with his name on it, meeting his end with the combination of style and sorrow that had marked him for the past few years. "Bran, I don't think I want to. Abandoning all of those soldiers, abandoning all of the citizens here who counted on us to defend them . . ."

"Sir, with all due respect," Malin urged, "it's not about you. You have a duty to carry on with this, with whatever we can salvage from the wreck of this world."

Morgan had appeared on Drakon's other side, her face twisted into exaggerated surprise. "Even he gets it right sometimes. General, let's go. We've got a while before those rocks hit and turn this place into trash, but once the mob finds out those rocks are coming, they'll riot and try to storm the landing fields."

They were right. Malin and Morgan had logic and reason on their side. But Drakon looked over at Iceni, who was gazing with a stony expression at the display. Sensing his eyes on her, she looked back at him. Iceni said nothing, but Drakon felt certain of the acquiescence she had just wordlessly conveyed to him. *Go ahead. Leave.*

Instead, he walked toward her, leaving Malin and Morgan. "Madam President," Drakon said formally, "you need to get to a shuttle. I'll order my soldiers to form perimeters around the landing fields. They should be able to hold back the crowds until the shuttles can load and lift."

She looked into his eyes. "And we would leave those soldiers? They would stand firm as we head for safety under their protection?"

"Soldiers do that, Madam President. Sometimes they have to. You'll be able to get clear."

"*I* will be able to get clear? What of *you*, General?"

Before he could answer, the command center supervisor called out. "We have a message coming in from the Alliance forces. It is addressed to President Iceni and General Drakon."

"Give us a private comm window here," Iceni directed.

Moments later, the virtual window appeared before them, invisible to everyone else. Drakon had seen images of Black Jack Geary before. The famous hero of the Alliance did not look like a hero. He looked like a man doing his job, a man who didn't think of himself as heroic. Drakon had liked that. At the moment, Black Jack didn't look happy about annihilating most of the enigma armada. Instead, he spoke in somber tones. "This is Admiral Geary. We have done our best to eliminate the enigma force, but some ships have gotten past us, and some of those have launched a bombardment aimed at your inhabited planet. We will continue our pursuit of the enigma ships but cannot stop the incoming bombardment. I urge you to take any possible measures to ensure the safety of your people. To the honor of our ancestors, Geary, out."

Morgan's scornful voice broke the silence following the message. "Was there anything in there that we didn't already know? General, let's go."

"He did everything he could," Iceni replied with a fiery glance at Morgan.

"Yes," Drakon agreed. "I can't fault Black Jack." But otherwise Morgan was right. It was past time to go. But he didn't move, feeling as if his feet were fastened to the floor, and neither did Iceni. In his mind's eye, Drakon saw the ranks of his soldiers, the men and women who had followed him for years in battles across a score of worlds, who had lost comrades on each of those worlds while carrying out his commands. He saw them standing firm to hold back panicked crowds while a shuttle carrying Drakon himself lifted to safety, leaving them to certain death. Beyond them he saw the white beaches of this world and the gentle slopes of its islands, he remembered the breezes off the wide waters and the setting of a sun whose particular size and tint had come to seem very familiar in a few years. To leave was one thing. To leave those soldiers and this world knowing that all would soon cease to exist was another and far harder thing.

Even after all the years climbing the ranks of the Syndicate hierarchy, even after all that had required, there were still some things that General Artur Drakon found impossible to do.

"General," Malin began again, though something in his tone conveyed his understanding that further pleas would be useless.

Drakon shook his head. "Accompany the President when she goes off planet, Colonel Malin. She'll need your advice and assistance."

Malin looked down, then back up at him. "I would rather stay, General."

"That's an order, Bran."

"I do not believe any punishment you threaten for disobeying orders would have much meaning under the circumstances," Malin pointed out. "We might be able to ride it out in the headquarters complex."

"Not too damned likely," Drakon grumbled. "All right, dammit. But get an escort set up to get President Iceni to the lift field. Make it strong. There's going to be mass panic soon."

Morgan was standing nearby, her posture strangely uncertain. Uncharacteristically, she didn't seem able to decide what to do, just watching Drakon with a fixed stare.

"Go ahead, Colonel Morgan," Drakon said. He looked over at Iceni, who herself was still standing, gazing across the command center, fists clenched at her sides. "You are to command the President's escort and ensure she gets on a shuttle, help her commandeer a freighter in orbit, then remain with her and guard her wherever she goes. Get her out of here, get her to safety, whether she wants to go or not, and you get out safe, too."

"No." Morgan shook her head like someone coming out of a daze. "You—"

"M-Madam President?" the supervisor called out. "Th-there's something happening."

"*What* is happening?" Iceni snapped, instantly focused on the situation again.

"Those six ships, Madam President. They're . . . they're doing something."

"What are they doing?" Iceni repeated in an even more forceful tone. But as she looked at the display, the anger was replaced by incomprehension. "What are they doing?" she repeated, baffled.

Almost forgotten until now, the six mystery ships had been driving steadily inward toward the star. Now they were diving back toward the plane of the star system, accelerating at a very impressive rate, their vectors aimed at—

"It's the bombardment," the supervisor said in a disbelieving voice. "They're aiming to intercept the bombardment."

"Why?" Iceni asked the question of the entire command center. "What's the point? What can they do?"

The supervisor, forced by his position to be the one to answer, faltered out a reply. "I . . . I don't know, Madam President."

Iceni spun to face Drakon. "Mobile forces cannot stop a bombardment. It's too hard a problem for the fire control systems. What are those ships doing?"

Colonel Malin answered. "Those aren't our ships. They're not Alliance ships. They're not *human* ships. Maybe they can do something ours can't."

Every eye stayed on the display as the six ships swooped down on the bombardment projectiles, sliding into position directly behind them in a maneuver that brought a gasp of admiration from Iceni and several others in the command center. The mystery ships began firing, somehow scoring hits, blows that did not destroy the solid metal bombardment projectiles but did divert their paths, sending them on courses that would never reach this planet.

Drakon watched, impressed even though he didn't understand the magnitude of the achievement, as the bombardment was diverted projectile by projectile. But he did note that the rate of success kept dropping as the bombardment pulled away from the six ships.

Finally, only one projectile remained on course for this world. Shots from the six ships blasted toward it again and again, with no results. Drakon began trying to calculate how much damage that one object would do when it struck this planet. "Any guesses?" he asked Malin and Morgan, both of whom shook their heads.

"It depends too much on where it hits," Malin explained.

The firing stopped. Drakon heard a vast sigh fill the command center as everyone at once seemed to let out disappointed breaths. To come so close to total success and not achieve it . . . But he couldn't complain, not when a planet-killing bombardment had been reduced to one rock that might be devastating but not a total disaster. "If you two have decided to start following orders again, calculate the trajectory on that rock and try to get an estimate of where it will hit," he ordered Morgan and Malin. "We need to—"

The six ships had fired again, a single volley.

Instead of reporting success, the supervisor sobbed with relief.

Iceni looked ready to reprimand him, then smiled and took a long, slow breath herself. "I don't know where they came from, I don't know what they are, but we are amazingly lucky that they were here."

"Perhaps it wasn't luck," Malin said. He had a calculating expression on his face as he eyed the depictions of the six strange ships.

Drakon glanced at Morgan for her reaction and saw the exact same expression on her face. "What do you think?"

Morgan grinned, all of her usual cockiness back. "We need what they've got."

"Don't start planning a boarding operation."

"And victory celebrations may be a bit premature," Malin added. "A second group of enigmas has launched a bombardment."

Drakon muttered a curse, swiveling to look at the display. Sure enough, the group headed for the gas giant had unleashed projectiles aimed at the mobile forces facility and the battleship still present there. "We need that thing to move."

"We couldn't send an order in time for it to be received," Iceni corrected him. "Whatever has happened, has already happened. Kapitan-Leytenant Kontos has shown some remarkable abilities in the past. I am sure he will realize the need to move that battleship before the bombardment reaches it. Kommodor Marphissa could not reach those enigma ships in time to stop their launch, but she will prevent them from doing more damage."

But, within moments, Iceni's surface serenity cracked. "What is he doing?"

Drakon squinted at the display, trying to understand what was happening. "The battleship has lit off its main propulsion."

"But it is still fastened to the mobile forces facility! It will rip the dock free and possibly damage the battleship as well to no purpose!" Iceni's opinion of Kapitan-Leytenant Kontos appeared to have undergone a radical change.

But as minutes went past, Iceni's expression shifted again, to incomprehension. "According to the data feed from the battleship, he's got his main propulsion going at almost full, but he's still tied to the facility. How is that possible?"

"The entire facility is moving," the command center supervisor reported helpfully.

"I can see that!" Iceni seethed. "Why isn't it coming apart under the strain? What the hell is Kontos doing?"

As if in answer to her, a transmission came in showing Kapitan-Leytenant Kontos on the bridge of the battleship *Midway*. As usual, the youthful Kontos showed an unruffled attitude despite the dire situation. "To President Iceni. When the alien force appeared in this star system, it occurred to me that there might be a need to protect this facility from the usual form of attack. Therefore, I ordered the shipyard workers to immediately begin reinforcing the battleship's ties to the facility, using all available means. They have worked steadily, and are still working to bolster those areas as I seek to use *Midway*'s propulsion to pull the facility out of the way of the incoming bombardment. I believe we have a reasonable chance of success. I have

informed Kommodor Marphissa of my actions as well. If we are successful in avoiding the bombardment, I will report on the outcome.
For the people, Kontos, out."

"He's crazy," somebody whispered clearly enough to be heard in
the hushed command center.

"It might work," the supervisor suggested.

Iceni looked as if she might explode. "He's risking the battleship . . .
my battleship . . . on a harebrained scheme that can't possibly—"

"Madam President?" a specialist asked with equal parts hesitancy
and daring. "Projections are that the mobile forces facility will just
clear the bombardment area."

"What? Are you certain?"

"From the data feeds we are getting, the known mass of the facility,
and the performance data on the battleship's main propulsion, yes,
Madam President."

Iceni stared at the display, wordless now, as the mobile forces facility and the battleship towing it moved with agonizing slowness away
from the danger zone. The enigma bombardment arrived, zipping
very close past the edge of the mobile forces facility before skipping
across the gas giant's atmosphere and zooming off into empty space.

"Colonel Rogero told me Kontos was good," Drakon remarked.

"Yes," Iceni agreed, her voice not quite steady yet. "He has a great
future. If I don't kill him first."

"There's one group left," Morgan interceded, as they watched Kommodor Marphissa's flotilla moving to intercept the enigmas who had
attacked the mobile forces facility. "The one heading for the gate."

Drakon eyed them sourly. "The mysterious six ships saved us from
the first group, Kapitan-Leytenant Kontos saved us from the second
with some help from Kommodor Marphissa when she catches those
enigmas, and now we have to depend on CEO Boyens to save us from
the third."

"Well, we've already seen at least one miracle today," Iceni replied.
"Maybe a second or third isn't too much to hope for."

As it turned out, the last group of enigma warships broke off their attack and headed for the jump point for Pele at the best speed they could, which was considerable. "They've had enough," Drakon observed. He had seen that often enough with human combatants. There always came a point when the will to fight faltered and failed. The better the fighters, the longer it took to reach that point, but sooner or later almost any force would break if subjected to enough damage. Whatever else was true of the enigmas, they were like humanity in that respect as well. There was some comfort in knowing that.

Knowing things. He looked at Black Jack's fleet, which had gone into enigma-controlled space and come back again, accompanied by the mysterious six ships as well as the massive ship being towed by Alliance battleships. "How much do you think he'll tell us of what he's learned?"

Iceni shook her head. "I can't guess. He may demand a price for what he has learned."

"What price? We don't have a lot."

"I don't know." But Iceni seemed worried, and Morgan bent a smirk her way as if Morgan knew the answer.

"We probably ought to say something to him," Drakon commented.

"Yes. Let's do it formally." Iceni led him back to the private office, where he once again sat beside her. "What do you wish to say?"

What did he want to say? Drakon glanced unobtrusively at Malin, who just as subtly communicated a suggestion to defer to Iceni. *All right. Better to be quiet than to sound stupid.* "I'll leave this one to you," he told Iceni. "We do need to tell Black Jack that we're not on good terms with Boyens and his flotilla."

"Of course. If we can get Black Jack to commit to us, CEO Boyens won't have a chance. Anything else?"

"No. I just want to make sure Black Jack sees us together so he knows we're jointly deciding on whatever is said."

Iceni inclined her head toward Drakon, then faced the pickup and gestured for the transmission to start. "We are in your debt again, Admiral Geary. I don't know the nature of your allies, but we owe them an immense debt as well.

"My warships will engage the enigmas heading for my battleship. I cannot control the actions of the flotilla near the hypernet gate. Do not trust that the flotilla there will act in our interest, Admiral. CEO Boyens, their commander, is known to you. If you make your orders clear to him, he may hesitate to act contrary to them. It is essential that Boyens understands that he is not in control of this star system and does not dictate what will happen here. For the people, Iceni, out."

She relaxed, then noticed Drakon looking at her. "Did I say something inappropriate?"

He motioned to Malin, indicating he should leave, then waited until the door sealed again before answering Iceni. "*My* battleship? *My* warships?"

"I said *my*? I thought I said *our*."

"No." A small thing, but also a clear unilateral claim on the most powerful military assets in this star system. Drakon realized that he was galled by recent events, that he had been forced to sit by with his soldiers and watch others defend and save Midway Star System. *I know ground forces couldn't have done anything against those threats. But it still annoys the hell out of me that her warships, and Black Jack's, did all the heavy lifting.*

Iceni tapped one finger on the table several times, watching it as if the gesture required concentration. "If that's a concern, then I will modify the description of the forces when next I speak of them." She looked over at him again, showing Drakon a poker face that left him wondering what Iceni was really feeling.

"Fine. As long as it is clear I have an equal level of control here."

"That has never been in question." Iceni locked her eyes on his. "General Drakon, we cannot afford to mistake who our allies are."

"Gwen . . . I regret our earlier misunderstanding."

"You mean when your officer threatened me?"

Iceni obviously wasn't going to make this easy. "It won't happen again. I'm going to make certain of that."

She looked carefully at the security lights glowing above the doorway, ensuring that no one could overhear their conversation. "Artur, the only way to be certain that officer does not act that way again is to get rid of her. You know that as well as I do."

"If you knew her history—" Drakon began stubbornly.

"I do know her history."

That shouldn't have been a surprise despite the highly classified nature of Morgan's early record. Iceni had done her homework. "Morgan had some bad breaks. If she couldn't do her job, that wouldn't serve as an excuse. But the fact is that she does get the job done. She found that snake agent in the command center way before anyone else."

Iceni leaned back, frowning at him. "It could have been a setup. The snakes still in hiding in this star system would have known we were closing in on that agent. They could have leaked that information to Morgan."

"Why?"

"To deflect suspicion from her."

Drakon had to pause, momentarily at a loss for words. "Gwen, seriously, if you knew more about Morgan, you'd know that's impossible. She really, truly, hates the snakes. She also hates the Syndicate. They messed her up, and while she won't admit that, Morgan wants revenge."

Iceni pursed her lips, thinking. "Confirm my data. She was *messed up* as you put it by mental conditioning for a suicide mission into enigma space when she was barely eighteen."

"Right. She spent about twenty years frozen in survival sleep, inside a hollowed-out asteroid headed for an enigma-occupied world. She, and the others in the mission, were supposed to be awakened just before atmospheric entry, reach the surface, and send back whatever information they could before the enigmas killed them. But the mission got canceled when the leading asteroids were destroyed by the enigmas, and Morgan and one other soldier were recovered to try to find out how their presence had been compromised to the enigmas."

"That matches," Iceni said. Whatever she was thinking was once again hidden behind her eyes. "Chronologically, she's twice her apparent age."

"Yeah. Biologically, she's about the same age as Malin. Not that either of them finds that a basis for getting along."

Iceni shook her head. "I can't tell you how to run your own staff. But I can tell you that she is, in my opinion, dangerous."

"You think she's a threat to me?" Drakon asked.

"Yes," Iceni replied, surprising him. "Don't get your back up until you hear me out. I do not believe that Colonel Morgan would intentionally do you harm. She has an intense loyalty toward you. What you ought to be worried about is where that loyalty could lead her, what actions she might take in the belief that they are in your best interests."

My best interests? Where have I heard that before? Drakon wondered.

Taroa. Morgan said exactly that. "General Drakon, everything I do is in your best interests." Even at the time he had wondered what that might mean.

But that it might constitute a threat to him? Morgan had her quirks, but she never would have gotten that medical waiver if she wasn't stable enough to meet Syndicate standards. Granted that Syndicate standards could be elastic, but they left no room for loose cannons who didn't have an important patron supporting them. And Morgan had not had any such patron.

Nonetheless, Drakon could understand Iceni's grounds for concern. "All right. I will ensure that Morgan knows that if anything happens to you, or to anyone else without my very clear and specific orders, all of her past service to me won't save her from the consequences."

Her eyes searched his for a long moment before Iceni replied. "This is a dilemma. I like you because you don't cast aside people who become inconvenient. But that character trait also makes life more difficult for me. Very well. Warn her. I'll be watching her."

"So will I," Drakon said. He gave her a skeptical look. "You like me?"

Iceni sighed and spread her hands. "A little. Is that so unusual?"

"As a matter of fact, yes." He smiled deprecatingly. "I'm not easy."

"And I'm not cheap," Iceni said, a momentary smile appearing, then vanishing again. "There's work I should be doing."

"Me, too." *Don't trust, don't get too close, don't mix your job and personal issues, never, ever, make the mistake of letting down your guard because of personal feelings.* The old warnings, which had saved him more than once while climbing the ranks of the Syndicate hierarchy, echoed in Drakon's head as they left the office.

But, dammit, I like her, too. A little.

"I reviewed the interrogation of the snake agent done by President Iceni's personnel," Colonel Malin reported. "I conducted my own as well. I agree with the results given to you. This particular snake agent knows nothing of use to us. Her disposal is awaiting your approval."

Drakon sat back in his chair, in his office, grateful to be back in his own headquarters complex, surrounded by people whose loyalty to him was beyond question. He ran Malin's last words through his mind again while Malin waited patiently, standing in the respectful and almost-at-attention posture that seemed the most casual attitude that he ever took toward Drakon.

"Disposal." That was one of the official and accepted Syndicate terms for executing someone. *Dispose of the prisoners. How many times have I heard that?* Drakon wondered.

He hated the word. He had hated it for a very long time.

But, exact wording aside, the woman's fate didn't have any room for debate. She had worked for the snakes. She had claimed, and the interrogation had borne out, that she had been blackmailed into cooperation by threats to her family, but that made no difference. She could expect no mercy even from her former coworkers. Letting her go was simply impossible.

And yet Drakon felt a strange reluctance to order her "disposal." "What about President Iceni? Has she given orders about the prisoner?"

"Her office approved disposal, General."

"*President Iceni* approved disposal, or *her office* approved disposal?" Drakon demanded.

Malin paused. "Sir, I will have to check on whether the President personally approved the decision."

Did something this routine fall under his agreement with Iceni? Probably. She should have coordinated with him before approving killing the agent. Especially since there was no need to rush the execution. But why delay it? It would be different if the snake agent was still of some use . . .

Drakon felt himself smiling. "Colonel Malin, suppose we kept her alive?"

"Alive?" For once in his life, Malin seemed to be baffled.

"Suppose you were the covert snakes still hidden on this planet, in this star system, and you knew we had captured that woman, then you learned that we hadn't executed her. What would you think?"

Malin puzzled over the question very briefly, then his expression cleared. "I would think that she was still of some use to us."

"Right. That she's still valuable to us. So what would you do?"

"Try to get to her. Eliminate her myself." Malin smiled approvingly at Drakon. "You want to keep her as bait to force some of the other snake agents in this star system to reveal themselves."

"That's the idea." Wasn't it? Maybe that was the only reason he had felt reluctant to dispose of the woman.

But he was sick to death of death. Gwen Iceni had been talking to him about something before the enigmas and Boyens had shown up, something about new ways of doing business that didn't involve casual executions and unchecked power for those in authority. "Bran, do you have anything on systems of government that contain limitations on power for those in charge?"

Malin nodded quickly. "Yes, sir. I can provide you some. Texts on political science and history."

"If politics is a science, it's a perverted one," Drakon grumbled. "I know why a lot of people support the kind of power CEOs can wield in the Syndicate system. They hope to become CEOs themselves and have that kind of clout."

"Don't underestimate the fear such a system generates," Malin cautioned. "Many fear to speak out when even innocuous words can be used to justify any penalty. And, if we are honest, many actually believe such power in the hands of those at the top is necessary to maintain order and security."

"Yet they hate the snakes," Drakon said derisively. "That's what the Syndicate system led to and justifies, an Internal Security Service that we feared more than we did the Alliance."

"Yes, sir. That's exactly what it leads to. I'll get you those texts, General."

Despite the absurdity of Iceni's suspicions about Morgan, they had kept nagging at him, and the mention of snakes had brought them to the forefront. "Colonel Malin, how certain are we of the information we have regarding Colonel Morgan's past? Is there anything important that I haven't seen?"

For a bare instant a trace of powerful emotion flashed in Malin's eyes, but the instant passed, and Drakon couldn't be sure what he had seen. Pain? That didn't make sense. Anger? Maybe. Frustration. Of course. Malin had probably spent long hours searching for any tiny bit of information that would condemn Morgan, and his inability to find such incriminating evidence must have caused him considerable disappointment.

Malin's voice came out as controlled as it usually did. "No, sir. What has she done now?"

"Nothing since her little show in the command center." Drakon rubbed his eyes, then looked back at Malin. "Is our information accurate? Is there any chance what we know of Morgan might be wrong?"

"No, sir. I am absolutely certain of the accuracy of what you know of Colonel Morgan."

"I know how you feel about her, so I'm going to ask this directly. Do you think there is any possibility at all that Morgan is working for the snakes?"

This time it was easy to see the exact emotion in Malin. Surprise. "No, sir. I can't imagine— She *does* hate them, sir."

"More than she hates you?"

Malin's smile was wan. "I doubt it, General. I am keeping an eye on Colonel Morgan."

And she's keeping an eye on you. We're all keeping an eye on each other. How the hell do we get anything else done? "Thank you, Bran. Make sure President Iceni's people know that the snake agent is to be kept alive. I want you to get custody of that agent and put her in a maximum-security setting with a few apparent holes in the security."

This time Malin smiled with understanding. "And complete surveillance of the holes so we can see who tries to use them. Yes, sir. I'll get it done right away."

PRESIDENT Iceni put on her best smile. That was a bit easier to do now that she had left the command center and returned to her own governing complex. Being on familiar ground, at her own desk, was a welcome thing after the tense days spent waiting for the enigmas to destroy them all. "Admiral Geary, I want to express my personal thanks for your actions in defending all of human-occupied space and the Midway Star System from renewed attack by the enigma race."

Now for the delicate part. "Midway continues to recognize its obligations under the treaties made with the Syndicate government on Prime," Iceni continued. "However, since we are now an independent star system, there will be a need to renegotiate agreements. I assure you that we seek agreements that will mutually benefit us and the Alliance, and do not anticipate any problems reaching such agreements." *There. Keep it short and a little vague. Don't say anything that sounds like groveling or threatening. CEO Boyens still has a flotilla hanging near the hypernet gate, and the last thing I need is to make Black Jack upset. But I can't have him taking me for granted, either.* "For the people, Iceni, out."

Iceni rubbed the back of her neck, trying to relax tense muscles. "Make sure a copy of that goes to General Drakon so he knows I'm not communicating with Black Jack behind his back," she instructed Togo. "Notify me the moment a reply comes in."

"Yes, Madam President."

"Nothing has come in from CEO Boyens?"

"No, Madam President. One of the light cruisers is on its way to be able to intercept tight-beam transmissions between the Syndicate flotilla and the Alliance flagship, but will not be in position for another hour."

She glowered at the display showing the light cruiser apparently creeping toward an orbit between the forces of Black Jack and Boyens. The display indicated the warship was actually moving at point two light speed, impressive by even space-travel standards. *I could berate Kommodor Marphissa about how long it is taking, but I know full well that her forces were tied up in chasing the enigmas by my orders. Not that such facts would have held back some of the CEOs I have had the misfortune to work for. But I did learn from such screamers that far from motivating people, such tactics usually cause them to slow down either out of resentment or fear. I hope Marphissa appreciates my restraint.*

"The ambassador from Taroa is waiting to see you," Togo said.

"Send him in."

Taroa, like other star systems that had revolted against the Syndicate, had suffered some serious attrition of older, more experienced officials. Some of those officials were dead, some had managed to flee, and others were in prison. The ambassador was one of the new officials, a former academic who had been rapidly boosted into high rank because of personal connections with the new government.

At least he knew that official protocol required visits like this to be in person.

Iceni smiled politely and gestured the ambassador to a seat, watching as he warily sat down and gazed back at her with the evident nervousness a more experienced official would have concealed. Iceni had been a CEO before retitling herself President; Syndicate citizens learned not to look CEOs in the eye, and a lifetime of habits died hard even for newly minted ambassadors. "You have received our offer?" Iceni asked.

The ambassador nodded. "Yes, Madam President. It appears to be . . . extremely generous."

"And you're wondering what the catch is?"

Her candor surprised him, setting the new ambassador off-balance, which had been what she intended.

"If you wish me to be blunt—" the Taroan ambassador began.

"Please. It saves time."

He smiled hesitantly. "You are offering us partial ownership of the main orbiting facility once more, as well as the battleship under construction there, and are asking only for certain mutual-defense agreements in exchange."

Iceni smiled back, broadcasting confidence and artificial candor. "You undervalue the importance to us of those agreements. Battleships we can get. We've already acquired two. But dependable allies in a region of space where threats may come from anywhere at any time is another and far harder thing to find. Midway can't stand alone, even with all of the advantages we get from our jump points and the hyper-net gate. Taroa can't stand alone, either. We were happy to help Taroa throw off the yoke of the Syndicate." It never hurt to toss in an explicit reminder of what Midway had done for the Free Taroans. "Together, with the resources of two star systems, we can much better defend ourselves, and even launch expeditions if necessary to help other star systems."

The ambassador nodded eagerly, giving away how much he wanted this deal to go through. "Yes. I'm certain that my government will understand that. No one wants to be reconquered by the Syndicate. Perhaps Kane could use help?"

The latest reports from Kane spoke of ongoing chaos, with dozens of small groups competing for control after the total collapse of Syndicate authority and subsequent failure of several weak successor governments. "Kane would be a dangerous place to intervene," Iceni said. "If Taroa wants that, we can talk about it. But my people believe that Kane is very likely to fracture into several competing governments within the star system. I am inclined to let that process shake out a little more before we commit our own, limited resources there."

"I understand, Madam President. Forgive me, but I need to be certain. Your offer is made on behalf of both you and General Drakon?"

"That's correct. You need to emphasize to your government that we cannot wait forever for an answer. If we get close enough to finishing that battleship in Taroa on our own, we won't require Taroa's assistance with that anymore."

"Yes, Madam President. I will emphasize the need for quick action."

"Thank you," Iceni said, her tone making clear that the meeting was over. The ambassador left, beaming with happiness at the offered agreement, which he would surely claim credit for negotiating.

Iceni gestured to Togo. "Get me an updated report on our agents of influence in Taroa. I want to ensure we have enough agents in the right positions to get that agreement approved without delay, and without too many questions about how much authority Midway will have under that agreement over military forces belonging to Taroa. Coordinate with Drakon's staff to ensure the agents reporting to his people have the same instructions. I want those instructions sent to Taroa on the same ship that carries the offer."

"Yes, Madam President. In order to ensure the rapid approval of the agreement by the Taroan government, it may be necessary to expend more in bribes than previously budgeted."

Iceni's smile this time was wry. "Perhaps not. I'm finding that bribing elected officials can be significantly cheaper than bribing appointed bureaucrats. The bureaucrats have a much clearer understanding of their value. But extra payments are authorized if needed. We can't afford to depend on Black Jack for defense of this star system." Colonel Malin deserved an under-the-table bonus for suggesting the agreement in the first place, but he would probably refuse it. Whatever Malin's motivations were, they didn't include a desire for wealth.

The reply from Black Jack to her message came six hours later, about as fast as it could have arrived given that the Alliance fleet, which had reassembled into a single massive formation, now orbited nearly three light-hours from the planet on which Iceni was located. Black Jack didn't look particularly triumphant. In fact, he looked about as overworked as Iceni felt. *I don't envy him being the most powerful person in human-occupied space. What do you do with that kind of power if you have a brain and a conscience?* Tired or not, his uniform looked immaculate. *He must have a very good assistant making certain he looks his best—*

Assistant? Or someone a bit closer than that? There have been rumors...

"This is Admiral Geary," Black Jack said. "I will leave negotiations on such matters to the two emissaries of the Alliance government who we have with us. They will be contacting you soon for that purpose. Of immediate concern, my auxiliaries are very low on raw materials. I would like your agreement for them to mine some of the asteroids in this star system for such materials so that we can begin to repair the battle damage suffered here.

"Please pass on to Kommodor Marphissa my personal appreciation for the efforts of her and her ships in working with us for the defense of this star system. They fought well. To the honor of our ancestors, Geary, out."

Iceni spent a moment considering her reply.

"He needs the raw materials badly," Togo said. Having arrived a few minutes earlier to deliver to Iceni an intercepted and decoded copy of the Taroan ambassador's highly secret message to his government about the defense agreement, Togo had been standing silently nearby. Now he spoke diffidently. "Black Jack would not have asked otherwise. Not in a Syndicate star system."

"We are no longer a Syndicate star system," Iceni replied.

"In their minds, we are, Madam President." It was impossible to tell from Togo's expression, or his voice, what he thought of that. "We have also had time to analyze the damage apparent on the Alliance warships. They have seen serious combat and have plainly needed extensive repair. He needs these materials."

"What are you suggesting?"

"A business transaction to our benefit, Madam President. We can bargain for profits that will enhance your stature and the security of your position."

Iceni considered that, too. *The idea is tempting. I have leverage to demand concessions and other things.*

Tempting.

Like bait for a trap?

Does Black Jack really need those raw materials that badly? He's going home, after all, and he has an immense amount of firepower. Even if those repair ships of his are riding empty, they could snag an asteroid in any star system they pass through without asking permission or offering payment.

He could do that here. He could take what he wants. He could simply say "you owe me this," and we could not object.

Instead, Black Jack, with overwhelming force at his back, asks.

Oh, you cunning master of misdirection, you. You want me to take the bait. To see what I do when given the chance to weasel and bargain and act like the very model of a Syndicate CEO. That's how he defeated us time and again, I suspect. Let us think we had the upper hand, then . . .

"We cannot afford to underestimate Black Jack," Iceni said.

"Madam President?"

"He wants us to bargain with him when we think he is in a position of weakness. He wants to see if we go for his throat at the first opportunity. We look at him and think he is just a simple sailor, making a straightforward request. Could someone like that have destroyed the mobile forces of the Syndicate Worlds? And then he distracts me with praise for Kommodor Marphissa, a very clever bit of manipulation designed to make him appear open and aboveboard. Black Jack is actually setting out a snare so carefully concealed that it could easily have tripped us up."

Surprise appeared on Togo's face for a moment. "Forgive me. I did not appreciate how devious Black Jack can be."

"But now we know. I'll give him what he wants. Graciously. Without bargaining." Iceni smiled grimly. "He'll know that he's dealing with someone smart enough to avoid his traps."

"Yes, Madam President." Togo raised a hand slightly. "We should ensure that whatever the Alliance does is coordinated with the space-resource-extraction authorities. That will enable us to monitor exactly what is done under the pretext of following standard procedures."

"Excellent idea. You tell the extraction authorities that they'll be hearing from the Alliance fleet soon and that they are to oblige the Alliance requests without hesitation." She sent a cheerful reply to Black Jack, granting him permission to mine, then forwarded the last part of his message to Marphissa, along with her congratulations.

"The mining authorities have been notified, Madam President," Togo reported.

"Good." She gave him a questioning look. Her earlier suspicions of Togo had faded considerably as he had continued to show nothing but appropriate deference to her and gratifying obedience to her orders. *I was rattled after the arrival of the enigmas, after everything that was happening. Easy enough to see dangers everywhere under such circumstances.* "Black Jack is surely trying to collect information about what we are doing here and in nearby star systems. His ships must be pulling in everything they can from transmissions and news reports and other sources. We need to ensure that the picture Black Jack builds is one that favors us."

Togo held very still, his eyes focused on some distant mental objective. "We need a method of sending him a narrative, telling him what he could otherwise learn but ensuring it does so in a way that we prefer," he observed.

"If we just sent him such a package it would be too obvious. We need at least a veneer of its being impartial."

"That would require a means of contacting the Alliance fleet officially without doing so . . . officially."

"And it's not like we have any friends on those warships of Black Jack's," Iceni grumbled.

Friends? On Black Jack's ships?

Togo started to say something more. She silenced him with a gesture, trying to catch the elusive thought. *Ah. That's it. A matter involving a certain subordinate of Drakon's and a certain subordinate of Black Jack's.* "Get General Drakon for me. I need to speak to him as soon as possible."

I don't like this, Drakon thought. "Are you all right with what I'm asking you to do?" he asked Colonel Rogero. *Actually, Iceni asked me to ask Rogero, but it was my decision to make that request, and I refuse to hide behind anyone else when doing it.*

Rogero nodded, outwardly impassive. "I appreciate the opportunity to send a . . . personal message, General."

"Donal, you've been open with me about what she means to

you even now. I know this isn't going to be easy for you, especially knowing that we're using this to send our own spin on recent events to Black Jack."

"I would rather be used by you and President Iceni than by the snakes, sir," Rogero replied with a very slight smile. "I am all right with it, General. It will let me say . . . good-bye. We never had that opportunity."

Drakon looked away, more uncomfortable than ever. "We'll send the message openly since we no longer have to worry about the snakes asking questions. Record what you want. I won't review that part. But you'll have to add this text worked up by the President's people. There's nothing objectionable in there, just an update on things that makes us all look good. The elections and all, and what we did at Taroa. Then I'll send it, personally, to Black Jack. There's no guarantee that Captain . . ."

"Bradamont."

It was amazing how much emotion could be invested in a single name, even when Rogero was clearly trying to suppress such feelings.

"That she'll get it," Drakon finished. "But I will ask Black Jack to forward it to her."

"Yes, sir. May I have a few minutes alone to do this?"

"Take the time you need. And, thank you, Donal. I wish things could work out differently."

"We both know that is impossible, sir. She is an Alliance fleet officer, and I was, until recently, a Syndicate ground forces officer. Fate brought us together, but neither of us ever believed anything but eventual separation would be the result."

Less than half an hour after that, Drakon sat behind his desk and tapped the command to send a message to the Alliance flagship. "I am asking a personal favor, Admiral Geary. I understand that you have no reason to grant that to a former enemy. However, the favor is not for me, but for one of my subordinates. Colonel Rogero is one of my most highly trusted and highly regarded officers. He has asked me to see if the attached message can be delivered to one of your subordinate officers. In light of his loyal service to me and as one professional to another, I am requesting that you forward the message to its intended recipient. In case any question arises, President Iceni is aware of this communication and the contents of the attached message and has no objections to either. I will answer any questions you have regarding this matter if you communicate them to me."

There. That was all he needed to say. But this was his first, and might be the only, individual message to Black Jack. Drakon imagined he could see the legendary Alliance admiral sitting across from him. *Are you as real a person as you seem? I hope so. This is what I'd say if you are really that man, as one combat commander to another.* "I'm glad we never met in battle during the war, Admiral. I'm not at all sure I would have survived that experience, though I would have given you the fight of your life before it was over. For the people, Drakon, out."

He was still sitting at the desk a few minutes later when Colonel Malin called. Even if Drakon hadn't been keyed up by recent events, he would have been alerted by Malin's grim expression. "What happened?"

"The snake agent is dead, General."

CHAPTER FIVE

DRAKON took a moment to calm himself before speaking. "How?"

"I took a full squad to the security cell to take custody of her, General," Malin said. "When we arrived at her cell, we found her dead. Medical readings from the cell had been spoofed to make it appear she was alive and well. An initial inspection suggests quick-acting poison as the cause."

"How long had she been dead?"

"Less than an hour. We'll get an exact time when the autopsy is complete."

The implications of that were pretty clear. "Someone didn't want us getting our hands on her. Who knew you were coming?"

"Senior members of President Iceni's staff," Malin said. "We couldn't just show up and take the prisoner without her knowledge."

"No." Iceni would raise hell if Drakon's people tried to step on her toes that way. "I suppose the security monitoring systems at the agent's cell show nothing?"

"Nothing," Malin confirmed. "I'm having them analyzed, but I'm sure we'll find that those systems were also hacked, and during the period when the agent was murdered, there will be false observations that reveal nothing. Sir, I take full responsibility for—"

"Don't," Drakon interrupted. "I should have told you to get that agent right away and personally called Iceni to approve the transfer. I let the snakes still hidden here get one step ahead of me. We need to start getting ahead of them."

"General, there are many things vying for your attention. The snakes only have to focus on sabotaging you and the President. You and President Iceni have to focus on dozens of issues." Malin nodded, his mouth set in determined lines. "I will work on this. And . . . I will notify Colonel Morgan if that is your wish. She needs to know about this since she is looking for hidden snakes."

Drakon raised an eyebrow at him. "She does need to know what happened, but if you tell her, she'll mock you for failing."

"I deserve the mockery, General. It will . . ." Malin's smile held a sharp edge. "It will motivate me to avoid any similar occurrence. I'll provide you with a detailed report when analysis of the agent's death and the circumstances around it is complete."

"Thanks." Drakon gazed past Malin, wondering why he had an odd sense of something left hanging. Something important? Or . . . something that should be important? "Colonel Malin, what was the agent's name?"

"Excuse me, General?" Malin seemed startled by the question.

"Her name. What was the name of the snake agent?"

Malin consulted his data pad. "Yvette Saludin, sir. Is that significant?"

"It was to her." Drakon closed his eyes. "The snakes were threatening her family if she didn't cooperate. Where is that family?"

"In Chako Star System, sir. According to the last information we have, Chako remains under firm Syndicate control."

"There's nothing we can do for them, then." Drakon opened his eyes and focused on Malin again. "Does that bother you?"

"Me, General?" Malin shook his head, perplexed. "No, sir. We had no alternative but to arrest her, and once she started working for the snakes, her eventual fate was certain. She was dead from that moment. I do regret not being able to use her to get leads on the covert snakes still hidden among us."

"Sure." For all his talk of rejecting the Syndicate system, Malin could be remarkably cold-blooded. Morgan would kill with a rush of fire in her veins, while Malin would do it with ice filling him. They were opposite sides of the same card, because the result would be the same for whoever had the misfortune to get in their sights. "Anything new on Boyens's flotilla?" Drakon asked, feeling a sudden desire to change the subject.

"No, sir. The mobile forces sent a light cruiser to drop surveillance satellites along the path between the Alliance fleet and the Syndicate flotilla. We have picked up a few transmissions, but they all consist of CEO Boyens inviting Black Jack and his fleet to leave and Black Jack or one of his subordinates telling CEO Boyens *after you*."

"I just sent Black Jack a message," Drakon said. "I don't know what impact it'll have. We'll have to wait and see."

THE message from the Alliance fleet had come not from Black Jack but from a woman identifying herself as Emissary of the Alliance Government Victoria Rione. Iceni regarded the image of the Alliance civilian skeptically. *An emissary? How much power does she actually have?*

But the woman's words quickly caught Iceni's attention.

"We have been speaking with CEO Boyens," Emissary Victoria Rione said. "As you are doubtless aware. Those discussions have not been particularly fruitful. He is eager for us to leave, for reasons you and I both know. CEO Boyens has already progressed from urging us to depart to issuing not-particularly-subtle threats, and when those do not work, I expect the threats to become overt.

"President Iceni, there is no question that CEO Boyens does not possess sufficient strength to threaten the Alliance forces here. I am told by the officers in this fleet that the flotilla CEO Boyens commands dares not leave the vicinity of the hypernet gate while we are here."

Rione's expression became more intense. "The next step is likely to be a threat to something that is very important to you and to us, something that CEO Boyens could strike at without moving his flotilla."

Iceni bit off a curse. *The hypernet gate. If Boyens threatens to damage it badly enough to cause it to collapse, we wouldn't be able to do anything to stop him. I'm not at all certain that Boyens would carry out such a threat because the Syndicate government would be very unhappy at the loss of that gate, but can we afford the consequences if he did? We would still have the trade traffic generated by our jump points, but the gate gives us access to a lot more.*

"There is a possible course of action that would frustrate such a threat," Rione continued.

As she listened, Iceni began smiling. *I'll need to convince Drakon.*

"YOU want to give the Alliance part ownership of the hypernet gate?" Drakon was staring at her as if wondering when insanity had set in. He had agreed without any argument to another private meeting in the former snake conference room that served as neutral ground for them. That quick agreement had left Iceni both pleased and wary of Drakon's motives, because as the old Syndicate saying went, every gift horse needed to be looked in the mouth.

"It checkmates Boyens," Iceni explained. "He can't threaten to damage the gate if it is partly owned by the Alliance. That would be an attack by the Syndicate Worlds on Alliance government property."

"It would break the peace treaty?"

"Clearly and without any doubt. Boyens has already identified himself as a representative of the Syndicate government and his flotilla as forces of that government. He could not possibly claim his actions were anything but an act of the Syndicate Worlds."

"The Syndicate government at Prime would have his head on a platter." Drakon stopped speaking, thoughts rushing behind his eyes. "How much?"

"How much of the gate? It doesn't matter how small the Alliance's ownership stake is. An attack on the gate would still be an attack on the Alliance. Would you be willing to consider one percent ownership for the Alliance?"

"One percent? What are we getting in return?"

"We already got it. We would grant the partial ownership in grateful acknowledgment of the defense of this star system from attacks by the enigma race."

Drakon thought some more. "Is this your idea?"

"I wish it had been. There's an Alliance politician with their fleet who proposed it. Rione is her name. We don't have much information on her, but what we do have identifies her as a vice president of the Callas Republic and senator of the Alliance."

"Sounds important," Drakon observed.

"It does. Which makes it odd that she only identified herself as an emissary of the Alliance government. We're a very long ways from the Alliance, but we've picked up faint rumors of disruptions there in the wake of the war. Nothing like the Syndicate Worlds has been facing, but problems." Iceni paused. "If Black Jack has taken over the Alliance, he would need politicians to handle some of the heavy lifting of ruling all those star systems. Rione's new title as an emissary, a personal emissary of Black Jack, might well be a lot more powerful than her former position."

Drakon nodded, glancing at the image of Rione visible on the display over the table. "She's good-looking enough. How personal do you think her relationship with Black Jack is?"

"I think," said Iceni, feeling the frost in her voice, "that this Rione struck me as very skilled, perhaps the closest to a Syndicate CEO's skills I have seen in anyone from the Alliance. I doubt she has had any need to use her body to advance her position."

"I didn't mean— Look, you know how things work. The one in charge decides the terms of employment, regardless of what the subordinates want and regardless of what the laws that everybody ignores say. It may not have been her choice if Black Jack wanted her."

"I know how things work in the Syndicate system," Iceni admitted, relenting. "You're right. He could have demanded that of her. But from the little I've seen and heard of Black Jack, he doesn't seem the type. Not everyone, even in the Syndicate, abuses their subordinates that way."

"I agree with you," Drakon said. "But we can safely assume that if this idea was presented by Black Jack's emissary, it actually came from Black Jack."

"It's the sort of extremely clever political maneuvering we've seen from Black Jack," Iceni agreed. She let Drakon see her internal unease for a moment. "We wouldn't want to disappoint Black Jack since we still need his protection. But we'll also be setting a precedent, in which we do as he . . . asks."

Drakon nodded twice. "There's not much we can do about that, is there? One percent. That's fine with me. The deal benefits both of us. I have to admit, I'd love to see Boyens's face when he hears about it." He gazed at the star-system display near one wall of the office. "Revolting against the Syndicate was a matter of survival for us. I didn't give much thought to some aspects of independence. Formal agreements, like this one with the Alliance. The one we've proposed to Taroa. Do we know enough to make sure we're doing them right?"

"Are you worried about my skills, General Drakon?"

"No. But we're going into very deep waters, here."

"Agreed." She altered the star display to show the entire region of nearby space. "We're building a fortress of sorts with these agreements, adding strength to our own by drawing on the strengths of others. If we did this wrong, we'd be draining our strength into theirs. But I am confident that we will get as much or more from these agreements as our partners in the deals."

"If we have enough time for their benefits to play out," Drakon said.

"Yes. We need time as well as more allies among nearby star systems. Taroa wants to intervene in Kane."

"I know." He grimaced. "Kane is a tar pit from all I've seen. The last thing we need is to show up and become the one guy everybody else there will combine to fight. I'm also a bit concerned about Ulindi."

"What have we heard from Ulindi?" Iceni asked.

"Very little. There's an information blockade. I'm trying to find out what's going on there that someone doesn't want outsiders to know about."

"Good. Unlike Ulindi, we're dependent on the space traffic using our jump points and hypernet gate and can't block ship movement to prevent anyone from learning what's going on here." She ran one hand through her hair. "Our preferred candidates appear to be well on their ways to winning the elections here. That will ensure stability."

"We shouldn't win every post," Drakon argued. "That will make it look like we did the Syndicate thing and just faked the results."

"We won't win all of them. Just enough." Iceni laughed. "And we won't have to manipulate results, apparently. Our stock, and that of our supporters, is very high after our heroic stands during the enigma attack. Does that feel strange to you?"

"What?"

"We're in charge because the people want us to be, not because we have the power to make them do what we want. Isn't that odd?"

"And if the people change their minds?"

"We still have the power if we need it," Iceni pointed out.

KOMMODOR Asima Marphissa sat on the bridge of her flagship, the heavy cruiser *Manticore*, painfully aware that of the various factions with mobile forces in Midway Star System, hers was the smallest and weakest. Half of her heavy cruisers remained at the gas giant, guarding the mobile forces dock there, leaving her to confront the Syndicate flotilla commanded by CEO Boyens with only two heavy cruisers, five light cruisers, and twelve Hunter-Killers. Her little flotilla would have been lost amid the Alliance fleet and was badly overmatched by the Syndicate flotilla of one battleship, six heavy cruisers, four light cruisers, and ten HuKs. She was inordinately proud of the tiny force, but she had no illusions about its size or capabilities.

Of course, I have a battleship, too. The Midway, *which can move but not fight. Actually right now it can't even move since Kapitan-Leytenant Kontos is still busy removing all of the braces tying the battleship to the main mobile forces facility. Only someone like Kontos could have figured out a way to use a battleship with no weapons to save that facility from the enigma attack.*

I wonder how badly Kontos wants my job? Can President Iceni and I trust someone that ambitious and brilliant once the battleship has working weaponry?

"Kommodor, we have a transmission from the Syndicate flotilla," the senior communications specialist reported, breaking into her gloomy train of thought.

"CEO Boyens has finally condescended to speak with me?" Marphissa asked. She had moved her flotilla much closer to the hypernet gate, less than five light-minutes from the Syndicate flotilla, openly taunting CEO Boyens and daring him to start a fight in which Black Jack and his fleet would hopefully intervene.

"It is not addressed to you, Kommodor. It was broadcast to our entire flotilla."

"Let me see it." She knew that workers and supervisors on every ship in the flotilla would be viewing that message, regardless of rules and regulations. Best to find out what Boyens was saying to them.

CEO Boyens wore the standard CEO smile for conversations with underlings (which naturally differed from the standard CEO smiles for conversations with equals or superiors). Marphissa had seen the patently insincere and patronizing expression often enough to instantly identify the smile, its exact shading based on the audience, and its lack of real meaning.

"Citizens," Boyens began in the tone of a disappointed father. "You've been misled and misdirected. Doubtless you have been forced to take actions that you have not wished to take. Now you face serious threats and have no one to count on to protect you and your families except the dictators who call themselves President and General. You need not bow to their will any longer."

Boyens's standard smile was replaced by the standard Syndicate CEO insincere look of sincerity. "I am authorized to grant you all immunity for any actions taken contrary to the laws of the Syndicate Worlds and for any actions against the people of the Syndicate Worlds. It is more important to reward the loyal than to try to punish those who mistakenly trusted in the wrong authorities. Take control of your ships once more. Bring them under my authority, where I can protect you from not only the brutal forces of the dictators but also from the fist of the barbaric Alliance forces with which the dictators have allied themselves.

"You will be welcomed, you will be protected, and you will be rewarded. All you have to do is act in the interests of yourselves and *of the people*. For the people, Boyens, out."

Marphissa glared sourly at where Boyens's image had been. *His message would have sounded a little more genuine if he hadn't rushed over that last "for the people" in a monotone. How should I reply to this?*

"He thinks we're fools," the senior communications specialist growled.

"He does," Marphissa agreed. "What would you say to him?"

The specialist hesitated through force of habit. Workers in the Syndicate system were trained not to speak their minds, and learned quickly enough that invitations by executives and CEOs to offer their opinions were simply traps. But he had seen how things had changed since the Midway Star System gained independence, how former-executive-now-Kommodor Marphissa led her crews, and so the specialist committed the formerly foolish acts of looking directly at her and saying what he really thought. "Kommodor, I would tell him that we are not fools. That we are not simple enough or crazy enough to believe the promises of a Syndicate CEO. That . . . that we have experienced the rule of the Syndicate Worlds and know it has nothing to do with the welfare of the people. That President Iceni and General Drakon have given us more freedom than we have ever known, and have also given us reasons, and the power, to laugh at the lies of a CEO!" The specialist stopped speaking, looking worried by the sort of outburst that would have resulted in serious punishment under Syndicate rules.

Marphissa looked around the bridge, seeing agreement with the specialist's speech on the face of every specialist and supervisor present. "I can't improve on your words, Senior Specialist Lehmann. Would you like to send that reply to the CEO?"

Lehmann looked taken aback, then more worried, then defiant. "Yes, Kommodor. If you would permit me to."

"I'll introduce you, then say what you did before. You don't need to make it longer or more elaborate. Just words from the heart." Marphissa tapped the transmit command, ensuring that the reply would go not only to Boyens but also to every warship in the CEO's flotilla as well as all of Marphissa's warships. "CEO Boyens, no one here will accept your offer. If anyone on any of *your* units wishes to find freedom, they are welcome to join us. Here is one of our senior specialists with his reply to your words."

Marphissa waited until Senior Specialist Lehmann had finished repeating his words, then refocused the pickup on her. "For the people," she said, stating each word slowly and with emphasis, "Marphissa, out."

She had let a line worker berate a CEO to his face. Marphissa felt a surge of elation at the act that overrode the fears of such an action created by a lifetime of experience and training.

The workers in Boyens's flotilla would hear the words of Specialist Lehmann, would hear her words. Perhaps they would act on them even though the snakes aboard Boyens's ships must be on constant alert and in larger numbers than before. It was a small hope, to cause some rebellion in the Syndicate warships, but all she could do besides watching others decide the fate of her star system.

"A message for both of us from Black Jack?" Drakon asked. He had come quickly when Iceni notified him. They could have linked displays, held a virtual meeting, but that would have involved an insane level of risk given the chance that someone would break into the link and monitor everything. Only a personal meeting, in a room confirmed clean of monitoring devices by both her and Drakon's techs, could offer enough security.

"Yes. Watch it, then tell me what you think." She tapped her controls, and the image of Black Jack appeared over the table.

Admiral Geary looked and sounded as formal as she had ever seen him. "President Iceni, General Drakon, I have two matters I need to place before you. First of all, President Iceni, I have to inform you that while in space controlled by the enigma race, we were able to locate and free some humans who had been kept prisoner by the enigmas, apparently for study. All of them, except those born in captivity, originated from Syndicate Worlds' colonies or ships. All have been checked as thoroughly as possible, and no signs of biological or other contamination or threat has been found.

"It is important for me to emphasize that none of them know anything about the enigmas. They were sealed inside an asteroid and never even saw any of their captors. They can tell no one anything about the enigmas. They have all been impacted mentally, physically, and emotionally by their long imprisonment. Given their condition, I intend taking the majority of them back to Alliance space, where I can arrange care and transport back to their home star systems elsewhere in the Syndicate Worlds. However, three of the prisoners say they or their parents came from Taroa, and fifteen others say they came from this star system. Those eighteen wish to return home now. We want to accommodate those wishes, but I desire first to know whatever else you can tell me about conditions at Taroa, and second to know your intentions toward the fifteen who came from Midway. I feel an obligation to see that they are treated well now that they have been freed."

Geary paused. "The second matter concerns formalizing our relationship with the new government of Midway."

Iceni had already heard this once, but still felt her heart leap at the words. *Formalizing our relationship. He's officially recognizing this star system as independent, and both Drakon and me as the legitimate rulers here. This is better than I had hoped for.*

"I am proposing," Geary continued, "to assign a senior Alliance officer here to represent the Alliance, to make plain our commitment to your star system, and to render whatever advice or assistance you might ask for in matters of defense and in your transition to a freer form of government. The officer whom I propose to assign here is Captain Bradamont, who has been serving as commanding officer of the battle cruiser *Dragon*. She is an excellent officer, and because she was at one point a prisoner of war, she has had some prior contact with Syndicate Worlds' officers and can work with them. Captain Bradamont has already agreed to this official posting, but I require your consent for such an assignment, which I think will be to the benefit of everyone involved. The emissaries of the Alliance government accompanying this fleet have already approved the posting of Captain Bradamont here, so all we require is the acceptance of your government.

"I await your reply on both of these matters. To the honor of our ancestors, Geary, out."

The message ended, yet Drakon sat for several seconds without saying anything. Finally, he looked at her. "Formalizing our relationship. Does that mean what I think it does?"

"Yes. He's giving us something very important, official recognition from the Alliance, official recognition from Black Jack himself, but with two complications."

"Let's tackle the easier one," Drakon suggested. "Those people the enigmas had."

"That's easier?" She regarded him steadily. "Do you believe Black Jack that none of them know anything about the enigmas?"

"Yes." Drakon grimaced. "Not because I tend to believe Alliance officers but because there wouldn't be any point in his lying about that if he intends giving them to us. If he were keeping them? Yes, then I'd be very suspicious. But after we get them, we can ask them anything we want."

"Once again, Black Jack proves he's a brilliant politician. He's giving us the truth and a deal we can't refuse." Iceni drummed her fingers on the arm of her chair. "Those citizens. We have to take them. If word ever got out that we'd been offered them and turned Black Jack down, there would be hell to pay. We'd be accused of conspiring with him to keep those citizens' knowledge of the enigmas hidden."

"Like you've said, he's tricky."

"If he has boxed us in on this issue, where can we put them? Where did he say the enigmas held them?"

"Inside an asteroid." Drakon rubbed his chin, thinking. "It sounds like they had spent a long time there. They wouldn't want to be dumped on a planet's surface. It would mess them up to have that much open around them."

"How do you know that?" Iceni asked. "Black Jack said they had been impacted by their imprisonment, but he didn't offer any details."

Drakon paused as if deciding whether to answer, then shrugged. "I knew some people who got released from a labor camp after a long time confined. They were . . . very uncomfortable without four walls around them."

Iceni wondered what to say. *How many of us know someone who was sent to the labor camps? Not many of us got to meet someone re-leased from the camps, though. Too many died in them.* "Were these people friends of yours?"

"Yeah." Drakon looked down, his expression hard and closed off.

All right. I won't ask more. I'll even change the subject for you.
"What are you suggesting for these former prisoners of the enigmas then?"

He looked up, obviously relieved that she had not pressed for more personal information. "The main orbiting facility. It's limited in size, it's somewhat like what they were used to, it's a mixed-use facility with military and citizens, security won't be a major issue since it will be easy to control access, and no one will be able to accuse us of locking them up for our own purposes."

"Hmmm." Iceni smiled. "We might even get some credit out of it with the citizens. Look! For the first time, someone has been brought out of space controlled by the enigmas. And here they are, free again, thanks to *our* relationship with Black Jack."

Drakon nodded, then fixed his gaze on her. "They're not really the first."

"To come out of enigma space?" Iceni asked. "I suppose Colonel Morgan does have the right to claim that. One thing you didn't tell me was why. Do you know why she volunteered for a suicide mission when she was barely eighteen years old?"

"No. She had been raised in an official orphanage, both parents dead in the war, but Morgan never says one word about it. However, she got a medical waiver to be commissioned after that mission."

"Oh? What does it say?"

Drakon scowled. "It doesn't say much beyond approving her for duty. She needed that waiver. Otherwise, Morgan would have been sent into combat as worker-level soldier cannon fodder. That's what happened to the other guy who was recovered from that mission. He died within a month of being shipped off to one of those battles where we and the Alliance kept feeding in men and women and ships and equipment as if eventually we could choke the machinery of slaughter by giving it enough victims."

She watched him, knowing the sorts of battles of which Drakon spoke and the awful sense of futility they had created, as if nothing and no one could stop the senseless dying. "But Morgan was saved from that fate when she was commissioned?" Iceni asked as if she had not already known that because of Togo's investigations. "She must have had a patron to get that waiver. Do you have any idea who her patron was?"

"No. I had to assume she passed the waiver requirements, because Morgan has no connections to anyone who could have arranged a deal."

"No connections that you know of," Iceni pressed.

"I've looked pretty hard," Drakon said in a way that made it clear his search had been exhaustive. "But you already know that about her, that she came back from enigma space. I brought that up because, well, we both know Morgan's got a few issues."

"That's putting it mildly."

"Some of those issues could have predated that mission and explained why she volunteered. There's no way to know. And," Drakon pushed on, "this all applies to these citizens who were held by the enigmas. We don't know who they are, what they did, how they ended up in enigma hands. If the enigmas have hands. Some of them might have issues now, too, and need a lot of help."

"I see." Iceni nodded judiciously. "I hadn't thought of that. Yes, until the citizens are evaluated, we can't just turn them loose. That will more than justify limiting access to them and keeping them secure. The fact that it's a valid reason will help keep anyone from questioning our motives."

"Do we have other motives with them?" Drakon asked.

She had to pause and think. "If they truly don't know anything? Probably not. I think your ideas for the released citizens are very good ones. We can keep the ones from Taroa up there, too, until we hear back from the Free Taroans." Iceni smiled wryly. "Though it may take a very long while for the still-interim government of Free Taroa to make a decision on the matter as they debate and argue and discuss."

"Hopefully, the Taroan citizens won't have died of old age while waiting," Drakon agreed. "We're already paying out enough bribes and applying other pressure to get the defense agreement approved before anyone at Taroa realizes how tightly they'll be tied to us by that agreement. We can't afford to invest effort right now into getting the Taroans to take the prisoners, too. Now, the other deal. You know about this Alliance officer, Bradamont."

"I know," Iceni said, careful once more to choose her words, "that she is linked to Colonel Rogero. And I know that we just used that link to pass our own version of events to Black Jack. I also know the snake records we captured contained a file on this Bradamont that identified her as a source code-named Mantis. Do you know the full story behind that?"

"I guess it's my day to talk about my staff." Drakon looked away, one hand to his mouth as he thought. "The short version is this. Several years back, Colonel Rogero and a small group of soldiers returning from visits home were drafted to serve as guards on a modified freighter hauling Alliance prisoners of war to a labor camp. On the way there, the freighter suffered a serious accident. Rogero let the Alliance prisoners out of confinement to save their lives, then let them assist in repairing the damage to the freighter to save everyone's lives."

Iceni shook her head. "The wise thing, the right thing, but also the contrary-to-regulations thing."

"Right. When they reached safety, Rogero was arrested. The CEO involved decided that since Rogero cared so much for the Alliance prisoners, he could spend more time with them by being assigned to the typically hellhole labor camp where they were confined. While serving there . . ." Drakon spread his hands. "Rogero and Bradamont fell in love."

"Rather odd circumstances for that," Iceni observed.

"Yes, but you see, they knew each other. Rogero told me Bradamont led the Alliance prisoners during the accident and while fixing the damage. She impressed the hell out of him. And she had seen Rogero risk his neck to save the Alliance prisoners."

Iceni nodded, finally understanding. "They knew some very important things about each other."

"While that was going on, I had been trying to find out why Rogero hadn't made it back from leave. I had just tracked him to the labor camp when the snakes there found out about him and Bradamont. I was told that the only question regarding Rogero's future was whether he would join the inhabitants at another labor camp or just be executed."

"What saved him?"

"I saved him," Drakon said, matter-of-factly and without any hint of boasting. "I suggested to the snakes that they could use Bradamont's affection for Rogero. Use that to turn this Bradamont so she'd report on Alliance stuff from the inside." Drakon grinned. "The snakes loved the idea. Of course, implementing it meant getting Bradamont back in the Alliance fleet, so the snakes arranged for her to be transported near the border with the Alliance and leaked the information. Her transport got intercepted, she got liberated by Alliance Marines and sent back to the Alliance fleet. Meanwhile, Rogero got sent back to me. I was told that was so he could pretend to send good intelligence to the Alliance in exchange for whatever Bradamont sent him, just as I'd proposed. But Rogero told me flat out that the snakes wanted him to spy on me, too."

"Naturally. But, by knowing who their spy was, you could better protect yourself from the snakes." Iceni rested her forehead on one palm. "The relationship is real? It seemed so from that message from Rogero that we passed to Black Jack."

"It's real."

"Did she really spy on the Alliance for us?"

"I seriously doubt it. What the snakes had Rogero send her was stuff the Alliance already knew, along with false information to mislead the Alliance. From what Rogero could tell, the stuff he got from her was the same sort of junk."

Iceni glanced at Drakon. "Do you think Alliance intelligence was using her the same way the snakes were using Rogero?"

"I'm certain of it."

"So she has been an agent of Alliance intelligence for some years already."

"Why else would they want to assign her here?" Drakon pointed out. "But she's also been, as Black Jack said, commanding officer of an Alliance battle cruiser."

"During Black Jack's campaign against the Syndicate Worlds," Iceni added thoughtfully. "What that woman must know about his way of fighting." She sat up straighter. "Black Jack said she would render advice and assistance. Including on defense matters. That knowledge could be invaluable to us. Oh, he is devious. Military advice to us, offered in a form that looks completely innocuous."

"You want to accept her, then?"

"We can't afford to turn her down! And if Colonel Rogero can really vouch for her . . ." Iceni chewed her lower lip as she thought. "It will be touchy. Very touchy. She's the enemy. Not officially, not anymore, but we've spent our lives seeing the uniform she wears as that of the enemy. An enemy who killed untold numbers of our citizens."

"We started it," Drakon said dryly.

"And you know how little that matters to the average worker." Iceni shook her head. "We'll have to figure out how to handle it. Formal recognition of our status as an independent star system by the Alliance, and an officer who both represents Black Jack and can advise on his tactics. We *cannot* turn this down."

Drakon nodded. "You're right, but you're also right about how hard it will be to get anyone to work with her. Do you want to confine her to the orbital facility for a while?"

"No. I want her free to go where she wants to go and do what she wants to do." Iceni smiled. "That way we'll learn where she wants to go and what she wants to do."

"Fair enough. We know she'll be telling Black Jack what's happening here."

"As long as she doesn't try to set up an Alliance spy ring, I can accept that."

Drakon played with the controls for a moment, and Iceni once again saw Geary speaking part of his message. ". . . in your transition to a freer form of government . . ."

"That might be a problem," Iceni conceded. "If he really expects us to keep offering the citizens more freedom and say in the government. We do have some measures under way already, such as the elections for low-level officials, that should gladden the heart of the Alliance."

"I have been getting advice that we should continue that process as far as we can safely take it," Drakon said. "For the sake of long-term stability and ensuring citizen buy-in to our government."

Where have I heard that before? That assistant of Drakon's. Colonel Malin. He must still be pushing the idea. "As long as the emphasis remains on *as far as we can safely take it*, I don't object to that concept in theory," Iceni said. "In any event, that's a long-term problem. We have one other short-term problem. What about your Colonel Rogero?"

Drakon brooded over the question for several seconds. "I want to leave it up to Colonel Rogero. I'll back whatever decision he makes."

As I could have guessed before I asked the question. "That could hurt him," Iceni said. "If the citizens learn that she is not only an Alliance officer but also served as a source for the snakes . . ."

"Rogero was technically a source, too. He misled the snakes at every turn, but their files list him as a source. Let's try to keep that quiet in both their cases."

"Let's." Iceni sat looking at Drakon. "Does anyone else know about Rogero and Bradamont? About Rogero's ties to the snakes?"

Drakon nodded heavily. "One person."

Something about the way he said it brought a lump of anxiety to life in her guts. *One person.* "Not her."

"Yeah. Colonel Morgan."

"Why *in the hell* did you tell—"

"I didn't tell her!" Drakon glared at Iceni. "She found out while checking for hidden snake agents after the mess with Colonel Dun. I told you she was good."

"Oh . . . *wonderful!*" Iceni tried to damp down her aggravation. "Can we keep her alive?"

"Morgan?"

"Bradamont!"

"Oh." Drakon's expression shaded to grim determination. "Yes. You don't have to worry about that."

"Pardon me, but I will be worrying about that!" Iceni sighed and managed to regain control. "If you tell me that Bradamont will be safe from . . . threats, then I will tell Black Jack that we will accept her and the citizens freed from the enigmas."

Drakon nodded and leaned forward to emphasize his words. "Ask if Bradamont will bring some intel about what Black Jack's fleet did in enigma space, and wherever they found the six mystery ships and that mammoth battleship. We haven't been told anything about those yet. If Black Jack really wants to formalize things, his representative should be willing to share some of that information. We're closer to the enigmas than any other star system. We need to know what he found out and what he found."

"Yes. Absolutely," Iceni agreed. "I will phrase it diplomatically, but I will make it clear that we hope for such information and regard it as of critical importance to the security of this star system." Another thought hit her then, causing Iceni to give Drakon a keen glance. "Bradamont's code name was Mantis. Why did the snakes call her that?"

He shrugged. "I have no idea. Snakes aren't in the habit of explaining things. Why does it matter? A mantis is an insect, right? Some sort of bug? The code name was probably intended as a put-down of Bradamont."

"I don't think so," Iceni said. "A mantis isn't just any insect. It's a very deadly insect. A predator. And a species in which the female mantises devour the males."

Drakon stared at Iceni, then shook his head. "Well, an Alliance battle cruiser commander. They're tough, right? Maybe that's what it was about. Or maybe it was the snakes' idea of a joke."

"Maybe. If she was working with Alliance intelligence, they would have given her their own code name. I wonder what Alliance intelligence called her?"

Iceni sat for a while after Drakon had left, letting thoughts tumble through her mind. Many of the issues bedeviling her could not be resolved quickly or easily or perhaps at all. *Like Morgan. I can't send Togo after her. He could take her. He's so good he even frightens me. But any link between me and whoever killed Morgan would kill any hope of working with Drakon again. He's far too obsessed with that loyalty thing.*

I need to contact Malin again. He refused to kill Morgan before. Maybe he'll agree now. Why wouldn't he want that woman dead? If he still won't get rid of her, I'll let him know that he had better keep her from doing anything against me or this Captain Bradamont. If Morgan does strike at me or her, Malin needs to know that I'll hold him *responsible.*

"KOMMODOR! A new warship has arrived at the hypernet gate!"

Marphissa bolted awake. She had been only fitfully sleeping, worn down by the long stalemate. Day after day of the Syndicate flotilla and the Midway Flotilla glaring at each other across five light-minutes of space, the Alliance fleet orbiting nearly two light-hours away checkmating any offensive action by the Syndicate CEO. Boyens couldn't attack, but he wouldn't leave, and she didn't have enough firepower to force him to go.

Despite her haste, Marphissa checked the passageway outside her door to ensure no one was waiting in ambush. Syndicate executives and CEOs got into those kinds of habits or fell prey to ambitious sub-ordinates looking to clear a few openings for promotion. That was changing. But there were still snake agents rumored to be hidden among the military and citizens of the star system, so old habits would remain current practice.

The way looking clear and her sidearm ready, Marphissa yanked open her hatch and ran for the bridge.

Inside, a sense of excitement had replaced the boredom that had been wearing at everyone. "A new warship? What is it?" Marphissa de-manded as she dropped into her command seat.

"Heavy cruiser, Kommodor," the senior watch specialist an-nounced. "Modified with extra cargo capacity and life support. They've seen the Syndicate flotilla and are running."

"Running?" Marphissa looked carefully over the situation por-trayed on her display before concentrating on the movement of the new heavy cruiser. "Do we have any ID yet?"

"It should have shown up at the same time we saw the cruiser's ar-rival, Kommodor," the watch specialist said. "We've seen nothing."

She took another look at the new arrival, whose first action upon seeing the Syndicate flotilla had been to run. "Send him our ID. I'll also send him a personal message."

Activity on the bridge paused for a moment as Kapitan Toirac ar-rived and hastily sat down in the seat next to Marphissa. "What's going on?"

She spared him a glance, thinking that just about every CEO, sub-CEO, and executive she had ever worked for would have publicly raked Toirac over the coals for getting to the bridge after his superior. "Check your display," she said, then turned to face the pickup for her own transmission. "To the unknown cruiser that just arrived at the hypernet gate, this is Kommodor Marphissa of the Midway Flotilla. We are a free and independent star system no longer answering to the authority of the Syndicate Worlds. If you wish to join with us, you will be welcome. If you are heading for another star system, close on our flotilla and we will defend you from the Syndicate flotilla in this star system and escort you to the jump exit of your choice. Our forces will assist in the defense of anyone seeking freedom from Syndicate tyranny. For the people, Marphissa, out."

"Kommodor," the senior watch specialist began urgently.

"I see." Alerts had appeared on her display as ships in the Syndicate flotilla began changing vectors. "Accelerating, coming around. All the heavy cruisers and all the Hunter-Killers."

"Are they going after the new cruiser?" Kapitan Toirac asked.

"It's a safe bet," Marphissa said. "We need to see if—"

"Kommodor?" the watch specialist said. "We have run the courses. If the Syndicate forces proceed at their best speed, then even at maximum acceleration we cannot reach that new cruiser before they do."

That watch specialist was overdue for a promotion. "Can the new cruiser get clear? He should have had enough of a head start."

"He's hauling a lot of extra mass, Kommodor. It's limiting his acceleration. If current projections hold, the Syndicate ships will catch him."

Damn. She glanced over at Kapitan Toirac, who was staring fixedly at his own display with the look of a man who was completely out of his depth and trying very hard not to let anyone notice. *I recommended he be given a shot as commanding officer of this ship. A lot of junior executives moved up fast when we cleaned out the Syndicate loyalists. Some of them could handle it. My old friend Toirac though . . . he was a good executive. Was that level of authority as much as he could handle?* "What do you think, Kapitan?" Marphissa prompted.

"Uh? Ah." Toirac focused intently on his display again. "We can't get there . . . and we're badly outnumbered . . . I don't see that we can do anything."

"Not doing anything is a choice, Kapitan," Marphissa said in a quiet voice. "An absence of action is an action. I will not choose to sit by while those others are wiped out by Syndicate forces."

Toirac flushed. "It could be a trap."

"A trap? The new cruiser as a decoy to lure us into trying to save it?" Marphissa pondered that. "That's possible. But they're being clumsy about it if that's the case. They should have set up the situation so it appears we can get to the new cruiser in time to help. What if it's not a trap? What can we do?"

Frowning with concentration, Toirac shrugged. "A demonstration of force? Something to distract the Syndicate forces?"

"I don't see—" Marphissa's gaze had settled on the Syndicate flagship. A battleship, far too powerful for her flotilla to engage. Only an insane commander would try to attack the battleship while almost all the Syndicate escorts were chasing the new cruiser. "Run this," she ordered. "An intercept on the Syndicate battleship. Can the Syndicate heavy cruisers and HuKs catch the new cruiser and get back to the battleship before we get there?"

Everyone from Toirac on down stared at her for a fraction of a second, then instincts instilled by Syndicate training in obedience to orders took over, and hands flew across displays. "No," Toirac announced before anyone else, smiling at having displayed his skill at maneuvering calculations. "That is, if we did that, they couldn't get back before we—"

"Then we're going." She had already set up the maneuver on her own display. "All units in the Midway Flotilla, this is Kommodor Marphissa. Execute attached maneuver immediately. Out."

FOUR hours later, on the inhabited planet, President Gwen Iceni watched the unfolding situation near the hypernet gate as the light from the events finally reached her. Alerted to the arrival of the new cruiser, she watched it begin to flee, watched the Syndicate flotilla, commanded by CEO Boyens, send a strong force in pursuit, saw her display confirm that the new cruiser was doomed, saw the ships of the Midway Flotilla, her warships, also accelerate into new vectors. *What is Kommodor Marphissa doing? She can't—*

Iceni stared in disbelief as the vectors on Marphissa's small group of warships steadied out. They were headed straight for an intercept on Boyens's battleship, a single warship that was more than a match for everything combined in the Midway Flotilla.

It had all happened four hours ago. Marphissa's entire flotilla—*No, my entire flotilla*—had probably already been wiped out.

CHAPTER SIX

"IF she has somehow survived, I will personally kill her!"

Togo, standing impassively near Iceni in response to her summons, wisely avoided saying anything.

It was a shame that Sub-CEO Akiri, who had briefly been on her personal staff, had been assassinated by a snake agent months ago. Right now she really wanted a mobile forces officer nearby so she could scream at him.

On the display above Iceni's desk, the Midway Flotilla had steadied out, accelerating for all it was worth toward an intercept with the Syndicate battleship. "Oh, isn't that wonderful! Icing on the cake!"

"Madam President?" Togo asked.

"Look! Do you see those two symbols? They mean that those two Hunter-Killer ships are on tracks to collide with the Syndicate battleship! Not a close firing run! A collision!"

A slight frown creased Togo's usually smooth brow. "How did the Kommodor convince the crews of those two ships to obey such an order?"

"She didn't have to! There are remote command circuits. With the right codes, Marphissa can take over control of other ships in her flotilla. I entrusted those codes to her, and now she's using them to do something that will cost me an immense amount of support!"

This time Togo nodded in understanding. "Because it will be perceived that you sent those two crews to their deaths. The crews of the other mobile forces units will not take that well."

"Nor will the citizens! I've been keeping the citizens happy with a trickle of changes that improve their lot and grant them more freedom. If I were a normal CEO, they wouldn't blink at my throwing away the lives of their fellow citizens like that, but they expect me to be different."

"You have codes that override the override codes that you gave to the Kommodor," Togo pointed out.

"And it would take four hours for my override of her override to get there! Which is about three hours too long," Iceni got out between gritted teeth.

"The action does not seem characteristic of Kommodor Marphissa," Togo offered.

Iceni glared at the display. "Characteristic or not, she's doing it. I want to get rid of Boyens and his flotilla, but not in a way that's going to undermine my position. News of this will spread to every nearby star system, and everyone will see me as nothing more than a typical CEO."

"They will respect you if—"

"I do not have enough firepower to rule this region of space through fear!" *Nor do I want to. I would have to do things to reinforce that fear, and I have done too many things like that already.* Togo knew of some of those things, had followed her orders to carry out some of them, but he did not know everything. Not by a long shot. "This action could destroy our chances of a much stronger mutual-defense agreement with Taroa."

She forced herself to sit down and breathe slowly. *How to deal with the fallout from this? Not only the loss of most of my flotilla but also the deliberate use of two warships and their crews as projectiles.*

Togo cleared his throat diffidently. "Some of the Syndicate ships are altering course."

Iceni looked up at the display, seeing the heavy cruisers and Hunter-Killers that had been sent in pursuit of the new cruiser turning back. "They're going to reinforce the defenses around the battleship." But Marphissa's warships continued on their attack run even though their mission had now become not simply hopeless but clearly impossible. *What is she trying to accomplish?*

The answer came to Iceni moments before she saw Marphissa's ships break off their attack and bend back toward their previous orbit. "It was a bluff. Damn her. She scared Boyens into letting that new cruiser go."

"CEO Boyens will be angry that they escaped," Togo said.

"Very angry, yes." *Can I use that? Oh my, yes. I can use that.* The frustrated anger of a short time earlier had become elation. Not only had Marphissa been far more clever than expected, but the recent events had given Iceni the sort of idea that could finally break the impasse between CEO Boyens and everyone else in this star system. "I need to contact that new cruiser. He could be very helpful to us. Notify General Drakon that I need to speak with him privately. Just him and me. Don't give me that look. There are still snakes around, and I can't risk any of them hearing the plan I just came up with."

"If Madam President no longer believes I can be counted upon—" Togo began, his posture and voice stiffer than usual.

"It's not that." *It's that this is exactly the sort of situation where I can use Colonel Malin's status as an information source to my advantage while also limiting the chances that anyone will guess what I'm planning.* She managed to muster up a reassuring smile for Togo. "You're too close to me. If you're known to be involved, everyone will try to find out what's going on."

Togo did not look comforted by the weak rationale. "Madam President, I must caution you that General Drakon is certain to be working against you. He will use any apparent closeness between you to his advantage."

"Closeness?" Iceni asked sharply.

"There have been . . . rumors."

"There will always be rumors. I can't let my actions be constrained by gossips who haven't matured since leaving school as children! Get that message to General Drakon while I contact the new cruiser."

DRAKON gazed steadily at Iceni, turning her proposal over in his mind. *I'm not expert on mobile forces tactics, but the concept seems sound.* "You think this might work?"

"I think it has a good chance," she said, "but we can't send Togo. Everyone will notice his absence and assume he's on some special mission for me."

"Who do we send? I agree it's too risky to put any of this into a transmission. One hint of what we're doing, and Boyens can thumb his nose at us."

Iceni made a casual gesture with one hand. "How about Colonels Malin and Morgan?"

"Two of my people? Going to personally meet with Black Jack?" His gaze on her narrowed. "You're willing to risk that I won't have them carry some other message as well?"

"Yes, I am," Iceni said calmly. "Are you saying that I shouldn't?"

"I'm saying that you and I both have a lot of experience with not taking those kinds of risks. What's changed?"

"I have gotten to know you better."

He wanted to believe that, which made him even more wary.

"In any event," Iceni continued, "I can have one of your officers wear a sealed monitor that will record everything said. That will ensure no unauthorized messages get passed to Black Jack."

"All right. I can see why you would suggest Colonel Malin. But why Morgan?"

Her smile this time was knowing. "Because if either of them had their own plans, the other would tell you."

"True enough." He went through the plan again in his mind, then nodded. "I agree. People will notice Malin and Morgan aren't around, but they'll assume they're on my business, which doesn't involve the mobile forces."

"Warships," Iceni corrected. "I want to get completely away from Syndicate terminology and Syndicate ways of thinking. I expect to hear from the new cruiser soon in response to our offer to use one of our heavy cruisers to escort him to his home star. As soon as he agrees, I'll notify you, and we can work out how to get your officers to Black Jack without anyone's knowing."

Drakon rubbed his lower face with one hand as he thought. "We could use that new Alliance liaison officer in this."

"Could we? Yes. You're right." Her smile this time appeared completely genuine. "We make a good team, Artur."

MARPHISSA stood at *Manticore*'s main air lock, waiting for the shuttle to finish sealing to the access. *What the hell is going on? Why did the President insist that I go to personally inspect progress on getting our battleship ready to fight?*

It had taken two days for *Manticore* to reach the gas giant, where the new battleship *Midway* continued her slow progress in fitting out. Now Marphissa was two days away from the rest of the flotilla and light-hours distant from knowing what was happening near the hypernet gate.

The shuttle took her directly to one of *Midway*'s air locks, where Marphissa found the young and brilliant Kapitan-Leytenant Kontos waiting by himself. "This way, Kommodor," Kontos said.

They started off alone through the battleship. Despite the shipyard workers and skeleton crew, the vast size of the battleship left many areas seemingly deserted. Marphissa felt a sense of unease as they headed down one such passageway. Kontos had shown no signs of dangerous ambition, and President Iceni had ordered her here, but this setup felt far too much like the sort of disappearance that occasionally afflicted senior Syndicate officers who had offended someone. And there had been rumors passed on to Marphissa by "friends" who had heard that Iceni had been very unhappy with the trick that had fooled Boyens into letting the new heavy cruiser escape. *Even if those stories are true, the President would not make me disappear. She is different.* "What's going on?" she asked Kontos in a low voice.

Kontos gave her an enigmatic look. "I can't tell you. It's important. You're . . . going to meet another officer. Someone who's supposed to join you on *Manticore*."

That was reassuring, since it meant she was supposed to return to *Manticore*, hopefully in one piece and not under arrest.

Kontos pulled out an envelope and passed it to her. "Orders. I have not read them, just a cover document that told me to pass them to you."

"*Written* orders?" Marphissa stared at the envelope as she took it.

"They don't want to risk any compromise of whatever is in there."

"I should say they don't! I've never seen orders written on paper before."

Kontos paused outside a hatch. "She's in here. I'm the only one aboard this ship who has seen her."

"Who the hell is it? Has the President herself secretly come aboard?"

"That would have been less surprising," Kontos said. He saluted. "I am to see you inside, seal the hatch, then wait until you call. There's a working comm panel keyed to my seat on the bridge. I'll wait there."

"Am I supposed to read these orders before I meet this officer?"

"I don't know, Kommodor."

"Fine. Let me in. I'll give you a call when I'm done." *Stupid secrecy,*

Marphissa thought. *What could be so hush-hush as to justify all of this—*

She got two steps inside the compartment and froze, barely aware of Kontos sealing the hatch behind her.

Standing next to one of the tables bolted to the deck was an Alliance fleet captain in full uniform.

Marphissa took a deep breath. An Alliance officer. She had seen prisoners, she had met Alliance ships in battle, but she had never actually talked to an Alliance officer, or anyone else from the Alliance for that matter. The war had lasted for a century. The people of the Alliance weren't just the enemy; they had always been the enemy, always the threat to her and her home. Meeting one of them couldn't have felt more alien than if there had been an enigma in that compartment.

But President Iceni had sent her here. There must be a good reason for this.

I have faced death. I can face an Alliance fleet officer.

"I'm Captain Bradamont," the officer said, standing as if at attention.

"Kommodor Marphissa," she replied automatically. Marphissa's eyes went to the left breast of Bradamont's uniform, where the combat awards and duty awards were displayed. But where on a Syndicate suit those awards would form a readable summary of someone's career, the Alliance decorations were all unknown, a riot of color and design that held no meaning to Marphissa. Who was this woman? "Why are you here?"

"You haven't been given any orders?"

"I . . ." Marphissa looked at the envelope she was still holding. "Maybe I had better read these now."

After some frustrating moments trying to figure out how it worked, Marphissa managed to split the seal on the envelope. She fumbled out the papers inside and read rapidly. *Liaison officer . . . assist in special project . . . authorized full access . . .* "What's this special project? Wait, there's another page."

An operation aimed at trapping the Syndicate flotilla into either fighting or leaving? Marphissa focused back on the Alliance officer. "Captain—?"

"Bradamont."

"I am completely at a loss here. I've never even imagined talking to someone like you. When the snakes were everywhere, it would have meant being charged with treason."

"Snakes? Oh. Internal Security."

The loathing in Bradamont's voice matched Marphissa's own feelings about the snakes. Marphissa found herself thawing slightly. "They're all gone. We killed them." *I personally killed one of them. Why do I feel a sudden need to boast about that, as if I need to top this woman with my own accomplishments? But I don't like to remember killing that snake. He deserved it, but I don't like to recall doing it.*

Bradamont had nodded at her words. "I know you got rid of your Internal Security. I wouldn't have agreed to stay in this star system if they had remained."

"Agreed?"

"I volunteered. Or, rather, Admiral Geary asked me to volunteer."

"Admiral Geary? Oh, you mean Black Jack. That would have been a hard request to turn down, I imagine. Were you on his staff?"

The Alliance officer shook her head. "I commanded *Dragon*. A battle cruiser."

The statement hadn't come out sounding like a boast, but it could have been. Marphissa came closer to Bradamont, eyeing her. "Why did you believe us when we told you the snakes were gone?"

"It's hard to miss the wreckage where the Internal Security installations used to be," Bradamont said. "And someone in this star system whom I trusted confirmed the fact."

"The Alliance had a spy in this star system?" Marphissa blurted out.

"No. Not even remotely. He's . . . a friend."

"A friend." A spy she could accept. A friend? How could that be?

A long pause followed as both seemed lost for anything to talk about. What did you say to the enemy? Even if she had ceased to be the enemy? Finally, Bradamont gestured vaguely around her. "I see that you've acquired a battleship."

"Yes." Marphissa said. "From Kane. We took it from the Syndicate orbital facility there."

"I got to see the action report," Bradamont said, startling Marphissa. "Your President sent it to me. That was some very good ship handling, Kommodor."

Marphissa almost jerked in shock at the praise, then felt herself warming more, though warily. *This woman was one of Black Jack's battle cruiser commanders, and she thinks I did a good job at Kane? Well, I did. But I never expected to hear an Alliance officer say that. Is she trying to get on my good side, flatter me to get me off guard?* "Thank you . . . Captain." Another uncomfortable pause. "Have you ever been on a battleship?" Marphissa asked.

"A Syndic battleship, you mean?" Bradamont asked. She tilted her head slightly in thought. "Just once. Leading a boarding party. That was at Ixchel."

Apparently there were no safe topics. "I'm not familiar with that engagement." There had been so many engagements. "I take it the Alliance won."

"If you define winning as being the last ones left alive, and not very many of you," Bradamont replied. "Then we left, and we blew it up."

Common ground. Not too surprising, really. "You lost a lot of people capturing the battleship, then you left and blew it up."

"It sounds like you've been through the same sort of thing."

"A few times." Another awkward silence fell as Marphissa gestured toward the chairs around the nearest table. This compartment would be an officers' lounge when finished. Though still lacking in many features, it did have the furniture installed. "Have a seat. Please."

"Thank you." Bradamont sat, her eyes on Marphissa. "In case you're wondering, I feel uncomfortable, too."

"I could tell. Because a few months ago we would have been trying to kill each other?"

"And we've spent all of our adult lives trying to kill each other, as did our parents and grandparents."

"But now we're, um . . ." Marphissa searched for the right word and failed. "What are we?"

"On the same side, I guess. What do you think of the plan to deal with the Syndic flotilla?"

"Risky. But . . . if it works . . ."

Bradamont smiled. "Right. If it works." She reached into a duffel near the table, pretending not to notice Marphissa tensing up, and lifted out a bottle. "I brought a small gift. A token of . . . um . . ."

"Greetings?" Marphissa asked, examining the label. "Whiskey? From Vernon? Do you know how much this is worth in Syndicate space? Nobody has been able to get this stuff except through the black market for . . . for a century."

"We're not in Syndicate space, are we?" Bradamont asked.

Marphissa grinned despite her worries. "No. We're not. Not anymore. Do you mind if I open it?"

"I was hoping you would." Bradamont smiled back. "I'll take the first drink so you can be sure it's not drugged or poisoned."

"You could have already taken an antidote," Marphissa pointed out. "Or, you might just want a head start on drinking this."

"You're pretty sharp for a—" Bradamont's smile faded. "Sorry."

"Force of habit," Marphissa said, pouring out two drinks. "I may call you something obscene without thinking about it. Try not to take it personally."

"Deal."

Marphissa took a cautious sip, marveling at the taste. "I admit to being baffled. How could you choose to put yourself in the hands of . . ."

"People who were Syndics not long ago? It wasn't easy." Emotion flashed through Bradamont's eyes. "I've been in a Syndic labor camp. I know what they're like."

"There are no more labor camps. Not where President Iceni's authority holds."

"So I was told." Bradamont smiled again. "You sound proud of that."

"I am. We . . . we are changing things here." Marphissa smiled once more, too. "President Iceni will help us build a government that truly is for the people."

Bradamont studied Marphissa for a long moment, then raised her own glass. "In that case, let us salute your President Iceni."

Marphissa matched the gesture. "To our President." She watched how much Bradamont drank, determined not to be more affected by the alcohol than the Alliance officer. But Bradamont had saluted Iceni . . . "You're just here to help with this operation?"

Bradamont shook her head. "I'm supposed to stay, when the fleet leaves. Liaison officer. To keep track of what's happening here and to provide any assistance I can that is consistent with Alliance interests."

"Assistance?" Marphissa laughed at a wild thought. "Tactics? Can you show us how Black Jack fights?"

"Yes."

Blessed ancestors! Marphissa took a bigger drink. Amazement warred with a feeling of resentment. "That's . . . can I explain my feelings to you? Because I'm having a hard time resolving them. On the one hand, I'm thinking how great it would be to have someone teach us a few of Black Jack's tricks. And with the Alliance fleet having vastly superior power to anything in what used to be Syndicate space, having one of Black Jack's former officers among us can't be a bad thing. So, for that I want to kiss you."

Bradamont took another sip of her drink, raising an eyebrow at Marphissa. "I take it I shouldn't be freshening my lip gloss right now, though."

"No, because on the other hand, your Black Jack humiliated us and annihilated our mobile forces, which were crewed by our comrades.

That's bad enough. But now one of his own is descending from on high to show us how to fight. For that, I want to slug you."

"You don't usually have that sort of mix of emotions about people, Kommodor?" Bradamont asked.

"Not usually. Or at least not at the same time. What are your emotions, Captain?"

Bradamont looked around again, taking another slow drink. "I understand your feelings. Any professional is going to feel pride in their own work, in their own abilities. They're going to resent any hint of condescending assistance. But you don't need any help with the fundamentals. If what you did at Kane is any indication, you are *good*, Kommodor. As for me, it's strange. I've been on Syndic, excuse me, Syndicate Worlds' planets before. As a prisoner. Part of me is screaming *escape, you fool!* Another part of me looks at you in that uniform and tells me I should hate you for all the deaths and destruction of a very long and very senseless war." She set down her glass and shook her head. "Parts of me are stuck in the past. The rest sees people who are trying to put the past behind them, to make something new, to throw off the bonds that have held them. And you are Colonel Rogero's people."

"Colonel Rogero?" Marphissa had to concentrate to remember who that was. "One of General Drakon's brigade commanders. *He* is your friend?"

"Yes."

The single word held more emotion than friends usually inspired. "Ah. All right. There must be an interesting story behind that."

"There is." Bradamont leaned back, draping one arm over the back of her chair. "The bottom line is that I knew, because of Colonel Rogero, that Syndics were human, too. That some of you were not just human but very fine humans. That couldn't change things during the war. I had to keep fighting all of you, and I had to do my best, because regardless of who each of you were as individuals, you were all fighting for something that I couldn't allow to win."

"I see." Marphissa sighed heavily, looking at the unfinished top of the table. "I didn't want the Syndicate to win, but I was afraid of what might happen when the Alliance won. They showed us pictures of the planets that had been fought over, bombarded— Don't. I know. We did it, too. I wanted to protect my home. That was all. They taught us you started the war. Did you know that? As kids, they told us it was all the Alliance's fault. Once you got old enough and high enough in the executive ranks you could learn the truth, that the Syndicate chose to start the war. But, by then, what were you going to do with the knowledge? By then . . . there wasn't anything left to do but keep fighting because what else could you do?"

Bradamont gazed back somberly. "You could have revolted while the war was still going on."

"Some did. Didn't you hear of those?" Marphissa shuddered and took a long drink, then refilled her glass. "When the Syndicate had mobile forces in abundance, they could deal with rebellion very easily. Traitors died," she said bitterly. "The worlds of traitors were reduced to ruins, the families of traitors died or were left to struggle amid the rubble of their cities, and the snakes were everywhere. Breathe the wrong words, and you disappeared. Offend a CEO, and your husband or wife or children disappeared. We could have revolted? Dammit, don't you think we tried?"

"I'm sorry." Bradamont sounded like she meant it. "In the Alliance fleet, we often complain about fighting our own government. But we've endured nothing like that. Nothing like that."

"They call us traitors now, the Syndicate," Marphissa continued. "But we're not. Do you know the funny thing? The entire Syndicate system encourages betrayal. Of your friends and your coworkers and even your spouse or your parents or your children. But then it says you must be loyal to the boss who has no loyalty to you. Damn them. Damn all of them." *Why am I saying this to her? But I could never say it to anyone. Not for all my life.*

Bradamont broke an uneasy silence. "But Iceni is different?"

"Yes."

"What about Drakon?"

"General Drakon? He supports the President. That's all I need to know."

"I thought he was a co-ruler," Bradamont said.

"I suppose technically he is," Marphissa conceded. "But I respond to orders from the President. What is Black Jack really like?"

"He's . . ." Bradamont frowned at her glass. "Not what anyone expected. Not less. More. He's real."

"Is he—? They say he— I mean, there's talk that he is more than—"

"He's human," Bradamont said.

"But was he sent? Is he an agent of more than the Alliance?" Marphissa demanded.

"He never claimed to be. I don't know. That's way above my pay grade." Bradamont bent a questioning look on her. "I thought Syndics didn't believe in that sort of thing."

"Religions? Faith? All of those have been officially discouraged. We were only supposed to believe in the Syndicate. But people hung on to the old beliefs." Marphissa shrugged. "Sometimes that was all we had to hang on to. Some people believed in the Syndicate, like somebody else would believe in a divine power, but a lot of them here were shaken in that faith when the Syndicate abandoned us to the enigmas. Did you really see some of the enigmas?"

Bradamont nodded, not fazed by the change in topic. "We saw one. Part of one. We actually learned very little about them. Admiral Geary is convinced that the enigmas would commit racial suicide to keep us from learning more."

That took a while to sink in. "A race even crazier than humanity? Wonderful."

"To them," Bradamont said, "it's not crazy. To the enigmas, what they're doing makes perfect sense. Kind of like how the war made sense to humanity."

"No, there you're wrong," Marphissa said, refilling her glass and

Bradamont's as well. "We've all known the war was crazy. No one could figure out how to end it. Fighting a war because we couldn't figure out how to end it. I guess the enigmas aren't crazier than we are after all. What about the fast ships we saw? The beautiful ships. Can you tell me about the ones in those?"

"The Dancers?" Bradamont couldn't help smiling. "They're very, very ugly. And they seem to think in some different ways than us. But there's still a connection there. They helped us."

"They saved our primary planet." Marphissa raised her glass in salute. "I couldn't believe it possible, actually managing to divert a launched bombardment. To the Dancers!"

"To the Dancers," Bradamont echoed. "But they are really ugly. Here's an image." She offered a data pad. "I'm going to deliver a report on them to your President."

Marphissa gaped at the image. "Like a wolf and spider having offspring. Seriously? This is how they look? But they drive ships like the ships were part of them. Incredibly graceful. How do their maneuvering systems manage that?"

Bradamont rolled a drink around in her mouth before swallowing it. "We're pretty sure they drive their ships manually."

Marphissa jerked in involuntary reaction. "Those kinds of maneuvers at those speeds? Done by manual control rather than automated systems? That's impossible."

"It is for us."

"What can you tell me about the huge ship?" Marphissa pressed.

"The *Invincible*? We captured it from the Kicks." Bradamont squinted as she studied the play of light in the amber liquid partially filling her glass. "They're cute. The Kicks. And crazy. Not *leave us alone* crazy like the enigmas. *Take over the universe if they could* crazy. And absolutely fanatical fighters. To the death. They're in the report for your President, too. Hopefully the Kicks will never make it to human space, but you need to know why you don't want to go to space controlled by the Kicks."

"Thank you." Maybe it was the booze. Maybe it was the shared experiences in warships. But Marphissa felt herself relaxing and smiling at Bradamont with real welcome. "I hope that includes how you captured that huge ship."

"It was . . . challenging," Bradamont commented. "Yeah. We can talk about how we, Admiral Geary's fleet, that is, beat our enemies."

Marphissa met the Alliance captain's eyes, feeling an inner chill that fought her previous sense of warming toward Bradamont. "Like us. How you beat the Syndicate mobile forces."

"Yes," Bradamont said in a softer tone as if sensing Marphissa's feelings. "I meant it when I said that. To help you work out ways to defeat the Syndicate Worlds' forces that come here to try to regain control of this star system. I can talk about what was done in different engagements, from Corvus all the way to Varandal. Admiral Geary authorized me to do that."

"Varandal? Isn't that Alliance space?"

"Yes. That's where we fought your Reserve Flotilla."

"Destroyed our Reserve Flotilla, you mean," Marphissa corrected. She stared at her glass. "I know. CEO Boyens told President Iceni that much, at least, though it seems he left out a lot of other things from when he was your prisoner. We had a lot of friends among the crews of those units. Some people had more-than-friends. The Reserve Flotilla spent a long time out here. They were based in this star system for decades." Her tones had turned sad, angry, and accusing. Unfair, she knew. It had been war. But, still . . .

"I'm sorry," Bradamont said again.

"We've both lost plenty of friends, I'm sure."

Silence for a few moments, then Bradamont spoke with forced cheerfulness. "Have you received a list of prisoners yet?"

"What?" Marphissa asked, wondering if she had heard right.

"A list of prisoners," Bradamont repeated. "The officers and crew members from the Reserve Flotilla we took prisoner at Varandal after their ships were destroyed."

Marphissa had been raising her glass for another drink, but now her hand froze in midmotion. "Prisoners? You took prisoners? Not just CEO Boyens?"

"Yes." Bradamont flinched. "Hadn't you heard that as soon as Admiral Geary took command, he banned the killing of prisoners?"

"I'd heard that, but I didn't believe it."

"It's true. We stopped executing prisoners—" Bradamont flushed this time. "I can't believe we ever did it. I can't believe we sank so low before he reminded us— The point is, we took prisoners. And if we didn't want prisoners and were in a Syndic-controlled star system, we let their escape pods go. Didn't you hear that?"

"We heard only what the Syndicate government wanted us to hear," Marphissa said.

"Oh, yeah. Security. It's funny what governments justify using security as a reason, isn't it? Well, I can tell you there are prisoners from your Reserve Flotilla being held at Varandal. A lot of them. I *know* that."

Marphissa just stared at Bradamont for what felt like a minute, then managed to speak again. "You're sure they're still at Varandal? Not dispersed to labor camps all over the Alliance?"

Once again Bradamont flushed, but this time in anger. "The Alliance never had *labor camps*. They would have been sent to prisoner-of-war camps. But they were still being processed when the war ended, then nobody wanted them sent to their star system to worry about. They've been stuck at Varandal, in the hands of fleet authorities, who have to worry about feeding them and housing them and guarding them and taking care of them until the prisoner-repatriation agreements are finalized. I know because so many of the officers there were complaining about it. The Syndics, I mean the Syndicate Worlds' government, is supposed to be working out procedures for prisoners of war to be sent home, but the whole process is dragging out, and meanwhile, the authorities at Varandal are stuck with a lot of Syndics they'd love to give back to someone."

Bradamont's flush faded into a thoughtful expression. "You guys are someone. You say you know the survivors of the Reserve Flotilla being held at Varandal. Why don't *you* send somebody to get them?"

"What? Us?" Marphissa asked, not quite believing what she was hearing.

"Send a converted freighter or two. How many would you need? More than two. Four. No, six. There are about four thousand prisoners from the Reserve Flotilla. It'll be a little tight, but six converted freighters can haul them if they're rigged to carry as many people as possible."

"We can rig—" Marphissa began eagerly before reality imposed itself on her thoughts. "Freighters. All the way across to the Alliance, through space where Syndicate authority is being contested or has already collapsed? Where any Syndicate authority that did exist would be gunning for ships operating on our behalf?" *I will not get my hopes up. I will not think this could happen.*

"You would have to send an escort," Bradamont agreed. "A few of your warships."

"Warships. We only have a few. And you want us to send a convoy escorted by warships to an Alliance star system?"

"That might not be a good idea." Bradamont took a drink, swirling the liquid in her mouth again for a moment before swallowing. "All right, here's how you could do it. Just a suggestion," she added wryly. "Go to Atalia. You've got the hypernet gate, so you can use that to get most of the way there. From Atalia, it's an easy jump to Varandal. Atalia has declared independence from the Syndicate Worlds like you have though it's not in nearly as good a shape as you are."

Marphissa nodded wordlessly. They didn't have to discuss the reasons for that. A border star system would have been pounded mercilessly over the decades.

"Atalia had a Hunter-Killer when we went through there last," Bradamont continued. "Just one. There's an Alliance courier ship there, too, maintaining a picket watch at the jump point for Varandal. Your convoy pops in to Atalia, then your warships wait at Atalia while the freighters go on to Varandal."

"What happens when six former Syndicate freighters show up at Varandal?" Marphissa asked.

"The Alliance authorities will demand to know why they're there. They won't destroy them right off the bat. Would you do that if Alliance freighters showed up here?"

"No." Obstacles. Objections. What could prevent this from working? "Would they release those prisoners to us?"

Bradamont grimaced, rubbing the back of her neck. "Technically, we're supposed to repatriate them to the Syndicate Worlds. But that's getting harder with every star system that bails out of the Syndicate Worlds. And we still don't like the Syndicate Worlds. It wouldn't be very humanitarian to take people from newly independent star systems and dump them back under Syndic control."

"Humanitarian?" Marphissa asked sarcastically.

Bradamont responded with a questioning look. "Why did you say humanitarian like that?"

"Because it's . . . a joke. No one ever says that and means it. Means what it actually is supposed to mean, whatever that is."

"Oh." Bradamont seemed briefly rattled, then refocused. "Then let's say that, in practical terms, the Alliance fleet wants to be rid of those prisoners at Varandal."

Marphissa sat her glass down carefully, aware of how her hand was shaking. "How many?" she whispered. "How many did you say?"

"I don't know exactly. Roughly four thousand. That's the number people kept throwing around."

"Four thousand." Out of how many? But so many times, when ships were destroyed, it happened in a flash, with no chance for survivors. For even four thousand to come out of that battle alive after their ships had been too badly crippled to fight reflected considerable luck. "We had no idea. Many of those men and women are our friends. They're from here, or nearby star systems."

"I'm sorry. I would have mentioned it right away if I'd realized—"

"That's all right." Marphissa sighed. "We just assumed they were all dead. We had to. That's how it's been."

"I know." Bradamont grimaced. "We assumed the same when forces were lost to Syndic hands."

"I'll need to get President Iceni's approval for it. We can't even think about doing this until the, uh, special operation to get rid of the Syndicate flotilla here succeeds. If that operation works, it will mean sending off a flotilla to escort those freighters, and they'll be gone awhile. That might be a hard sell when we have so few units. To be honest, if it were anyone but President Iceni, it would be an impossible sell. I think our President will jump at the opportunity, but there will be advisers trying to convince her not to do it. Where's the profit in it?" Marphissa added bitterly. "And General Drakon might be hard to sell on it as well."

"From what I have heard of General Drakon, he's not that bad. But he might still need a strong reason." Bradamont gazed at her somberly, then gestured around them. "This battleship of yours is still being fitted out. Do you have a crew for it?"

"Just a skeleton crew," Marphissa admitted. "Finding enough trained mobile forces personnel to fill out the crew of a battleship is proving to be a serious challenge, and there's another under construction at Taroa that will eventually require a crew, too. Our ambitions and hardware exceed our available supply of skilled personnel."

"Four thousand survivors of the Reserve Flotilla might help you out with that problem," Bradamont noted.

"That's right." Marphissa looked around her at the unfinished compartment they were in, imagining it completed and filled with people she had never expected to see again. "They're alive, they're trained, a lot of them thought of Midway as home before they got yanked out of here, and with those reasons, I've got a good chance of convincing people in charge to let us go get them. Damn you, I think I do want to kiss you, you Alliance monster."

Bradamont grinned. "Keep your filthy hands off me, you Syndic scum."

"Your people also exchange insults to express friendship, Alliance demon?"

"We reserve those kinds of insults for the best of people, Syndic shrew."

"Thank you for the compliment, Alliance fiend."

"You're welcome, Syndic savage."

"No problem, Alliance ghoul."

"Happy to oblige, Syndic devil."

Marphissa paused, realizing that the booze had gone to her head and not caring except that it made concentrating more difficult. She hauled out her comm unit. "Excuse me while I look up some more words."

"Is it all right if I have another drink while I wait?" Bradamont asked.

"Be my guest, you . . . Alliance . . . harpy."

"Thank you." Bradamont was checking her own personal unit. "We're supposed to be getting to know each other, you Syndic . . . sleaze. I can keep it up as long as you can."

When Kapitan-Leytenant Kontos, looking worried, finally checked up on them, the bottle was empty and they were leaning on each other, crying over the friends they had each lost.

Marphissa called *Manticore* to let them know her inspection of the *Midway* was taking longer than expected.

The next day, hangover controlled but not eliminated by a generous dose of painkillers, she transmitted a "report" of her inspection of the *Midway* that included the code phrase called for in her written orders ("everything can be done on schedule with proper support"), then led Captain Bradamont, her uniform hidden under standard-issue Syndicate-crew coveralls adorned with the insignia of a Midway Kapitan, to *Manticore*'s shuttle. Kontos joined her there, unhappy at leaving *Midway* but obedient to his own orders to also transfer temporarily to *Manticore*.

—————

A couple of days after that, in company with the newly arrived cruiser, *Manticore* approached the jump point for the star Maui. Officially, *Manticore* would escort the cruiser all the way to the home star of most of its crew, Kiribati.

Only three people aboard *Manticore* knew that in fact she would leave the cruiser when it was most of the way to Kiribati. Kommodor Marphissa, Kapitan-Leytenant Kontos, and the mysterious VIP going by the name of Kapitan Bascare knew that *Manticore* would jog off to one side, heading for the star named Taniwah, where another hypernet gate could be found.

From the hypernet gate at Taniwah, *Manticore* would leap back to Midway.

To arrive nose to nose with the Syndicate flotilla commanded by CEO Boyens.

CHAPTER SEVEN

"COME to full-combat alert twenty minutes before we arrive at Midway," Marphissa ordered.

Kapitan Toirac eyed her worriedly. They were in Marphissa's stateroom, which was nothing luxurious on a heavy cruiser but large enough for two people without feeling claustrophobic. "We're going to drop into the lap of the Syndicate flotilla, and we'll be moving at only point zero two light speed in normal space."

"That's the idea. We want them to chase us. The moment we arrive at the gate, command of the *Manticore* will temporarily shift to Kapitan Bascare."

"What? Asima— Excuse me, Kommodor, I don't even know who this Bascare is."

"You'll find out." Marphissa couldn't yet tell Toirac that "Bascare" was actually Alliance Fleet Captain Bradamont, but she unbent enough to explain more. "Trust me. These are the orders of President Iceni, to carry out an operation planned by her. But we have to do our part."

"I don't know." Toirac looked around, uncertainty written all over his expression and posture. It had become an all-too-familiar look for him, whether in private or on the bridge.

Marphissa licked her lips, trying to find the right words. "Ygor, we've known each other for a while. I recommended you for command of this ship."

"You did? Why didn't you—"

"Wait." She fixed him with a hard look. "You've got the skills to run this ship, but you're not demonstrating the strength to command it. You're slow, you hesitate, you allow your specialists and junior officers to decide things that you should be deciding. It's one thing to delegate some authority and responsibility. I believe in the wisdom of that, contrary to the teachings of the Syndicate. But you can go too far. Delegation is one thing. Effectively ceding command decisions to your subordinates is another."

Kapitan Toirac scowled, looking away. "I'm doing my best. This is very difficult. I'm trying to avoid the mistakes of the Syndicate."

"Fine; you don't want to run the ship with an iron hand. I understand that. But you're going too far in the other direction. You can't command this ship unless you *command* it! I will back you, Ygor. I will give you what advice I can. I know Kapitan-Leytenant Kontos has been speaking to you, trying to help. But he says you're not listening."

"Kontos! A few weeks ago, he was a subexecutive! I know more about being in charge than he does."

"He's good, Ygor. Kontos knows how to do things so that subordinates look to him as a leader. You need to cultivate the same traits, the same approach to command—"

"If you're so unhappy with me," Toirac grumbled, "why not just drop the hammer?"

"Because I want to help you succeed," Marphissa insisted, trying not to let Toirac's behavior aggravate her too much.

"Tearing me down is not helping me."

"Have you heard anything that I've said? Have you noticed how your officers and specialists are acting toward you and around you?"

Toirac's mouth set stubbornly. "If you're so unhappy with me, maybe this ship would be better off with another commanding officer."

She glared at him. "I don't want that, but since you raised the topic I have no choice but to warn you that unless you start acting like the commanding officer of *Manticore*, I will have no choice but to recommend that you be replaced."

He stared at her, the gaze turning dark. "It didn't take long, did it, Asima? All that talk of things being different now, but once you got your hands on power, you're just another Sub-CEO trying to suck up to her CEO—"

Marphissa leaped to her feet, her mind filled with anger. "I will pretend those last words were not said! Listen to yourself! I am trying to offer you help, and you're answering me with insults! If I were being a typical Sub-CEO I would've relieved you of command weeks ago! But I've been waiting. Waiting to see you assert yourself."

Toirac avoided her eyes. "Yes, Kommodor."

"Damn you, Ygor. Are you trying to back me into a corner?"

"The Kommodor can act as she sees fit. I understand and will comply."

"Get out of here!" Marphissa nearly yelled, worried that she would say something far worse if Toirac continued to display attitude rather than intelligence.

He saluted, the gesture stiff and formal, then left, only the hatch closing mechanism preventing it from slamming under the force of Toirac's push.

She sat down, trying to control her anger. *I tried. And he answers me with "I understand and will comply," as if I really am some Syndicate thug abusing her authority. It's a lot easier to complain about the boss than to be the boss. But if Toirac can't tell the difference between me and a Syndicate bootlicker, he's not just weak, he's also a fool.*

Don't decide now. You're too angry. But Toirac had better show me a lot better performance and do it fast.

"Kommodor?" The question was accompanied by a knock on her hatch.

Marphissa looked up, calming herself. "Enter."

Bradamont eyed her from the hatch. "Is everything all right?" Behind her, Kontos was looking up and down the passageway, keeping an eye out for trouble. Bradamont and Kontos were already in survival suits, prepared for combat.

Both Kontos and Marphissa had noticed that the Alliance officer focused a lot on the ship, on the state of equipment, cleanliness, and other material issues, but didn't seem to worry about the crew. Bradamont paid attention to the crew, displaying unmistakable interest in them and their jobs, but she didn't appear to *worry* about them as a potential source of danger. The implications of that attitude, what it might say about the Alliance fleet versus Syndicate practices that still haunted this ship, bothered Marphissa a great deal.

"Personnel issues," Marphissa explained. "We're half an hour from arrival, aren't we? I need to focus on that. We're going to have to do everything just right."

"It's nothing you can't handle," Bradamont said.

"You're going to be in temporary command. You have to call the maneuvers. I'm sure that's what President Iceni wants." Marphissa managed a smile. "Besides, I want to watch you maneuver a ship in combat."

"I wish to watch that as well," Kontos offered.

"Are you sure your crew will be all right when they find out who I am?"

"They know me. They believe in the President. They also know Kapitan-Leytenant Kontos by reputation. And . . . they're conditioned by training to do as they're told. Those things should keep the crew from blowing up until we get the job done."

Marphissa quickly pulled on her own survival suit, then led the way to the bridge, taking her seat next to a visibly sulking Kapitan Toirac, who had not yet donned a suit himself. The specialists on watch took in the survival suits on her, Bradamont, and Kontos, and unobtrusively began passing the word to their friends in other parts of the ship that something was up. Two of the specialists glanced Toirac's way, said something to each other in very low voices, and grinned.

Marphissa suppressed a sigh, mentally running through candidates to replace Toirac. Kapitan-Leytenant Diaz came quickly to mind. As second-in-command of *Manticore*, he had done his best to support Toirac and had not undermined him in any way that Marphissa was aware of. Diaz lacked apparent ambition, which could foretell problems if he was promoted above his comfort zone, but his actions commended him.

Kontos, standing at the back of the bridge next to Bradamont, cleared his throat.

Marphissa checked the time. "Kapitan, it is nineteen minutes until we arrive at Midway."

Toirac ignored her.

Fine. You're gone. But I won't do it formally until after this operation is over. We don't need the disruption a change of command could cause when we're this close to action. "Bring *Manticore* to full-combat readiness," Marphissa ordered the specialists on the bridge.

"Yes, Kommodor!"

The specialists popped open lockers near their watch stations and pulled on their own survival suits, outfits that were far inferior to the battle armor worn by ground forces but provided some protection from shrapnel and small arms as well as providing oxygen if the ship was holed by the enemy. The helmets stayed open, unpressurized hoods draped loosely behind their shoulders, to conserve the suits' life support until it was needed. Readiness reports flowed in, green markers popping up on Marphissa's display as weapons, sensors, shields, and propulsion as well as a host of other less critical areas reported full-combat status.

Kapitan Toirac, moving with obvious slowness, took out his own emergency suit and put it on as well.

"The ship is at full-combat readiness, Kommodor," the senior specialist reported.

"Five minutes. You can do better," Marphissa said. "Next time, make it four. Everyone on the bridge, listen. The moment *Manticore* leaves the hypernet and arrives at Midway, Kapitan Bascare will become temporary commanding officer of this ship. You will respond to her every order as if it were mine, regardless of what happens. Is that clearly understood? There must be no hesitation, no questions."

The specialists all nodded and saluted. The seniormost specialist smiled as he did so. "I understand and will comply, Kommodor." But he gave the old words of subservience an aura of pride that made Marphissa smile in return.

Bradamont came to stand beside Marphissa.

Kontos caught Marphissa's eye and tilted an inquiring eye toward Toirac. She shook her head and mouthed "later" in reply.

Marphissa readied a command for *Manticore*'s identification broadcast, ensuring that the broadcast was disabled and wouldn't send anything until she activated it. The sensors in CEO Boyens's flotilla would know *Manticore* without any official ID being broadcast. They had seen her hull too many times and knew every unique feature and mark it had accumulated in space. But the identification contained in the broadcast this time would give them a very unpleasant surprise.

Five minutes. "Everyone listen," Marphissa said. "If Kapitan Bascare sends a message, she will use a different name and rank. She is here by personal order of President Iceni. Do not let that name and rank cause you to hesitate. Is that clear?"

Once again, everyone nodded. Everyone but Kapitan Toirac.

"Disable main propulsion unit two," Marphissa ordered. "Ensure it does not light off when maneuvering orders are given, not until you are told to reactivate it."

"Yes, Kommodor," the engineering specialist said. "Deactivating main propulsion unit two. Unit two is deactivated."

Marphissa looked at Bradamont. "Do you need this seat?"

"No. The weapons are yours. I can give whatever maneuvering commands are needed while standing here."

One minute. "Shields at maximum, all weapons ready," Marphissa said to Bradamont.

Kontos hadn't moved, but his eyes were locked on Bradamont.

They exited the gate at Midway, the nothing outside of *Manticore* abruptly being replaced by countless stars and endless space. "I have command," Bradamont announced. "Come starboard one seven zero degrees, down two zero degrees, maximum acceleration on main propulsion units one, three, and four."

Manticore swung around and accelerated, her vector altering to head for the other ships of the Midway Flotilla, five light-minutes away.

"Boyens is still here," Marphissa observed, as her display updated.

Bradamont nodded and pointed to another area relatively close to the hypernet gate. When they had left, the entire Alliance fleet had been two light-hours from the gate, but now a substantial force of battle cruisers and other warships orbited only ten light-minutes away.

"The Syndicate flotilla is maneuvering," the senior specialist announced. "Heavy cruisers and Hunter-Killers. They're coming around to an intercept."

Bradamont nodded again. "When will they come within weapons range of us?"

The specialists exchanged glances. "We were not moving fast coming out of the gate, Kapitan Bascare, and with one propulsion unit disabled, we are accelerating at less than an optimum rate. The Syndicate heavy cruisers will be within missile range in seventeen minutes."

"Good. How long will it take to bring main propulsion unit two back online?"

"Five seconds, Kapitan. Then another five seconds for it to achieve full thrust." The specialist gave her a quizzical glance, wondering why an officer of such rank did not know such basic information about a ship built by the Syndicate Worlds. They had seen Kapitan Bascare practicing maneuvering *Manticore* during some of the transits through star systems while escorting the other cruiser and knew from that she was experienced in handling ships, making her lack of knowledge all the more puzzling.

Bradamont smiled slightly. "Sixteen minutes," she told Marphissa.

Her confidence was so palpable that the crew, despite their nervousness as the Syndicate pursuit force lunged toward them, waited without question as the bubble on their displays marking missile-engagement range for the Syndicate warships drew steadily closer to *Manticore*.

"The Alliance ships are moving! They are . . . heading toward the Syndicate flotilla!" The operations specialist blinked at her display in disbelief, then grinned. "They are coming to help us? Black Jack is coming!"

Not the Alliance, Marphissa noted. Black Jack. She would remember that.

An alert pulsed on the displays, warning that the Syndicate warships would be within missile range in one minute.

"Steady," Bradamont said. "Engineering, I will order main propulsion unit two back online in one minute and ten seconds. Is that understood? Wait for the command."

"Yes, Kapitan."

Marphissa glanced at Bradamont. "Now?"

"Forty seconds," Bradamont replied. "The information has to reach the Syndic warships too late for them to change their actions."

Exactly forty seconds later, Marphissa tapped a control. *Manticore*'s identification broadcast lit off, telling the universe that the warship was—

"Kommodor?" the communications specialist asked, bewildered. "Our unit identification says we are . . . Alliance."

"Alliance-flagged," Marphissa said. "Not the same thing. Listen to Kapitan Bascare."

"Activate main propulsion unit two, full thrust," Bradamont

ordered, then tapped Marphissa's comm controls. "Units of the Syndicate Worlds, this is Captain Bradamont of the Alliance fleet, commanding a chartered warship on official Alliance business. You are to cease threatening activity immediately."

"Missiles have launched!" The warning came just as Bradamont finished speaking. Seconds later, *Manticore* lurched in response to a significant increase in her acceleration, the inertial dampers not quite masking the effects of propulsion unit two coming on line at full power.

Then Bradamont's last words struck home and everyone on the bridge but Kontos and Marphissa stared at her in disbelief. "Stand by!" Kontos said sharply, bringing everyone's attention back to their duties.

There were twenty-four missiles inbound. Their targeting solutions had been badly thrown off by the sudden increase in *Manticore*'s acceleration, but the missiles' targeting systems could compensate for that to some extent. "Come port one four degrees," Bradamont ordered. "Down six degrees."

"The Midway Flotilla is altering vectors," the operations specialist said. "They are on an intercept with the Syndicate heavy cruisers pursuing us, Kapi— Kapitan . . . Bascare."

Marphissa, her gaze darting from one point on her display to the next, noticed that Bradamont's small vector change had placed the pursuing missiles into a stern chase, coming in from directly behind *Manticore*. That meant the relative speed of the missiles had been reduced as much as possible, making them easier targets. A small thing, but an important thing.

"Wait!" Kapitan Toirac, glaring at Bradamont, had started up from his seat. "We can't accept orders from this—"

"Shut up!" Marphissa snapped, her patience with her former friend exhausted.

"I will not—"

But Toirac did stop speaking, his face rigid. Marphissa leaned back enough to see that Kontos had drawn his sidearm and had the barrel planted on Kapitan Toirac's spine. At that range, Toirac's survival suit wouldn't stop a shot, and Toirac knew it. *Sometimes the old ways may be the best.*

"Incoming," Bradamont prodded, her eyes turned away from the small tableau. She gave no sign of what she thought of Syndicate command procedures.

But Bradamont probably was not impressed. Angrily refocusing on the engagement, Marphissa authorized the hell-lance weapons that faced aft to open fire, watching as the particle beams lashed out at the oncoming missiles. Two, then three, then four missiles were knocked out.

That left twenty.

Bradamont had been watching the missiles, counting the time since their launch, watching the display to see remaining endurance data based on the precise capabilities of the Syndicate missiles. "It's a lot easier to estimate this when you know exactly what the missiles can do," she commented to Marphissa. "All main propulsion units to zero thrust," she ordered.

Marphissa and Kontos both swiveled to look at the engineering specialist, but he had already moved to implement the command. "All main propulsion units at zero, Kapitan."

"Maneuvering thrusters pitch up one seven eight degrees."

The thrusters fired, pushing *Manticore*'s bow up and over until the bow pointed back down the opposite way the ship was still traveling. With her heaviest armament now facing the oncoming missiles, *Manticore*'s hell lances knocked out several more.

"All main propulsion units at maximum," Bradamont ordered.

The engineering specialist hesitated only a fraction of a second. "All units at maximum."

Manticore moaned as pressure on her hull built rapidly. Her main propulsion, facing in the direction the ship was still going stern first, was braking her velocity at a rate that caused danger warnings to pop up on displays. Those not seated had to brace themselves as the forces of deceleration leaked past the overloaded inertial dampers.

"How long can she hold it?" Bradamont murmured to Marphissa.

Marphissa studied the hull-stress readings climbing quickly into red zones. "Ten seconds at this rate. No more."

"That's enough."

The missiles, accelerating for all they were worth for the point where *Manticore* would have been if she had kept accelerating all out, now found themselves having to swing onto much shorter intercepts as *Manticore* decelerated as quickly as the heavy cruiser could. The turns required of the missiles to do that were extremely tight. Far too tight for the structure of the missiles to withstand in most cases. As the missiles slewed about, many of them broke apart under the stress.

Six survived, but their radical maneuvers had brought them, for a few crucial seconds, to nearly a standstill relative to *Manticore*.

Hell lances stabbed out again, nailing every surviving missile.

"Reduce thrust on all main propulsion units to two-thirds," Bradamont ordered. The strain on *Manticore* eased immediately, the stress warnings hesitating before they began shading back down into safe territory.

"All of the Syndicate ships are changing vectors," the operations specialist said. "Kapitan, the Syndicate flotilla is heading for the hypernet gate."

"A smart move," Marphissa remarked, feeling satisfaction that shaded into disappointment. The heavy cruisers pursuing *Manticore* had veered off and were moving quickly to join up with the Syndicate battleship once more. "Unfortunately. They're not staying to fight."

The Alliance warships were storming toward the Syndicate warships but, according to the projections on her display, would not get within weapons range before the Syndicate flotilla could use the gate to escape. "Why couldn't Black Jack catch them?" Marphissa muttered to Bradamont.

"The plan was to get rid of the flotilla," Bradamont murmured back. "With or without actual fighting. We successfully tricked Boyens's ships into firing onto an Alliance-flagged warship, giving Admiral Geary grounds for shooting back. But if CEO Boyens chooses to avoid contact, Admiral Geary can't force it. This trick will force the Syndicate Worlds' flotilla to leave, though."

Still feeling disgruntled, Marphissa checked the track on the rest of the Midway Flotilla, which was coming on a slightly curving intercept aimed at the heavy cruisers hastening back to the Syndicate battleship. The odds in a heavy cruiser–to–heavy cruiser fight hadn't gotten any better. "This is Kommodor Marphissa to the Midway Flotilla. Ensure that you remain out of range of the Syndicate weapons unless one of the Syndicate ships tries to defect to us."

"What are the chances of that?" Bradamont asked as she altered *Manticore*'s vector again, bringing the ship on track to join up with the rest of the Midway Flotilla.

"They could be good," Marphissa said. "It depends on how many snakes are aboard each ship, how alert they are, how loyal to the Syndicate the officers and crew are, and a lot of luck. But if the Syndicate flotilla is going to use the hypernet gate, there's little time left for anyone to try a mutiny."

"Kommodor—!" the communications specialist began, then stopped abruptly, looking puzzled.

Marphissa had barely begun to look that way when an urgent alert on her display began pulsing near the Syndicate battleship. "A Syndicate light cruiser just blew up." It took her a moment to realize that she had said those words. "What happened?"

"There has been no firing from the Syndicate flotilla except the missiles launched at us," the operations specialist confirmed.

"From the signature of the explosion," the engineering specialist said, "it was a power-core overload. There were no precursors, no warning signs. It just overloaded."

"How can that happen?" Marphissa demanded. "There are safety interlocks, physical and in the software. There are passwords, there are sequences that must be followed, there are automatic corrective measures. How could a power core overload without any warning?"

"Kommodor," the communications specialist said, her voice subdued. "I think I know. Just before the light cruiser exploded, we received a message broadcast toward us by directional beam. The message ID tagged it as from CL-347. All I heard was *freedom or*—and then it cut off."

Marphissa covered her face with one hand, aware of the silence that had fallen on the bridge. She took a long moment to compose herself, then lowered the hand and looked around. "The snakes have a new trick. Or the Syndicate CEOs. They would rather destroy a ship than let the crew escape." There was no need to drive the point home. Everyone already hated the snakes and the bosses. This incident would only reinforce their determination to fight to the death rather than surrender.

"The Syndicate flotilla has entered the hypernet gate," the operations specialist said. "The star system is free of Syndicate military forces."

Bradamont nodded to acknowledge the report. "The operation is complete." Her voice sounded subdued as well, the death of the light cruiser having cast a pall over any desire to celebrate. "Kommodor, to whom do I return command of *Manticore*? You or . . . ?"

Kapitan Toirac stiffened at the question but stayed silent. Kontos, standing behind him, had holstered his sidearm, but Toirac couldn't see that.

Perhaps, despite everything that had come before, Marphissa would have hesitated to take the final step. But not after watching that light cruiser be destroyed. Her mood left no room for further tolerance of someone who could not, would not, fulfill his responsibilities.

She tapped an internal comm control. "Kapitan-Leytenant Diaz, come to the bridge."

It only took a little more than a minute, but seemed far longer, before Diaz appeared. "Yes, Kommodor?"

This was not a moment she had sought. Marphissa had to steel

herself as she stood up to face Diaz. "Kapitan Toirac, for failure to
carry out your responsibilities you are relieved of command and of all
duties. Kapitan-Leytenant Diaz, you are promoted to Kapitan and will
assume command of *Manticore* effective immediately."

Diaz, his expression aghast, then saddened, glanced toward Toirac.
He nodded and saluted. "Yes, Kommodor."

"Kapitan Toirac, you are confined to quarters," Marphissa said,
fighting to keep her voice from quavering. *Why did you force me to do
this?*

Toirac got up and stomped off the bridge without a salute or other
acknowledgment of Marphissa.

"I'll make sure he gets there without any . . . difficulties," Kontos
said. "By your leave, Kommodor."

"Yes. Go." She watched Kontos go quickly after Toirac to make sure
he didn't attempt any mischief, then faced Diaz again. "You know why
I took this action. Take *command* of this ship, Kapitan Diaz."

"I will." Diaz glanced at Bradamont.

"I relinquish command to Kapitan Diaz," Bradamont said.

"Thank you, Kapitan . . . Bascare?"

"Bradamont. I am Captain Bradamont."

Marphissa placed one hand on her shoulder. "She is Black Jack's,
sent to assist President Iceni and aid us in getting rid of the Syndicate flotilla. Captain Bradamont will be leaving *Manticore* soon, but
she will remain in this star system when Black Jack's fleet leaves because Black Jack wants everyone to know that he supports the freedom
of Midway Star System."

She could feel emotions on the bridge wavering.

"An Alliance officer?" Diaz asked, doubtful.

"One of Black Jack's officers," Marphissa corrected, her voice firm.
"One of his battle cruiser commanders." They all understood the sig-
nificance of that, their expressions taking on grudging respect.

"Kommodor," the senior specialist asked, his voice hesitant, "she
will not command us?"

"No. It was necessary this time, to place the Syndicate flotilla in the position of having fired on a ship under Alliance charter and with an Alliance officer in temporary command. That gave Black Jack justification to destroy the Syndicate flotilla, which unfortunately escaped. But she is not here to command us. Captain Bradamont is here to mark Black Jack's commitment to our freedom."

"Why would Black Jack require justification for whatever he wanted to do?" the operations specialist asked.

Marphissa almost snapped back at the bold question, but Bradamont forestalled her. "Because Admiral Geary, the man you call Black Jack, is not a Syndicate Worlds CEO. He does not do whatever he wants. He follows the law."

That impressed them. They were still wary, but the worker specialists looked at Marphissa and nodded, then the senior specialist stood and saluted. "We understand, Kommodor."

As Marphissa and Bradamont left the bridge, Bradamont sighed. "I get the feeling I'd better stay confined to my quarters as well."

"I'm sorry, but you're right. It will be safer."

"I can't complain. If there were a Syndic officer on an Alliance warship, she or he would face the same attitudes."

"I'll find out whether President Iceni wants you picked up by a freighter on a regular supply run or sent on a Hunter-Killer or other warship." Marphissa said. "Until then, I'll post a guard outside your stateroom. I hope you understand."

"You'd better post a guard at that Kapitan's stateroom as well," Bradamont said.

"I'm sorry you saw that." Marphissa made a muddled gesture, half-angry and half-frustrated. "Why did he make it so hard?"

"They always do," Bradamont commiserated. "The ones who can't do their jobs always make everything as hard as possible for everyone else as well."

"He was my friend."

"Ouch. You got promoted pretty fast, didn't you? Welcome to the joys of higher rank. Being willing to do what you have to do, but don't want to do, is a big part of it. Some people can handle that. Some can't."

Marphissa grimaced. "I'll miss you, Captain. Good luck once you leave *Manticore*."

"You'll see me again, Kommodor. We'll need to convince your bosses to let you recover some prisoners of war even though it will mean sending some of your warships a long ways away. That's going to be a harder sell now. Admiral Geary is going to be leaving this star system soon since the Syndic flotilla has been chased off, so Midway will be on its own again as far as defenses go."

"PRESIDENT Iceni, we have encountered an unusual situation. We can't access the hypernet gates at Indras, Praja, Kachin, or Taniwah," Black Jack said. "CEO Boyens warned that the Syndicate government would make our journey back harder than we hoped, but we didn't expect that they would drop the Syndicate Worlds' hypernet system. According to our hypernet key, the only gate now accessible is at Sobek."

Drakon, who had come to the command center to watch the departure of Geary's fleet, shook his head in disbelief at the message. "Prime dropped almost every hypernet gate? That will cripple what's left of the Syndicate Worlds. The economic impact alone will be huge, but it will also seriously hinder its ability to shift military forces to deal with internal and external threats. Did they kill their chances to hold some stars together in the Syndicate Worlds just to make Black Jack's journey home more difficult?"

"It does seem like tearing your hair out to avoid going bald," Iceni agreed. She knew she had been moody lately and had been trying to shake it. But Boyens had escaped instead of having his flotilla destroyed. Black Jack's fleet was leaving, taking with it all the protection for Midway Star System that such a mass of warships could provide.

There was at least one snake agent still hidden close enough to plant an agent inside the planetary command center. On top of all that, she had found herself increasingly bothered by a vague sense that there were other plans under way, involving people and events she wasn't even aware of, like the slow movements of continents that you did not feel except when earthquakes suddenly and devastatingly brought it all to your attention.

And now this.

"Where is Sobek?" Iceni asked, her brow furrowed with concern. The answer popped up on the display, a window showing a region of space much closer to the Alliance. "Why would Sobek's gate be spared?"

"It doesn't make a lot of sense," Drakon said. "Maybe Prime ordered it and something went wrong at Sobek, so its gate didn't collapse as ordered."

"But *that* doesn't make sense! Prime ordering the elimination of their own hypernet? Why not just commit suicide outright?" She lowered her head, fighting for control with an effort she knew must be obvious to those around her. "Do you have any idea what impact this will have on us? It means our gate has become nearly useless."

"We still have all the jump points," Drakon pointed out.

"Yes. Relatively speaking, that will leave us with an advantage, but . . . damn them."

"Could Black Jack be lying about this?"

"Why would he? The instant another ship showed up from another gate, it would tell us he had lied. Togo, I want our techs checking that gate. I want a full, remote diagnostic and a check of accessible gates using our monitoring software."

"Yes, Madam President." Togo paused in a listening attitude, one hand to the phone relay in his ear. "I had already ordered our technicians here to check on the remote status signals from the gate. They indicate no problems with the functioning of the gate."

"If there's no problem with our gate, then all of those other gates really are gone!" Iceni said. "Get a ship out there. I want techs check-ing that gate in person, not remotely. Boyens was near that gate a long time. Maybe he managed to sneak something onto the gate-control mechanisms that is producing this problem."

"In theory," Togo said, "such a mechanism would be detected due to its interference with the gate-control mechanisms."

"I didn't ask for a lecture on theory! According to what the Alli-ance found, the technology for those gates came from the enigmas. We know far too little about the hypernet and the gates. Do as I have instructed!" Iceni turned a furious look on Drakon. "What have those bastards who rule the Syndicate Worlds done to us? Are they pulling everything down around them just to ensure we lose as well?"

But Drakon wasn't really listening to her, instead gazing at the display intently. She managed to damp down her anger before it ex-ploded. "Is there something up there I don't see?" Iceni asked through clenched teeth.

"No." Drakon shook his head, still half-lost in thought. "There's only one gate left, at Sobek. Why Sobek?"

"I already asked you that."

"This means Black Jack has to take his fleet to Sobek," Drakon pointed out.

"Of course, it—" Iceni halted in midsentence as she realized the point of what Drakon was saying. "Prime wants Black Jack to go to Sobek, and only to Sobek."

"Yeah." Drakon frowned and shook his head. "That would explain why Sobek was the only gate left standing, so that Black Jack would be forced to take a path home that Prime wants him to take. And he has no choice, the way I read it. He has to stick his head in that lion's mouth in order to get back to Alliance space in any reasonable amount of time. Using jump drives all the way back would take way too long. But it doesn't explain why Prime would take the extreme step of dropping the rest of their hypernet in order to force Black Jack to go to Sobek."

"The Dancers?" Iceni felt a coldness sweep through her at the thought. "Would stopping them from reaching Alliance space be worth that cost to the Syndicate Worlds?"

"That's possible." Drakon looked even grimmer than before. "The first human contact with a nonhuman intelligence, if you don't count the enigmas, and I don't think you can. There's no contact with the enigmas. Just war. But the Dancers are different. It would be just like the CEOs on Prime to want to destroy the Syndicate Worlds if necessary in order to keep the Alliance from gaining friendly contact with an alien species."

"That could explain it. There's also that superbattleship. Boyens kept pushing for access to that long after it was clear that Black Jack would never allow him within a light-hour of it. All Black Jack told us was that there was potentially new technology on that Kick ship and, hopefully, more information about the Kicks themselves. Maybe that's all he knows. But that Kick technology could be of immense value, and Prime would want to deny that to the Alliance as well." Iceni made a fist and rapped it against her own forehead. "But, all of those are long-term concerns. Short term, the impact on business in the Syndicate Worlds would be catastrophic. I just don't see how they could do that. I'll tell Black Jack we have no idea what the problem is but that we'll do all we can to find out."

"Do you want to warn him about going to Sobek?" Drakon asked.

"Do I have to?"

"No. If we saw the threat there, we can be certain that Black Jack saw it, too."

Iceni headed for the secure office off the command center that she had been using lately, followed closely by Togo. "When was the last time we know that the hypernet gate could access other stars than Sobek?" she asked Togo, as they walked.

Togo consulted his data pad. "Two days. A freighter came in from Nanggal."

"Nothing since then? That's unusual but not too unusual. No wonder this came as a surprise."

She entered the room, Togo behind her pausing to ensure the door closed securely, she glancing back to check the green glow of the lights pronouncing the room safe, reaching the desk, and beginning to walk around it to the chair—

"Freeze!"

Togo did not use that word or that tone of command unless it was very, very necessary.

Iceni jerked herself to a stop so quickly that a muscle protested. But she ignored that pain, concentrating on not moving.

She saw Togo come past her, studying one of his security devices, his eyes flicking toward the desk beside Iceni. His motions slowed, becoming very cautious and deliberate, as Togo knelt to look beneath the desk. He remained there for several seconds that felt much longer to Iceni, who was even trying to breathe without making any excess motion.

Togo stood up, his movements still careful but no longer minimized. "A bomb, Madam President, planted under the desk, invisible to the naked eye because it is formed into a thin sheet which was applied to the undersurface of the desk. Directional explosive. It would have cut you in half."

"Am I still in danger?"

"Not where you are standing, Madam President. It is aimed at the chair." Togo paused, no emotion visible on his face. "The fuse uses a biometric trigger, keyed to your physical traits."

"Biometric." Keyed on her. The bomb would not have exploded if anyone else sat in that chair. But if she had sat there again, she would have suffered certain death. "I've heard of those kinds of assassination devices. They're not easy to acquire." She wondered why she suddenly felt so calm.

"The Syndicate government kept tight control of them," Togo agreed. He had knelt again and was working under the desk. "It is deactivated."

Iceni relaxed, standing up straight. She looked toward the door of the room and the panel above it, where the lights still glowed green to indicate there were no taps, no bugs, no bombs, no threats of any kind in this office. Obviously, someone had not only planted the bomb but also hacked the supposedly secure sensors that would warn of the bomb. And of other things. *How long ago was that done? Is this room bugged as well? How private have the conversations held in here really been?*

The momentary calm was being replaced by anger again. "This room was compromised. How?"

Togo lowered his head in apology. "I do not know, Madam President. I will find out."

"You'd damn well better. You saved my life, but if you'd done your job right, my life never would have been in peril. I need to know how someone got in here, everything they did, how the room got compromised without anyone's detecting it, and most importantly, who it was."

"I will find the answers, Madam President." Togo indicated the desk. "But the answer to the last question may already be before us. This device contains explosives with military tags embedded in it."

Military? Snakes had access to their own explosives, which contained no tags allowing them to be traced to their sources. The only people on Midway who would have access to specialized military explosives of this sort would have to be—

Togo was speaking again, his tone that of someone pronouncing sentence on the guilty. "General Drakon. Or someone on his staff."

CHAPTER EIGHT

UNDER the circumstances, Iceni thought she sounded appropriately concerned but not as rattled as someone who had narrowly escaped assassination. She had chosen another secure room in the command center at random, had it swept for hazards, then sat down to send her reply to Black Jack. "A freighter arrived two days ago from the gate with Nanggal and did not report any problems. I assure you that we are extremely concerned by the news you have given us. We cannot explain the problems you are having accessing gates elsewhere in the Syndicate hypernet. My information prior to our break with the Syndicate was that every standing gate had already been equipped to prevent collapse by remote means. I cannot believe that the new government on Prime would have deliberately destroyed almost all of their hypernet. The impact on corporate activity and profits would be incalculable.

"That said, we have no idea what has happened. There are no indications that our own gate is suffering any problems or malfunctions. We have closely monitored it for any signs of software or hardware sabotage, especially during the period when CEO Boyens's flotilla was in this star system.

"If you discover anything, or find any anomalies in the operation of the gate, we would be grateful if you would provide us with that information. For the people. Iceni, out."

As she gazed at the small display above the desk, it occurred to her that if Black Jack had departed as scheduled, the bomb aimed at her would have gone off either just after his fleet left this star system or so close to that time that news of the event could not have reached Black Jack before his fleet entered the hypernet gate. *Whoever did that did not want Black Jack to know. That tells me something very important— that Black Jack was not involved.*

The big question now was what to do. Strike back? Syndicate etiquette called for an equivalent response, which would mean an attempt to put an end to Drakon.

Iceni kept her eyes on the display, but she wasn't seeing the play of ships through the star system anymore. *What am I feeling? Disappointment. No, something more than that.*

How could Drakon have done such a thing? Or, if he didn't order the attempt, let someone like that insane Morgan go after me? They should have known that even if the plot succeeded the military-tagged explosives would point—

Her eyes refocused. So did her brain.

Yes. They should have known. Get a grip, Gwen. Would Drakon or one of his close staff, people with access to commercial explosives, people who overran and control the snakes' old headquarters facilities and so must have access to snake explosives, use military explosives that would clearly implicate them?

I must be getting old. Why did it take me so long to spot that?

She sat back, thinking, running through every fact, every event. After several minutes, Iceni keyed in a comm address. "General Drakon, I need to speak with you. Alone. Not at the command center. I have learned that at least some of the supposedly secure rooms here have been compromised."

Drakon watched her, his eyes questioning. Concerned. She could tell he was worried, but his next words caught her off guard. "Are you all right?"

His first question was about her? She was what he was concerned about? Iceni's mind floundered for a moment, surprised. "I'm fine. Where do you want to meet? We need somewhere new, somewhere secure, where no one would have expected us to meet."

"There's only one place I know of that fits that description, but you might not want to go there."

"Tell me."

DRAKON waited at the entrance to the office once occupied by CEO Hardrad, former head of the Internal Security Service in the Midway Star System. The snake headquarters complex had been badly shot up when Drakon's troops took the heavily fortified building, but Hardrad's office deep inside it bore only one sign of the fate of both CEO Hardrad and the snakes on this planet. On one wall, behind Hardrad's former desk, stains were still visible, marking where Hardrad had been standing when Colonel Morgan put a bullet through his head.

Iceni arrived with a couple of bodyguards, whom she told to wait outside before entering. She looked around, grimacing. "I have no fond memories of this room."

"Me, neither," Drakon agreed, gesturing to Colonel Malin to close the door and remain outside. "But the one place on this planet guaranteed to be without recording or listening devices is this office."

"Ironic, isn't it?" Iceni said. She glanced at the desk and Hardrad's former chair, shook her head, then sat down in one of the comfortable chairs arrayed about a small table to one side of the office. "The snakes bugged every place they could except the office of their boss."

"Snake CEOs don't want anyone to know what they've done, or ordered," Drakon observed, taking a seat opposite Iceni. "What happened?"

She eyed him for a few seconds before replying. "Someone tried to kill me. Or someone tried to make it look like someone tried to kill me."

Drakon's face went cold and hard. Inside, he felt the same way. "An assassination attempt? Aimed at you?"

"There was a biometric trigger on the bomb."

He could feel warmth rushing to his face now, anger replacing the coldness. "I'll— Hold on. You said someone might have *tried* to make it look like an assassination attempt?"

"Possibly." Iceni watched him, looking puzzled. "You are a dilemma, General. Let me be frank. The bomb aimed at me contained military-tagged directional explosives."

"What?" She kept throwing revelations at him, and it was taking time to absorb each new one. "Military-tagged?" The implications hit, and his anger grew. "Someone tried to implicate me in it? Someone wanted you to think I authorized that?"

"You didn't?"

"No!"

The vehemence of his reply surprised him, but Iceni just gazed back at him speculatively. "What about members of your staff? Someone close to you?"

"Absolutely not," Drakon said. "You mean Colonel Morgan, don't you?"

"Among other possibilities."

"It wasn't Morgan," Drakon said, "because if it had been her, you would be dead. How did the bomb get spotted?"

"Someone detected it before I sat down."

"Lucky they were behind the desk."

Iceni paused. "Why do you say that?" Her voice sounded a bit too calm, too controlled as she asked the question.

"You said it used directional explosives," Drakon explained. "The trigger would only have been scanning in the direction the explosives would strike."

"Yes," Iceni agreed. "So the trigger could only be detected in that direction? Interesting."

Drakon gave her a demanding look. "Why?"

She watched him again for a while before replying. He wished he could hear the thoughts behind Iceni's eyes.

Suddenly, Iceni made a small movement that caused a compact but very lethal and powerful weapon to appear in her hand. "You know that I could kill you right now."

"I know that you could try. You must know that I have the same sort of defenses."

"Yes." Another twitch and the weapon disappeared into conceal-ment again. "Why didn't you tense when I displayed my weapon?"

Drakon gestured toward her face. "I was watching your eyes, not the weapon. When someone intends using a weapon, you can read it in the eyes first. You didn't have the look."

"I'll have to work on that. I thought maybe you . . . trusted me. My experience in life," Iceni said, "everything I have learned while climb-ing to the rank of CEO in the Syndicate, tells me to trust no one. There is only one person in this star system who I can be certain is not work-ing against me."

He started to smile, only to stop as she continued.

"That person is the Alliance liaison officer. I know she is not a snake. I know she is not working for you, or for any other faction in this star system, or for anyone in any nearby star system."

"You think she doesn't have any agendas?" Drakon challenged, his voice harsh.

"I know she does. And I know those agendas should correspond to mine."

"Really? Are you ready for those free-and-open elections the Alli-ance always boasts about?"

Iceni didn't answer immediately, instead sitting back and running one hand through her hair as she looked to the side. "You brought that up before. The citizens seem to be content with the bones we're throwing them," she finally said.

"I assume you've seen the same reports that I have," Drakon said, pushing his point. "Some elements are already dissatisfied, already pushing for elections for all positions up to and including yours."

Her eyes went back to him, challenging this time. "But not yours."

"Because I don't fill that kind of job. But those elements of the citizens expect me to obey whomever they elect to *your* job. I'm not thrilled at the idea," Drakon added. "At some point, we'll have to confront those citizens. That means keeping the majority of the citizens on our side and the majority of the elected offices on our side. I understand what that means. So do you. That Alliance officer? Very likely not."

Iceni nodded, her eyes still on him. "You're right. What are you telling me, Artur?"

"I'm telling you that the reason we decided to work together in the first place is still valid. If we're going to survive, if we're going to win, we need to work as a team." *I don't know why I want her to believe that so badly, but I do. Anyway, it's true. Alone, either one of us will be toast.*

She finally smiled. "I wanted to hear you say that. I agree with you, but I wanted to know that you still understood what we're facing. But does everyone else understand? Everyone who works for us?"

"No." There wasn't any sense in beating around the bush. "Not for me, anyway."

"Not for me, either." Iceni stood up, then reached a hand toward him. "Is there anyone *you* trust in this star system?"

He had to think carefully before answering, then stood as well and very briefly grasped her offered hand. "Yes."

He knew Iceni was waiting to hear more before they both headed for the door, but, still smarting from her statement that she could only trust the Alliance liaison officer, Drakon said nothing else.

BLACK Jack's fleet had departed but had left something behind that required Drakon's personal presence in the main orbiting facility. The Syndicate citizens who had been captured and kept imprisoned by the alien enigma race had all chosen to stay at Midway, all three hundred and thirty-three of them. Black Jack had offered them eighteen, but at the critical moment, when the former prisoners would have been separated from each other, the rest of the group had changed their minds. It was the sort of thing you would expect from people suffering the effects of long imprisonment together. But now they were all free, and they were all coming here. They knew nothing about the enigmas, but their presence at Midway would still be a diplomatic coup of sorts.

Drakon sat alone in the passenger compartment of a military shuttle as it rose above the atmosphere. The large display at the front of the compartment was set for a split screen, one half looking upward to endless dark and endless stars, the other half down to where white clouds drifted above vast expanses of water broken by chains of islands and a couple of small island-continents. He had a sensation of being suspended between extremes, a feeling that his own decisions and actions could keep him here, balanced between the heavens and a living world, or propel him down to a fiery reentry or up to be lost in the cold dark.

The urgent chime of his comm unit provided a welcome interruption to the disturbing reverie. "What's up?" he asked as the image of Colonel Malin appeared. "Is President Iceni going to be delayed?" Iceni was taking her own shuttle up. While the public image of them riding together might have helped cement the citizens' view of Drakon and Iceni as co-rulers working in what passed for harmony under a Syndicate definition of the term, the risk of having two extremely lucrative targets in one vehicle had been judged far too great. Besides, accidents did happen. Real accidents, as opposed to the sort of accidents that conveniently removed rivals.

"No, sir," Malin replied. "The President's shuttle has lifted. But we have an interesting development. A freighter arrived at the hypernet gate a few hours ago. It came from Taniwah."

He started to dismiss the news as inconsequential, then stared at Malin. "Taniwah? Not Sobek? You're certain?"

"Yes, sir. When the freighter showed up, Kommodor Marphissa ordered *Kraken* to approach the gate and search for destinations. Every known gate in the Syndicate Worlds hypernet, except those like Kalixa, which were previously destroyed, was listed as an option."

Drakon sat back, rubbing his chin. "We've got access to the entire hypernet again. The CEOs on Prime didn't destroy the Syndicate hypernet."

"No, sir. What they did do was somehow temporarily block access to any gate except Sobek for any ship or ships leaving here."

"I didn't know that was possible."

"It's not supposed to be possible," Malin replied. "We don't know how to do it. However, we have to assume that Prime now knows how to do it."

"Wonderful. Where did you get this information?"

"It was forwarded to us from the planetary command center by order of President Iceni, General."

"What are the chances that our spies in Syndicate space can find out how to work that trick with the hypernet, and maybe how to counter it?"

"I will send instructions to our sources in Syndicate-controlled space," Malin said. "But since the instructions must go along with routine freighter movements that will take circuitous routes to avoid the official Syndicate blockade of us, it will take some time for those instructions to be received, and I do not know whether any of our sources can achieve the access needed to get that information. The Syndicate is certain to be holding it in the most-highly-classified channels."

"What about our techs? Can they come up with the answer now that they know it can be done?"

"They have been notified, General. I understand that President Iceni has made that research a priority."

"Good. Thank you." As Malin's image vanished, Drakon turned his gaze back to the display at the front of the compartment, where the stars and the surface of the planet offered their visions of opposing but equally dire fates.

THE buzz of conversation among the main orbiting facility workers and family members who had gathered to view the arrival of those who had been captured by the enigmas rose as Drakon walked into view. He did his best to look casual, stopping to speak with the soldiers who were providing security in the shuttle-dock area for the event. "How does it feel?" he asked the major in charge of the guard force. "Do you have enough troops on hand?"

"The citizens are excited, General," the major replied. "No anxiety, no sense of trouble brewing, though. No one thinks we're hiding anything. We've got plenty of soldiers here if something unexpected happens."

Drakon nodded, his eyes on the hatch through which the liberated prisoners would come. "I don't know about you, Major, but I'm discovering that it's sort of nice to be on the same side as the citizens."

The major grinned, as did the soldiers within earshot. "Yes, sir. Instead of doing the dirty work for the snakes and the CEOs, we're working for the people. I could get used to that."

"It's a welcome change, isn't it?" These soldiers, and many others, had been used for security details often in the past. The snakes wouldn't deign to dirty their hands with routine crowd control, or riot suppression, or other "mass internal security" actions, so the CEOs would order regular troops to do the disagreeable tasks.

But as Drakon took in the attitudes of his soldiers, saw that they stood and reacted toward the crowd as if they were part of it rather than a separate force to control it, he wondered what would happen if orders were given to use force against this crowd or any other. Iceni had said that she and Drakon still had the ability to use force to control the citizens, but looking at the situation here and now, Drakon wondered if that was still true.

I'll check with my brigade commanders for their impressions when I get back to the surface. First, this operation has to be done right. "Stay alert when the prisoners start coming out," Drakon ordered. "There was some trouble when they were picked up by our shuttles."

The major's smile faded into a frown. "The Alliance?"

"No. Apparently the Alliance treated them well. The trouble was because these citizens have been imprisoned by the enigmas. They're fragile."

"Oh, yes, sir. Like someone out of a labor camp? I'll pass the word."

The background drone of conversation rose to a roar as Gwen Iceni walked onto the dock, waving to the citizens behind the security barricades. "I-cen-eh! I-cen-eh!" the crowds chanted between cheers.

Drakon walked to meet her. "You're popular," he observed.

She eyed him, unexpectedly smiled, then grabbed his hand with one of hers and raised both high while turning to face the crowds full on. Drakon felt uncomfortable as the cheers redoubled and he heard cries of "Dra-kon!" and "the General!" mixed with the adulation for Iceni.

"I don't trust it," he muttered to Iceni, as she lowered her arm and released his hand.

"The hero worship from the mob?" she asked. "You're right not to trust it. It can shift like the weather, and they'd be howling for our blood instead of chanting our names worshipfully. It was a good idea to meet up here together. It lets everyone see us doing something jointly, as a team."

"Maybe we should look for anyone who appears unhappy at that," Drakon commented.

"That's not a bad idea." She spoke into her personal comm. "My security detail will do a software search of security-camera imagery for discontented expressions."

"Where are your bodyguards?"

"If the need arises for them, you'll see them." She smiled. "Yours?"

"I've got soldiers on hand."

"Do you know of any specific threats?"

"No," Drakon replied. "That bothers me. Somebody should be mouthing off, somebody should be getting drunk and boasting about what he or she would do someday, somebody who hates the CEOs should be planning to hit us because of our past. And then there's the hidden snake agents out there. Why aren't I hearing anything? Somebody went after you."

"True. We can't let our guards down, and the lack of reported threats to either of us is odd. We're going to have to worry about threats to Captain Bradamont now as well. She will be coming off the ship first. We need our citizens to see this Alliance officer as a friend. How better to do so than by having her release to us the prisoners liberated by Black Jack?"

"It won't be enough, but it'll be a start," Drakon conceded. "There goes the hatch. Let's hope this doesn't turn into a fiasco."

The background noise of talking and shouting among the citizens dwindled rapidly as Captain Bradamont came walking out of the hatch, heading straight for Drakon and Iceni. Her Alliance uniform was impossible to miss, as was the fact that she was not walking like a prisoner. The conversation among the citizens died out completely before a few angry shouts erupted.

By then, Bradamont had reached Drakon and Iceni. She came to attention and saluted in the Alliance fashion, the fingertips of her right hand to her right brow, holding the gesture as she spoke. "President Iceni, General Drakon," she said in a voice that easily carried. "It is my great pleasure to deliver to you on behalf of the Alliance the citizens who were formerly held captive by the enigma alien race. We have brought them home, as they wished, and now release them to the care of their friends, families, and loved ones."

Drakon returned a Syndic salute, right fist coming across to rest on his left breast. "Thank you."

Iceni nodded. "We are all in debt to Black Jack, who liberated these citizens from the enigmas, brought them back to us through great dangers, and asked for *nothing* in return for them."

The buzz of conversation this time was much more subdued as the citizens reacted to the show that been put on for their benefit. Drakon suspected that Bradamont's little speech had been edited by Iceni before the freighter carrying her arrived.

Bradamont stepped a little closer and spoke much more quietly. "Watch the liberated prisoners carefully when they come out and handle them gently if they start to act up. They're very jumpy. Not dangerous. Just scared."

"Got it," Drakon said, watching as the liberated prisoners began coming out of the hatch. Some wore new overalls and other clothing provided by the Alliance, while many others clung to the patchwork assortment of clothing they had worn when liberated. They walked in a group, staying together like a herd of animals seeking protection, some looking around in wonder and others staring fixedly ahead. Most of them broke into relieved smiles as they saw images and uniforms that told them they were indeed home.

One of them, an elderly man, saw Drakon and pulled himself away from the others. He straightened and saluted in a jerky, rusty way, as if the gesture were something dimly remembered.

"Line Worker Olan Paster," he announced. "Reporting for duty."

Drakon regarded the old man somberly as he returned the salute. "What is your unit?"

"Hunter-Killer 9356G, sir."

"G-model Hunter-Killers haven't been constructed for decades," Iceni said. She looked up from a quick data check. "HuK 9356G is listed as having disappeared at Pele forty-five years ago."

"It has been that long?" The old man blinked in confusion. "We had no way to track time. The Alliance told us the universal date, but we wondered. I'm sorry. I don't know the clothes you wear, so I don't know what title to give you."

"We've discarded standard Syndic outfits," Drakon told him. "I'm General Drakon, this is President Iceni. We are no longer part of the Syndicate Worlds."

"Not . . . Syndicate?"

"No," Iceni said, smiling reassuringly now. "There are no snakes in this star system," she announced to all of the former prisoners. "We are no longer servants to the Syndicate, no longer slaves to the CEOs on Prime. We, and you, are free. You will be given living quarters on this station and treated well. As soon as any family members in this star system are identified, they will be allowed to visit you. Cooperate to the best of your ability in answering all questions. Citizens from Taroa, we have accepted temporary custody of you pending your acceptance by the new government in Taroa Star System. The rest of you are welcome here while we locate your homes and try to arrange transportation."

A woman of late middle age stared at Drakon. "What has happened to the Syndicate Worlds? The Alliance workers told us they had won the war, that it was over. We didn't believe them."

"Did the Alliance treat you well?" Iceni asked for the benefit of the onlookers.

"Yes. Yes, they were good to us."

"The war *is* over," Drakon said. "You'll have access to current news as well as archives and history so you can catch up on events."

"Thank you, honored CEO—"

"General," Drakon interrupted. "My rank is General. The civilian leader of this star system is *President* Iceni. CEOs no longer rule here."

"For the people!" Iceni said loudly, drawing renewed cheers from the onlookers as doctors began leading the liberated prisoners toward the room block set aside for them.

A small child, who must have never known freedom, broke away from the group and ran up to Captain Bradamont. "Thank you! Thank you for saving us!" the child cried before her mother caught up and led her back to the group.

Drakon glanced at Iceni and saw her smiling. That little incident would play very well on every newscast and other form of media. *I wonder if Gwen somehow set that up, too?*

Captain Bradamont watched the prisoners leave, then faced Drakon and Iceni again. "I am at your service."

She was putting up a good act. He had to give Bradamont credit for that. But Drakon could see the nervousness behind her unruffled façade.

"So I understand," Drakon said. "Come along. Your bags will be brought down later."

He and Iceni began walking back toward the VIP boarding area, Bradamont between them. It felt odd to walk side by side with an Alliance officer. Very odd. Soldiers formed security a ways before and behind as they walked, as did several men and women dressed as citizens who stayed well away but who were exceptionally alert and radiated a dangerous competence.

"My office," Iceni said, "is issuing a public announcement about you, Captain Bradamont. Everyone in Midway Star System is being told that you are here as a personal representative of Black Jack. Do you know the term 'scion'?"

Bradamont shook her head.

"There are several sorts of patronage arrangements in the Syndicate system," Iceni explained. "We still default to that system. People still think in those terms and understand those terms. Most patronage arrangements are informal, reflecting varying degrees of interest by a higher-up in the career and life of a particular subordinate."

"I understand that sort of thing," Bradamont said.

"Then there is a scion," Iceni continued. "A scion is a formal designation of patronage. When someone is declared the scion of a high-ranking official, it says that anything that happens to the scion, any threat made to the scion, is the same as if it was done to the high-ranking patron. My office is identifying you to every citizen as a scion of Black Jack and a scion of both General Drakon and myself."

Iceni gave Bradamont a wry look. "There has probably never been a scion with that amount of firepower in her corner. Congratulations."

"Thank you, but that wasn't necessary—"

"Yes, it was," Drakon said. "Everyone had to know that any attempt to harm you or mistreat you would be regarded in the exact same way as a personal attack on myself or President Iceni. That won't keep you safe from anyone gunning for either of us, but it will stave off attempts by anyone tempted to settles scores from the war."

"It will also," Iceni added, "ensure that you are treated appropriately to your rank. Anyone who insults you will know they are insulting us as well." She brought out a comm unit and passed it to Bradamont. "This is yours. It is loaded with personal contact numbers for myself, General Drakon, and some of our high-ranking assistants. If you use this unit to call any of the official numbers it will automatically encrypt the conversation. That does not mean no one can intercept the signal or decipher what is being said. Never say anything confidential on this unit or in public. Save such conversations for face-to-face talks in secure environments."

"We've set up quarters for you at my command complex," Drakon said. "There's a suite there for visiting VIPs. It's a lot more than an officer of your rank would normally get, but then you're also sort of an ambassador. Having you inside the command complex perimeter will make security a lot easier."

Bradamont just nodded this time, looking at the military and civilian guards around them. Her thoughts couldn't be read from her expression, but Drakon found himself wondering if this level of guards and security would have been found around comparable Alliance leaders. *Probably. The Syndicate didn't have an exclusive monopoly on crazies. But for someone much lower on the ladder like Bradamont, this amount of personal security must feel weird.*

They reached the access to the VIP dock, shedding most of the guards and all of the onlookers as they left the public areas. "Tell me," Iceni said to Bradamont, "your impression of Kommodor Marphissa."

"She is talented and has a great deal of potential," Bradamont said without hesitation. "Due to her rapid rise in rank, she has some experience to gain, but I have no doubt she will pick that up quickly."

"I understand that you witnessed the removal from command of Kapitan Toirac," Iceni continued.

"I did."

"What was your impression of Kapitan Toirac?"

This time Bradamont did pause before speaking, each word coming out with thought behind it. "Promoted well above his level of competence. Unable to handle the responsibilities. Unwilling to address his weak areas. Now so embittered that I would not trust him in any position of authority."

"I see." Iceni halted, causing the rest of them to stop walking as well, and studied Bradamont. "Did you discuss the matter with Kommodor Marphissa?"

"Yes, ma'am."

"And Kapitan-Leytenant Kontos? What did you think of him?"

Bradamont smiled slightly. "He is impressive. He has a lot to learn, but I have no doubt he will pick everything up fast. He's the closest thing to a natural I've ever met."

"A natural?" Iceni asked.

Drakon answered. "Someone with an instinctive grasp for the right thing to do and how to do it. That was Colonel Rogero's impression of Kontos as well."

Bradamont kept her expression controlled but her eyes went to Drakon as he said Rogero's name.

Iceni noticed that as well, raising an eyebrow at Drakon. "I will leave you here, Captain Bradamont. General Drakon and I are traveling by separate shuttles for security reasons. I have in hand a proposal from Kommodor Marphissa for a very hazardous mission. I want to talk to you about that soon. General, you will have to be at that meeting as well. The proposed mission will require some ground forces as security."

"Yes," Bradamont said. "I do want to talk about that as soon as possible. But I don't think it can be done now that the Syndic hypernet is gone."

"You didn't hear? A freighter arrived via hypernet a few hours ago. Everything is working again."

Bradamont stared at Iceni. "You— The Syndicate Worlds can do that? Selectively shut off your hypernet?"

"The Syndicate apparently can do it," Drakon said. "But we can't." Iceni turned a reproachful look on him. He knew why and answered her unspoken rebuke. "Captain Bradamont needs to know that. She needs to tell the Alliance we still have a hypernet gate that is of great value to them and that *we* did not block Black Jack's fleet from reaching other destinations."

Iceni thought about it for all of two seconds, then nodded. "You're right, General. The arrival of that freighter came as a great shock to us, Captain Bradamont."

"I do need to get word of that back home as fast as I can," Bradamont agreed. "Before you go, Madam President, I should deliver these to you and General Drakon." She put a hand into one pocket, apparently oblivious to the way the remaining bodyguards focused intently on her motion, and brought out two data coins. "From Admiral Geary. These are reports on what we found in enigma space, Kick space, and Dancer space, as well as what information we have on each species."

Drakon took one of the discs. "These are identical?"

"The discs? Yes, sir. One for each of you."

"How diplomatic," Iceni commented, taking hers. "Are there any surprises on here?"

"I don't know," Bradamont replied. "I know Admiral Geary already told you some things. He said to me that you are on the front lines of humanity's contact with these species and therefore need to know as much as possible about them."

"A pity he did not allow some of our technicians to board the captured alien superbattleship," Iceni said pointedly.

Bradamont made an apologetic gesture with one hand. "Even our own techs haven't been allowed on board. There's a security force on *Invincible*, but we don't dare touch anything until we get her back to Alliance space."

Drakon had to admit that the explanation made sense, but it was the same sort of excuse he would have offered to anyone who wanted to stick their nose in somewhere he didn't want them to go. *At least Black Jack is being polite when he tells us to go to hell.* "Let me know about that meeting," Drakon told Iceni, then led Bradamont into his shuttle.

The guard at the entry ramp was doing her best not to stare at Bradamont, as was the shuttle pilot waiting inside. Drakon gestured for Bradamont to enter, then followed her into the passenger compartment, seating himself next to Bradamont.

As the hatch sealed, she took a sudden breath. Glancing down, Drakon saw one hand tightly gripping her armrest. *The last time she was locked in with someone like me she really was locked in. A prisoner. Now she's back around the same kind of people, having put herself totally at our mercy.* "Do you know what snakes are?" he asked.

Bradamont nodded. "Both the reptile kind and the human variety."

"The human-variety snakes were almost completely eliminated in this star system. We're hunting a few hidden remnants."

"Colonel Rogero told me." She nodded again, still tense. "I hope you understand there is a difference between knowing that and accepting it."

"I do," Drakon admitted. "I still have trouble with that myself. But it is in our best interests to treat you right, Captain Bradamont, and I intend making sure you are treated right."

Bradamont looked right at him. "No escorts for us on this shuttle?"

"You're a guest. Why would we need guards?" Drakon studied her as the shuttle undocked and began the transit and descent to the planet below. "Colonel Rogero has worked directly for me for some years. He's one of the best officers I've ever had."

She met his eyes. "And?"

"If you're wondering why he wasn't the one who met you, it's because I wanted to size you up in person. You almost got him killed, you know."

"Yes. I know."

"But he was an equal partner in that," Drakon continued. "All I care about is whether we can work with an Alliance officer. From what I've heard, you did all right on *Manticore*."

"I was mostly an observer, there for the legal niceties," Bradamont said.

"I recognize some of those ribbons you're wearing, Captain. You didn't earn them observing things." He pointed to one, with red, green, and silver bands. "I know that one. It's for Ajatar, right?"

"Yes, sir. How did you know?"

"One of those intelligence summaries," Drakon explained. "I didn't really need to know what all the Alliance ribbons and badges stood for, but that one caught my eye because I was at Ajatar. On the ground."

Her eyes met his again. "Ground forces? The second planet."

"Yeah. We got our butts kicked pretty bad."

She shook her head. "Our ground forces people were saying afterward that they couldn't believe you held out until a Syndic flotilla arrived that was strong enough to drive us out of the star system."

Drakon shrugged, looking away as memories flooded into his mind. "It wasn't easy. There weren't a lot of us left by then. I was a . . . you'd call the rank major, I guess. I arrived on the planet with a battalion. When we finally got relieved I had about a platoon's worth still alive."

"It was bad in space, too. I was just an ensign on a heavy cruiser.

The *Sallet*. We got shot to pieces. About forty of us made it off in escape pods before the power core blew."

"Damn. Funny you were on one of the ships dropping rocks on my head. Small galaxy, isn't it?" Drakon sighed, then shrugged again. "I'm glad it's over."

"Is it?"

"Nah. We're all still fighting, aren't we? The enemies have just changed. But I like to pretend."

"That can be a bad habit in senior officers," Bradamont observed.

The blunt observation could have upset him with its borderline insubordination, but instead Drakon found himself smiling wryly. "A very bad habit, especially when planning operations. I think I'm beginning to see what Colonel Rogero sees in you and why Black Jack picked you for this assignment."

"Will I be . . . General, this is a purely personal question. Will I be allowed to see Colonel Rogero?"

"Allowed? You'll be required to see him. He's going to be your official handler though he'll retain his primary job as one of my brigade commanders."

Bradamont swallowed, eyes wide. "Thank you, General."

"I did it for him," Drakon said, feeling uncomfortable at her obvious gratitude. "You'll have some guards assigned to you, but they'll respect your privacy. Remember what President Iceni said. Anything you say in public or on a comm line will probably be overheard."

"I thought the snakes were gone," Bradamont said.

"Most of them. We're certain there is at least one snake operative hidden among the citizens or the military. But snakes aren't the only ones who tap into conversations. You know how that is."

Her gaze back at him was perplexed. Clearly, this Alliance officer didn't know how it was. "General, are you talking about official or unofficial snoops?"

"Both. Internal politics and competition for promotions can get really hardball." She had to understand that aspect of things.

"Hardball," Bradamont repeated. "You mean politicking?"

"No, I mean blackmail, spying, and assassinations."

She stared back at him. "I'm waiting for you to say *just kidding.*"

"That doesn't happen in the Alliance?" Drakon asked.

"No. I mean, in rare cases. But it is rare." Bradamont looked down, her expression concerned. "Some of the things Colonel Rogero said to me. I assumed I'd misinterpreted them."

"You didn't." Drakon gave her his sternest look. "You need to know how things work here. How things *have* worked because I always hated that junk and will do my best to stamp it out. There's a reason why officers always carry sidearms, and it's not because we expect an Alliance invasion at any second. There's a reason why I often have bodyguards around me. I'm going to do my best to keep you alive, and I'm sure that Colonel Rogero will do the same. But you need to know what's going on so you'll stay alert for trouble."

"I . . . will do that, General." She looked up at the large display mounted on the front of the passenger compartment. It was now displaying a single external view of the planet below them as the shuttle dropped ever lower. "It's beautiful."

"I've seen a lot worse planets," Drakon agreed. "Are you going to be all right, Captain?"

She switched her gaze, and he saw an Alliance battle cruiser commander looking back at him. Tough. Smart. Not just competent, but skilled. "I'll be all right, General."

He had wondered what could have led Rogero to fall in love with an enemy prisoner of war. Having finally met her, he found that Rogero's fall wasn't all that surprising. "We'll land next to my headquarters complex. Colonel Rogero is standing by there. He doesn't know why, by the way."

"He'll have seen the news reports—"

"No, he won't. As far as Colonel Rogero knows, you left with Black Jack's fleet."

She smiled. "You're an evil man, General."

"Most people who have said that really mean it, you know."

"I doubt that. General, may I make a request?"

COLONEL Rogero tried not to look as aggravated as he felt. It was not by any means the first time he had been pulled away from his unit on vague orders from General Drakon. It also wasn't the first time he had been escorted to a secure conference room in the main command complex to await the General and a briefing on orders too sensitive to be passed on by any other means.

But he had been sitting here for hours, alone in a conference room that was not just secure but also sealed. He hadn't been able to access any comm lines, hadn't been able to check on alerts or current events or anything else outside the four walls confining him. *I wanted to see the former enigma prisoners arrive. There were rumors that the General would be at the main orbiting facility for that. Why am I a virtual prisoner in here when there is so much going on outside?*

It wasn't just the former prisoners coming in, though their arrival could arouse a wave of rumors and even instability among the citizens. There were still snakes hidden out there, and he couldn't hunt for them while confined in a room that didn't even allow him to call out.

Is my own loyalty suspected? Colonel Morgan has been acting guarded around me for a while, but Colonel Malin knows me well enough to know I would not betray General Drakon. But, if knowledge of my ties with the snakes has become more widely known . . .

Rogero looked toward the door with a sinking feeling. *Protective custody? Is that what this is? To keep my own troops from murdering me as a snake agent? Surely Drakon would tell them the truth, that I misled the snakes and protected the General. But would they listen?*

He saw the door latch move, then the portal swung open. General Drakon himself, looking unconcerned. "I'm sorry you've been kept on ice for a while, Donal. There was something I needed to take care of."

"General," Rogero said, rising from his seat a bit faster than he usually would have, "is there anything—"

Drakon waved a dismissive hand. "You're all right. I brought you here to tell you that you're getting another collateral duty."

"Another collateral duty?" That wasn't welcome news. Extra jobs on the side tended to take an inordinate amount of time away from your primary job. But compared to his earlier worries, it was a very small inconvenience. "What is it?"

"I'll show you. Come on."

Rogero followed, mystified, as Drakon led the way through the complex. "How's your unit doing?"

"They're fine, General. Morale is good."

"Excellent. I need to talk to you later about your impressions of the troops and their attitudes toward the citizens." Drakon stopped before the closed door of a small automated snack bar for use by headquarters personnel. "But that can wait a few hours. Here we are."

"General?"

Drakon glanced at Rogero. "Your new, extra responsibility is inside. It's something that only you can deal with, Colonel."

"In . . . a snack bar?"

"Take your time. When you're done in there, report to VIP Quarters One. Understand?"

"VIP—?"

"Just do as you're told, Colonel." Drakon partially opened the door, took Rogero by one arm, and urged him through the gap.

Mystified, and a bit worried again, Rogero started to turn back as he heard the door click shut behind him. Instead, he spun to face the inside of the room as someone stood up from one of the tables.

For one of the few times in his life, Donal Rogero could only stare, unable to think or talk.

"I bought you a drink," Captain Bradamont said, offering a bottle. "I didn't have any of the local currency, so your General lent me some."

The Alliance dress uniform she wore was clean and neat, not like the torn and burn-marked battle uniform that Bradamont had worn on the prisoner transport ship and in the labor camp. A command pin had been added to the decorations she wore, along with some new campaign and battle ribbons. But she herself had not changed at all. "Honore?" Rogero finally said as his brain gradually began working again. "Is this real?"

She walked up to him, offering the bottle once more. "It's real. I told you that I'd buy you a drink someday. Your General said this is a popular drink here."

"He was joking," Rogero said, feeling dizzy. "The troops call it *croak* because of the taste. We use it to clean brass."

"Oh, sorry." She paused, looking at him. "You said you'd buy dinner."

"Yes. I did." Rogero shook his head. "I . . . I don't understand."

"I've been detached from the Alliance fleet with orders to serve as liaison officer to the Midway Star System."

"It's . . . not possible. General Drakon knows. He knows about us."

"Yes. So does Admiral Geary."

"Then . . . why?"

"Because they know us," Bradamont said. "They know that we held to honor despite everything and that we never failed in our duties. We never betrayed them, we never betrayed our worlds, and we never betrayed each other. Maybe that qualifies us to show our respective peoples how to work together. There were some other reasons why I ended up being asked to volunteer for this assignment, but we can discuss those another time."

Enough neurons finally started firing in Rogero's brain for him to think. "General Drakon set this up? How did he know that the last thing you said to me was that you would buy me a drink someday?"

"I told him." She smiled. "He seems like a hard boss, but a good one."

"He's a very good boss. He's . . . he's . . . Dammit, Honore, may I hold you? May I kiss you?"

"Why the hell are you asking instead of doing it, Donal? But be careful not to muss the uniform."

DRAKON waited until an escort arrived to get Bradamont safely to her quarters, telling them to wait until Colonel Rogero opened the door. As he walked away, he saw Morgan standing at the end of the hallway, her eyes locked on the door to the snack bar.

"Is what I heard true?" she demanded.

Instead of replying, Drakon bent a stern look her way. "Is that the proper tone of voice to use with me?"

She made an obvious effort to control herself. "Pardon me, sir. Is it true that an Alliance fleet officer is in that room and *not* under arrest?"

"We're not at war with them anymore, Colonel Morgan. In fact, they're acting a lot like allies."

"Sir—"

"Yes. An Alliance fleet captain is in that room. She is an official representative to President Iceni and me, and she is under the personal protection of President Iceni and me. She is my scion. Understand? Nothing is to happen to her, and she is to be treated with the respect appropriate to her rank."

"Your . . . *scion*." Morgan stared at him, her eyes wide and alight with fury. "An Alliance officer. They killed—"

"We all killed, Colonel Morgan. The war has ended. We have plenty of enemies in common. We start over now. Even if that weren't true, we need the backing from Black Jack that woman gives us. She might be the one thing that buys us enough time to get our forces strong enough to stand on our own."

The way she regained full control almost instantaneously was startling and more than a little alarming. The fire in Morgan's eyes died, replaced by a cold shield that revealed neither thoughts nor feeling. Her expression smoothed out into a similarly shielded exterior. "Yes,

General. I understand." Even her voice was now perfectly professional and properly respectful.

"Colonel Morgan . . . Roh . . . we need to do things differently. For a long time, the past, the present, and the future were all the same. The same war then, the same war now, the same war to come. That pattern has finally been broken. The future can be different than the past. The future can be better than the past."

Emotion came back. Morgan nodded, smiling in total agreement. "Yes, sir. The future will be better. *We* will build our strength, and we will make a better future."

"You understand that declaring Captain Bradamont to be a scion of myself and President Iceni is to ensure her safety?"

Morgan smiled and nodded. "It doesn't mean she's really your heir in any way."

"That's right. Come along with me. I want to talk about finding the snakes still hiding on this planet or elsewhere in this star system."

"I've been digging. Got a few leads," Morgan said as she walked beside him. They went out the front of the headquarters complex into the open area before it, guards automatically falling into place around Drakon. He glanced at the turf covering much of the plaza facing his headquarters, his mind as usual briefly recalling how much effort the Syndicate had insisted go into keeping that grass perfect, including the use of the most sophisticated genetic manipulation to create grass of just the "right" shade of green and just the right thickness of each blade of grass. He had looked at the official specifications for grass once, marveling at how much effort could be invested in something so relatively unimportant, especially given the Syndicate bureaucracy's tendency to blow off issues regarding the safety of the soldiers who were prohibited from walking on the grass except during official functions.

Behind them, the front of the headquarters complex did not look like the fortress that it was, the armor and defenses hidden behind false windows, façades, and other decoration. In one of its odder decisions, the Syndicate bureaucracy had mandated no fences or other barriers or defenses on the other three sides of the parade plaza, declaring that ground forces headquarters must appear open and accessible to the citizens. Or perhaps the decision hadn't been so odd since it had meant the snakes inside their Internal Security Service facilities had been better protected behind their defensive walls than the soldiers of the ground forces.

"We should fix some of this," Drakon commented to Morgan. "Now that we can. Get some unobtrusive defenses set up along the outer perimeter of the parade area. No citizens are allowed on it anyway." He scanned the other three sides of the plaza, where low, multiuse buildings of various designs sat across from an access road that formally separated the headquarters area from the rest of the city. A lot of the citizens were in sight, going about their business and, out of long habit, avoiding even glancing toward the headquarters. The snakes had liked to haul in anyone suspected of "surveillance," even if the evidence for that had consisted only of a single fleeting look toward a government building.

"Now you're talking," Morgan agreed, and began describing a set of defenses that would have withstood a full-scale attack by an entire army.

"Maybe a little less than that," Drakon suggested dryly, glad that he had gotten Morgan's mind off the Alliance officer. "Have you found any leads yet on—"

Drakon would never know just what had tipped off one of his bodyguards. The woman had begun to shout a warning, her weapon out and coming up to aim, when alarms tied to automated sensors watching the area blared to life, followed a second later by shots erupting from three sides.

CHAPTER NINE

ICENI, head lowered in thought, bolted to attention as an urgent signal echoed in her office. "What is it?"

The staff official looking at her through the virtual window that had popped up beside her desk spoke rapidly. "We have reports of weapons being fired near General Drakon's headquarters. Automated collection systems show an ongoing firefight."

"A *firefight*?" Iceni demanded. "Not just a few shots?"

"There are scores of shots already recorded, Madam President. I have dispatched emergency tactical teams from the nearest police stations and notified the nearest hospitals to send assistance."

"Good." She was taking deep breaths, trying to control her heartbeat, which had begun racing.

"Hundreds of messages, alerts, and bulletins in news channels and other media about the fighting are being held up by the censoring software."

"Keep doing that until we find out what's going on," Iceni ordered.

The officer looked to one side, his expression going from concerned to horrified. "Dozens of unconfirmed media reports saying that

General Drakon is dead are coming in and being blocked from further transmission, Madam President."

Dead? No. Impossible. Not him. She inhaled slowly again. "Hold those as well. I want to know everything as fast as we learn it."

"But if General Drakon is—"

"He's not dead!"

The officer stared, then nodded. "I understand, Madam President. I will send a constant data feed to your desk."

"Get it going," Iceni said, her voice under control again. As the officer's image vanished, her hand went to her comm unit, then hesitated. *If he's alive, and people are shooting at him, he doesn't need distractions.*

Where the hell is Togo?

THE female bodyguard died before she could get off a shot, as did two other guards, but her warning had given Drakon the extra instant he needed to dive for cover and avoid subsequent shots aimed at him. Not that there was much cover in this open area, by order of the Syndicate bureaucracy.

Drakon sprawled behind the body of one of his guards, his weapon in his hand, trying to spot some of the locations where the shots were coming from as solid projectiles and energy bursts tore holes in the very-carefully-maintained turf near him. Even under these circumstances, a small part of his mind couldn't help recalling certain bosses he had suffered under who would have been far more upset about the damage to the grass than the deaths of the bodyguards.

Two meters away, Morgan, her face a mask of rage, was lying near another dead guard, her weapon out, one hand supporting her weapon hand as she fired with steady, careful accuracy. Other defensive fire was going out, the surviving bodyguards and the sentries at the entrance to the headquarters hurling shots at the places among the low buildings surrounding the plaza from which the attackers were firing.

Spotting the location of one attacker, Drakon aimed and squeezed off three carefully spaced shots. *It's been about fifteen seconds since they opened fire,* another part of his mind calculated with cold precision. *The reaction security force inside headquarters will be out here within another forty-five seconds.*

The attackers had ceased aiming at the guards and now were concentrating their fire on Drakon. He wondered if forty-five seconds would be too long. Bad enough to be the target of so many attackers when in battle armor, but right now all he had were the defenses in his uniform, which while sufficient for some protection would not stop the sort of barrage that was directed at him.

Morgan glanced back at him, sizing up his situation and his peril in an instant, her eyes dark and wide.

She bolted to her feet, instantly becoming the most prominent target on the plaza.

"Morgan!" Drakon shouted, firing rapidly at a couple of spots from which shots were coming. "Get down!"

She ignored his command, not just charging furiously ahead but also screaming defiance and firing as she ran to generate the maximum amount of attention. Morgan could move like a ghost when she wanted to. Right now, she was doing all that she could to attract the fire of the attackers to her, and away from Drakon. Morgan was dodging as she moved to make shots aimed at her more difficult, but was still hideously exposed. In full battle armor, such a maneuver would be very risky. With Morgan wearing no armor at all, her charge was insane.

Unable to stop her, Drakon took advantage of the distraction Morgan had provided to rise to one knee and aim, ignoring the shots still aimed at him that tore into the turf or zipped past his head. His next shot caused a figure to fall. He shifted targets, firing several more times.

Soldiers were spilling out of the headquarters entrance and secondary exits, menacing in armor, carrying combat weapons, and searching for targets.

The remaining fire aimed at Drakon dropped off so rapidly that he knew the attackers must be bolting for safety.

Morgan had reached her objective, miraculously not having been hit. She leaped over a railing, one hand staying locked on the top rail to help her pivot in midair and come down on those sheltered behind the ankle-high wall topped by the open fence. Drakon saw her weapon firing and Morgan's free hand rising to strike down viciously.

"General!" The captain in charge of the response force and a dozen of his soldiers raced into place around Drakon, forming an armored perimeter.

Drakon pointed, speaking coolly and clearly. "Shots came from there, there, there, and there. Colonel Morgan has taken out whoever fired from that location."

"We've got troops in full pursuit, sir."

Drakon heard the sirens from headquarters cut off but heard other sirens approaching. "There will be police responding to this gunfire. Make sure our troops don't engage them by accident."

"Yes, sir!"

Drakon looked around, realizing that firing had completely ceased. The soldiers forming an armored wall about him moved outward as they were reinforced, leaving him standing in a small, circular, open area where the grass smoked in dozens of places that marked the impacts of shots.

Two of the soldiers moved slightly, opening a temporary gap between them. Morgan came strolling through that gap. She was dragging a limp body with her by one leg, the body's torso and head thumping along over the ground. Reaching Drakon, Morgan dropped the leg and stood by her trophy, grinning wolfishly.

"Roh," Drakon said, "if you ever—"

"You're all right, General?" Morgan interrupted, her chest still heaving from exertion, her eyes alight with something more feral than adrenaline-fueled energy.

"I'm fine. That was insane."

She grinned wider. "I got a medical waiver saying I'm good enough for government work, General. I had to draw their fire."

"No, you didn't," Drakon snapped.

"Yes, sir, I did," Morgan said with an intensity that surprised him. "Nobody's going to kill you if I can stop it. And I got us a prisoner."

"How many did you see?" Drakon asked, deciding not to further berate Morgan in public, not that his words seemed to be having any impact on her. He also knew that she was very likely right. If she hadn't drawn some of the fire aimed at him, he wouldn't have made it until the soldiers had arrived.

"Two," Morgan said nonchalantly. "The other one at that spot is dead."

Shaking his head, Drakon knelt to examine the man. "He's not military."

"Nah. Civilian. He had a suicide belt on, but I left that with his buddy. I can't wait to see what this guy says under interrogation."

"Me, too." Drakon jerked back as the limp body suddenly jolted, then went slack in a different manner than before. In the near distance, two explosions resounded at nearly the same moment, the crashes so close together that they nearly merged into one blast that echoed from nearby walls.

Morgan scowled. "Someone set off those suicide belts." She knelt as well, peeling back one eyelid on her former prisoner. "Looks like brain-bake nanos. The same someone who triggered the belts figured out we had this guy and activated a backup method of keeping him quiet."

"Damn. We've still got two bodies."

"One body, boss," Morgan pointed out. "And parts of another."

"All right. There should be enough parts left for some identification. Let's find out who they both are, so the police can go talk to their friends before the friends can go underground." He stood up, grimacing at the sight of the dead bodyguards. "Somebody besides those two you took care of is going to pay a price for this."

"Say the word and name the target," Morgan said, her grin fully exposing her canines.

His comm unit buzzed in a particular pattern. Drakon pulled it out. "Here."

"Artur?" Iceni sounded very worried. Most of him felt good about that, but part of him couldn't help wondering if it was because a plan of hers might have misfired. "Are you hurt?"

"I'm fine, but I lost three guards."

"What happened? All I heard was a firefight. Someone tried to flood the media with reports you were dead."

"Did they?" Drakon asked. "Can you trace those back to their source?"

"We're trying. Did you get any of them?"

"Two, at least. One was alive, but he had remote-suicide nanos in him. Somebody is definitely playing for keeps."

A pause, then Iceni spoke again. "Is there anything you need from me?"

"Just make sure the police and my troops don't knock heads. I have a feeling the attackers who took off have already vanished into the woodwork."

"I'll do that. Take care of yourself."

Drakon put away his comm unit, noticing that Morgan was looking down at the dead attacker with an inquiring gaze. "See something?" he asked.

"Who really wants you out of the way?" Morgan answered him with a question of her own.

"Besides whatever snakes remain in this star system? You tell me."

"Madam President." Morgan nodded toward the dead man. "Who has access to that kind of nano? And those kind of weapons?"

"The snakes," Drakon said patiently.

"They're not the only ones." She used her toe to push back one sleeve and expose the man's forearm. "See that?"

It was impossible to miss. "A labor-camp mark."

"How many citizens who spent time in a labor camp are going to have anything to do with snakes?"

He didn't have any answer to that.

COLONEL Malin had been extremely upset when he returned to headquarters, making up for his absence when Drakon was attacked with a whirlwind of activity. "The police have hauled in every known associate of the two dead men," he told Drakon. They were in a secure conference room, along with Morgan.

Malin brought up an image on the display, showing every shot fired during the engagement. "From an analysis of the firing patterns, they initially aimed for your guards, General, then, after the first volley, shifted their attack to you and Colonel Morgan. That split in their targeting is what kept you from being hit, sir. For the first several seconds, only half the available weapons were firing at you."

Drakon glared at the image, then at Malin. "Colonel Morgan drew their fire deliberately."

"Yes, sir," Malin agreed, while Morgan smirked at him. "But there were a lot of shots being aimed at her before she did that, almost as many as were fired at you."

The implications of that were pretty obvious. "Colonel Morgan was a primary target, too? Why?"

"I believe, sir, that the attackers targeted her in error."

Morgan, leaning back in her seat with one foot on the table, her leg extended in a way guaranteed to draw the eye, grinned. "You're just jealous."

"Not at all," Malin said. "I'm certain they thought you were someone else."

"Who else could she have been?" Drakon demanded.

"It was widely known that you met the new Alliance liaison officer on the main orbiting facility, and that she left in company with you and President Iceni. President Iceni's shuttle landed, and she was seen leaving it alone. Your shuttle landed in a secure area, but one visible to long-distance snooping that would have identified a woman leaving the shuttle with you."

"They thought I was walking Captain Bradamont around? Morgan doesn't look anything like Bradamont."

Malin gestured toward Morgan. "A wig, a uniform change, some other cosmetics, and their physical builds are close enough that an observer could conclude that the Alliance officer was the one accompanying you."

"They thought I was that Alliance bitch?" Morgan asked. "Now I'm insulted."

"Colonel Morgan . . ." Drakon began.

"Pardon me, sir," Morgan replied. "I will endeavor to avoid using such language about our new friend and ally in the future."

"We have IDs on the individuals Colonel Morgan took out," Malin continued, bending his head briefly in Morgan's direction. "They both belong to an extreme group called The People's Word, which wants immediate, full democracy."

Drakon scowled at that. "They want to elect all their leaders now?"

"No, sir. They don't want any leaders. They want all decisions to be made by direct vote."

Morgan's laughter echoed scornfully from the walls. "Oh, yeah, that'll work."

"For once, I agree with Colonel Morgan," Malin said. "However, the attackers' affiliation with The People's Word raises a big question. Their philosophy could explain their attack on you, General. It does not explain why they would target an Alliance officer."

"They'd want that Alliance presence here, wouldn't they?" Drakon asked, rubbing his chin.

"At the very least, they would regard her as sympathetic to their own agenda," Malin agreed.

Morgan was pretending to examine her knife, testing the edge.

"Where did these People's Weird guys get the weapons they used to try to kill us?"

"You think there was a deal?" Drakon asked.

"Yes, sir." Morgan balanced her knife, its point on her forefinger tip. "Somebody offered them the weapons to kill you in return for their agreeing to also take out the Alliance . . . woman."

"That could be so," Malin agreed.

"Or," Morgan continued, "they planned to take out the woman in addition to you to make it look like an anti-Alliance hit that just happened to take you in as well."

Malin glanced at Drakon. "Sir, I think we do have to assume you were both targets until we learn more."

"Where were you, anyway?" Morgan asked, flipping her knife in one hand and catching it by the hilt.

"I was running down leads about the snakes, per General Drakon's orders."

Drakon nodded. "I knew where he was. Colonel Malin is not a suspect."

"What about our President and her hatchet man Togo?"

"I don't believe that President Iceni was involved," Drakon said.

"With all due respect, sir," Morgan said, "*don't believe* isn't the same as knowing."

"I'm aware of that." He must have made that statement with extra force because Morgan raised an eyebrow at him. "Colonel Malin, I want you to check on any possible connection between the President's staff and the attempt to kill Colonel Morgan and me."

"General?" Morgan said, her tone playful again. "What if they targeted you and me knowing it was me? Who would want to do that?" She smiled at Malin.

"Do you have any proof?" Drakon said.

"Not yet."

"Nothing happens to anyone until you get proof, show me the

proof, and get clear, unequivocal orders about what to do. Is that clear, Colonel Morgan?"

"Yes, sir." She sat up, her eyes still on Malin, the knife now unmoving in her hand. "I'll get proof."

ICENI watched Captain Bradamont enter the room and stand before the long table behind which she and Drakon sat. Bradamont was on unfamiliar terrain, but she looked and acted as if she were in the most well-known and secure of environments. *She is a dangerous woman. Is that all the code name Mantis referred to, or is there more that I haven't seen yet?* "Kommodor Marphissa has proposed that we undertake a long and hazardous mission. She said she did so on the basis of your information and recommendations," Iceni said.

"That is correct," Bradamont replied.

"I won't play games with you, Captain. You know your presence here is valuable to us. You also surely know that your presence here creates some problems for us."

"That was made very clear to me soon after I arrived," Bradamont said, her eyes going to General Drakon where he sat next to Iceni. "I am sorry for the deaths that occurred in what might have been an attempted attack on me."

Iceni made a short, angry gesture. "The motives, and targets, involved in that attack are still being investigated. But the incident does highlight our most critical concern. We cannot afford to be seen as lackeys to Admiral Geary."

"Admiral Geary knows nothing of this proposal, Madam President."

"You are talking about what we know. I am talking about what others will perceive." Iceni tapped her data pad. "I have gone through Kommodor Marphissa's proposal. She makes a good case for the benefits that could accrue to us from recovering the survivors of the Reserve Flotilla. She pays less attention to the potential risks, however."

Bradamont shook her head slightly. "I have not seen the proposal myself. I don't deny there are risks involved. There are ways to minimize those risks."

"Yes, I know." Iceni kept her expression nonrevealing as she turned to glance at the readout. "The Kommodor proposes to minimize the risks by taking two heavy cruisers, half of what we have, plus four light cruisers and six Hunter-Killers. Plus six freighters. Twelve warships and their crews, as well as the Kommodor commanding the flotilla that defends this star system. This is a huge investment for us."

"The return, Madam President, would be even larger," Bradamont said. "Admiral Geary asked me to suggest anything that could strengthen the defenses of this star system. You need those trained personnel, Madam President."

Iceni wagged one remonstrative forefinger at Bradamont. "Never tell someone in charge what they *need*, Captain. I'll decide what I need. I do admit there is a strong case to be made for the benefits to be gained from recovering those personnel. However, if they return to find this star system reconquered by the Syndicate, we will gain no benefits at all."

"Do you wish me to speak bluntly, Madam President?"

Iceni leaned back, smiling tightly. "Please do."

Bradamont nodded toward Iceni's data pad. "Your entire force of warships is insufficient to defend this star system if the Syndicate Worlds sends another flotilla of the same strength as that CEO Boyens came here with. The one thing that will place you in a decent defensive position is your battleship, but only when it is completely outfitted, all of the weapons operational, and is properly crewed. You can outfit that ship, you can get the weapons operational, but can you find enough trained personnel to crew her?"

Drakon, who had seemed to be understandably preoccupied since the attempt on his life the day before, bent a glance Iceni's way. He didn't have to say anything. Drakon's look clearly told her *this is your call, not mine.*

"Captain Bradamont," Iceni said, "you know the threats any force from Midway would face as it went to Alliance space and returned. Yet we cannot possibly risk sending more of our very limited numbers of warships than Kommodor Marphissa has already proposed. We need to maintain a warship presence here in case someone other than the Syndicate tries something. What do we have that might balance the odds for the flotilla we send on this proposed mission?"

Bradamont frowned as she considered the question. "Kommodor Marphissa has displayed skill as a combat commander, Madam President."

"Can she command a force as well as Black Jack?"

"No, but—"

"How much experience does Kommodor Marphissa have with Black Jack's ways of fighting? His tactics? His ways of gaining victory under even unfavorable circumstances?"

Bradamont shook her head. "She does not have any of those things, Madam President. We have discussed them a bit, but there wasn't time for extensive training."

"But *you* do have that experience and that training," Iceni said.

Bradamont finally showed uncertainty. Out of the corner of her eye, Iceni could see Drakon trying not to smile at her reaction. They had already talked this out, and it had been Drakon's suggestion that had tilted Iceni toward her decision. "Your orders," Iceni continued, "are to assist us as you believe appropriate. Do you, Captain Bradamont, consider assisting in the successful pickup and return of the prisoners from Varandal as falling within that mandate?"

"Madam President, your warships will not operate under my command. The crews won't accept it. I had proof of that aboard *Manticore*."

"Did I say you would command? I said *assist*. I will approve this proposal only if you, Captain Bradamont, agree to accompany my ships, not as commander but as adviser in matters tactical and political. Your mere physical presence accompanying the mission, a captain of the Alliance fleet, may be of great value. Your presence at Atalia and Varandal could be decisive in ensuring that our freighters are allowed access to Alliance space and successfully recover the survivors from the Reserve Flotilla."

Bradamont paused, thinking, then nodded. "I agree with your reasoning, Madam President, and I believe this form of assistance falls within the orders given to me by Admiral Geary. I will accompany the mission."

"Good," Iceni said, a little disappointed at how easily she had been able to maneuver Bradamont into agreement. But then, the Alliance captain was a fleet officer, not an Alliance politician, and certainly not someone as cunning as Black Jack. "Prepare to leave immediately."

"Immediately?" Bradamont's gaze went from Iceni to Drakon. "The freighters will need to be prepared."

"The freighters are standing by," Drakon said. "We have six that were modified to carry troops when we assisted Taroa in its revolt against the Syndicate. We got back from that mission not long before the Syndicate flotilla showed up here, followed by the enigmas, then Black Jack, so we kept the freighters in orbit to use if we needed to evacuate some of the citizens."

"I haven't enjoyed having unused assets boring holes in space and through my budget while we waited to see if we needed them," Iceni added. "But now they will come in very handy. It is critical that we get this operation moving fast. My technicians are of the opinion that the blocking of the Syndicate hypernet that Black Jack encountered does indeed shut down access to the gates affected. That means they can't be used by the Syndicate, either, when they're blocked. The Syndicate would only employ such a device in very specific circumstances for limited times because of the economic and military impact. But if they learn that we are planning this operation, they might again block our hypernet access to frustrate our attempt to gain thousands of trained mobile forces personnel."

Drakon spoke up. "We'll be sending soldiers along for security aboard the freighters after you pick up the Reserve Flotilla personnel. We don't know if any snakes are among those captured personnel. We don't know how many of those personnel will be more loyal to the Syndicate government than to the idea of joining us. It should be a minority, maybe a small minority, but we can't have them in a position where some of them could seize control of one or more freighters. The ground forces personnel will be commanded by an officer of sufficient seniority to deal with any matters that arise."

Drakon paused as Bradamont's eyes fixed on him. "That officer will be Colonel Rogero."

Bradamont smiled ruefully and shook her head. "I have too little experience in negotiating with Syndics."

"We're not Syndicate anymore, Captain," Drakon said, "which is why I will also tell you that you'll be on one of the heavy cruisers along with the Kommodor, and Colonel Rogero will be on one of the freighters. Until you reach Atalia. Then you'll transfer to Colonel Rogero's ship."

"So near yet so far?" Bradamont asked. "You don't need to send Colonel Rogero, General. I already agreed to go."

"Rogero's going," Drakon said. "Because he's the best officer for the mission and because I know you and he can work together to get this done."

Iceni nodded. "That was General Drakon's judgment, and I have agreed with his reasoning. The fact that you have proven your ability to work with Kommodor Marphissa is also a factor in my decision. Do you have any questions? No? If there is anything you feel is needed for this mission to succeed that you do not have, inform me or General Drakon personally. Now, I have one question for you that does not pertain to this mission. When Black Jack first came to this star system he gave his rank as fleet admiral. It has been brought to my attention," she added with a sidelong look at Drakon, "that he has consistently referred to himself as admiral and worn an Alliance admiral's insignia during the last two times he was here. Are you aware of the circumstances behind the use of a lower rank by Black Jack?"

"Everyone in the fleet knows that, Madam President," Bradamont replied. "He was a fleet admiral during the final campaign of the war with the Syndicate Worlds, but his current rank is admiral."

"Which is a lower rank than fleet admiral?" Iceni pressed. "Captain Bradamont, why is Black Jack using a lower rank than he did when his fleet first repelled the enigmas from this star system?"

"He reverted to captain when we returned to Alliance space after that engagement, then he was promoted back to admiral."

"Why?" Iceni asked, not bothering to hide her bafflement.

"I don't know all of the reasons, but I know the reversion to captain rank was at least partly a personal matter."

"A personal matter?"

"Captain Desjani," Bradamont said, as if that explained everything.

"Who is?" Iceni prompted.

"Geary's wife. Captain Tanya Desjani." Bradamont looked from Iceni to Drakon. "You hadn't heard? I assumed Syndic intelligence would have learned that. It's no secret in Alliance space. Not at all."

Iceni stared at Bradamont. "We are a long ways from Alliance space, Captain Bradamont, and Syndicate intelligence isn't in the habit of forwarding reports to star systems in rebellion. Admiral Geary was interested in a subordinate? And instead of just sleeping with her, he accepted a lower rank to legitimize it?"

Bradamont's expression didn't change, but her posture stiffened. "Regulations in the Alliance fleet do not permit relations between officers and their subordinates in the chain of command."

"We have similar rules," Iceni said, openly amused. "Those with power don't need to pay attention to them."

She noticed that Drakon didn't quite avoid a flinch at that. *Feeling guilty about your drunken roll in the hay with that crazy female*

Morgan at Taroa, General? You should *feel guilty. Or are you just afraid that I'll learn about it, not knowing I already have?*

"Admiral Geary behaved with honor," Bradamont replied. "He is a man of honor as our ancestors understood it. Admiral Geary and Captain Desjani followed the rules and regulations of the fleet and acted honorably."

"I see. Thank you, Captain. Once you've been escorted back to General Drakon's headquarters, get in touch with Colonel Rogero. He'll work you into the troop lifts up to the freighters."

Iceni watched Bradamont leave. "Have you noticed that even when that Alliance officer is at her most relaxed with us, there is still a barrier?"

"That's scarcely surprising," Drakon replied. "To her, we still look like the enemy."

"I don't think it's just that. Kommodor Marphissa and Kapitan-Leytenant Kontos in their reports to me both said they did not feel Bradamont was holding back on them. Yet I see that sense of reserve in her when dealing with us."

Drakon snorted derisively. "Kommodor Marphissa was a lower-midranked executive. She didn't make decisions, but she paid the price for decisions made by her superiors. That's even more true of Kontos. You and I were CEOs, part of the hierarchy of the Syndicate Worlds. We called the shots."

"Not as much as we would have liked to," Iceni said, her voice subdued.

"Yeah. That's why we're here. But it's not surprising that, to an Alliance officer, we're in a different category from more junior personnel. We were CEOs. We did things."

She looked back at him for a while before answering, trying to sort out her feelings. "I did what I had to do. So did you."

"Yeah," Drakon repeated.

Only one word, yet the feeling behind it came through clearly to

Iceni. A feeling she understood all too well. *"I did what I had to do"* *isn't what anyone would want carved on their memorial.* Unhappy at the direction the conversation had taken, Iceni gestured upward. "The Syndicate is ahead of us on tricks with the hypernet. I have a strong feeling the Alliance is even farther behind than we are."

"A feeling?" Drakon pressed.

"There are some facts. Black Jack wanted the device from me that would keep a gate from being collapsed by remote command. That meant the Alliance didn't have it."

"You gave him that?"

She paused, then nodded, not looking at him. "Yes. It was a deal."

"Are there any other deals?"

Iceni turned her head to look directly into his eyes. "None that you are unaware of. I made that deal with Black Jack before we revolted, Artur. I couldn't coordinate it with you, I couldn't even talk to you about it, not with the snakes still everywhere. Do you know what I find most intriguing about that interview with Captain Bradamont?" It was a very clumsy change of subject. *Why am I never at my best with Drakon anymore? He's rattling me for some reason.*

Drakon didn't call her on the awkward segue though. "No. What did you find intriguing?"

"The bit about Black Jack's rank. Despite Captain Bradamont's impassioned defense of his honor, Black Jack must have manipulated his rank to technically avoid violating Alliance rules about marrying a subordinate. But why? Why bother with the theater? Why did he then choose only to advance back to the rank of admiral? And what do we know about this Captain Desjani?"

Drakon poked in a query. "Battle cruiser captain. *Dauntless.* Rated highly effective based on what we were able to learn of her. As a lieutenant, led a boarding party in an operation that won her the Alliance Fleet Cross. That's about it. No, wait. In the report Morgan and Malin gave me when they got back from talking to Black Jack to set up that trick we pulled on Boyens. Captain Desjani was there. Black Jack insisted that she be present. That confirms the relationship that Bradamont told us about."

Iceni rested her chin on one hand as she thought. "The whole show must have something to do with Alliance rules and protocol. Maybe he had to justify what he did to their fleet and their citizens. How that translated into playing games with rank, I don't know. Maybe, with time, Captain Bradamont will tell us more about it. I didn't want to push her during this meeting. She's acting very open with us, as if there's not a secret in her pretty little head. But she has a hidden agenda. People always have hidden agendas."

He took a few moments to reply, looking steadily toward the far wall, then finally glanced at Iceni. "My first impressions of her were that she was exactly what she looked like. Not much hidden. I've talked to Colonel Rogero again since then, and he says she is trustworthy. That evaluation means a lot in my mind."

Iceni laughed sharply before she could stop herself. "A man in love trusts the object of his affections? Just how many tragedies have been set into motion by that?"

"That's . . . a point."

Iceni gave him another searching look. "What I just said didn't make you happy."

"Is it that obvious?" Drakon shrugged. "You know Colonel Gaiene. That is, you know who he is now."

"A drunken letch who always seems to be seeking out the next woman to share his bed. But I saw the reports for Taroa. He was highly effective. Are you saying he trusted the wrong woman?"

"In combat, he can forget for a few moments. But it wasn't a matter of betrayed trust. It was exactly the opposite." Drakon grimaced, clearly unhappy at the memories this conversation was calling up. "Here's the quick and dirty. Lara was a major in another unit. She and Conner Gaiene never had eyes for anyone else. Conner's outfit got caught in an ambush and were being cut to ribbons. I had my hands full repulsing a major counterattack. Somehow, Lara pulled together all of the soldiers close to her and punched through to Gaiene. She saved Conner and about half of his unit, but she never knew that because she died during the final push that broke through the Alliance forces trapping him."

"Oh." Iceni looked away and didn't speak for several seconds. "That's why he's like that."

"Yes. Conner Gaiene had his dream woman once. Just about every day I'm reminded of what happened to him when he lost her."

"And you don't want to see that happen to Colonel Rogero."

"No. If this Bradamont is bad, and I don't think she is, she'd hurt him. If she's as good as she seems, she could hurt him a lot worse."

"Not every man falls apart when he loses a woman," Iceni said. *Have you avoided relationships out of fear of that, Artur Drakon? The snakes and the Syndicate couldn't break you, but you worry that a woman could?* "You must have lost someone in the past."

"This isn't about me," Drakon objected, a little too fast and a little too emphatically.

"What if it were?"

He looked down, away, then back at her. "It isn't."

"Then you listen to me, Artur Drakon," Iceni said heatedly. "From what you say, this Lara was an exceptional woman who gave her all to save the life of the man she loved. And that man has rewarded her sacrifice by wasting the life she died to save. If I ever gave my life to save a man I loved, that man had damned well better live the rest of his life in a manner that justifies the sacrifice that I made for him! Is that clear?"

Drakon looked steadily back at her. "Absolutely clear. Why do I need to know that?"

"I don't know! But now you do. Be certain that you do not forget it."

"I won't."

She sat alone in the room for a while after Drakon had left, staring at the display but not really seeing it. *Why am I more upset about the attempt on his life than I am about the bomb aimed at me?*

It's because I do like that big lunk. He's a better man than he realizes he is. He's—

I like him too much.

You can't do this, Gwen. Mixing personal feelings and politics is a guarantee for disaster. He is a man, and he obviously doesn't have any particular feelings for me, so he would either use my feelings to get what he wants, or if he's not quite that awful, he would laugh at me. Either of those would be better than his feeling pity for me because he couldn't return such feelings. I will never accept pity from anyone.

Never.

THE hopefully named Recovery Flotilla had departed only the day before. Drakon had watched it go, taking along with it not only Colonel Rogero and six platoons from his brigade, but also a substantial portion of the warships available to defend this star system. The Alliance captain had been right. Even all of the warships they had couldn't adequately protect Midway. But that was something the brain knew. The gut still watched those warships go and felt the desperate need to call them back.

And, inevitably, because the universe seems to enjoy mocking the hopes and the plans of mere humans, a freighter carrying urgent news had arrived at the jump point from Maui Star System within an hour of the departure of the Recovery Flotilla.

Which was why he was once again meeting with Gwen Iceni, who had seemed unusually irritable since their last one-on-one meeting. This time, though, Colonel Malin was briefing them while Iceni's assistant Togo watched with the closest thing to disapproval his deadpan expression ever revealed.

"The news from Maui concerns the Supreme CEO in Ulindi Star System," Malin reported.

"Supreme CEO?" Drakon checked the star display. Ulindi was one of three stars that could be reached from Maui. Another one of those stars was Midway itself. "What does that mean?"

"I'd say it was pretty self-explanatory," Iceni commented shortly.

Malin, experienced in dealing with superiors who didn't always get along with each other, continued speaking as if he hadn't heard the remark. "From what we have learned despite all attempts to keep anyone from finding out what is happening at Ulindi, it means that CEO Haris managed to kill the other CEOs in that star system and overawe all opposition."

Drakon squinted at his display, mistrusting what he was reading. "Haris is the snake CEO. How did he get the Syndicate government to sign off on a title like Supreme CEO?"

"Haris is no longer answering to the Syndicate government."

"A senior snake rebelled?"

"Yes, sir."

Drakon looked toward Iceni. "Do you know Haris at all?"

She shook her head. "No. I never associated with snakes." Relenting a bit, she added more. "Even snakes can be ambitious. This Haris might have seen his chances of gaining more power falling away with every star system that left Syndicate control."

"So he decided to start his own little empire?"

Malin brought up a new image on the display. "General, reports from Maui say there is a strong flotilla there from Ulindi. It was on its way to the jump point for Midway, but halted that movement when merchant ships arrived reporting the presence of the Alliance fleet. That news was outdated when they got it. Black Jack had left Midway soon after the freighters carrying the news to Maui."

"It bought us time," Iceni said. "Good."

"A little time. It leaves us with six days to act, Madam President," Malin explained. "A freighter headed for Rongo via Maui left Midway three days ago, doubtless taking word of Black Jack's departure with it. The freighter would have taken four and one-half days in jump space to reach Maui, would have passed on its information, and the Ulindi flotilla would have headed for the jump point for Midway. It would probably be half a day before they reached it and jumped for Midway, after which another four and half days would bring them here. Factoring in everything, the Ulindi flotilla should arrive six days from now."

"That is *very* little time," Iceni complained. "I can't argue with your timeline, though. They won't delay any longer once they hear that Black Jack is gone. Apparently, Haris wants to expand his little empire. But that flotilla at Maui does not look like a force aimed at conquering this star system."

"No, Madam President, it is not. The Ulindi flotilla consists of a single C-class battle cruiser and four Hunter-Killers. If there are ground forces embarked, their numbers are very limited."

"No ground forces?" Drakon pondered that. A flotilla built around a battle cruiser could do a lot of damage to a star system. But it couldn't take over that star system. Even if Midway surrendered under the threat of bombardment, Ulindi's control of this star would last only as long as it took the battle cruiser to leave. "How much else does Ulindi have?"

"According to our best information, only one heavy cruiser, which must have remained at Ulindi to protect Haris. The ground forces at Ulindi total perhaps a division, but most of that is recently raised and barely trained. Less than a single brigade of former Syndicate soldiers form the core of Haris's ground forces. The rest of internal security at Ulindi is handled by local militia, police, and snakes."

"Not much to build an empire on. That sounds like barely enough to maintain control of Ulindi. What's he planning then?"

Drakon had addressed the question to both Iceni and Malin. Iceni frowned and spoke first. "He must know that we intervened at Taroa. Maybe he heard about our push to get a much tighter defense agreement with Taroa even though the government there is supposed to be keeping it secret."

Malin shook his head. "Our offer to Taroa is widely known all over that star system. More than one Free Taroan government official must have talked freely."

"Which means Haris heard about it," Drakon said.

Iceni made a fist and almost slammed it onto the table before controlling herself. "I should have realized that trying to tie Taroa much more closely to us would cause local problems. Haris sees us as a threat to his ambitions and wants to hit our mobile forces before we can take advantage of Taroa's resources as well."

"That makes sense," Drakon agreed. "Anyone planning on empire-building out here could well see us as rivals who need to be taken down as soon as possible."

Malin spoke diffidently. "There is another possibility given the composition of the Ulindi flotilla. In Kommodor Marphissa's absence I discussed the situation with Kapitan-Leytenant Kontos."

"You did?" Drakon glanced at Iceni again. "What did Kontos say?"

"He thinks they want the battleship."

CHAPTER TEN

DRAKON had to pause, startled. "The battleship?"

"Of course," Iceni said in a low voice. "We've tried to keep the battleship's status secret, but there's probably not a soul in this star system and every nearby star system who doesn't know it still has a skeleton crew and is far from combat capable. They plan to swoop in, take the battleship, then haul it home to finish it."

"Which is how we got the battleship from Kane in the first place."

She gave him an aggravated look. "I fully intend that our theft of the battleship will be the last *successful* attempt to steal it. If Supreme CEO Haris wants to become a local power, he needs more firepower, and it looks like he's trying to build that up the same way we are, by taking it from someone else less prepared to defend it. Why did Haris have to have a battle cruiser?"

"Is there any chance we can take them with what we've got?" Drakon asked.

Iceni shook her head impatiently. "Even if the Recovery Flotilla hadn't hauled half of our strength with them, it would have been very touch-and-go to defeat a flotilla built around a battle cruiser."

"Any ideas?" Drakon asked Malin.

"No good ones, sir," Malin replied. "Our mobile forces are simply too badly outmatched. We could try sending the battleship somewhere else and leaving it there until Haris's flotilla leaves."

"We couldn't have the battleship stay here and avoid that flotilla?" Drakon asked.

Iceni shook her head. "No battleship can outrun a battle cruiser. They'd be run down in fairly short order. The same thing might happen if we send the *Midway* to some other star system. Anyone else who saw it would see a perfect and very valuable target to acquire for themselves."

"In that case," Malin continued, "the best remaining option available to us may be to lure the battle cruiser close to the battleship, then blow up the battleship, taking the battle cruiser with it."

"That is *not* an option!" Iceni insisted, her face flushing with anger. "We need that battleship."

"Madam President," Malin said, "if we have no other means of stopping Haris from taking the battleship, using it to eliminate his battle cruiser would at least leave him without the capability of threatening us."

"And how much good will that do us when the Syndicate sends another flotilla here?" Iceni demanded.

Malin hesitated, then shook his head. "None, Madam President."

"Blowing up both ships is a lousy option," Drakon said, "but what else can we do?"

Iceni turned her frustration on him. "You tell me! You're the military expert, General! I have some experience with mobile forces, but it wasn't my career."

"My experience is with ground forces," Drakon pointed out, keeping his voice level. "I've been in this kind of situation before, where every option is bad, and it's a matter of choosing the one that hurts the least. But we can't change the reality of what we're facing."

She glared at him, then looked away, breathing in slowly and regaining control. "You can't think of anything?"

Drakon barely masked his surprise at the disappointment he saw in her. Disappointment in him? She expected him to pull more mobile forces out of his hat to save the day? "I've got a few basic principles for how to fight. One of those principles is that it is a mistake to confront the enemy's strength with your weakness, or his strength with your strength. Instead, you should confront the enemy's weakness with your strength."

"How can that work here?" Iceni asked.

"It can't. Ground forces can't take on mobile forces unless the mobile forces come to them and make themselves targets, and there's no reason why—" He broke off, trying to figure out why his last statement felt very important.

"General?" Iceni said, studying him.

"Madam President," Drakon said, his words coming out slowly as he mentally groped to uncover the idea hanging barely out of reach, "how will that battle cruiser try to capture the battleship?"

"There's only one way to do it," Iceni said. "Send a boarding party over. One large enough to defeat the skeleton crew on the battleship."

"Using shuttles?"

"No. A single battle cruiser only has a few shuttles. They couldn't carry nearly enough people for an attack, and if the battleship had even a few weapons working, the shuttles could make easy targets."

"We used shuttles to capture that battleship at Kane," Drakon pointed out.

"And," Iceni added, tapping her forefinger hard against the desk to emphasize her words, "we were extremely worried that the shuttles would be destroyed on approach. We used them because we had to, but we knew we might lose them. I would not have chosen that method of attack if I had been able to launch an attack directly from my own warships. Not with only a few shuttles."

"You need overwhelming force applied quickly," Drakon said.

"Yes. Exactly. Is that so different from ground forces operations?"

"No." Drakon looked into the distance, thinking. "I haven't done any boarding operations. Walk me through what the battle cruiser will do."

Iceni shrugged. "It's pretty simple in this case. The battleship doesn't have working weapons or a crew large enough to operate it. Running wouldn't make any sense because the battle cruiser could easily overtake it. The battle cruiser will pull up close alongside the battleship, matching any movement so the two ships are motionless relative to each other. Then a boarding party will jump across the gap between the ships, arriving at several main hatches simultaneously, entering the battleship, and overwhelming any defenders. Kapitan-Leytenant Kontos and his crew can hole up inside the defensive citadels for the bridge, propulsion, and weapons, but the boarding party will be equipped with the means to crack open those citadels in fairly short order."

"Close?" Drakon questioned. "How big a gap between ships?"

"Fifty meters. Maybe a hundred, depending on how risk-averse the battle cruiser's commander is."

"How big will the boarding party be?"

Iceni spread her hands. "That depends. A battle cruiser should have about fifteen hundred in the crew. Syndicate doctrine spells out how many to send in a boarding party based on the target and its condition but sets a maximum of half the available crew."

"Seven hundred? Eight hundred maximum?" Drakon asked.

"If Haris's commander follows Syndicate doctrine."

Malin had gotten what Drakon was driving at. He smiled thinly. "Seven hundred mobile forces personnel in survival suits with hand weapons?"

"Yeah," Drakon agreed. "Maybe some special forces among them, but that would only be a couple of platoons, at most."

"One platoon, at most," Iceni corrected. "And more likely Haris's snakes than special forces. What are you thinking, General?"

"I'm thinking, Madam President, that if this comes down to a boarding operation, we're dealing with a situation in which ground forces could balance the odds." Drakon leaned toward her. "If that battleship were full of mobile forces personnel, we couldn't pack it with armored ground forces. But it's almost empty. There's lots of room for soldiers. And if that battle cruiser can send its boarding party jumping across the gap between ships, my soldiers can jump that same gap onto the battle cruiser."

"It's not that simple." Iceni bit her lip, her eyes calculating. "But it could be done. My mobile forces people can tell your people what defenses the battle cruiser would have against a counterboarding operation. It would have to be a total surprise, too. They couldn't know we had a lot of soldiers waiting on the battleship."

"Six days." Drakon looked at Malin. "Can we do it? Can we get a substantial number of soldiers onto that battleship before our preparations can be spotted by Haris's force when it arrives?"

Malin's eyes were hooded as he ran through mental calculations, then he nodded. "I'll have to confirm my estimate, sir, but we should be able to if we can get our people into orbit quickly. There's a freighter in orbit, a converted passenger hauler, that's getting ready to depart. If the President's warships tell that freighter to wait, we can use it."

Iceni turned to Togo. "Notify orbital control that the freighter is not to leave orbit." She faced Drakon again. "You have no experience with boarding operations?"

"No. But I think we should try this, and I should command this operation."

She bent her head, elbows resting on the table, forehead against her clenched hands, and said nothing for a couple of minutes. "Are you saying we should try it because it seems to be the only option?" she finally asked Drakon. "Or because it could work?"

"It's not the only option. As Colonel Malin pointed out, we could blow up both ships. But I do think a counterboarding operation could work. If what you told me about what the battle cruiser will do is right, this is worth a try."

"And if Haris only wants to destroy our battleship?"

Drakon thought about that, unhappy at the prospect. "We'd be screwed."

"We'd lose the battleship," Iceni said, "and everyone on it. Crew, soldiers, and whoever the on-scene commander was. General, we can't afford to lose you."

Drakon raised both eyebrows at her as he leaned back. "Was that an imperial *we* you used?"

"If you want to think of it that way." Iceni scowled at him. "Who takes your place as ground forces commander if you died out there? Who takes your place as co-ruler? I'm not a fool. I know there are people who follow you who would not follow me. Someone else has to command this operation."

"It's nice to think that you don't want anything to happen to me, but giving me orders—"

"I can't make you see sense, and I can't make you follow my orders, but I know I don't have to." Iceni nodded toward him. "You're smart enough to know that I'm right."

Drakon looked away, frowning. *She's brilliant. Openly praising me for being smart enough to know she's right, so if I argue, I'll be acting like I'm* not *so smart.*

Colonel Malin cleared his throat. "Sir, Colonel Gaiene has conducted at least one boarding operation."

"He has?" Drakon pondered that, grateful for the out that Malin's suggestion offered. "He would be good for this operation. It calls for his talents."

"Colonel Gaiene?" Iceni asked icily. "His talents? Does the operation involve consuming large quantities of alcohol and the attempted seduction of any female who comes within groping range of Gaiene?"

Drakon shook his head at her. "Conner Gaiene knows where to draw the line. He's also good at exactly what this operation will require."

"I find that hard to believe," Iceni said.

"You know why he's like he is. You also know how he did on Taroa."

Drakon rested his fist on the table between them. "I will not sideline Colonel Gaiene."

She eyed him for a long moment. "Because he would not last long without responsibilities to tether him to some semblance of the man he once was?" Iceni finally asked.

Drakon hesitated, then made a deliberately vague gesture. "Because he can do it, because he's the best officer for the job."

"If Colonel Rogero were here, I might still argue the point. What about Colonel Kai?"

"Colonel Kai," Malin said, "has no experience in space operations."

Iceni looked downward for several seconds, then nodded. "All right. Gaiene can command." She leaned close, her eyes on Drakon, and spoke very softly. "You have too many walking wounded on your staff, General."

"War does that to people," Drakon replied in the same low voice.

"Does that include you?"

"Hell, yes."

She sat back again, her eyes on his. "This has to be my decision."

"Why?"

"It's mobile forces. If we do this, it involves a lot of your people. But ultimately, it's a mobile forces action. It's my responsibility to make the call."

Drakon smiled crookedly. "You didn't learn that while becoming a Syndicate CEO."

"Taking responsibility for my decisions? No. I didn't learn that from the Syndicate." Iceni sighed. "I say we go with it."

Drakon turned back to Malin. "Get in contact with Colonel Gaiene. Tell him a substantial part of his brigade has to be ready to lift yesterday. Full combat gear and supplies for two weeks. How much troop lift do we have?"

"We have plenty of shuttles," Malin said.

"Have we told the freighter to remain in orbit?" Iceni asked Togo.

"Yes, Madam President." There was no telling what Togo thought of the plan that had just been decided upon. "It was supposed to have left for Kahiki in another hour, but it was told to hold off departing. The freighter's executive has registered a protest."

"Oh, dear. A protest." Iceni laughed. "Tell the executive that freighter has just been chartered, and the executive can either accept the charter with grace and the chance of reward, or . . ."

Togo almost smiled. "The executive will certainly understand the consequences of refusing an offer from the President."

"General," Malin said, looking up from his data pad, "if we load in less than eight hours, the freighter should be able to reach the gas giant with less than a day to spare."

"Then let's see how many troops we can pack into it in eight hours," Drakon ordered. "And get everyone and everything off the freighter that we don't need."

After Malin had left to pass on the orders, Drakon held up a hand to forestall Iceni. "Can we talk privately?"

She looked toward Togo and pointed at the door. Togo hesitated, then nodded and walked out. "What do you need?"

"I need to know what the problem is the last few days. Did someone tell you I planted that bomb at your desk?"

Iceni smiled humorlessly. "Of course someone did. I have no evidence to support that charge, though."

"It looks like you believe it," Drakon said, his voice sounding rougher than he had intended.

"I— Why are you saying that?"

"The way you're acting toward me," Drakon said bluntly. "Look, I understand that you don't like me. If that's the way it is, fine. But I thought we could work together."

Iceni looked back at him, perplexed. "You think I don't like you?"

"I'm not a fool."

"On that point, we may be in serious disagreement, General Drakon."

"What?"

She sighed, looked upward as if beseeching aid from the deities they had been taught not to believe in, then back at Drakon. "I don't don't like you."

"What?" Drakon said again. "You don't don't like me?"

"That's what I said."

"Can you explain what it means?"

"It means we can work together," Iceni said, looking exasperated. "Artur, you can't be that big an idiot!"

Is she trying to make me angry? Something clicked in his head. "Hold on, if you don't don't like me—"

"Ancestors!" Iceni cried, looking upward again. "Save me!" She glared at Drakon. "I must be a bigger idiot than you are!"

His anger grew in response to hers. "What in the hell are you talking about?"

"Perhaps you'll figure it out before one of us is dead! Now, if you'll excuse me, we have a battleship to save!"

Iceni swept out, leaving Drakon sitting there, mystified.

"I should do it," Morgan complained.

"Gaiene can handle it," Drakon replied.

"Him and that brat on the battleship?"

Drakon rested the left side of his chin on one fist as he looked at her. "You don't like Kontos? I understood that you'd been sending him long, chatty communications."

Instead of acting guilty, Morgan just grinned. "I'm flirting with him like crazy."

"'Flirting' is a fairly innocent term," Drakon observed.

"Maybe it's a bit more than flirting, then. I want the kid interested in me. I want him willing to do what I want, what *you* want, with that battleship of his."

"You're trying to turn Kontos against Iceni?" Part of him, the part that looked at cold reality and its demands, saw the merit in such tactics. Another part of him, the part that knew Gwen Iceni, rejected the idea of undermining her authority with a mobile forces officer.

On the other hand, if Morgan can turn Kontos, Gwen needs to know that. Gwen has been acting like I annoy her no end, but she still deserves my support, and I still need her support.

"How's your plan going?" Drakon asked.

Morgan made a diffident wave with one hand. "It's a work in progress. If I can get him alone, he and I together, I think I can make the innocent young lad forget all about Her Royal Majesty the President."

Drakon shook his head, trying to mask the reaction her words created in him. "I'm uncomfortable with those kinds of tactics."

"Kontos won't actually get any," Morgan said with a grin. "It's holding out the possibility that makes men do really stupid things." As if realizing that Drakon might take that as a derisive reference to what had happened at Taroa, Morgan's smile abruptly vanished. "Besides, I don't sleep around, no matter what that worm Malin tells you."

"Colonel Malin is not part of this conversation and has not made such accusations." *Given how much Malin dislikes Morgan, it is a bit odd that he has never even implied that Morgan is promiscuous, but then, Malin doesn't seem the type to heedlessly use that sort of slur as a weapon against a woman. He might have tried to kill her during that incident in orbit, or he might instead have saved her from being killed by someone else as he claims despite the improbability of his doing that, but he's never called her a slut. I guess his mother raised Malin right.* "Even if all you're doing is offering something you don't intend to ever deliver on, the whole thing strikes me as too much like what the snakes would do to entrap somebody."

Morgan shrugged. "If the enemy does something smart, do you reject using the same idea because the enemy came up with it? General, it would be extremely useful for us to have effective control of that battleship. You still don't know who sicced those assassins on you, and maybe on me, but you can't rule out the possibility that our President wants to clear the field of competitors. If you want Gaiene to lead this op, that's fine. Let me go along so I can do some, uh, close-in maneuvering with Kontos and get him really interested in doing what *we* want."

"No offense, Roh, but that tactic wasn't too successful when you tried it on Black Jack."

She made a scornful sound. "That slug Malin was there cramping my style. And that woman, the one that Black Jack was obviously sleeping with. I still could have gotten to Black Jack if Malin hadn't been there. That Alliance drab wasn't anything special."

Drakon laughed. "She was an Alliance battle cruiser commander. And Black Jack's wife."

"Wife?" Morgan cocked on eyebrow at Drakon. "When did that happen?"

"Not too long ago, I guess."

"He'll get restless. Now, what about our boy Kontos?"

I don't like it, and I don't want to do anything that would feed any suspicions that Gwen has of me. But I have to put this in terms that Morgan can understand. "Here's the thing, Colonel. If you make an explicit play for Kontos, and he doesn't bite but instead reports it to his superiors, where does that place us? You'll be on his ship. He can record everything you say and do with him even if you two are supposedly in an unmonitored compartment."

Morgan scowled at that. "He probably would, too. Just to protect himself. If that happens, our own plans could be exposed."

"I need you here, anyway," Drakon added. "You're right that we need to run down whoever ordered the attack that almost got you and me. You're the best for that job."

"Damn right I am. Whoever set that up covered their tracks really well." Mollified by Drakon's praise, Morgan saluted jauntily. "But I'll find whoever it was."

"And then you will tell me, and I will decide what to do. Right?"

"Yes, sir," Morgan replied with another grin.

"*Especially* if you think either Colonel Malin or President Iceni were involved," Drakon emphasized with his hardest glare. "Nothing is to happen to President Iceni."

Morgan's smile didn't waver. "Yes, sir."

"MADAM President, the military explosives used in the bomb at your desk have been traced to the armory of a subunit of the brigade commanded by Colonel Rogero of General Drakon's division," Togo reported dispassionately.

"Someone must have issued those explosives," Iceni observed. They were in her office, as secure a place to talk as possible. Her desk display showed a stream of shuttles heading upward from one of Drakon's camps toward a single freighter in orbit.

Togo, standing facing her desk, nodded diffidently. "Interrogations were begun to determine who had issued the explosives and under what pretenses. One of the supply sergeants, however, was found dead in his quarters before questioning began. The cause of death appeared to be an overdose of the illegal drug known as Rapture."

"An overdose? Before questioning began? How very convenient for someone. Who knew that questioning of those personnel was to be conducted?"

"General Drakon's office was notified twenty minutes before our team arrived at the armory," Togo said.

"Twenty minutes? Who gave that much warning of an interrogation raid?" Iceni demanded. "Do I have to personally supervise the carrying out of even the most basic security actions?"

"The interrogation personnel were delayed by a breakdown of their vehicle," Togo said without emotion. "I accept full responsibility for the failure."

"That won't bring back that supply sergeant and whatever he knew." Iceni sat back, rubbing her mouth with one hand as she thought. "But he might not have known anything. I have experience in the mobile forces, remember. Even with the tightest controls, it is possible to acquire the small amount of explosives used in that bomb by legitimate means. All you have to do is draw some for training or for demonstration purposes and draw a bit more than you really need."

The sub-CEO who had taught her such tools for dealing with rivals had been a charming man who had appointed himself her mentor, seeking to bed Iceni through guile rather than coercion. He might eventually have succeeded in that if his wife hadn't blown him and his bed to bits over yet another woman. In the end, he had taught Gwen a few more lessons than he had intended.

"The fact remains, Madam President," Togo persisted, "that the explosives have been traced to the command of Colonel Rogero, who is a loyal follower of General Drakon."

"And that doesn't make you suspicious?" Iceni said, letting ice form on her words. "Neither of those men is stupid." *Though you wouldn't know it from Drakon's oblivious behavior in personal matters.* "Draw the explosives from a source directly traceable to them? Even the lowest level subexecutive knows better than to point such an accusing finger at themselves."

"Perhaps that was the goal," Togo suggested after a pause. "They know you would regard such a move as hopelessly amateurish, so by pointing the evidence so clearly toward themselves, they would convince you that they were not involved."

Iceni laughed scornfully. "That's the sort of thing that happens in bad novels. Drakon is a successful commander. He knows how foolish it is to base your plans on the assumption that your opponent will act exactly as you wish, and the more convoluted your wishes, the less likely it is that your opponent will take the steps you desire. What can you tell me about the trigger for the bomb?"

"It was as I said, Madam President. Tuned to your biometrics and focused on the chair behind the desk."

She sat forward, eyes intent on Togo. "Then how did you detect its presence from the door?"

Togo didn't hesitate. "There was a wave-guide leak. A pinhole that allowed some signal strength to emanate back and to the side."

"I see. How fortunate. Are there any leads yet as to who set up the attack on General Drakon and whether or not the Alliance officer was also a target?"

"No, Madam President. Most of the members of The People's Word have proven to be unaware of the actions by their most radical associates. Others have disappeared though remains linked to several indicate they might have been victims of suicide belts that exploded. Three were found dead from the actions of injected nanos."

"The same type of nanos that killed the one captured by Colonel Morgan?"

Togo visibly tensed at Morgan's name, but his voice remained unemotional. "Yes, Madam President."

"I expect better results, on both issues, and I expect them soon. These internal threats have to be dealt with. We have enough to worry about with external threats." Her eyes went back to her display, watching the shuttles rising to orbit and dropping back down to the surface.

"Madam President," Togo said, "may I suggest that the assassination attempt aimed at General Drakon might have been staged? That his survival was because the attackers were told not to kill him?"

"Are you saying that Drakon himself set it up? That they did really want to kill the Alliance officer and only her?"

"It is possible. That officer had already worked with Kommodor Marphissa and might be perceived to be in your camp, and the close ties between you and Black Jack are widely known."

"What does that— What if the attack were aimed only at Colonel Morgan?" *We won't discuss my personal life. But as for the rest, you opened this can of worms. Tell me where you think this part of it leads.*

Togo paused for several seconds. "If that were the case, then, speaking solely in terms of your self-interest, Madam President, it is unfortunate that it did not succeed."

Iceni almost smiled before she caught herself. "Let me know of anything else you find out as soon as you learn it."

After Togo had left, she went back to gazing at the shuttles. Less than six days to set this up. The freighter should be pulling out of orbit within the next hour.

Her gaze shifted to the hypernet gate near the edge of the star system. Marphissa and the others were still on their way to Indras Star System. They wouldn't pop out of the gate at Indras until after the matter of Haris's flotilla was resolved, wouldn't know until they got back whether or not the battleship *Midway* would still be here to receive the hoped-for thousands of crew members who had been formerly assigned to the Reserve Flotilla. That was assuming the Recovery Flotilla made it safely to Varandal, succeeded in convincing the Alliance authorities there to hand over the prisoners, then made it back to Midway Star System in one piece.

And someone, or some ones, here had either tried to separately kill her and General Drakon, or had tried to make it look like they were trying to kill the pair of them, or that she and Drakon were trying to kill each other.

"Madam President?" The call came over her routine comm channel. "The press crews have arrived for your statement supporting the low-level political-office elections. They may try to ask questions."

Iceni sighed and keyed her reply. "That's fine. Send them in, and tell them I will answer any questions that I deem appropriate."

No matter how hard those questions were, they would surely be easier than the questions privately bedeviling her.

"I don't like this," Kapitan Stein complained, looking as unhappy as she sounded. Her heavy cruiser, one of two that were orbiting the gas giant in order to protect the battleship *Midway* and the orbiting dock where the battleship was moored, was within two light-seconds of where Gaiene was on that orbiting dock, so there was no noticeable delay in the conversation.

Colonel Conner Gaiene made a half-apologetic shrug, both palms facing upward in the eternal gesture meaning *what can we do?* "You're only pretending to run away."

"If we didn't have orders from the President herself, *Gryphon* and *Basilisk* would stay near this facility and fight!"

Had he ever been as enthusiastic as this Kapitan Stein? It was hard to remember. Like many of the mobile forces officers, Stein was young for her rank, the more senior officers often having suffered varying but unfortunate fates when the star system revolted against the Syndicate. "Don't go too far. We may need you to chase off the four Hunter-Killers with the battle cruiser."

"We'll do more than chase them off," Stein promised. "Don't let Kontos give you any lip," she added.

"Now, Kapitan, I know Kapitan-Leytenant Kontos has been promoted quite rapidly, but haven't we all?"

Stein smiled. "Not you in the ground forces. You should have killed more of your supervisors."

"I was one of those supervisors," Gaiene reminded her. "And I am very comfortable where I am in the command hierarchy. If you ever get to visit the surface, you should look me up, and we can discuss the matter over drinks."

Kapitan Stein got that *is-he-really-hitting-on-me?* look, then apparently decided Gaiene wasn't serious. "The jump point from Maui is two and a half light-hours from us at this point in the gas giant's orbit. We'll wait until at least three hours after we see the enemy flotilla arrive, by which point they should have settled onto vectors clearly indicating they are coming this way, then we'll pretend to pull away and leave you to your fate."

"Don't try to tangle with that monster on my account," Gaiene warned. "I don't want to have to do an alas, poor *Gryphon* speech."

Stein laughed, either because she got the joke or because she was being polite. He had noticed that, as the years went on, younger women were beginning to treat him politely, which was a very bad sign for any man with lecherous intent. At least, Gaiene thought as Stein ended her call, young women weren't laughing *at* him yet. *There's still time to seek an honorable death in battle before that happens, or a dishonorable death at the hands of an enraged relative of a lover. I wonder how much longer it will be before I cease to care which it turns out to be?*

"THEY'RE here." Lieutenant Colonel Safir, who had been promoted to fill the second-in-command slot in the brigade after Lieutenant Colonel Lyr had been promoted to command the orbiting dockyards at Taroa, tapped a control to bring a display near her to life.

Colonel Gaiene cocked his head to one side as if studying the image intently. "Just a few specks of light."

"I can zoom it in." The tiny dots of light blossomed into the lean shark shapes that ground forces had learned to fear and hate. One massive shark led the way, four much smaller shapes following in its wake like remoras.

"Our target," Gaiene commented. "Why did I volunteer for this?"

"You didn't," Safir pointed out. "None of us did. We just got told to do it."

"Was that what happened?"

Safir grinned. She had no trouble with his banter, recognizing when he was serious and when he was just trying to ward off emotion, and had also made it clear she wasn't interested in any closer relationship even if Gaiene had dared to try it in the face of Drakon's orders to avoid his own subordinates. All in all, a very valuable second-in-command. "When did that freighter leave?" he asked.

"Six hours ago." Safir pointed to a part of the display showing space nearby. "Just poking along as if it were a routine supply ship on its way home. We got the final soldier and the last of the equipment under cover five hours ago."

"Well done!" Gaiene waved an extravagant gesture of praise. "Our new friends from Ulindi will see nothing untoward here."

"Just a nonoperational battleship, with hardly anyone on board, ripe for the plucking." Safir sobered, eyeing Gaiene skeptically. "What do you think our odds are?"

"If our foes are confident? Not bad at all. And we have given them every reason to be confident, especially since if we had had a day or two less of warning, their confidence would have been fully justified, and this battleship would be doomed." Gaiene pursed his mouth in thought. "Mind you, we will have to move carefully and make sure our people are distributed properly to provide an appropriate welcome when our guests arrive. How fast are our guests moving?"

"Point one light speed. The mobile forces called that right."

"This is their battlefield, after all." Gaiene looked at those far-off shark shapes and the vector data displayed under them. "If they don't change their speed, we'll have more than an entire standard day to get ready for them."

Safir smiled again. "It doesn't seem right to watch your opponent spend twenty-five hours charging at you. Like they're stuck in something and moving very slowly."

"Whereas they are actually in nothing and moving very quickly." Gaiene glanced at Safir. "You have done ship boardings, haven't you?"

"Only one, as a junior executive. It's been a while."

"It's been too long for all of us," Gaiene said with mock-sadness, drawing a grin from Safir at the barely masked innuendo. "But we were talking about boarding operations, not personal problems. We ground forces types are out of our element in space. Space is too big, too fast, too strange compared to operating on a planet or an asteroid or orbital facility. So we minimize the time we spend in space for this engagement. We fight here on this ship, then we fight there on that ship. Simple enough."

"Except that everything that's simple is very difficult."

Gaiene nodded with an appreciative expression. "You've been reading the classics. Very good. Are you planning to command this brigade?"

Safir smiled again, though gently. "I'm happy as second-in-command."

"So was I." The former brigade commander had died in the same action that . . . Gaiene felt the darkness weighing on his spirit again and tried to shift the topic. "Let's go over where everyone will take up position inside this large mobile unit. I want the entire brigade ready an hour before our guests come knocking."

"Yes, sir." Safir brought up a schematic of the battleship's deck plan on the display, and they went to work.

Battleships normally carried a couple of thousand personnel. Until very recently, the *Midway* had only a couple of hundred aboard, and a good proportion of those were outfitters, construction specialists instead of mobile forces personnel. They could have put up a small fight against the kind of boarding party likely to come off of a battle cruiser, but with no chance of success.

But a warship big enough to carry a couple of thousand crew members could also carry a thousand soldiers with room to spare.

"THE last of the outfitters have left the *Midway* and are sheltering inside the dock facility," the very-young-looking Kapitan-Leytenant Kontos reported to Colonel Gaiene. "If the battle cruiser conducts a high-speed, heavy-braking maneuver as I expect, they will be next to us in just under an hour."

Like the rest of his soldiers, Gaiene was in battle armor and waiting at the spot inside the battleship from which he would begin the fight. He regarded the youthful Kapitan-Leytenant with an approving look that hid any trace of melancholy or wistfulness. He had been that young once, that enthusiastic once. That had been a long time ago, it seemed, but every once in a while someone like Kontos helped him remember. "Did the outfitters put on a convincing display of panic?" Gaiene asked.

"If I had not known it was an act, I would have believed it myself," Kontos advised cheerfully. "Between you and me, I suspect some of the outfitters really are feeling a bit panicky."

"I suspect you are right."

"*Gryphon* and *Basilisk* are two light-minutes away from us. They look exactly like they are waiting for an excuse to run a lot farther and a lot faster. Both cruisers have received offers to defect to Supreme CEO Haris's forces with promises of wealth, promotion, and happiness beyond the measure of men and women."

Gaiene smiled again though only with his lips. Anyone who looked into his eyes would have seen no humor there. "Sounds tempting."

"I don't think *Gryphon* and *Basilisk* will be tempted," Kontos replied with utter seriousness. "The mobile forces personnel still aboard *Midway* are all in the citadels. We will seal them when the battle cruiser approaches." Kontos looked distressed. "I wish I could do more to assist your assault, but if any of our few operational weapons fire, they might well hit your own soldiers."

"And the battle cruiser would shoot back," Gaiene said. "We don't want this pretty new ship of yours banged up. Your President wouldn't like that, and I am endeavoring to stay on her good side."

"President Iceni is a great leader," Kontos replied.

He really believes that. Perhaps he's right. What he doesn't realize, because he lacks the experience, is that even great leaders can lead people into great disasters. Hopefully, this won't be one of them. Iceni is a damned fine woman, though. Too bad she's never made a pass at me. I wouldn't dare make a pass at her. If she didn't kill me, General Drakon would. "She is impressive," Gaiene said out loud.

"Yes." Kontos sounded almost reverent.

He worships the woman. Poor boy. I hope the impact when he encounters reality won't leave too big a crater inside him.

"I have received another transmission from the battle cruiser," Kontos said, his tone returning to a businesslike cadence.

"Your own offer of wealth, promotion, etc.?"

"No. I have received no such offer, possibly because the enemy commander knows that I would never betray our President."

Or possibly because the enemy commander doesn't see the need to offer you anything, believing that this battleship is fruit ripe for an easy plucking. "What are they saying?" Gaiene asked.

"They demand that I acknowledge their last demand to surrender."

"Tell them no. Tell them that you'll defend this ship to your dying breath."

The image of Kontos squinted at Gaiene, puzzled. "I want them to expect strong resistance?"

"What you want," Gaiene explained patiently, "is to make them expect you to resist as hard as you can. Which shouldn't be very hard, of course, given how few people they think you have aboard this battleship. But the prospect of determined resistance by your small contingent will cause them to put together a boarding party large enough to quickly overwhelm your skeleton crew. Then, when that boarding party gets here, my soldiers will destroy it and face correspondingly fewer crew members on the battle cruiser itself."

"Ah. I see. I should act desperate and determined."

"Absolutely." Gaiene managed to muster another smile for the young Kapitan-Leytenant.

"I can do that," Kontos said in a quieter voice. "I know how it feels. At Kane. On this battleship, on this bridge, waiting for the snakes to break through, day after day."

Gaiene regarded Kontos with a different gaze. *The boy has been through a lot. It's easy to forget. He doesn't let the scars show very often. But they are there, aren't they, lad? Sometimes, they fade with time. If you're lucky.* "That was an exceptional job you did at Kane, Kapitan-Leytenant Kontos. After that, this little operation should be easy. It either works very quickly, and we all celebrate, or it fails miserably, and we all very quickly die."

Kontos smiled in turn and nodded, his eyes on Gaiene. "That is so. I will keep the battle cruiser's commander entertained and his attention occupied. Let me know if there is anything I can do to assist your actions."

"Just keep your citadels locked tight. We'll take care of everything else this time."

Kontos saluted with formal dignity, then the scene changed to an outside view.

"Just under an hour," Gaiene told the soldiers of his brigade over the command circuit. "I want full-combat readiness in half an hour."

Over the next forty-five minutes, Gaiene watched the battle cruiser swooping in, starting out as a flaring spot of light marked by the propulsion units straining to bring it to a halt relative to the battleship, then growing dramatically in size as it reduced speed, creating the illusion that the massive warship was expanding at an ever-slowing rate as it got closer.

"I never liked these boarding operations," Lieutenant Colonel Safir commented from her location elsewhere in the battleship. The nearly one thousand soldiers they had brought with them were dispersed among four large loading docks spaced along the battleship's hull. Fitting almost two hundred and fifty armored soldiers into each of those docks in such a way that almost all could engage attackers had taken some careful arranging despite the size of the compartments. "I've only done the one, and I don't have fond memories."

"We'll enjoy this one more than they will," Gaiene replied. The universe had long been a drab thing for him, illuminated only by the highs brought on by combat or alcohol or women. Memories could have provided more light and color, but along with the light and color came pain, so he did his best to block them out.

The ring on his left hand was concealed under the gauntlet of his battle armor, but he always knew it was there. Nothing else remained, but the ring did.

His spirit felt the lift that imminent battle carried before it, and for a moment, Gaiene could forget the emptiness he fought every day and the memories he fought to avoid every minute of every day.

The link to the battleship's external sensors showed the battle cruiser looming very close now. "Five minutes," the voice of Kapitan-Leytenant Kontos warned over the battleship's announcing system. "Both *Gryphon* and *Basilisk* have broadcast acceptance of the offer from Haris and are altering vectors to join up with the battle cruiser!"

CHAPTER ELEVEN

"THEY betrayed us?" Lieutenant Colonel Safir asked Gaiene.

"I doubt it." Gaiene hoped he was right about that and about his evaluation of Kapitan Stein. When it came to judging women, or men for that matter, he wasn't always successful.

Five minutes and four seconds later, the battle cruiser came to a stop relative to the battleship, only about fifty meters separating the sides of the two massive vessels. Openings suddenly gaped in the hull facing the battleship as the battle cruiser opened all four of its cargo hatches on this side, openings five meters high and ten meters wide, which were almost immediately obscured by a flurry of shapes coming out on trajectories aimed at where similar still-sealed hatches could be found on the outer hull of the battleship.

Gaiene and part of his brigade waited patiently behind one such hatch, other portions of his brigade behind other hatches, close to a thousand soldiers in full battle armor with weapons at ready. He would have liked to have more, but one freighter could only carry so many (life support had been almost overloaded on their way to the gas giant as it was), and a thousand should be enough.

"All scouts launch," Gaiene ordered.

Clinging to the outside of the battleship's hull where they had taken position half an hour ago were scouts in stealth armor, invisible to the attackers. At Gaiene's command, those scouts pushed themselves toward the battleship, passing unseen through the oncoming ranks of the Ulindi boarding party and toward the big hatches on the battle cruiser from which the attackers had come.

Spotting and counting objects was one of the things automated sensors were very good at. Within seconds, the battleship's sensors reported the result. Seven hundred and twenty. "Almost half the crew of the battle cruiser," Safir commented.

"Excellent," Gaiene agreed.

The impacts of a bit more than seven hundred attackers coming to a halt on the battleship's hull couldn't be felt by humans in armor, but once again the battleship's sensors reported the arrival of the boarding party, pinpointing the positions of all of them and passing that information on to the combat systems in the soldiers' armor. Gaiene watched, feeling his excitement ramp up, enjoying what he knew would be brief sensations of being truly alive.

The attackers attached overrides to the hatch controls on the battleship. Other attackers waited nearby with breaching charges to use if necessary, but Gaiene knew those would not be needed. Kontos had set the hatch controls to yield easily to the hacking. He didn't want his new battleship scratched up any more than necessary.

"Stand by," Gaiene said, feeling a deepening awareness of his heart beating and his breath flowing in and out. His hands gripped his pulse rifle, feeling metal and composites and death under their touch. "Follow the assault plan. All units, weapons green."

He knelt to provide a steadier aim, leveling his weapon at the hatch before him as it swung open. On either side of him, hundreds of other weapons came to bear on the hatch. The battleship hatches, burdened by much more armor than those of a battle cruiser's hull, moved more slowly than those of the other warship but still opened with gratifying speed.

The attackers came swarming in at all four hatches in a coordinated assault that would have swamped the number of defenders expected aboard the battleship. Among the boarding party were only two squads of special forces in armor like that of Gaiene's soldiers, heavily armed and trained for face-to-face combat. As was usually the case, the rest of the boarding party were crew from the battle cruiser in survival suits and carrying a variety of hand weapons. All of the attackers were expecting to face a meager number of defenders similarly lightly armed and lightly protected. As they entered the battleship, the attackers were forced to bunch up at the hatches, coming in from the top, the bottom, and both sides, silhouetted against empty space behind them, forming perfect targets.

Gaiene's sight automatically zoomed in on his target, a single figure in a survival suit, clean and clear and bright in the rifle's sight. He forgot everything else for a moment, forgot the past, forgot the pain, felt only the unholy joy of having a clean shot and a powerful weapon and the sensation of his hand tightening as his finger squeezed the trigger, then the shock as the weapon fired and the target jerked from the impact of a hit that blew open the suit and tore a hole through the chest of the unfortunate man or woman who wore it.

He instinctively sought a second target, but the rest of his soldiers had opened fire at the same moment as their colonel, and there were very few targets left.

Of the seven hundred twenty attackers in the boarding party who had tried to board through the four cargo hatches, over six hundred died in the first volley.

"Forward!" Gaiene shouted.

As the survivors of the attack force tried to gather their wits, Gaiene's thousand hurled themselves forward, overrunning and annihilating the remnants of the attackers, then launching themselves without hesitating into open space toward the battle cruiser.

Fifty meters is not a large distance, even when measured against the standards of a planet's surface. In space, it is nothing, unless it is the distance between you and safety, between you and your target, between life and death. Men and women who had literally jumped off one ship to hurl themselves toward the other crossed that fifty meters in only a few seconds that felt much, much longer. Sufficiently alert sentries in the battle cruiser's cargo holds could have seen them coming, could have slammed shut the outer hatches in that brief time available, possibly giving the battle cruiser time to accelerate away before the soldiers could breach those outer hatches.

But the few sentries posted at the battle cruiser's outer hatches were all dead and dying, slain by Gaiene's scouts, whose presence the guards had never suspected until too late.

Gaiene felt a dizzy sense of elation and disorientation as a brief stretch of star-littered space flew past, infinity on all sides, the hull of the battleship forming an armored wall behind him and that of the battle cruiser an expanse before him, the cargo-loading dock that was his objective growing very quickly before him as if he were falling into it. He barely had time to override the panicked reaction of his instincts, keeping his sense of orientation—*It is ahead of me, not beneath me*—then he had plummeted inside the loading dock he had aimed for on the battle cruiser, landing with a practiced ease that kept him on his feet, weapon ready for immediate use. His soldiers had varying amounts of experience with the maneuvers required to leap from one artificial gravity field through a gap of zero gravity and land in another artificial gravity field. Some kept their feet like Gaiene, some skidded to a running halt, and others tumbled, rolling along the deck before scrambling to their feet. The least experienced hit hard, flailing, disoriented and confused by the abrupt shifts in where up and down were.

Against strong defenses at the hatches, Gaiene's troops might have taken significant losses as they hit the deck with varied degrees of skill. But the battle cruiser's commander had seen no need to leave strong forces at the hatches, instead throwing his entire assault force into the attack. Before the battle cruiser crew realized what was happening, more than seven hundred of their comrades were dead and nearly a thousand armored soldiers were inside the hull of their ship. A battle cruiser constructed by the Syndicate Worlds, whose deck plans had been easily available to help Gaiene prepare this counterattack, whose operating systems, hardware, and software were as well-known to the soldiers of Midway as they were to the crew of the battle cruiser.

Gaiene moved past the bodies of two dead sentries as the outer hatches finally swung shut, this time under the command of his own soldiers. *"Try to keep from blowing out the atmosphere in the ship,"* Drakon had ordered. *"The mobile forces people say their ships can handle vacuum inside, but it can make a real mess, and we're supposed to take this ship as intact as possible."*

Some of Gaiene's troops had attached small Bedlam Boxes to the comm terminals and sensors in the loading docks, the devices generating a stream of misleading and deceptive messages, warnings, and reassurances into the sensors and internal comm systems of the battle cruiser. The officers and crew of the ship, trying to figure out what was happening and where, would waste precious moments trying to grasp the situation as confusing data poured in.

The instant the outer hatches sealed and safety interlocks glowed green, his soldiers got the inner hatches open and began pouring into the passageways of the battle cruiser.

In places where emergency locks had been activated in time, breaching charges blew out those inner hatches, a delay of only a few more seconds before the rest of Gaiene's forces were heading for their objectives. "Remember the General's orders," Gaiene broadcast. "Give the crew members a chance to surrender if you have time."

Gaiene was one of the first out of the loading dock where he had landed, finding himself facing a half-dozen crew members of the battle cruiser who had been racing toward the dock. A single shot ricocheted off of Gaiene's battle armor before he and the soldiers closest to him opened fire and riddled the sailors through their relatively flimsy survival suits. "Didn't have time," the sergeant nearest Gaiene noted apologetically.

"No. But that was their own fault," Gaiene said, as his column moved along the passageways. The interior of a warship could be a maze to someone unfamiliar with it, but the heads-up displays on the soldiers' armor provided clear maps of the routes they needed to take to their objectives, with occasional helpful reminders such as "turn right here and take the next ladder down."

Gaiene's column shrank as squads peeled off but remained strong since his ultimate objective was the battle cruiser's bridge, securely nestled deep inside the hull. Alarms had begun blaring through the ship, interspersed with frantic orders shouted into the general announcing circuit.

"Most of the remaining crew are at their duty stations," Lieutenant Colonel Safir reported. "We're rolling them up."

"There are a few wandering around loose," Gaiene warned, as his own column encountered another group of sailors still trying to scramble into survival suits. For an instant the two groups stared at each other, then the sailors' hands bolted upward, coming to rest palm first on their heads as they slammed their backs against the bulkheads. "Good lads," Gaiene told them. "Leave a fire team here to guard this batch," he ordered the sergeant.

The next group of crew members they ran into was either more highly motivated or simply had a lot less common sense. Weapons carried by the crew members swung to bear, but before they could fire, Gaiene's soldiers opened up and wiped out the pocket of resistance, the soldiers scarcely pausing in their movement, rushing onward as the last of the dead crew members were still falling limply to the deck.

Gaiene kept one eye on the directions to the bridge his heads-up display was providing, used his other eye to monitor the progress of the whole assault on another portion of his heads-up display, and used his other eye to watch for immediate danger. *"That's three eyes,"* a young Conner Gaiene had protested to the veteran who had told him what commanding an assault required. The veteran had smiled sadly. *"By the time you reach command, if you're any good, you'll know how to make two eyes do the work of three. Or you'll die."*

Gaiene hadn't died though that particular veteran had, not long after imparting some painfully acquired wisdom to him. It sometimes bothered Gaiene that he had trouble remembering what the woman had looked like before an Alliance bombardment projectile had blown her into tiny pieces.

"Looking good," Safir's voice reported to Gaiene.

The brigade was seizing more and more of the ship, resistance in most places crumbling as what was happening became clear to the survivors in the crew. "Don't relax," Gaiene warned everyone. "Mobile forces can fight well when their backs are to the wall, and there are supposed to be a lot of snakes aboard this can."

"We found some of them!" a unit leader warned on the heels of Gaiene's words. "Snakes!" Brighter symbols popped up in an area far from Gaiene, showing a bastion of resistance where Internal Security Service agents were putting up a fierce fight near the central weapons-control citadel.

"Handle that, Safir," Gaiene directed. Weapons control was Safir's objective, so she was already in that area.

Battle cruisers were almost as large as battleships but longer and leaner, presenting an apparently endless series of passageways leading to an apparently endless series of more passageways. The command staff in the battle cruiser's bridge citadel had awoken to their peril and were trying to lock isolation and blast barriers in place to seal off routes through the ship, but Gaiene's soldiers had brought the means to either blow holes through those barriers or locally override the lock commands.

Shouts of triumph erupted across the command circuit. Annoyed by the noise, Gaiene checked his display and saw that the nest of snakes had been eliminated. All dead, of course. General Drakon might issue orders that opponents be allowed to surrender, but snakes rarely tried to surrender and, if they did, were killed by vengeful soldiers anyway. The General surely wouldn't mind, as he knew as well as the rest of them did that snakes occupied a different category than regular forces did.

Gaiene and the soldiers with him ran past a group of crew members waving enthusiastic greetings and bloodied implements. At their feet lay two others, both newly dead, both wearing the standard suits for Internal Security Service snakes. Another fire team broke off to guard the new volunteers who had formerly worked for Supreme CEO Haris before tendering their resignations in blood.

Most of the ship had been overrun, the survivors of the crew being herded into compartments under guard, but the three citadels were locked down, armor sealed and defenses active. While the controls on another blast door were hacked, Gaiene paused, evaluating the situation.

Main propulsion-control citadel, weapons-control citadel, bridge citadel. The last-ditch defensive barriers put in place on Syndicate ships to defend against enemy boarding parties, as well as against mutiny by crews of workers who lacked loyalty to their masters and were kept in line by discipline, fear, and the ever-present snakes of the ISS. "How does it look, Safir?"

Lieutenant Colonel Safir sounded annoyed. "Not too bad. We lost some people taking out the snake stronghold. The power core has been overrun and the remote operating cables cut, so the snakes or the other Ulindis can't overload it. I think the propulsion citadel will surrender, but I'm guessing we'll have to crack open the weapons citadel."

"Get into the weapons citadel and make sure they can't fire on the battleship, which they may realize they can attempt if they are given time to think. I'm closing in on the bridge citadel," Gaiene said. The blast barrier blocking him whooshed open, and he took off at a trot, surrounded by the soldiers with him, their movements in the power-assisted armor oddly dainty as they used the gliding steps most effective inside a warship's confined spaces. "I'll give the bridge crew a chance to do this the easy way as soon as I get into position."

Danger signs popped up on Gaiene's display, warning that the defenses around the bridge citadel were near. He had the means to break those defenses and get into the citadel, but that would cost time and lives as well as messing up parts of this ship. Gaiene ordered the soldiers with him to halt in a safe area outside the bridge-citadel defenses and looked around for a comm panel. "Here we are. Bridge. Acknowledge, you fools."

The panel lit to show a mobile forces officer in the command seat on the bridge. Gaiene knew the look in the man's eyes. He had seen it many times before. Disbelief. Shock. Fear. Confusion. That look meant Gaiene had to keep pushing, keep the man from recovering, keep him from thinking clearly. "We have your unit under our control and will soon breach your citadels. However, in the interest of avoiding excessive damage, we are willing to offer you the chance to surrender, open the citadels, and deactivate their defenses. *If* you surrender, you will be allowed to live, and given your freedom. We'll keep our word. We're not snakes. Every snake in this star system is dead. *If* you refuse to surrender, and we have to blast our way in, there will be no mercy shown, and your dead bodies will be tossed into space. Or perhaps you'll only be mostly dead when we toss you into space. We'll keep that promise as well. Make your decision now. I am not a patient man."

Shouting could be heard in the background of the bridge citadel while the battle cruiser's commander stared at Gaiene. After several seconds Gaiene prodded him. "Now. Surrender or die. I won't ask a third time."

The man looked toward something behind him and must have seen what he needed to see, since he turned back to face Gaiene and nodded in a jerky fashion. "I agree. Surrender. I surrender the ship." A hand that Gaiene could see was trembling danced spasmodically over the controls at the command seat. "Deactivating defenses."

"Make sure the other citadels do the same."

"I don't have control of the weapons citadel! Haris's snakes are in there!"

"Lieutenant Colonel Safir, the weapons citadel *is* occupied by snakes. You will have to take that one the hard way."

Safir replied with grim satisfaction. "I thought so. Everything's ready. Commencing assault."

The danger markers on Gaiene's display were winking out as defenses around the bridge citadel shut down. He gestured, and several soldiers scuttled forward, around the corner of the passageway and toward the massive armored hatch sealing off the bridge.

No attacks erupted from hidden traps, so Gaiene and the rest of his soldiers followed, additional units closing in on the bridge from other sides and the decks above and below it. Armor and defenses were in place in those locations, too, but the ship's commander appeared to be abiding by his agreement to surrender.

Vibration could be felt as the heavy bolts holding the hatch locked ponderously retracted, then the hatch itself pulled back.

Soldiers stormed inside, their weapons ready. Gaiene came with them, a last rush of adrenaline fueling the elation of victory.

The bridge crew were standing with raised arms, hands resting on their heads, most of them at their duty stations. But several were gathered around the spot where a man and a woman in the standard suits of the ISS lay on the deck. Gaiene gave the snakes a dismissive glance that took in the unnatural angles of their heads that bespoke broken necks. "Make sure they're dead," he ordered one of the officers with him. "Make sure everyone else up here is disarmed, then get them down to one of the holding areas. Lieutenant Bulgori, get on the comm controls and let the battleship know we have the bridge of this unit and will soon have the rest in hand."

A series of faint shocks registered through the hull of the battle cruiser. Gaiene switched his attention and his display to a close-up on Lieutenant Colonel Safir's portion of the brigade. The defenses outside the weapons-control citadel had been destroyed, allowing soldiers to get close enough to place breaching charges powerful enough to defeat even the protection around a citadel. The shocks had marked holes being blown in the armor guarding the citadel, and now antipersonnel and electromagnetic-pulse grenades were being fired in through the openings, followed by assault forces with rifles blazing.

A few snakes were still standing, their outlines barely visible through the murk created in the weapons-control citadel by the breaching charges and grenades. Gaiene barely had time to focus on the remote images before the shapes of the snakes were torn ragged by scores of shots and tossed aside.

"We have the propulsion-control and weapons-control citadels," Safir reported. "Propulsion surrendered as soon as their defenses deactivated."

"Thank you," Gaiene replied. "I fear we're going to hear some complaints from our shipyard people about the damage to the weapons-control area."

"We did try to minimize the damage," Safir said with a grin.

"Yes, but the repair people will be unreasonable. You know how they are. *You broke it.* It's our job to break things, but they never understand that. Speaking of jobs, you did a good one as second-in-command, fulfilling every expectation of your superiors in the finest tradition of etc., etc., etc. Let's get the internal sensors back online and make certain there aren't any crew members hiding in out-of-the-way places."

"We're on it, Colonel. It looks like we captured between four and five hundred crew members. This ship was a little short-handed."

"Not as much as it is now."

"We have comms with the *Midway*," Lieutenant Bulgori reported. "A minute after our attack began, *Gryphon* and *Basilisk* opened fire at close range on the four HuKs escorting this battle cruiser. Three of them were destroyed, and the fourth surrendered after taking propulsion damage."

Thank you, Kapitan Stein. A pity you don't seem inclined to cele-brate our victory with me in a very inappropriate fashion. Gaiene looked around, weary, sensing the color flowing out of the world once more. They had won. It didn't really matter, nothing really mattered, but at least the attack had provided a momentary lift to his deadened spirits. And it had provided a victory for Artur Drakon, who had kept him from dying in a labor camp or a gutter. It was all as good as any-thing could be in a universe that had ceased to hold meaning.

The commander's seat on the battle cruiser's bridge lay vacant and somehow forlorn. Gaiene walked over to it and sat down, half of his mind monitoring his soldiers as they went about the business of mak-ing secure the battle cruiser they had just captured, and the other half wondering how long it would be before he could get drunk again. Secure the ship, turn it over to the mobile forces people, then find out where the shipyard workers kept their booze.

It was always good to plan things out.

GIVEN how their last private conversation had ended, Drakon was surprised to see Iceni smiling at him when she called on their secure line.

"I wanted to thank you, General, for my lovely new battle cruiser."

"*Your* lovely new battle cruiser?" Drakon asked.

"Now, don't spoil the present by getting tightfisted." Iceni smiled wider. "I may be a witch at times, but I'm not an ungrateful witch. In all seriousness, I know I owe this to your soldiers and your decision to participate in the operation. Once we get the battle cruiser back in shape and the battleship operational, we'll have a defense for this star system that will knock Boyens on his butt if he shows up here again."

"Colonel Gaiene said there wasn't much damage to the battle cruiser," Drakon said.

She laughed, a sound he found unexpectedly pleasant after their strained relationship of recent weeks. "That's a ground forces assessment. Your soldiers, and I know they had no choice, trashed some important equipment, blew out a lot of hatches, and even blew some holes in bulkheads that aren't supposed to have holes in them. That all has to be fixed. Most of the survivors among the crew appear willing to join us, but there aren't that many survivors compared to the size of the crew a battle cruiser needs."

"If we're lucky, Colonel Rogero and your Kommodor will solve that problem. They should be bringing back enough veterans to crew both *Midway* and the new battle cruiser."

"Yes. What should we name it, Artur?" She gave him a happily inquiring look. "I named the battleship. You should give a name to our new battle cruiser."

"Really?" Gwen *was* in a good mood. Of course, he couldn't expect to produce a battle cruiser for her every time she got inexplicably moody, but, hopefully, that wouldn't be necessary too often. "Do you want to name battle cruisers after stars, too?"

"I think it would be a good idea. But . . ." Iceni pursed her lips in thought. "If we name the ship after one of the nearby stars, they might either take that as an indication we feel a sense of ownership toward them or give them the mistaken impression that they have some rights to the battle cruiser."

"That's a concern," Drakon agreed. "How about if we name the battle cruiser after a star nobody occupies? Pele."

"Pele? A star occupied by the enigmas?"

"The enigmas kicked the Syndicate out of Pele," Drakon said, "but according to what Black Jack's fleet found, there's no enigma presence there."

"Hmmm." Iceni looked sideways, considering. "We are the front-line defense of humanity against the enigmas. Declaring some sort of tie to Pele would emphasize that."

"It might not please the enigmas," Drakon felt constrained to point out.

"Who the hell cares what pleases the enigmas? Who the hell *knows* what pleases the enigmas? Even Black Jack couldn't find out. The enigmas just keep attacking us and tried to depopulate this entire planet." Iceni nodded. "I'm good with *Pele*. And I will freely admit that you were right in your assessment of Colonel Gaiene. Kapitan-Leytenant Kontos was very leery of your colonel, but was awestruck by how well he and his unit carried out the capture of the battle cruiser." Her smile became tentative. "I'm going to have to learn to . . . trust . . . your assessments."

Trust? And she hadn't used the word in a mocking way. "Are you sure?"

The smile faded away completely, replaced by a serious gaze at him. "No. I may never be sure. Can you live with that?"

"I have so far."

"You've lived with far worse than that from me, General Drakon, even if you seem curiously unable to figure out such things. But you pushed me to approve an action that has left me in a far stronger position. Either you truly intend to work alongside me without betrayal, or you are the biggest fool in the history of humanity, or you are far more subtle and cunning than Black Jack."

Drakon smiled sardonically. "I don't think I'm a fool. Not usually, anyway. And I know I'm not Black Jack."

"A man doesn't have to be Black Jack to be important to— To this star system," Iceni finished. "Thank you again, Artur."

It was only after she had signed off that Drakon realized Iceni had been worried. Was that why she had been so upset at their last meeting—because she had known that if the attack on the battle cruiser succeeded, Drakon's own soldiers would then have control of the most powerful warship in the star system? She hadn't known for certain that he would abide by their agreement, their partnership, and turn the battle cruiser over to Iceni's mobile forces personnel as soon as the warship was confirmed secure.

Why didn't it even occur to me that I could have double-crossed her and ended up with both the most powerful mobile forces and ground forces here? But it didn't. We made a deal. I don't break deals. Even when someone is being as unpleasant and cold as . . .

She's not going to betray me. If Iceni had planned to stick a knife in me, she would have been all sweetness and light the last few weeks, and especially the last week, trying to lull me into doing what she wanted. Standard CEO tactics. Of course I'm your friend . . . sucker. *Then when she had her hands on the battle cruiser, she would have gone all ice and fire on me. But she did the opposite.*

Why didn't the option of keeping the battle cruiser occur to Malin? Maybe it did, but he just assumed that I must have already considered the option and rejected it. But that doesn't explain why Morgan hasn't gone ballistic at the idea of turning the battle cruiser over to Iceni. Morgan hasn't objected to the operation at all.

Because, he realized, it had never occurred to Morgan that he *would* give the battle cruiser to Iceni. *She assumed I was keeping it. When she finds out I didn't—*

Maybe when she sees that this is working to everyone's benefit, that this sort of strategy and cooperation makes us all stronger, Morgan will finally make some progress on trusting and accepting other people again. I've spent the last decade trying to get her to realize that cynicism and manipulation only gets you so far, and wherever it gets you isn't worth the price. Besides, it's the Syndicate way, and she hates the Syndicate much more than I do.

But she is going to raise hell while I explain that all again.

"General?" his comm panel called. "Colonel Morgan is here. She says she needs to see you immediately."

And, here we go. "Send her in."

ON the bridge of the heavy cruiser *Manticore*, Kommodor Marphissa awaited her flotilla's imminent arrival at Indras Star System. She had just come from speaking with Captain Bradamont, who had spent most of the time since leaving Midway in her stateroom, where her presence was least disruptive to the crew. *When Admiral Geary's fleet came through Indras on the way to Midway months ago, the star system was still firmly loyal to the Syndicate Worlds,* Bradamont had repeated. *They didn't try to oppose our movement through Indras, but then they lacked the means to oppose us or stop us.*

What was at Indras now? Had they gained more warships, more defenses? Was Indras still loyal to the Syndicate or had its leaders, or its people, struck off on their own as so many other star systems had in recent months? She, and the rest of the Recovery Flotilla, would learn the answers in a few minutes.

Her display had a row of green lights indicating full-combat readiness on *Manticore.* The other warships of the flotilla should also be as ready as they could be. The freighters could do little but hope that the warships could defend them.

"One minute," the senior watch specialist informed Kapitan Diaz.

"We are ready, Kommodor," Diaz told Marphissa.

"Let's hope so," she muttered in reply. For a moment, she wondered where former Kapitan Toirac was right now. On President Iceni's orders, Marphissa had sent Toirac under guard back to the primary world at Midway. She had wanted to avoid seeing him again, but a sense of duty had driven Marphissa to be at the air lock when Toirac was escorted off of the ship, her last sight of him being his accusing eyes staring at her from a slack and unanimated face.

She shook her head to dispel the image from her mind as the flotilla left the hypernet with the usual lack of any sensory effect. One moment, nothing surrounded the flotilla in its bubble of something. The next, the bubble was gone, the stars shone upon them, and the flotilla was moving away from the gate at Indras.

"What are communications telling us?" she asked the comm specialist.

The woman was watching her screens intently and listening. "They're still Syndicate, Kommodor. All of the message traffic I can see and hear is consistent with that. There are snake ciphers being used for some of it. We can't read them. The snake ciphers we captured at Midway must have been superseded."

That settled the matter since those messages had been sent hours before the arrival of the flotilla and so couldn't be a deception designed to fool the newly arrived ships. Marphissa adjusted her suit. As much as she detested Syndicate uniforms, it had been necessary to don one for this performance, though it was a suit for a much higher rank than she had ever actually achieved.

She adopted the look of haughty superiority that she had seen so many times in Syndicate CEOs, then tapped her comm controls. "To the authorities at Indras Star System, this is CEO Manetas, commanding a flotilla en route to an internal security mission at Atalia Star System. I do not require your assistance at this time," Marphissa drawled with as much arrogance as she could manage. President Iceni had stressed the need for that. *Syndicate CEOs never ask, and they never show any trace of humility or weakness.*

"For the people, Manetas, out." It had taken a special effort to say "for the people" in the standard Syndicate manner, rapidly, with the words slurred together into the meaningless phrase it was for the leaders of the Syndicate.

She ended the transmission and inhaled deeply. "We'll see how well that works."

Diaz bent an amused look her way. "I'll bet you never expected to wear a CEO suit."

"Never expected and never wanted," Marphissa said. "I feel unclean in this thing. But the imposture is necessary. We need to convince the authorities at Indras that we're a legitimate Syndicate flotilla on our way to hammer Atalia. If we can do that, then even if they learn the truth when we show up again on way back to Midway, they won't have time to activate the hypernet gate block, however that works."

"They might be able to do it from here," Diaz suggested.

"But they won't, not without approval from Prime," Marphissa insisted. "Do you think Prime is going to authorize anyone but themselves the power to shut down hypernet commerce and military movements? Indras will have to ask permission, and by the time they get it, we'll be home at Midway."

"I see your point," Diaz admitted. "What if they see through us before we leave for Atalia?"

"Then we push on and hope the gate isn't blocked when we get back," Marphissa said. She pointed to her display. "All they have here in the way of mobile forces is two light cruisers and two HuKs orbiting thirty light-minutes from the star. Enough to overawe the local citizens but not enough to stop us, and not in any position to threaten us."

Diaz licked his lips, his eyes on his display. "Should we destroy them? Try to lure the light cruisers and HuKs in close and take them out so the locals have a chance to rebel against the Syndicate?"

Marphissa hesitated, feeling a strong temptation to agree. It took a major effort of will to suppress the desire to say yes. "We can't. We have a mission, a primary responsibility."

"But—" Diaz began, turning a disappointed look her way.

"No. Listen. You're in command of a warship now. You have to see the big picture. One part of that is, if something happens to us when we try to take out the Syndicate mobile forces here, or if our action provides enough notice for the hypernet to be blocked against our return, how do we get back? Who picks up the survivors from the Reserve Flotilla? We are their only hope for rescue from the Alliance camps where they are being held."

"That's true, Kommodor, but still—"

"And if we succeed, if we destroy all four Syndicate warships here, can the local citizens do anything? What about the ground forces? What about the snakes? You know the snakes plant weapons of mass destruction in cities as a last-ditch means of defeating rebellion."

"I had heard that," Diaz admitted.

"It's true. President Iceni received a full briefing on what General

Drakon's soldiers found when they captured the snake headquarters. The snakes had nukes under every city on Midway's primary world, and they were trying to set them off when General Drakon and his ground forces stopped them."

"That could happen here," Diaz said, his eyes hooded. "If the citizens aren't ready, if they don't have the ground forces on their side—"

"And if *we* start things rolling, the end result could be their cities vanishing into nuclear fire and rubble," Marphissa concluded. "President Iceni and General Drakon planned and coordinated their rebellion. That's why it worked. We can't just jump-start another rebellion here."

Diaz gave her an admiring look. "You've picked up a lot in a short time. It seems like only yesterday, you were an executive."

"It was only yesterday in some ways," Marphissa said. "And now look at me in a CEO suit! I can't wait to get this thing off, but I have to see what kind of reply we get first. Do you want to know where I'm learning some of these things?"

"Sure."

"From the Alliance officer." Marphissa ignored Diaz's jolt of dismay. "Captain Bradamont has been around a while longer than you and I, and she's been a senior officer a lot longer, too. She's had to think about these things, and she's telling me about them."

"If she's telling you what to do—" Diaz began.

"*No.* She is showing me how to think! What I should think about. The big picture. What might happen, as opposed to what I might want to happen. The consequences of my actions. I knew some of this, even if I didn't think in those terms, but she's helping me understand. She wants us to win, Kapitan Diaz. Not because the Alliance has designs on Midway Star System, but because . . . well, she has personal reasons for wanting us to be free and strong."

Diaz looked around, his mouth working, then back at Marphissa. "And because it weakens the Syndicate?"

"Certainly that, too. Look, Chintan, she hates the Syndicate, we hate the Syndicate. She spent time in a labor camp. We don't have to like each other, but we can help each other."

"True." Diaz gave her a twisted smile. "But you do like her."

Marphissa started to deny it, then spread her hands in a helpless gesture. "We get along."

"Will she talk to me?"

"Of course she will. That's why Black Jack sent her to us."

Diaz nodded slowly, his eyes once more on his display, his expression thoughtful.

THE reply from the authorities in Indras took exactly one hour and one minute longer than transmission times across the vast gulf of interplanetary space required. That timing made it obvious a snub was being delivered, an impression confirmed for Marphissa when CEO Yamada, a man of late middle age who had obviously lived many of those years too well, began speaking. "CEO Manetas, I have not heard of you."

"He knows you're a fake!" Diaz cried.

"No," Marphissa said. "President Iceni told me I might hear something like that. It's a CEO put-down. He's saying I can't be all that important because he never heard of me. It means they fell for it."

Yamada had continued speaking as if the conversation held no interest for him. "I do not have any need for your assistance. You may continue on your assigned duties. I will expect you to leave both heavy cruisers here when you return as I have use for them. Enjoy your trip through Kalixa. For the people, Yamada, out."

Diaz and Marphissa both laughed. "He did buy it!" Diaz said.

"He's going to be very disappointed when we come back," Marphissa said, "and tell him and every other CEO in this star system where they can stuff their expectations." She got up. "I am changing out of this awful suit and putting on a uniform I am proud to wear,"

Marphissa announced for the benefit of the bridge watch specialists. "Keep me informed of developments, Kapitan Diaz."

"Yes, Kommodor Marphissa," Diaz replied with a grin.

She stopped by Bradamont's stateroom on the way to her own. "Our deception worked. Can you believe they thought I was a real Syndicate CEO?"

Bradamont nodded approvingly. "Good work. I was just watching my display and remembering the last time I came through here. It never occurred to me I'd come back aboard a former Syndic cruiser." She nodded again, this time at her display. "Indras is far enough from the border with the Alliance that it didn't get hit too often. It's a shame a decent star system like this is still part of the Syndicate Worlds."

Marphissa leaned against the side of the entry. "It's all a lie, you know. Everything you're seeing is fake. Those big manufacturing centers and transportation hubs? They're full of inefficiencies, shoddy work, theft, and diversion of goods to the black market, thanks to workers who know the system is rigged against them and so don't care about their jobs, and thanks to supervisors who owe their promotions to superiors who only care whether the supervisors tell them what they want to hear. The schools and universities teach technical subjects fairly well, but everything else they teach is lies. The houses and apartment complexes look neat and secure and safe, but they're full of families and individuals who live every moment in fear that the Internal Security Service will come knocking because the snakes suspect them of something or they were accused of something or just because some snake supervisor needs to fill an arrest quota. That's the real Syndicate system."

"I'm sorry," Bradamont said. "No one should have to live that way."

"*Should* has nothing to do with it. It's the way it is. The way it has been. But not at Midway anymore. We'll get strong enough to help other star systems, too, like we did Taroa. Someday, the Syndicate will just be a bad memory."

"And then somebody will start a new version of it," Bradamont commented gloomily. "There's been a lot of speculation in the Alliance that the Syndic leaders kept the war going because it helped hold together the Syndicate Worlds and allowed them to justify repression and everything else."

"They didn't need the war to justify repression," Marphissa scoffed. "They stopped trying to justify things a long time ago. But it is true that we couldn't rebel while people were worried about what the Alliance would do to us. Why swap one set of tyrants for another set?"

"The Alliance isn't run by tyrants," Bradamont said, startled. "The instability there these days is precisely because we can vote out our leaders. The people are doing that, and not always for the right reasons."

"You're talking about the way things are in the Alliance," Marphissa pointed out. "I'm talking about what we were told about the Alliance. We knew what we were told was probably lies, but we didn't know the truth. What we did know was that people in power were corrupt and cared nothing for those beneath them. Why should we expect your leaders to differ from ours?"

Bradamont shook her head. "How did you come out the way you did, Asima? You're not a bad person. Not at all."

"I knew I could either be like the people I hated, or I could be something else. I decided to be something else." Marphissa paused. "The CEO here made some mocking comment about enjoying our trip through Kalixa. I know that's where a hypernet gate collapsed and caused a lot of damage. How bad is it?"

"Bad," Bradamont said. "Very bad."

THEY were still twelve hours away from the jump point when Marphissa was awakened from sleep in her stateroom by an urgent summons. "We've received a snake message," Diaz said. "We can't read it, but it's high-priority and addressed to the fake Syndic hull identification we've been broadcasting."

Marphissa stared at him, puzzled, then felt horror replacing her bafflement. "They want the snakes on our ships to check in with them! There haven't been any snake status reports sent from our ships!"

"Damn! I should have—"

"We all should have thought of that! Quick. Have a message made up using as templates some of those snake messages we captured after we killed them. Use the snake encryption we brought from Midway. It will be old, but it's the best we've got. Tell them . . . tell the snakes in Indras that there are new procedures. ISS agents on ships are supposed to maintain comm silence as much as possible to keep rebels from knowing which ships are still loyal."

"Kommodor, that is really weak," Diaz said, "but it's a lot stronger than anything I've thought of. I'll get the message ready and send it to you for approval."

Marphissa sat on the edge of her bunk, staring into her darkened stateroom. *So close. We almost made it out of Indras without being uncovered. But it looks like we're going to be busted before we leave here, and that might mean getting home will be a nightmare.*

CHAPTER TWELVE

"THERE'S no way the snakes in Indras would accept silence in response to their demand," Marphissa said to Bradamont, who, along with Kapitan Diaz, had come to Marphissa's stateroom in response to a summons.

"Then it sounds like you have no choice but to try your bluff," Bradamont agreed, looking unhappy.

"Can you think of anything more plausible?"

"Plausible? To a snake?" Bradamont laughed shortly. "Actually, from what I know of them and other bureaucracies, the stupider the directive, the more realistic it might seem to them. How many really dumb directives did you get in the course of a year before you revolted against the Syndicate Worlds?"

"You should measure that in days, not years," Diaz said. "Otherwise, the number gets too big."

"They might think this is legitimate because it doesn't make much sense?" Marphissa asked Bradamont. "You know, that's possible. That's really possible. All right, I'm approving the message," she said to Diaz. "Transmit, and if you still believe in any deities, pray to them to convince the snakes to believe this when they get it."

Further sleep was impossible. Marphissa tried to work in her stateroom, got irritable, went to the bridge, almost bit the head off of a watch specialist who made a friendly comment to another specialist in too loud a voice, went back to her stateroom, then finally went to Bradamont and sat talking with her.

One hour short of the jump point for Atalia, Marphissa returned to *Manticore*'s bridge, aware that she looked like hell and feeling just as bad as she looked. "No response from the snakes?" she demanded of Diaz.

"No, Kommodor." Diaz rubbed his eyes wearily, then slapped onto his arm one of the stimulant devices that everyone called an up patch. "No reply."

She tried to remember the last time she had come onto the bridge and not seen him there. Diaz had apparently kept himself on duty for the entire transit. "No signs of alerts in the star system?" Marphissa pressed. "Still no indications of any reaction? No fast ships suddenly heading for the hypernet gate as if they were carrying an urgent message?"

"No, Kommodor."

What are they doing? Marphissa glared at her display. *The snakes must at least suspect something. Are they laying some trap? Are they awaiting approval from some CEO who has strict instructions not to be awakened unless Black Jack himself comes storming in here with his fleet?* "We keep going. We get to the jump point and head for Atalia, no matter what happens from this moment on."

To her surprise, the tension level on the bridge seemed to relax considerably. She gave Diaz a questioning look.

"The uncertainty," he said to her in a low voice. "It's driving us all crazy. But you just gave them some certainty. We're going to keep going. Now they know what's going to happen."

"What's going to happen in the next hour," Marphissa grumbled. "After that, it's anybody's guess."

"It could be worse," Diaz suggested. "We could still be wearing Syndicate suits, and there could be a snake standing at the back of the bridge listening to our every word." He paused, an intent expression crossing his face. "That would really suck."

"Have you been taking too many meds?" Marphissa demanded.

"Maybe." Diaz leaned back, his eyes on the overhead. "I don't think I like Indras. Wouldn't it be great if we had a big display over us that looked like the stars so it would be like we were on the outside of the hull and had a window above us?"

"Kapitan Diaz, one minute after we enter jump for Atalia, you are ordered to turn over the bridge to another officer, go to your stateroom, take a crash patch, and get at least eight hours' sleep. Is that understood?"

"Uh . . . yes, Kommodor."

"I know you're feeling the responsibilities of being a ship's commanding officer, but the point is not to stay on duty until you are half-delusional unless there is no alternative. The point is to get sufficient rest so that you can make decent decisions and be at your best when it's needed. And, yes, I am fully aware that I have done a poor job of that in the last several hours. I'm going to be crashing once we enter jump, too."

"Incoming transmission," the comm specialist warned. "Snake cipher, the same one we used."

Marphissa closed her eyes, exhaled slowly to calm herself, then answered the specialist. "What do the snakes say?"

"Just . . . we understand."

"What? They said what?"

"That's all, Kommodor. The entire message. *We understand.*"

Diaz roused himself to glare at the specialist. "Are we certain that there is no worm or virus or Trojan horse attached to that message?"

"There is nothing, Kapitan. It's far too small to carry any of those, and there are no attachments. It's just the address header and those two words."

Marphissa exhaled again, this time heavily. "They know. They're playing with us. The snakes have figured out we're not who we say we are. But they probably don't know who we are. Maybe they hope that message will provoke us into telling them by implying they know more than they do."

"That's an old snake trick," Diaz agreed.

"And they don't know why we're going to Atalia, and I will bet my life that the snakes have no idea that we intend going to Alliance space from there. They've probably got hidden agents in Atalia, and they'll find a way to get those agents to report on what we're doing." She turned a triumphant look on Diaz. "But we'll have more firepower than anyone else in Atalia if Captain Bradamont's information is still good. We'll block anyone from leaving Atalia for Indras until the freighters return from Varandal and we jump out. The snakes won't know what we were up to until we get back here; and then it will be too late for them to interfere with us."

I hope.

Forty minutes later, they reached the jump point. "All units in Recovery Flotilla, jump now," Marphissa ordered. She barely felt the mental jolt of entering jump space, barely noticed the stars and blackness of normal space replaced by the unending gray sameness of jump space, and only noted in passing the blooming off to one side of *Manticore* of one of the strange and unexplained lights that came and went in jump space. "I'm getting some sleep. So are you, Kapitan Diaz. Make sure I am notified of any emergencies," she added to the watch specialists, then marched off the bridge toward her stateroom.

THEY had to go through Kalixa to get to Atalia. Kalixa had been a fairly well-off star system, bristling with defenses and home to many millions.

Then the enigmas had caused Kalixa's hypernet gate to collapse in hopes that it would set off a wave of retaliatory actions by the Syndicate and the Alliance against each other.

"There's nothing left," Kapitan Diaz breathed in shock as he gazed at the dead remnants of the star system. "Even the star has become unstable."

"You can still see some ruins on what used to be the habitable planet," Marphissa replied somberly. "There's not much atmosphere left to block our view of them. If the enigma plan had succeeded, a lot of star systems belonging to the Syndicate and the Alliance would be like this."

They couldn't rush through Kalixa, not with the freighters along, but they made the best time they could to the jump point for Atalia, and everyone breathed a sigh of relief as the gray of jump space replaced the dead remnants of Kalixa.

CAPTAIN Bradamont's information about Atalia was still good.

Marphissa relaxed as her display updated to show only a single Hunter-Killer orbiting near the star system's primary inhabited world and a single Alliance courier ship hanging near the jump point for Varandal. Getting out of the eerie gray isolation of jump space, returning to normal space, where stars glowed all around once more, was always a relief. But it was often also rendered tense by wondering what might be waiting outside the jump exit.

"That's it," she told Bradamont, who had come to the bridge to observe the entry to Atalia just in case other Alliance ships were present. "Let's get you over to that freighter. I'm going to keep *Manticore* and *Kraken* here near the jump point for Kalixa to keep anyone from going on to Indras and taking word to the snakes of what's happening. The light cruisers and our HuKs will escort your freighters to the jump point for Varandal, then wait there for you to return."

"For me to return with your shipmates," Bradamont corrected.

"If it can be done, you'll do it," Marphissa said. As she stood to accompany Bradamont to the shuttle, Marphissa was surprised to hear the senior watch specialist call out to Bradamont.

"Good luck, Kapitan!"

"Yes," another specialist agreed. "One of those guys from the Reserve Flotilla owes me money. I hope you bring him back!"

Bradamont grinned, waved, and followed Marphissa off the bridge.

"That was surprising," Marphissa muttered, as they made their way toward the air lock.

"They must be getting used to me," Bradamont offered. "And they idolize you—"

"Don't be absurd."

"They do. So when they see that you trust me, it rubs off a little on me." They reached the hatch, and Bradamont paused. "If Admiral Geary is already at Varandal, this will be a piece of cake."

"And if he's not, you said this Admiral Timbale will cut a deal," Marphissa said. "Be careful. I don't want to lose you. And you and Colonel Rogero behave yourselves once you're on the same ship. No sneaking off for a little private recreation."

Bradamont laughed. "That's unlikely. You are the only other person in this flotilla who knows about Donal Rogero and me. He thinks his soldiers will take it all right, but we don't want to create too many problems with the Reserve Flotilla survivors when they get on the same ship with us."

"Smart move." Marphissa hesitated, feeling unusually diffident. "What do you say? May the stars protect you? Something like that?"

"Something like that. May the living stars watch over you."

It was only after Bradamont had sealed the hatch behind her that Marphissa realized that she had not simply given Marphissa the correct phrase, but spoken the wish on her behalf as well. *Good luck, you Alliance scum. Come back safely to us.*

Several hours later, Bradamont called Marphissa from the freighter she was on. The freighters and their escorts had left the two heavy cruisers behind, plodding at the best rate the freighters could manage for the jump point for Varandal.

Bradamont looked unhappy. "The courier ship confirmed that Admiral Geary has not yet brought the fleet back through Atalia en route to Varandal. That's not unexpected since he had to go to Sobek, then transit a number of star systems and jumps before getting here, but it means we'll get to Varandal before he does. We can't wait around since it could be days or weeks before Admiral Geary makes it here hauling along that Kick superbattleship, which makes these freighters look like racing yachts by comparison. We'll continue on to Varandal."

Black Jack is taking longer to get back? Marphissa thought. *We did expect that. But I'm worried. The Syndicate wanted him to go to Sobek, and the Syndicate never plays fair. Ha! Listen to yourself. You're worried about the safety of an Alliance fleet.*

But I am. Things have changed.

COLONEL Rogero had been careful to act toward Bradamont only in the most professional and impersonal of ways. But once they returned to her tiny cabin on the freighter after sending her message to Kommodor Marphissa, alone with no one else around, he gave her a concerned look. "You're worried."

"I'm some Alliance officer that you never met before, remember? You're not supposed to know me that well, Colonel," Bradamont replied with a small smile.

"But I do, Honore. Do you expect trouble in Varandal?"

"I don't know," she confessed. "There shouldn't be. But. These freighters are Syndicate Worlds' construction. You and your soldiers are former Syndicate. Someone might throw up obstacles."

"What are you still not saying?" Rogero pressed.

"Oh, hell, why do I try to lie to you?" She sat down on the single chair in the cramped cabin. "You're the senior officer. You may have to sign for the released prisoners. And you're . . ."

"A man in whom your intelligence people might be interested?"

Bradamont nodded unhappily. "If they have files tying Colonel Donal Rogero to the Alliance source known as Red Wizard, they might insist on taking you into custody. They wouldn't call it that, but that's what they'd be doing."

"But what of you? What did Alliance intelligence call you?"

She rolled her eyes. "White Witch."

"Seriously?"

"Don't. Make. A. Joke."

"I wouldn't," Rogero protested. "But that means that Alliance intelligence might have a great deal of interest in you as well."

"Yes." She grimaced. "I'm going to need to communicate with Admiral Timbale. Admiral Geary provided me with some special codes I can use to do that. But it would be wise to avoid letting anyone else in Varandal know that I'm along for this ride. The wrong words in the right ears could cause me and you to be hauled off and detained, along with perhaps all six freighters. It's going to be interesting, Donal. And even though we're on the same ship, I can't even touch you."

"Our dreams kept us going for a long time. What's a little longer? Do you think that Alliance intelligence or the snakes can beat me and you together?"

Bradamont smiled and rendered him a casual salute in the Alliance style. "No, sir. We are going to get this done."

IT was hard leaving behind the light cruisers and HuKs when the freighters entered the jump for Varandal. They were, after all, not just jumping to an Alliance-controlled star system but one that was a military stronghold crawling with defenses. Even though the freighter supervisors and crews were not military and usually regarded Syndicate mobile forces as only one step better than Alliance warships when it came to rapacious threats, even they were rattled by the prospect of arriving at Varandal completely unescorted.

Colonel Rogero listened carefully to the conversations around him during the four days in jump space required to reach Varandal from Atalia. He tried to talk to the freighter supervisors about jump space, but they knew little of the theory behind it and the jump drives. Practical men and women, they knew how to keep their equipment working and what that equipment should do. But they didn't know whether jump space truly was a different universe in which no star or planet had ever formed and in which distances were much shorter than the human universe. It was something they went through to get where they needed to go within a reasonable period of time. That was all they needed to know.

He didn't have a lot of ground forces on each freighter, just a platoon per ship. As much room as possible had to be left open for accommodating freed prisoners. Rogero's troops were leery of Bradamont, but the knowledge that General Drakon had ordered her to be along on this mission (for that was what Rogero told them) led the soldiers to accept the odd presence of an unconfined Alliance officer among them.

Bradamont had also arranged to "accidentally" reveal in the presence of some of the soldiers the place on her arm where the Syndicate labor-camp mark was still visible. Anyone who had been through a labor camp and survived automatically earned some degree of sympathy and respect from those like Rogero's soldiers, who had lived under the Syndicate.

But now that period of waiting was coming to an end. Rogero had escorted Bradamont to the cramped bridge of the freighter, where the freighter executive waited with ill-concealed nervousness for the exit from jump space.

"They won't shoot?" the freighter executive asked Bradamont for the third time despite her having said *no* the first two times.

"Probably not," she replied on this occasion, without visible concern. "If they do, we'll probably be able to make the escape pod before the ship blows up. We won't all fit, though, so I hope you're a fast runner."

Behind the freighter executive, Rogero grinned at Bradamont, but she kept a serious expression.

The drop out of jump space interrupted whatever reply the merchant executive might have mustered.

Two Alliance destroyers were within five light-seconds of the jump exit.

Rogero felt his breath catch as instinct born of a lifetime of war warned of serious danger.

But Bradamont gestured to him with an encouraging look, pointing to the freighter's transmitter. *All right. Let's see how good I am at talking to the Alliance.* "This is Colonel Rogero of the independent Midway Star System. We are here at the invitation of Admiral Geary, on a peaceful mission to recover prisoners of war from the Syndicate Reserve Flotilla. Please notify Admiral Timbale that we have information regarding Admiral Geary and the success of his mission, and would like to speak with him."

Bradamont made a quick warning gesture and Rogero managed not to speak his next intended words. "Rogero, out."

"I should have warned you earlier," she said. "Saying *for the people* would tag you as Syndics."

"They'll probably tag us as Syndicate, anyway. But, with any luck," Rogero commented, "they'll be curious enough about the information on Black Jack to avoid destroying us."

"They know that Admiral Timbale will be curious," Bradamont replied. "And they won't want to make him mad."

Rogero watched the freighter's limited display update, an apparently endless array of warships, support craft, civilian ships, repair facilities, and defensive installations popping up in fits and starts. "Black Jack isn't even here," Rogero murmured. "And look at all of it."

Bradamont heard. "There aren't that many warships present, and those here are cruisers and smaller."

"That's more than big enough for us to worry about," the freighter executive grumbled.

Less than thirty seconds passed before a reply came in from one of the destroyers. "This is Lieutenant Commander Baader of the Alliance destroyer *Sai*. Your status and your political allegiance are unknown to us, Colonel Rogero. You and your ships look Syndic."

Bradamont made an encouraging gesture, and Rogero tapped the controls again. "I am a colonel in the ground forces of the free and independent star system of Midway. My allegiance is to our President Iceni, and to my commander, General Drakon. We no longer answer to the Syndicate. The Syndicate is our enemy. We are at peace with the Alliance and have fought alongside your Admiral Geary at Midway."

This time almost a minute passed before Lieutenant Commander Baader's image once more appeared. "We have forwarded your message to Admiral Timbale, Colonel Rogero. Your freighters are to remain in this orbit until we receive clearance for you to proceed farther."

"More waiting?" Rogero asked.

"More waiting," Bradamont agreed. "They've bumped the matter upstairs, which was the smartest thing they could do."

Light crawled across the light-hours to the massive orbiting Ambaru station where Admiral Timbale had his headquarters, then crawled back. Awoken from a restless sleep by the freighter's second officer, Rogero returned to the bridge, collecting Bradamont along the way.

"This is Admiral Timbale." The admiral looked thoughtful as well as suspicious, which Rogero thought a good sign. "We would of course be happy to repatriate the Syndic prisoners currently held here, especially to representatives of a star system that has thrown off the Syndic yoke. But this is a delicate issue given the history between our two peoples. I will need to request guidance from higher authority. Your ships will have to wait here until I receive an answer, which will require at least two weeks."

Rogero looked over at Captain Bradamont, who made a face. "That was worst case," she said. "But now we have a transmission ID that I can send a reply to. Can this ship's comm gear handle a tight beam, secure, eyes only send?"

"It couldn't before we installed some upgrades for the mission to Taroa," Rogero replied. "That's not standard freighter comm gear. But to use the upgraded equipment we'll need to go to a compartment we rigged up for that."

He led her along the passageways of the freighter, nearly empty at this hour of ship's time, to a hatch leading into a small compartment which from the smells still lingering inside had once been used to store potatoes and onions. One of Rogero's soldiers maintained a lone watch over the equipment despite the unlikelihood of any messages coming in aimed at its parameters. "Are you going to send it in the clear?" Rogero asked Bradamont.

She held up a data coin. "This contains the necessary Alliance codes. Admiral Geary provided me with them in case I needed to send an encoded message through your channels."

"Very well." Rogero gestured to the comm operator. "Up and out."

The operator stood, saluted, and left the compartment without a word.

"Your people don't tend to ask questions," Bradamont observed as she sat down at the comm station.

"The Syndicate hierarchy frowns on workers asking questions," Rogero replied as he closed and locked the hatch. "For my soldiers, it's a lesson learned over a lifetime and not easily broken."

She looked at him for a moment, a brief smile showing. "You don't seem to have learned that lesson."

"No, and you saw what happened to me. I went from being ordered to labor-camp staff to being one step from becoming the occupant of a labor camp myself. If not for General Drakon, I would have probably died in one."

"Me, too," Bradamont said, her eyes back on the comm gear. "Until you told me, I never realized that he was the one who suggested to the snakes that our relationship could be used by them. If not for that, the snakes wouldn't have leaked the information about my transfer to another labor camp to the Alliance, so I could be liberated."

Rogero nodded. "He is a good man. He no longer believes he is a good man, but I believe it."

Another short pause as Bradamont looked at him. "Why? Why does Drakon have such an opinion of himself?"

"He was a CEO. To reach the ranks of a CEO, to survive in such a system, requires doing things that would eat the soul of any person. I have met all too many CEOs who showed no signs of missing their souls. General Drakon somehow retained most of his." Rogero tapped his chest. "But that means he also knows in his heart the wrongs he did."

"Ignorance is bliss," Bradamont muttered. "It was an ugly war. Has any war ever been anything but ugly? We all carry scars inside us from that."

"It wasn't just the war, Honore. It was the system. The Syndicate system. You ate others, or the system ate you."

She nodded, not looking at him this time. "But you got rid of that way of doing things. You're going to make a better way. If General Drakon and President Iceni don't screw it up." Bradamont sat back, running her hands through her hair. "It's ready for the transmission. How do I look?"

"More beautiful than ever."

Bradamont laughed. "It's a good thing we're alone in here."

"And an unfortunate thing that we can't stay alone in here long, and that it is so confining."

"Maybe that's a blessing in disguise. All right. Move over that way as far as you can. We want to be sure you don't show in the image."

Rogero scrunched over as far as he could, waiting.

Bradamont tapped a control, her eyes on the video pickup. "Admiral Timbale, this is Captain Honore Bradamont, formerly commanding officer of *Dragon*. Admiral Geary detached me from the fleet when it returned to Midway Star System and ordered me to serve as a liaison officer to the government and military there. Midway Star System is completely independent of the Syndicate Worlds. It has a stable government that is pursuing a more democratic course and has assisted nearby star systems in throwing off Syndicate Worlds' authority. Their warships assisted our fleet in the most recent battle there against the enigmas. They need the personnel from the Reserve Flotilla to crew warships that are under construction to defend them against attempts by the Syndicate Worlds to reconquer the Midway Star System.

"Admiral Geary's fleet is on its way back from Midway but was delayed by Syndic interference. I don't know exactly what he has run into, but we have learned that the Syndics have a means for temporarily blocking use of their hypernet. That forced Admiral Geary to take his fleet to Sobek. He is doubtless proceeding homeward from there but may have run into Syndic opposition despite the peace agreement. The fleet took considerable combat damage fighting our way through enigma space, during combat with a second alien species, and when defeating a renewed enigma assault on Midway Star System. It is also burdened by the presence of a captured alien warship, which is being brought back to Alliance space, and six ships belonging to a third alien species, which seeks friendly relations with us.

"I can provide you with further information regarding Admiral Geary's successful mission, but given the extreme sensitivity of the information and my assignment by him to duty at Midway, I do not want it known that I am back at Varandal. Fleet headquarters would surely negate my orders from Admiral Geary as a liaison officer, order me to report to them and provide them with all I know regardless of how Admiral Geary wants to present that information upon his return.

"I am, of course, subject to your orders here. But my interpretation of Admiral Geary's orders to me is that I should do my utmost to ensure those prisoners of war are returned to Midway Star System, and thereafter continue to monitor the situation there and provide whatever reports I can back to Alliance authorities. I respectfully request that we undertake as soon as possible a transfer of all Syndic prisoners of war in this star system to the freighters under Colonel Rogero's command.

"Captain Bradamont, out."

Rogero waited until Bradamont had cut the connection before saying anything. "That ought to be a wide-awake call when he gets it."

"Oh, yeah."

Rogero eyed her a moment longer, wondering if he should ask the next question, but finally decided to do so. "Do you believe it? What you said about President Iceni and General Drakon."

She returned his look. "What did I say? You mean that your government is stable and undertaking democratic reforms? As far as I can tell, it is."

"What do you think of President Iceni?"

"Are you collecting intelligence on me for your boss, Colonel Rogero?" Bradamont asked. Her tone was light, but there was a real challenge in her eyes.

"No. I want to know what you think. I won't tell anyone else."

She paused, frowned, then looked at him. "I think she is one very tough bitch. And I mean that in a good way."

"You can mean that in a good way?" Rogero asked. "So, you think she really will do things for the people?"

"Yeah, I do. Don't get in her way. I think people who get in Iceni's way regret it big-time."

"What about her primary assistant? That man Togo."

Bradamont shook her head. "He's a cipher to me. I haven't seen enough of him. Now, you answer something for me about your General's two assistants."

Rogero laughed. "What a pair, eh? But they are very, very good at what they do, Honore. Individually, each is impressive. Together, they give General Drakon the type of support that equals another brigade of troops, if not more."

"Do they hate each other as much as it seems?"

"More," Rogero said. "Morgan had been here a few years when Malin showed up. Instant, mutual hatred. Too much alike if you ask me."

"Alike?" Bradamont questioned. "Those two?"

"Sure. They just handle things differently. Morgan would laugh while she put a bullet in you. But she would have what she thought a good reason to do it. Malin would, maybe, feel a little sorry when he killed you in cold blood for what he thought was a good reason. But you would be dead, either way. I think they both have big plans. Very different plans, but plans that place them at the center of things."

Rogero paused. "There was an operation that both Malin and Morgan were on, to take an orbiting platform. This was right after we killed the snakes. It turned out the commander of the platform was a covert snake. While the snake was being killed, Malin put a shot so close to nailing Morgan in the back that it looked like he barely missed a chance to end their feud permanently. But the General didn't toss him out because that shot killed the snake right before she would have killed Morgan. Funny, isn't that? If Malin did try to kill her, he instead saved her life. If he did try to save her life . . . well, he saved her life! And she damned near killed him right after that because she thought he'd tried to kill her. Only the friendly-fire inhibits in her weapons saved Malin."

"I would not want to get on her bad side," Bradamont said.

"The entire universe is on Morgan's bad side," Rogero explained. "I don't know the details. Some special mission when she was young. The mission messed her up bad. There's only one person who has Morgan's undying loyalty. That person is General Drakon, who gave her a chance when no one else would."

"She's been nice to me," Bradamont said. "Respectful. It's a little scary."

Rogero felt a bit of a chill, too. "Morgan doesn't fake nice unless she has a reason. If she's acting that way, she thinks you are important to her. Or to General Drakon, which may be the same thing in her mind."

"Why does he keep her around?"

"Because he's trying to help her. And because General Drakon doesn't throw away people. And because if he fired her, sent her away, she would be dead within a month. She might take an entire planet with her when she died, but she wouldn't survive very long without General Drakon's guidance and support."

"That's tough," Bradamont said. "I take it if you ever said that to her, she would go completely berserk."

"Yes. Don't do that."

"Thanks for the advice." Bradamont stood up with a longing expression as she looked at him. "Now open that hatch before I lock it and have my way with you, or your soldiers try to break it down to save you from me."

"Alas, I can be free of the Syndicate, but I can never be free of you," Rogero said as he opened the hatch.

THEIR first reply to Bradamont's message came from the Alliance destroyers.

"You are to follow the attached vector in-system toward the vicinity of Ambaru station," Lieutenant Commander Baader informed Rogero. "All six freighters must conform to the indicated velocity and course. *Sai* and *Assegai* will accompany your ships to ensure that you remain on vector. Baader, out."

"Get moving," Rogero told the freighter executive. "Make sure the other ships do the same."

"Those Alliance destroyers aren't escorting us," the executive complained. "They'll stay close so they can blow us apart if we go off vector."

"Then don't go off vector."

Bradamont came by the bridge, waving at him. "Your comm watch says there's an incoming message using Alliance encryption."

"Let's go see what it says," Rogero said. He followed her to the tiny comm compartment, waited while the soldier on duty left, then pulled the hatch shut. The small size of the compartment meant that he had to stand near Bradamont, but that wasn't exactly a hardship.

"Captain Bradamont, this is Admiral Timbale. I am, needless to say, surprised." Timbale gazed out from the comm display as if he could actually see Bradamont in real time. "That's good news about Admiral Geary's being on his way back and having successfully completed his mission. And that's bad news about the Syndics being able to play games with the hypernet. I want to know everything you can tell me about what has happened to Admiral Geary and his fleet since they left Varandal. Do I understand correctly that three intelligent nonhuman species have been discovered? That is remarkable.

"You've given me all of the reasons I need to hand over those prisoners. I've wanted to get rid of them for some time, but no one would take them." Timbale scratched one cheek, his eyes on something beside him. "I've got five thousand two hundred and fifty-one Syndic prisoners here. Most of them from that Reserve Flotilla, but several hundred from other sources. Can you take them all? Let me know as soon as possible. If we have to sort out the Reserve Flotilla survivors from the others, it might take a while.

"Now, the hard part. There has to be a physical transfer of custody," Timbale insisted, tapping one finger on his desk for emphasis. "There's no exception allowed under these circumstances. Someone has to be handed the agreement and make a legally binding statement of acceptance *in my presence*. Needless to say, I can't go to the Syndics. To the people of Midway, rather. The symbolism would be very bad since they still look too much like Syndics. One of them, their senior officer, has to come to us, has to arrive at Ambaru station so we can meet the physical requirements for turnover of the prisoners."

"Damn," Bradamont muttered.

"That would be me," Rogero said. "Can I trust Timbale?"

"Yes. He wouldn't approve of trapping you, not when you're here at Admiral Geary's behest. He'd give me some sort of subtle sign that everything wasn't on the up and up."

"I'm aware of the risk to Colonel Rogero that this might entail," Timbale continued. "By the way, the fact that they've started using military ranks instead of the Syndic executives and CEOs thing really helped me make up my mind to agree with this. Nonetheless, legally, I have to cover my butt on the transfer, or compliance officers might throw up obstacles that will put a stop to the transfer for who knows how long. We'll keep the meeting as low-profile as possible, which won't be much. Some word will leak out, especially among the civilians in the dock area when it actually goes down, but I'll have plenty of Marines there to provide security on the dock."

"You can't ask for better than that," Bradamont said.

"Alliance Marines?" Rogero asked. "Is the prospect of being surrounded by Alliance Marines supposed to comfort me?"

"They're damned good fighters, Donal!"

"I know! I've fought them! That's why the idea of being surrounded by them does not make me feel better!"

Timbale was finishing up. "It will take those tubs you're riding a while to get close to Ambaru. Not too close, mind you. No one wants Syndic-origin freighters getting within danger range of this station. But the time required for your trip will give me time to get those prisoners up here and ready to shuttle over to you. Timbale, out."

Bradamont gave Rogero a demanding look. "Can I tell him we're good with this?"

"*We're* good with it? I'm the one who is going to have set foot on that station. What is Alliance intelligence going to do when they hear that Colonel Donal Rogero is literally on their doorstep?"

"First," Bradamont insisted, "they have to figure out that the Midway Colonel Rogero is the same as Sub-CEO Donal Rogero of the Syndicate Worlds' ground forces. Second, if they do, the Marines will be there. Third, if somehow Alliance intelligence does get its hands on you, I will personally go onto that station and get you back no matter what it takes. I will not have you treated here as I was by the Syndics even if I have to do things that neither Admiral Timbale nor Admiral Geary would approve of."

Rogero looked at her and felt himself smiling. "How was it you characterized President Iceni?"

"What? Why did you bring that up?"

"No reason. Tell your Admiral Timbale that I'll be there."

She gave him another look, this one suspicious, then hit the send command. "Admiral Timbale, thank you. I will provide what I can via this message about Admiral Geary and our activities in alien-controlled space. Before I begin, Colonel Rogero has agreed to the physical turnover of prisoners aboard Ambaru. I assured him that there would be no danger to him when you had promised his safety. I must, however, inform you that it is very likely that Colonel Rogero has a high-priority flag on his files in our intelligence system. It is purely an intelligence matter. It has nothing to do with his actions in the war. You have my word of honor, sir, that it is *not* a war-crimes flag.

"Here is a summary of what Admiral Geary's fleet encountered . . ."

AFTER a long, plodding voyage that was the best the freighters could manage, they were close enough to Ambaru station, within a few light-seconds, for the communication delays to be almost unnoticeable. "Believe it or not, Captain Bradamont," Admiral Timbale said, "I have some qualms about turning some of these Syndics over to those Midway people. There's no doubt that at least a few of the prisoners are die-hard Syndicate Worlds' patriots. What will your Midway people do with them?"

"Are any of them snakes, Admiral?" Bradamont asked, exchanging a glance with Rogero.

"Snakes?"

"Syndic Internal Security Service."

"Oh, those guys. No. None of them are tagged with that."

Rogero leaned in. "Admiral Timbale, only ISS agents would face danger at our hands, and that is because of the blood of our people on their hands. Each of our freighters has a small ground forces unit aboard for security, so we need not fear actions by the Syndicate loyalists. We will drop off along the way to Midway anyone who does not want to join us."

Timbale paused, then spoke heavily. "Drop off? Admiral Geary has had some influence on me, Colonel. I would feel guilty if I turned over to you prisoners who were subsequently pushed out of air locks to get rid of them."

Rogero shook his head firmly. "We will not do that. General Drakon's orders."

"What's that?"

"We have orders not to kill prisoners. We will obey those orders, Admiral. Any prisoners released to us who do not wish to join with us will be delivered to one of the Syndicate-controlled star systems we pass through on our way home. *Safely* delivered."

Timbale studied Rogero, then nodded. "Very well, Colonel. The first shuttle is on its way to the freighter carrying you. Ride it back here, and we'll get this done. Don't worry, I'm not going to wait for the completion of the physical turnover before we start shoveling Syndic prisoners at you. Make sure those freighters are ready to take a lot of prisoners and take them fast."

Bradamont spoke warily. "Are there any grounds for concern, Admiral? Any security threats?"

"I don't have ironclad control of every unit in this star system, Captain. Not even close. So far, I've presented a very carefully tailored account of what's going to happen to everyone. But at some point, some of the Alliance military forces that don't answer to me might get orders from some other high-ranking officer to do things that you and I and Colonel Rogero wouldn't like at all, especially given what you told me about possible Alliance intelligence interest in Rogero. The faster we get this done, the better."

"That does not sound good," Rogero said after Timbale had signed off.

"No," Bradamont agreed. "Get in, get out, get back here in one piece."

"I'll do my best."

CHAPTER THIRTEEN

HE had entered Alliance orbital installations before. He had done so wearing combat armor, at the head of soldiers, fighting against defenders sometimes frantic and sometimes determined, but almost always tough. In Colonel Rogero's mind, the thought of an Alliance orbital installation conjured up images of torn metal, smoke filling those passageways not open to vacuum, and death walking all about him as attackers and defenders fought and bled.

It felt unreal now to step from a shuttle, an *Alliance* shuttle, onto the clean, smooth surface of an undamaged loading dock, out into an open passageway beyond.

But Alliance Marines waited there, armed and armored for combat, though their face shields were open in a small gesture of peace. Despite the open face shields, the Marines' weapons looked to Rogero as if they were all powered-up and ready to fire, which did nothing for his peace of mind. Alliance Marines in combat armor aroused some very unpleasant memories for him. But he remembered that Honore Bradamont had walked onto a former Syndicate warship, surrounded by former Syndicate officers and crew, to do her duty. *I can do no less than her.*

The Marine officer in command gestured wordlessly to Rogero, then led the way into a larger area where crowds of civilians were visible on either hand. The crowds were held back by more Marines as the numbers of civilians swelled rapidly. Apparently, word of his visit had spread quickly but only recently so that spectators were rushing to view the event.

Admiral Timbale waited in the center of the open area, standing stiffly as if on sentry.

As Rogero appeared among the ranks of the Marines, a low sound arose from the crowds, the murmur of many voices speaking at once so no one voice could be understood. He could not hear the words, but he could sense the feelings behind them. The crowds sounded . . . curious. He didn't wear a Syndicate uniform. He wasn't a prisoner. For so long the universe had been divided into two sides. You were Alliance, including the much lesser allies like the Callas Republic or the Rift Federation, or you were Syndicate. But Rogero looked like something else. Something new. What?

He wished he could be sure of the answer to that himself.

Rogero came to attention before the Alliance Admiral and saluted, bringing his right fist across to touch his left breast. Would the people here recognize that as a Syndicate-style salute? It had been at least fifty years since Syndicate personnel had been ordered never to salute Alliance officers, in one of the more petty lowerings of common courtesies and humanity that had characterized the war as it dragged on. Quite likely no one but prisoners of war would have seen Syndicate workers exchanging salutes.

Admiral Timbale, his eyes studying Rogero intently, returned the salute in the Alliance fashion, bringing up his right hand to touch his right temple. "Welcome aboard Ambaru station, Colonel Rogero of the independent and free Midway Star System." Timbale recited the words slowly and clearly, ensuring they could be heard by the crowds and entered into the official record exactly as he said them.

Bradamont had told him what to say, and now Rogero paused to be certain he recalled the words properly. "As an official representative of the independent and free Midway Star System, I express my thanks for your assistance in the . . . humanitarian mission in which I am engaged." It had been hard to say *humanitarian* without giving the word the usual Syndicate sarcastic lilt, but Bradamont had drilled him on it. "Admiral Geary has defended our star system and all of human-occupied space twice against the attacks of the enigma race. Our forces were honored to fight alongside his during the last engagement." *You have to mention Admiral Geary,* Bradamont had urged. *Tell them he accepted you as allies. And don't call him Black Jack. The Alliance people may call him that to your face, but you have to appear more respectful.* "We hope this is just the beginning of a new chapter in our relations with the people of the Alliance."

Another murmur of conversation arose from the crowd. It still didn't sound threatening, but it didn't sound welcoming, either. Skeptical, perhaps. Well, he couldn't hold that against them. He had his own share of skepticism about working with the Alliance. The countless dead in the very-long and only-recently-ended war would stand between him and these people for long years to come.

An officer just behind Timbale stepped up next to him and offered a data pad. Timbale took the pad, looked over the screen, then offered it in turn to Rogero.

Rogero read the screen carefully even though it appeared to contain the same wording as the agreement previously sent to him. He touched the record tab, activating the pad. "I, Colonel Donal Hideki Rogero, as an authorized and appointed representative of Gwen Iceni, President of the Midway Star System, accept full custody of the former prisoners from Syndicate Worlds' military forces held by the government of the Alliance in the Varandal Star System, and agree to abide by the terms of the agreement set forth here."

Timbale took back the data pad, passing it to his aide, who stepped back again, then looked Rogero over once more. "A hundred years of hate," Timbale said in a low voice, "is not easily overcome."

"Yet we must," Rogero said, "so that the next generation has a chance to live without that hate."

"True enough, but if you still wore a Syndic uniform, I'd be hard-pressed to believe you meant it." Timbale nodded toward the crowd. "They've been told that Admiral Geary supports your government, so they're willing to listen. Tell your leaders not to blow that chance. The people of the Alliance may not listen a second time if they get betrayed again."

"I understand." Rogero saluted once more. "For the people." Remembering Bradamont's comments, he made the words sound as if they really did mean something, which drew a skeptical look from Timbale.

"To the honor of our ancestors," Timbale replied, returning the salute again. "Perhaps—" he began.

A bustle of noise and activity drew their attention. Rogero saw a large number of Alliance soldiers in uniforms he recognized. Elite commandos. They were coming this way as fast as they could push through the crowds.

Timbale spun to face the Marine officer. "Get him back to his shuttle. Now. Make sure he gets aboard and the boarding hatch is sealed. Block anyone from reaching him."

The Marine hastily saluted, then he and the other Marines began quickly herding Rogero back to the dock entry. Rogero felt a curious reluctance to retreat like this. Part of him wanted to turn and face those commandos. Face them down, fight them, as he had more than once.

But that would be foolish, and senseless. He couldn't win. It would imperil his mission.

And if he were captured by those commandos, he did not doubt that Honore would live up to her promise to come after him, no matter the cost to her. That decided him.

The Marines formed a solid wall in the passageway behind Rogero as he reached the dock. Their armor alone made a formidable barrier, in addition to which most of the Marines were facing outward, weapons held at a port arms position in a nonthreatening but obvious way. He could hear Admiral Timbale ordering the commandos to stop, orders that were being repeated, which meant they likely were not being obeyed. There was no telling how much time he had, or what the Alliance Marines would do when the commandos reached them. But Rogero still paused long enough to look into the eyes of the Alliance Marine officer, one professional to another, one veteran to another. "Thank you."

The Marine looked back, his face expressionless but his eyes both hostile and puzzled. Then the hostility cleared a small amount, and the Marine nodded to acknowledge the words.

No more than that, but it was something.

Rogero walked quickly up the ramp and onto the shuttle, hearing the hatches sealing behind him.

"Strap down fast!" the pilot called over the intercom. "I've got direct orders from the admiral to blast out of here!"

He had barely gotten into a seat before acceleration pressed Rogero back hard enough to drive the breath from him. He managed to get the straps fastened as the shuttle swung wildly from side to side and up and down as if following a roller-coaster track through space. *Pilots. They're all crazy. This one is probably enjoying tearing out from the station and whipping through all of the traffic around us even though we're probably avoiding swift death by only centimeters at times.*

Bradamont had been right. The ground forces here had attempted to intervene, had doubtless aimed to detain him. Perhaps the intelligence service of the Alliance had prompted that, recognizing Rogero with certainty when he had recited his full name for the turnover ceremony. But Bradamont had also been right that Timbale was to be trusted.

I was protected by Alliance Marines, Rogero realized. *They defended me. No one will believe it.*

I'm not sure I believe it myself, and I was there.

Rogero looked toward the display positioned near his seat, wondering if he was allowed to touch it. All it showed now was an outside view, stars and other bright objects glittering against the black of space, the dots of light blurring into streaks as the shuttle spun onto new vectors. The shuttle rolled again, and the small disc of a not-too-distant planet spun across the display, bottom to top before vanishing again.

"There's a lot of shuttles out," the pilot suddenly said, startling Rogero. "From the markers on them, they're loaded with personnel. Must be your guys."

Once again, Admiral Timbale is true to his word. He did order the movement of the prisoners begun while I was still on the way to the station to see him.

What exactly happened on the station? Why would Alliance military personnel refuse to obey the orders of a senior officer, even if he was of the fleet and they of the ground forces? No Syndicate worker would have defied orders from a CEO because the CEO was not their assigned supervisor.

But if a snake CEO had ordered an action, other CEOs would have had a hard time stopping it.

There's a stench of political maneuvering here. I didn't expect it in the Alliance. Despite what Honore has told me, I thought they would be fanatically pure in their dedication to only military issues. Not like us, riddled with politics. Most of the Syndicate, or now former Syndicate, officials that I know felt like that. Strange that we should have believed our foes to be superior to us in such a way. I feel strangely disappointed. If we had to lose, why couldn't the enemy who beat us have been superhuman?

"Thank you," he said to the pilot. "How long until we reach my ship?"

No response came, the pilot perhaps already regretting volunteering information. Or perhaps the pilot had suddenly remembered who his passenger was.

Any thrill that came from the wild ride had long since subsided by the time the shuttle began braking hard. Fortunately, the rough-and-tumble shuttle trip had also eased off as they got farther from Ambaru. Rogero gripped the armrests tightly as the braking maneuver went on and on, then abruptly ceased. A few moments later, a gentle bump announced their arrival at the air lock of the freighter. A fast approach, one long burn, and a gentle arrival with no last-minute thrust adjustments. The pilot was showing off, even under these conditions. Rogero grinned, heady with relief. "Well done!" he called to the pilot. "You're good."

As he headed for the air lock, the pilot offered a single word in reply. "Thanks."

Rogero had no sooner left the lock and stepped onto the freighter than he felt the shuttle disconnect.

Lieutenant Foster, the commander of the platoon of Rogero's soldiers aboard this freighter, was standing by with several of his troops. "We were told the first load of prisoners would be here within minutes, sir," he explained.

"Get them in and moved away from the air lock," Rogero ordered, trying to adjust emotionally to the rapid transition from being surrounded by the Alliance to now being back among his own soldiers. "Fast, clean, no holdups. Any questions?"

"No, sir."

More than five thousand to pack onto six freighters. They would be stacked in the passageways as well as the Spartan living quarters, and there wasn't time to do an elegant job of the stacking.

The air lock opened again. Men and women began coming onto the deck of the freighter, all of them wearing faded Syndicate uniforms that bore the marks of amateur repairs of rips and tears as well as burn marks. They looked healthy enough, but their eyes bore the wariness and resignation of those who had spent their lives expecting nothing but worry and uncertainty. Rogero knew that look. Most workers under the Syndicate had it though they disguised it as best they could.

"Welcome," Rogero said, using his voice of authority. "We are here to take you back to Midway. You are no longer prisoners of the Alliance."

A woman in the dilapidated outfit of a senior line worker straightened and spoke to him in the tones expected of a worker. "Honored CEO—"

"I am not a CEO. I was a sub-CEO. Now I am a Colonel in the ground forces of the independent star system of Midway. You know us. Now, obey instructions. We must get everyone on board as quickly as possible."

Looking more dazed than ever, murmuring among themselves, the freed prisoners followed one of the soldiers down the passageway.

Lieutenant Foster watched them come off the shuttle with growing amazement. "How many are on there?"

"As many as the Alliance could safely fit," Rogero said. "They have little with them but the clothes on their backs. No luggage, no bulky garments or survival suits, so each individual doesn't take up much room."

The next hour was a blur as shuttle after shuttle docked, discharged its passengers, then pulled away to make room for the next, while Foster's platoon labored to move the freed prisoners away from the air lock and get them packed in somewhere to make room for the next load. The sense of urgency from the Alliance shuttles was easy to pick up, but as load after load accumulated, the process began slowing down as people clogged the passageways on the freighter. Even though the freed workers were trained to unquestioning obedience, they were disoriented and confused, many looking around as if awaiting the moment when they would wake up from this dream.

"Move!" Rogero bellowed at one group that had unaccountably stopped dead, completely clogging a major intersection of passageways. As the workers bolted into motion like frightened deer, he heard his name being called.

"Donal!"

Colonel Rogero recognized the man and woman pushing their way toward him, but he had to search his memory for a moment to place them. Sub-CEO Garadun and Executive Ito. From . . . a battle cruiser. He couldn't remember which one. They had met several times at official meetings and official social events related to those meetings. Not that social events were casual or that he had learned all that much about the other Syndicate officials he met there, including these two. Everyone at official social events assumed there would be covert snakes salted through the attendees, not to mention plenty of surveillance gear, all listening for any hint of disloyalty. Official Syndicate social gatherings did usually have unlimited, free drinks, but since that was aimed at getting people drunk enough to blurt out compromising statements, wise citizens limited their intake. It all made for "casual" gatherings that were extremely formal, everyone watching their actions and words, as well as the actions and words of those around them.

Garadun stopped before Rogero, his face split by a huge grin. "Then it's true! You came for us! For once the ground forces have bailed out the mobile forces!"

"We're from BC-77D," Ito said, coming to a halt beside Garadun. "in case you don't remember. A lot of our crew got off when the unit was destroyed, and they're with us now." She was smiling almost as widely as Garadun. "Is it true? The Syndicate government is gone?"

"Not gone," Rogero advised. "It still exists on Prime. But we've thrown them out of Midway."

"The snakes . . . ?"

"Dead. We took them down." Rogero heard pride in his voice as he said that. Well, why not? It was true.

Garadun and Ito exchanged glances. "It's obvious you've got ground forces. Do you have any mobile forces?" Garadun asked.

"Why do you think we're here? We need trained crews."

"How did you know to come here?" Ito asked. "How did you know any of us were alive?"

Rogero cleared his throat before speaking to buy a few seconds. "How much do you know? About what happened after . . ."

"After we were captured?" Garadun said. "Not much. The Alliance guards claim that the war is over, that they won. Maybe they did. We didn't believe them, but we don't know. Since you're here to get us, maybe we won."

"They won," Rogero said. "Black Jack."

Ito shook her head, her eyes dark. "He is not human. A demon. He has to be."

"He saved us," Rogero blurted out, seeing the shock on their faces. "After he broke the Syndicate government and forced an end to the war. He led his fleet to Midway and threw back an enigma attempt to take over the star system."

"He beat the enigmas?" Garadun stared at Rogero.

"A demon," Ito repeated.

It was not a good time to bring up the complicated events that had led the infamous Black Jack to be the savior of Midway Star System, Rogero thought. "Anyway, the Syndicate government failed. The Syndicate way of doing things failed. It all failed. President Iceni and General Drakon are running things at Midway now. We are free." He saw the reactions to the word "free" and smiled again. "We've got an escort waiting at Atalia. Cruisers and destroyers loyal to us and commanded by Kommodor Marphissa—"

"Kommodor?" This time Garadun shook his head. "The name Marphissa isn't familiar to me."

"She was an executive on a heavy cruiser. Clearing out the Syndicate loyalists left some big gaps in the chain of command and improved promotion opportunities. Listen, we have very limited ability to screen all of you. What can you tell me about the physical condition of everyone? Most of those we're picking up in seem to be in good health. I'm not spotting any old, untreated injuries." He didn't have to explain why he had looked for those. In a Syndicate labor camp, something like that was routine.

Garadun looked away, glowering.

Ito gave him a sympathetic glance, then nodded to Rogero. "The Alliance scum took good care of us, much as we hate to admit it. Nothing great. Bland food, but enough of it. Some cleanup duties at the camp where we were held, but no hard labor. Medical care when needed, though nothing but what was needed. They treated us as prisoners, but we weren't abused."

"It was Black Jack," Garadun grumbled. "The guards talked about him. He crushed our flotilla, he killed so many of our friends, and yet we owed decent treatment to him. We're fine, Donal. You shouldn't find any serious health problems." He focused on Rogero skeptically. "There are no CEOs? You said Iceni and Drakon are still running things."

"Not as CEOs." Rogero nodded to the personnel streaming past. "They sent us to get you. Very risky, very expensive, but they sent us to get you."

That went home. The casual callousness of Syndicate leaders toward workers and junior executives was simply taken for granted. "I guess if they did that, they aren't just CEOs with different titles," Garadun remarked.

"What do you need us to do?" Ito asked.

"Help keep things under control. Keep people moving. We have to cram ten kilos of workers into a five-kilo bag. After that, we've got a long ways back. Sort out anyone who wants to stay loyal to the Syndicate. We'll drop them off in a Syndicate-controlled star system. Are there any snakes among you?"

"Oddly enough," Ito commented with a gentle smile at odds with the lack of feeling in her voice, "none of the snakes with our flotilla survived."

"Good." Rogero stopped speaking as silence fell around him. He saw Garadun and Ito staring behind him and turned to see Brada-mont there. She had been in the comm compartment, out of sight. Only something urgent would have brought her out.

"Admiral Timbale says we need to leave as soon as possible," Brad-amont reported. "A courier ship has left the star system. Timbale sus-pects that he may be relieved of command when it returns."

"We're already getting everyone on board as quickly as we can," Rogero agreed. "Sub-CEO Garadun, Executive Ito, this is Captain Brad-amont of the Alliance fleet. She is the official Alliance liaison officer to President Iceni and General Drakon."

Garadun and Ito were still staring at Bradamont, their expressions like stone.

Bradamont faced Rogero. "Do you require anything else, Colonel Rogero? If not, I will continue to monitor the situation and inform you of any significant developments."

He barely suppressed a grin. Bradamont's statement had sounded very much like a subordinate reporting to a superior. She had done that on purpose, establishing before these others that he was in charge here. "No, Captain Bradamont, I do not require anything else. Keep me informed."

As Bradamont left, Rogero gestured to Garadun and Ito. "She's the only Alliance citizen on any of these ships."

"She's answering to you?" Garadun asked in a disbelieving voice.

"That's right." Rogero paused to slap the nearest comm panel. "Ex-ecutive Barchi," he called to the freighter's commander, who was on the ship's bridge. "Tell the other ships to ensure they are getting people aboard as fast as they can move them. The moment we have the last individual off the last Alliance shuttle, we are heading for the jump point at the best acceleration these ships can manage."

As he finished, Ito came close, grasping Rogero's chin to stare into his eyes. "Donal, is this real? You haven't been turned? This isn't some sick Alliance trick to break our morale, where just as we're about to leave this star system, they'll jump out of the bulkheads to tell us it was all a game to mess with our heads? Is this real, Donal? Is that Alliance officer really doing what you say and have you told us what is really going on at Midway?"

Rogero gazed back into Ito's eyes. "It is all true. You're going home. We're going to jump for Atalia as soon as we can reach the jump point, and there you'll find Kommodor Marphissa's flotilla waiting for us."

Ito nodded and let her hand fall. "Even a CEO couldn't lie that well. Keep that Alliance bitch away from our people, though. There's no telling what they might do."

Rogero stiffened. He could let the words pass, and after all they were what any Syndicate citizen would have said, but this was Bradamont. "Executive Ito, that officer, that Alliance Captain, is the only reason we are here. She told us of you, she helped convince our leaders to send this mission, she helped us get here, and she convinced her own leaders to release you to us. *Her* fleet, *her* people, took losses defending our homes from the enigmas. During the war, she was captured and spent time in a Syndicate labor camp. Yet she fought for *us*."

Neither one wanted to hear it, but Garadun finally answered in a gruff voice. "A labor camp? All right. As long as she answers to you."

Ito was watching Rogero closely. "Yes. Since it seems to be important to you."

"Colonel Rogero?" Lieutenant Foster sounded worried as he pushed through the crowd toward him. "We need you to talk to the Alliance shuttle pilots. There's some problem with timing between deliveries. And, sir, there's another Alliance destroyer on an intercept with us."

Rogero nodded briskly to Garadun and Ito, dashing off with gratitude for the interruption. Ito had plainly sensed that his opinion of Bradamont was not purely a professional matter.

He reached the small command deck of the freighter and squeezed in near Foster and Executive Barchi. "Where's the destroyer?"

Barchi pointed. "Here. There's its track. It will be here in about half an hour if I'm reading this right."

"What happened to the other two? *Sai* and, uh . . ."

"*Assagei.* They headed back for the jump point a few hours ago."

"Velocity . . ." Rogero muttered, trying to find that data. He was used to displays for ground equipment, not those for spacecraft. "There it is. Point zero three light. Is that fast?"

Barchi made a dismissive gesture in response to Rogero's question. "On a planet? Fast as hell. Up here? A mobile forces unit? He's loafing along."

"He's not in a hurry?" Rogero pressed.

"A ship like that, they don't think anything of ramping up to point zero five light or point one light," the executive explained. "He's taking his time. But then, he knows we can't outrun him. Why rush when we're sitting ducks? Even if we bent on full acceleration, he could catch us within an hour or so."

Rogero kept his eyes on the display, not wanting to look at the freighter executive who simply accepted his helplessness. Rogero had always been in the ground forces, always been able to fight or run or perhaps fight and run. It was easy to forget how things were for those without weapons or speed to serve them. Men and women like this freighter executive, who had spent the years of the war knowing that if the enemy appeared, they had no good options, no chances unless distances were great enough or the freighter too small a prize for the enemy to bother with. Without them and the cargoes they hauled between stars and planets, the war could not have continued, but they had always been prey in that war. It was a strange and ugly irony.

He called down to the tiny comm compartment, where Bradamont had again taken up her watch. "Captain, there is an Alliance destroyer on its way to intercept us."

"I'll see what I can find out," Bradamont called back. "What's her velocity?"

"Point zero three light."

"That's all? What are the Alliance shuttles doing?"

"Still off-loading."

"They'd break off if there was impending action. Let me know if any start heading away before off-loading."

Lieutenant Foster had relaxed since Rogero arrived. Someone of higher authority was here to make the decisions, and Rogero knew his soldiers had confidence in him. *I earned that confidence the hard way. But now I'm putting on an act for the lieutenant and everyone else. Calm. Confident. Everything may be hectic, but otherwise it's fine. Except if that Alliance warship comes in shooting, we're all dead.*

"Colonel Rogero?" Bradamont's voice had rarely been so welcome.

"Here."

"Destroyer *Bandolier* is being sent to provide close escort for us. Admiral Timbale is increasingly concerned that someone might try to interfere with the prisoner transfer or try to board one or more of the freighters. He's also going to send the light cruiser *Coupe* over to us. They have orders to accompany us until we jump for Atalia."

"Thank you, Captain," Rogero said, trying to sound as dispassionately professional as possible in a this-woman-is-merely-a-fellow-officer manner. *Someone might try to interfere? The Alliance ground forces people. Or maybe their intelligence branch. Or maybe other people I don't even know about. I hope Admiral Timbale can keep them off our backs.* "That's it, then," he told Lieutenant Foster. "We're getting an escort."

"An escort?" Foster asked. "Alliance mobile forces are going to escort us?"

"I know it feels strange. Think how strange it will feel for them."

"More likely," Executive Barchi grumbled, "they'll be along to nail us immediately if we do anything suspicious."

"We won't do anything suspicious. Let's get those people aboard our ships and get out of this star system."

"Yes, sir!" Foster agreed.

There wouldn't be any need to motivate everyone to keep working quickly. Not this time. Nobody wanted to stay here, where the Alliance ruled and evidence of Alliance military power loomed with deadly menace on all sides.

"Um, Colonel?" the freighter executive asked, sounding and looking like the bearer of bad news. "My line workers say we've got a problem in the internal communications. Some of that new stuff you installed seems to be interfering with it, so if you need to talk to anybody inside this ship before we get it sorted out, you'll need to send a runner."

Rogero's immediate frown caused the executive to look a lot more nervous. "Are external comms impacted at all?"

Lieutenant Foster was already shaking his head when the executive answered. "No. No. No problem there. It's your external comm gear that is somehow interfering with internal comms. We could probably fix the internals really fast if we shut down the externals for a few—"

"We can't afford to lose external comms," Rogero said. "Not for any length of time." Not being able to talk to the Alliance shuttles and the other freighters would be a major problem, but a temporary loss of internal communications in this freighter was only annoying, not serious. "Let me know as soon as internal comms are fixed."

The executive nodded with visible relief that Rogero's response hadn't been worse.

"Lieutenant Foster, with internal comms down, I want you to check on conditions personally and report back here."

Foster saluted and rushed off.

Another shuttle came and went. Another shuttle docked.

"How are we doing, Lieutenant?" Rogero asked, as Foster returned, looking like he had just run a race.

"We're tight, but there's room, sir. We can take more. No discipline problems."

"We're almost done," Executive Barchi reported. "Only two or three shuttle loads per freighter left to go. Another half an hour to forty-five minutes, and we can get the hell out of Dod."

"Just where is Dod?" Rogero asked, his eyes on the freighter's display.

"I dunno. Some star system nobody wanted to stay in, I guess. It's not even on the charts."

Rogero had barely begun to absorb the executive's good news when Bradamont burst onto the command deck. "What the hell happened to internal comms on this ship? Commandos have launched from Ambaru! We've got to get moving *now!*"

CHAPTER FOURTEEN

"COMMANDOS?" Rogero's eyes were going back to the display as he felt a surge of adrenaline hit. His body was shifting to combat mode without any prompting. "I can't see—"

Bradamont shook her head. "They're in stealth-configured shuttles. The best the Alliance has got. The sensors on these freighters wouldn't see them even if those stealth shuttles were doing loops around us."

"Admiral Timbale—"

"Is losing control of the situation! He still has the fleet units and the Marines responding to him, but both ground forces and aerospace forces in this star system are acting on orders from the generals in command of them. For the love of our ancestors, get these freighters moving!"

Rogero pointed to the display, letting his frustration fill his voice. "We've still got shuttleloads of personnel to get on board. Are you saying we have to abandon them?"

"How many?" Bradamont pushed people aside until she stood at the freighter's maneuvering controls. "Give me a minute." Her hands started flying over the controls and the display.

"She's setting up a maneuvering plan," Ito said. Rogero abruptly became aware that both Garadun and Ito had followed Bradamont onto the control deck, making it very crowded indeed. "She was trying to get up here and being blocked by our workers in the passageways so we came along and told everyone to clear a path. What do you know about her? Does she know mobile forces?"

"She was a battle cruiser commander."

"Alliance battle cruiser," Ito murmured. "Which one?"

"*Dragon*."

Bradamont looked over at him. "You can do this. Because these freighters accelerate at about the rate of glaciers going downhill on a good day, the Alliance passenger shuttles can keep up for more than half an hour. They can proceed along with us and off-load those remaining passengers before we build up enough velocity that they would have to break off. There's not much room for error, but we can do it."

Nonetheless, Rogero hesitated, thinking of those remaining loads of workers, of people who might find themselves watching freedom accelerate away from them when it had been almost within touching distance.

Ito pushed next to Bradamont, her eyes narrowed as she studied the display. "She's right. I'm rusty at this, but if the shuttle-performance levels she input are good, then it works."

"We have to go now," Bradamont insisted. "That doesn't mean we'll get clear. I don't know exactly where those commando shuttles are. It might already be too late. But if we don't start getting out of here immediately, then we have no chance of outrunning the commandos' shuttles. And if those commandos catch us, then your soldiers on these freighters will not stand a chance."

Running. Again. "Those commandos would not find my soldiers to be easy opponents," Rogero said, hearing the stiffness in his voice. "They would pay."

"I have no doubt of that, but you would still lose! There aren't enough of you. And how many of the people you've just picked up would die in the cross fire? I know how hard it is to turn your back on an enemy. *I know.* That's why you're in command, because General Drakon knew you would make the hard decisions when they were the right decisions."

Was it because Bradamont was making these arguments, or because he would have known the truth of those words regardless of who said them? Rogero nodded abruptly. "All right. Let's do it."

Ito hit some controls. "I've sent the maneuvering plan to all of the other freighters. You, you're the executive in charge of this freighter? Implement the plan. Get us moving."

Executive Barchi began slapping controls.

Rogero felt the freighter respond with an all-too-gentle nudge. "Lieutenant," he ordered, "tell the Alliance shuttles that we need to start leaving now. If any of them ask why, tell them it was orders from their admiral. Tell those shuttles to keep up until they've dropped off the last passenger. Tell the other freighters to redouble their loading speed. Get our people on board as fast as they can move them even if we have to pile the last load in the air locks."

Garadun was beside him, peering at the display. "Good thing these freighters were all pointed in the right direction already. It would have taken close to half an hour just to pivot them around one-eighty. Did she suggest that, too?"

"Yes," Rogero said, realizing only now just how important that piece of advice had been.

"She knows ships. I'll give her that," Garadun conceded. "Funny, you said the war was over, and here we are being chased by Alliance commandos."

"I guess they didn't get the memo." An old joke. How could he think of a joke right now?

"What is he doing?" Ito demanded to Bradamont, pointing to the display. "That Alliance destroyer."

"He was coming this way already," Rogero said. "To escort us back to the jump point for Atalia."

"He's *accelerating*," Ito pointed out caustically.

Tension levels ramped up even higher, suspicious looks aimed at Bradamont as she studied the movement of the Alliance warship.

Bradamont suddenly began laughing, drawing shocked looks from everyone. "*Bandolier* is moving to foul the approach of the commando shuttles. Look, she's not only accelerating but also bending her track a bit. Her vector is going to carry her short of us, but across the route that would have to be used by anything coming toward us from Ambaru. See that light cruiser? *Coupe* is doing the same though she's coming in from farther out. The commando shuttles can avoid them, but the extra maneuvering will slow them down a little."

"How do they know where the stealth shuttles are?" Garadun asked skeptically.

Bradamont shook her head. "I won't give you the details of how the Alliance tracks its own stealth equipment. I wouldn't expect you to give me details of how the Syndicate Worlds does it. But you know you can track your own gear, and so can we."

"Those warships are buying us time?" Rogero asked.

"A little. Not much, but hopefully enough."

He watched the data as the shuttle off-loads proceeded with now-frantic haste, and the vector data on the clumsy freighters showed them very gradually building up velocity, headed outward away from Ambaru station and toward the jump point for Atalia. But Rogero's mind was consumed by other matters as well. "How did you learn about the commando launches?" he asked Bradamont.

"Admiral Timbale warned us."

"I don't understand. Are you saying the Alliance forces here are working against each other? That some of them are not obeying orders?"

Bradamont nodded heavily. "I told you that. They're not obeying Admiral Timbale's orders. The Alliance military is badly fractured.

Force levels and funding are being chopped, and the different branches are fighting to keep as much as each of them can. The fleet and the Marines have the advantage of being firmly allied, while the ground forces and the aerospace forces distrust each other as much as they do the fleet and the Marines. Right now, in this star system, the ground forces commander and the aerospace forces commander are no longer working with the fleet commander, Admiral Timbale, even though he's supposed to be in overall command. I don't know what they think is happening, but they've been convinced to try to stop us."

She looked at Rogero, her expression bleak. "You know what the war did to the Syndicate Worlds. Do you think the Alliance paid less of a price? We won. That didn't replace the dead, repair the destruction, or pay the costs. The strains of the war tore apart the Syndicate Worlds. I don't know what those strains may yet do to the Alliance, but the military is as frayed as everything else."

Rogero's mind was filled with images of the revolt at Midway, Syndicate unit against Syndicate unit. "Are you talking fighting? Combat between Alliance forces?"

"No!" Bradamont seemed shocked at the suggestion. "I don't see any of the forces involved shooting at each other. Not over this. Not over *anything*. But that means none of them will shoot to protect these freighters. The fleet units are trying to delay the commandos without engaging them, and doing it in a way they can claim was accidental. That is the best we can hope for."

"The fixed defenses," Garadun said harshly. "The Alliance must have a lot in this star system. Whose orders are they responding to?"

"Ground forces or aerospace," Bradamont answered. "But even these freighters can dodge shots fired from at least several light-minutes away. We'd be in trouble if we were heading for a site being defended, but we can avoid those."

"What about a barrage?"

Bradamont shrugged irritably. "That might be challenging. All we can do is try to dodge."

"We?" Ito asked.

"I'm aboard this ship, too."

Garadun gave Bradamont an appraising look. "Every one of these freighters has talented personnel on board, people who can make mobile forces dance to their tune. If we have to, we'll show the Alliance how it's done."

"When will we know we're clear of the commandos?" Rogero asked.

"When they don't get here," Bradamont answered. "If we started accelerating soon enough and can prolong their approach long enough, they'll have to turn back because of fuel constraints. They can't sustain a long tail chase. I'd guess that if they haven't caught up with us in an hour, we can breathe easier."

Rogero turned to Foster. "Lieutenant. All soldiers are to go to full-combat footing. Armor sealed and weapons powered. Threat is Alliance commandos boarding from stealth shuttles. As soon as the last passenger shuttle breaks free, all hatches on the freighters are to be sealed and guarded."

"The commandos are likely to be in stealth armor, too," Bradamont said. "And they can get in by other means than using hatches."

He looked at her, startled by the sudden catch in her voice, and saw that Bradamont looked as if she were physically ill.

She met his eyes. "They're Alliance," she said in a low voice.

Of course. Her own people. Bradamont was helping him prepare to fight those she had fought alongside. If the commandos boarded, some of them would die, and many if not all of Rogero's soldiers would die.

And, quite possibly, Rogero, too.

"You should go to your quarters," he told Bradamont. "It would be safer."

"I will not hide down there," she said. "I will be here if they enter this command deck."

He had to accept that because he knew she would not bend on it.

Ito gave him a speculative look, though, and glanced at Bradamont.

"The last five Alliance shuttles are mating for the transfer now," Lieutenant Foster said. "Their pilots are complaining about our acceleration."

"Just tell them to get our people off those shuttles," Rogero said. "As soon as the last is clear, they can head home."

"The shuttles are off-loading very quickly," Lieutenant Foster commented.

"Good old-fashioned fear-of-death motivation. It's the Syndicate way."

Everybody on the command deck but Bradamont laughed when Rogero repeated a joke that was old in the Syndicate Worlds, though the laughter held some nervousness as eyes kept straying to the display, as if the Alliance stealth shuttles would miraculously become visible on it.

"An hour?" Garadun asked Bradamont as he studied the freighter's acceleration rate with a disgusted look.

"That's just an estimate. I can't be certain."

"I hate being stalked by invisible enemies." His eyes grew shadowed by dark memories. "Like the enigmas. How did Black Jack beat them?"

"We found out they'd been messing with your sensors," Bradamont said. "Ours, too. Worms in the systems controlled what we saw whenever the enigmas wanted to be invisible."

"What kind of worms couldn't be found by our security scans?" Ito demanded.

"Quantum-coded worms," Bradamont replied. "Don't ask me how. I don't think anyone human has figured out how to do it, yet. But we figured out how to cancel them out."

"I suppose Black Jack figured that out, too?" Garadun said, his tone bitter.

"No. Captain Cresida. One of the battle cruiser commanders." Bradamont closed her eyes for a moment. "She died in the battle with your flotilla when her ship was destroyed."

Nobody said anything because there wasn't anything that could be said. Instead, they all watched the displays where the vectors of the freighters grew longer with agonizing slowness as the clumsy ships accelerated at the snail's pace that was the best they could manage.

After several minutes, Ito broke the silence. "Why are these commandos chasing us? Why do they want to recapture us? The Alliance guards never made any secret of the fact that they wanted to be rid of us."

"Some of them want you back because you might be leaving under circumstances they don't like," Rogero suggested. "It is also likely that they want me, specifically."

"Why?"

"Because," Rogero replied with the ease of someone taught to lie well by the demands of the Syndicate system, "I went to Ambaru station and am known as the one in charge. I then got away from them thanks to their Admiral Timbale. So they want me. They may also have records related to the months I spent as part of the staff of a Syndicate labor camp. That might make me a criminal in their eyes."

Garadun scowled in frustration. "No weapons to defend ourselves, lousy acceleration and maneuverability, and the best the Alliance has got coming for us. I've fought under better circumstances."

"Sir?" Lieutenant Foster asked. "Shouldn't we get some armor up here for us?"

Rogero shook his head. "Not until we've gotten those last shuttles off-loaded. Then you go join your unit. I'll stay here."

"But—"

"They want me, Lieutenant. There's no sense in everyone else's dying when I can—"

"Colonel Rogero," Bradamont interrupted, "they want you, but they'll hold the entire ship. You and everyone and everything on it. They won't just take you and let everyone else go on their way."

"I can take the escape craft—"

"If you eject, they'll assume you're trying to divert them from this ship for a reason. They'll leave you drifting in the escape pod to pick up at their leisure and keep coming for this ship and any other of the freighters they can catch." Bradamont took a quick breath. "I'm not just trying to save your butt, Colonel. If the commandos catch us, they will hold all of us indefinitely. The entire mission will fail. That's the best case if they catch us. In my estimation, there is a strong chance they will come in shooting because someone in their chain of command has decided that the whole independent-star-system bit is a trick, and everyone aboard these freighters are actually Syndics on some covert mission that violates the peace agreement. Stop thinking about ways to sacrifice yourself. None of them would do any good."

"What about you?" Ito asked Bradamont. "What happens to you if these freighters are taken?"

She made an angry, helpless gesture. "I have orders from Admiral Geary that justify my being here. I seriously doubt that would do me much good once I'm in the hands of the ground forces or aerospace forces under these circumstances." Bradamont looked at Rogero, her glance exchanging understanding of the matter they could not openly refer to, her and Rogero's involvement with both Syndicate snakes and Alliance intelligence.

He didn't know what to say, what would be safe to say, but Ito came to his rescue. "I know what the snakes would do to me if I they caught me on an Alliance ship helping them," she said.

"The last Alliance shuttle has finished off-loading," Lieutenant Foster cried out in relief, then immediately looked embarrassed at his outburst. "He is breaking free now. Our detachments on the other freighters report all personnel have been brought on board, all hatches are being sealed, and all soldiers report ready for action."

The Alliance shuttles dropped back quickly, pivoting around to head back to Ambaru for recovery and refueling. For a moment, as the shuttles accelerated in the opposite direction, there was an illusion of the freighters leaping ahead with a burst of speed, but the displays made it clear just what a fantasy that was. The velocity of the freighters was climbing, but with the same dogged slowness as before.

"Lieutenant Foster," Rogero ordered, "get your armor on and rejoin your unit."

As Foster rushed off of the freighter's bridge, he had to veer around the other people blocking him in the crowded and confined area. Bradamont stared after Foster, then her hands flew over the maneuvering planning system again. "Colonel Rogero, there's something else we can do. If the freighters use their thrusters to nudge them onto a different vector, the commando shuttles will change their intercept vectors to match. If we then thrust back in the opposite direction, it will force the commando shuttles to swing back."

"They'll lose ground?" Rogero asked. "And we won't slow down if we change the direction we're going?"

"No. Not for a change this minor. You're in space. We'd just be altering direction enough to force the commando shuttles to change their vectors. That means they'll have more ground to cover to reach us, which will take longer even though they won't slow down either."

"And if they're close," Garadun added, "it will mess up their final approaches. Five-degree course change?"

"Seven," Ito suggested.

Bradamont nodded. "We can do seven, even in these freighters, since we're not worried about how wide the turn would be. Up and to the left. That should maximize how much of a change the commando shuttles would have to make."

"What about that Alliance destroyer?" Executive Barchi demanded. "What's he going to do when we veer off our vector?"

"We're not veering far enough to threaten anything in this star system," Bradamont snapped at him. "Nor for long. And he's going to be under orders from Admiral Timbale to protect us. We'll be fine."

"Do it," Rogero ordered.

The orders went to the other freighters, and within seconds a slight pressure announced the thrusters on this freighter firing along with those on the other ships.

Was it working? The vectors of the freighters altered with agonizing slowness, but it was impossible for Rogero or anyone else to tell whether or not the commando shuttles were reacting as hoped. "Twenty minutes?" Ito asked, but directed the question to Bradamont rather than Rogero.

"That's as good a guess as any," Bradamont replied. "Were you a battle cruiser driver, too?"

"That's right." Ito turned a superior look on Rogero. "We're the best."

He just nodded in reply, only belatedly realizing that Ito had included Bradamont in that *we*. Shared danger could go a long way to breaking down barriers.

The freighter lurched slightly, causing Rogero to flex his hand as if it held the weapon still holstered by his side. *That's it. We didn't make it. That lurch must have marked a stealth shuttle making contact with the hull of this freighter. How long until the commandos reach this place on the ship?*

The others must have been asking themselves the same question, all except the freighter executive who was listening to something. "We got internal comms back," Barchi announced with a cheerfulness that shocked the others.

"Wonderful," Garadun muttered.

"Colonel," the executive continued, "can you tell your people not to shift crowds all at once? These units aren't made to deal with rapid changes in load locations."

Rogero squinted at the executive, unable to understand the man's apparent obliviousness. "What do you mean?"

"That lurch. Didn't you feel it? My workers say your people rushed a whole bunch of the ones we picked up over two compartments. That's a lot of mass to shift that fast."

"The lurch . . ." Rogero grinned, looking at the smiles breaking out on the faces of the others. "That's what it was?"

"Yes," Executive Barchi said, giving him a puzzled look. "Is that funny?"

"No. Not funny. Just very good news."

Bradamont, rigid with tension a moment before, had sagged against the maneuvering controls. "Five more minutes, then we'll swing back."

"Weaving?" The executive scratched his head. "We don't usually burn thrusters for no reason. That's money down the drain."

"We have a reason," Rogero assured him.

"Here comes that cruiser," Ito announced.

The Alliance light cruiser *Coupe* slid past astern of the freighters like a sleek shark cruising behind a pod of clumsy whales. Rogero watched the cruiser tear past, wondering if it was as close as it seemed to be to him.

Apparently it was. Ito shook her head. "If that cruiser came between us and the commando shuttles, they are way too close."

"Yes," Bradamont agreed. "Let's swing back now."

The orders went out, and the motion of the freighters up and to the left gradually slowed, stopped, then was replaced by a glacial sway to the right and down.

Five minutes. Ten. Twenty. "How long until we're clear?" Rogero asked.

"I don't know," Bradamont replied.

"The destroyer is coming back," Ito warned.

All eyes went to that warship on the display as *Bandolier* came in barely astern of the freighters. But instead of sailing past, the Alliance destroyer was braking, her main propulsion units flaring to bring the destroyer to a stop relative to the freighters and not very far behind them at all.

"What is she . . . ?" Bradamont began.

Bandolier's thrusters lit off. The warship was vastly more agile than the clumsy freighters, so her hull almost immediately began pivoting, still holding position just astern of the freighters. The bow came up and over and around, the entire ship pivoting in a circle as if it were a hand on a clock of ancient design.

"They're being fairly obvious about fouling the shuttles' approach, aren't they?" Garadun commented. He looked to Rogero as if Garadun couldn't decide whether to be admiring of the maneuver or amused by it but was too tense to do either. "They're very close astern as such things are measured in space."

"Meaning the commando shuttles are, too," Bradamont agreed, herself radiating nothing but tension. "Whatever *Bandolier* does next will tell us whether or not that last obstruction trapped the shuttles into an impossibly long stern chase."

The Alliance destroyer's bow finished spinning through a full three hundred sixty degrees.

Rogero realized that he was holding his breath, watching the Alliance destroyer, waiting to see what its next move would be.

Instead of continuing around again, *Bandolier* rolled and pivoted to one side, coming out pointed in the same direction as the freighters.

Bradamont nodded wearily. "That did it. They're just accompanying us now. I expect that *Coupe* will come back and join up with *Bandolier*."

Rogero felt the same sense of tiredness as his body finally relaxed. "They'll stay back there until we reach the jump point?"

"Once the commando shuttles give up the chase, there's a chance *Bandolier* and *Coupe* will maneuver around us, taking up different positions relative to the freighters, to make it hard for any fixed defenses to throw rocks at us without risking hitting them. That's what I would do."

"Thank you, Captain Bradamont," Rogero said. "I'm going to tell the soldiers on the other units to stand down and locate Lieutenant

Foster to tell him we can relax on this freighter. It would be a good idea for you to return to the comm compartment, where you can see if Admiral Timbale has sent any further messages."

She nodded, then, with a small smile, stood at attention and saluted him.

Rogero returned the salute with crisp professionalism, knowing that they would never have made it out of danger without her.

Garadun gestured to Ito. "Since Alliance forces are escorting us, we'll provide an escort for this Alliance officer. She's not safe in the passageways of this unit if she's moving alone. You should assign some of those ground forces soldiers to guard her now that this freighter is full of veterans from the Reserve Flotilla."

"Thank you. I'll do that."

Bradamont had paused, her eyes on the display. Was it his imagination that those eyes held a yearning in them? She had given up those Alliance ships to serve as a liaison officer, and now could only watch as others rode those decks and ordered those ships about.

She looked away, catching him watching her. No, he wasn't mistaken about her feelings.

"Thank you," Rogero said, this time only to her. He was certain she knew he meant it for far more than just her help in this latest incident. "I'll accompany you as well. It's on my way."

He, Bradamont, Garadun, and Ito moved off the command deck and into the passageways, now crowded with survivors from the Reserve Flotilla. Bradamont's Alliance fleet uniform drew looks of surprise that almost immediately changed to anger and hate. Shouts sounded, hands reached to punch and push, but Garadun and Ito shouted back. A year as prisoners of war had done nothing to fray the iron discipline drilled into Syndicate forces. At the commands from a sub-CEO and an executive, men and women fell back, faces going blank as they came to attention.

And Ito, at least, had gone into full executive mode, her voice booming through the passageway and surely carrying a good distance down it. "You will *now* hear this! *All* line workers, *all* line supervisors, *all* junior-executive ranks *will* treat *this* Alliance officer as a *direct* assistant to Colonel Rogero. *Anything* said to her *will* be appropriate to her status, and *any* physical action against her *will* be treated as *deliberate assault* against a *supervisor.* Is that *clear*?"

Everyone in the passageway waited for the two-second beat required, then thundered their response. "Yes, Madam Executive!"

The rest of the walk to the tiny comm compartment was met by silence, and everyone lined up along the bulkheads as word spread ahead faster than the small group could walk. As Bradamont said good-bye to Rogero she beckoned him close. "Did their treatment of me really outrage her that much?"

Rogero replied in a low voice. "I believe Executive Ito was very unhappy with the treatment you were receiving. But that's because of your actions. She sees you as an equal if also a recent enemy. What made her outraged was to see line workers and supervisors behaving that way toward someone of executive rank, as well as the lack of discipline in their showing such behavior in the presence of her and Sub-CEO Garadun."

"I see." Bradamont smiled wryly. "I guess I should be grateful, whatever the reasons."

"I'll have two soldiers here before you leave. You'll have an escort from now on."

"It looks very much as if Ito's instructions are being followed," Bradamont pointed out.

Rogero paused, realizing how little Bradamont knew of the Syndicate way of doing things. It was hard to think of her as being innocent, yet when it came to the underside of Syndicate life, she knew almost nothing despite the attack on General Drakon soon after her arrival. "You understood the need for bodyguards on the planet."

"Yes. That necessity was pretty heavily underlined by the attack on your General right after I arrived. But that was a much-less-controlled environment than this. I can see the discipline these people were trained to follow."

How to explain? "Very rigid control can mask and create a great deal that happens out of sight," Rogero said. "There is the surface, and there is what goes on beneath it. I routinely sleep with a sidearm handy because assassinations happen. Personal disputes, the desire for a promotion opportunity, an opportunity to blame a rival for the deed, there are many reasons. Disputes are resolved in ways that never see the light of day. Rules are meant to be twisted, or ways are meant to be found around rules, all without anyone in authority admitting to anything. You deserve whatever you can get away with, and if you get caught or simply accused, no mercy will be expected or given unless you have a patron powerful enough to protect you. That is how things have been done, in *all* aspects of Syndicate society. That is what President Iceni and General Drakon rebelled against."

She gazed somberly at him. "General Drakon told me the same thing. The snakes, the Internal Security Service, were a symptom, not a foreign element."

"Sadly, that is true. Which is why, when the Syndicate grew weak enough, everyone who could began revolting against it. Wait for the escorts to arrive before you leave." He drew out his sidearm, holding it out to her. "And keep this handy. Don't worry. I've got another."

BRADAMONT'S estimates proved accurate. The Alliance destroyer and light cruiser were eventually joined by another destroyer, all of them weaving around the freighters in a frequent shifting of positions that must have caused a huge amount of frustration for the fixed defenses in the star system. No rocks were fired at them from the rail guns occupying many defense sites throughout the star system; though whether that was because they could not get a clean shot or they had been told not to fire remained unknown.

Admiral Timbale had sent Bradamont one final message, urging them to keep going, then ceased communicating to protect himself.

No one called them, in fact. The six freighters might have been in a bubble insulated from any form of communication, except that they could tap into the Alliance news broadcasts filling the space between planets.

Where is Black Jack? seemed to be the most common theme.

"These are not a happy people," Sub-CEO Garadun observed in the tiny meal compartment of the freighter, which had become an executive dining room. He sat on one side of the small table, looking across it at Rogero on the other side. "I used to imagine them gloating over their victory, assuming they really had won. It doesn't seem to have brought them much joy, though."

"I wonder if there were any winners," Rogero said. "The Syndicate Worlds lost, but did the Alliance win? Or did they suffer a lesser form of defeat?"

"If not for Black Jack . . ."

"Yes. He made the difference, just when he was most needed, just as the legends of the Alliance claimed." Rogero turned a questioning look on Garadun. "According to the people of the Alliance, that was the work of the living stars."

"More likely coincidence."

"Hell of a coincidence," Rogero observed.

Garadun raised an eyebrow toward Rogero. "Have you been hanging around the workers too much, Donal? Listening to their myths about ancestors and stars and other mystical powers that care what happens to us? What's the policy toward that at Midway? Is it still officially discouraged?"

Rogero shook his head, looking down toward the table's well-worn and blemished surface. "No. It's not being encouraged, either. It's just allowed. If citizens want to believe in something, that's their business." He looked directly at Garadun again. "The Syndicate taught us to believe in nothing. And eventually they taught us so well that we didn't believe in the Syndicate anymore either."

"That's a point." Garadun set down his drink, a pouch of *Ground Forces Fluid Maintenance and Vitamin Supplement, lemonade flavor (contains no lemons),* and looked back at Rogero. "I've been thinking. I don't blame you for revolting and wiping out the snakes in your star system. Hell, I'm happy for you. But Midway isn't home for me. I need to get back to Darus."

"We don't know what the situation is at Darus," Rogero replied. "And we can use you. Midway is building a bigger flotilla. But it's your choice."

"Are you going to drop the loyalists off at Atalia?"

"I don't know," Rogero said. "Maybe there, maybe at Indras. It will be up to Kommodor Marphissa. I'd say Atalia for sure, since we can use the room on the freighters, but Atalia is also independent now. They probably won't appreciate having a thousand or so Syndicate loyalists dropped in their laps."

"I'm scarcely loyal," Garadun said. "But . . . look, Donal. I know you get on all right with that Alliance officer, but it's very hard for me. If Midway is a place where the Alliance has a strong voice . . . then it isn't somewhere I can accept yet. There's too much history, too much pain, for me to be part of that."

"I understand. But that officer *is* the Alliance voice at Midway. She's all there is, and she has only as much authority and influence as we grant her."

"Hmmm. But still," Garadun noted, "she has Black Jack and his fleet behind her. The fleet Midway needs to protect itself."

"President Iceni knows she has a lot of leverage because of how much Black Jack needs Midway. According to what General Drakon has told me, she's playing her side of the game well." Rogero tapped the tiny table between them. "The Alliance doesn't want the enigmas getting any closer to it. And only through Midway can the Alliance access the other two alien races that Black Jack found."

Garadun stared back at Rogero. "Two more? Different than the enigmas?"

"Very different."

"How did you find out about them?"

"Black Jack told us about them." Rogero sat back as far as the cramped seat would allow, which wasn't far. "It's strange. Do you know what Captain Bradamont told me? Black Jack was in survival sleep during the war. The whole time since it began until he was found recently. He never knew the war. He didn't grow up hating us or knowing how many of his friends and relatives had died during the war. So it's much easier for Black Jack to imagine getting along with us. Not the Syndicate. Us. It's not emotional for him. He can still believe in peace."

Garadun didn't answer for a while, brooding over what Rogero had said. "I can't believe in peace," he finally said. "Not yet. Not even after that Bradamont did so well getting us out of that mess. I can see her professional skills and accept them and even admire them. But that's not the same as accepting *her*."

So many think that way. I love her. But those around me distrust her at best. They see the enemy, where I see the woman. Will that ever change? But Rogero kept those thoughts hidden. "You are far from alone in that. We can't forget. If for no other reason than we owe that to those who died not to forget them. But if we let the past rule us, we'll be condemned to endless war and endless dying, and we all know how that feels."

"All too well," Garadun said. "What do we know about those two new sets of aliens? Did you see them?"

"Images of some of them, and records the Alliance provided." Rogero paused, remembering his first sight of the alien spacecraft when Black Jack's fleet arrived at Midway. "One of them is dangerous. The other is friendly. The friendly ones helped us. They stopped a bombardment aimed at our primary world—"

"You're joking."

"No, they did it. We've got a lot to learn about them, besides making Midway safe against any threat from the Syndicate government on Prime. Are you sure you don't want to help?"

"Not as sure as I was." Garadun looked outward, his eyes distant. "I wanted to be a scout when I was young. An explorer. As a young boy, I dreamed of being the one to finally find another intelligent species. The existence of the enigmas was a deep secret, so I thought I could still be the first to find aliens. But there weren't any job openings. No scouts required. Everyone had to support the war effort. No resources could be wasted on exploration, and besides, the frontier was sealed for reasons that were so secret no one would even say they were secret. I went into mobile forces training with a vague hope that someday, when the war ended, I'd be able to use those skills to become a scout and see new star systems." He sighed, saddened by the memories. "I gave up those dreams a long time ago. They died with each inhuman bureaucratic decision I had to live with and with every battle at every star where I fought."

Garadun played with his drink pouch for a few moments before giving Rogero a searching look. "But, maybe, like Black Jack, my dreams aren't really dead. Maybe they just went to sleep so deeply I didn't realize they still lived. I need to see my family at Darus. But afterward, if a former sub-CEO can make his way to Midway, maybe with his family, would there be room there for him?"

"I'm certain of it." Rogero gestured vaguely. "Or on Taroa if you prefer there. Didn't you once tell me you liked it?"

"Taroa? Sure I liked it. Lovely place. What's happened there?"

"Revolt. The people rule there, but it's not a mob. They've got a government that we're supporting. They also lost a lot of people during the revolt and could use immigrants. Especially immigrants with the right skills and training," Rogero added.

"I'll think about it," Garadun promised.

"What about Ito? Any idea how she feels?"

"Ask her." Garadun took a drink and grinned. "She'll want at least a heavy cruiser."

"I don't know that I can promise that."

"Just tell her you'll try. All she wants is an excuse to go. Most of the former crews will go, too. Not that they love their supervisors." Garadun laughed at the idea. "But they think we'll look after them, they think of Midway as home, and a lot of them have family there, and since we've been living without snakes for a while, they've gotten used to that and like it. They'll need a firm hand, though. Ito can provide that." He laughed again. "One of the snakes on our ship almost made it to the escape craft. I saw Ito shoot him before he made it to the hatch. She'll go with you." Garadun laughed a third time, accompanied with a sly look at Rogero. "Ito told me she thought you were hot for that Alliance captain. Can you imagine? Women see that sort of thing everywhere."

"I guess so," Rogero said, hoping that he had revealed no reaction to Garadun's words and deciding to change the subject as quickly as possible. "How certain are you that there aren't any snakes or snake agents among the workers and supervisors that we recovered?"

Garadun shrugged. "As certain as we can be. You know how often snakes on stricken mobile forces units *mysteriously* fail to make it to escape craft. When we were picked up by the Alliance, there weren't any openly known snakes among us. Every once in a while, someone among the prisoners would get tagged by their fellows as a covert snake. We'd hold a trial, without the Alliance guards knowing, of course, and if the charges held up, we'd deal with the snake. Then we'd turn the body over to the guards with one of the usual excuses about falling down stairs or off a building or something." He gave Rogero a knowing look this time. "It's a little worrisome how easily the workers came up with excuses like that. I can't swear there aren't still some covert snakes among our numbers. I don't think so. But they can be very hard to spot."

"I know," Rogero agreed. "How many of those with us do you estimate will want to be let off?"

"Off the top of my head? Maybe fifteen hundred. No more than that. Most of those won't be loyalists any more than I am. They'll be people wanting to go to their families at places other than Midway, or people who can't stomach even a whiff of Alliance involvement with you, or both. How long until we jump?"

Rogero checked his data pad. "Assuming nothing happens between now and then, about five hours."

"It can't happen a minute too soon for me." Garadun stared toward the hatch leading into the passageway where workers sat with their backs against the bulkheads. "I never thought that I'd leave here, not unless it was on some prison transport taking me to a camp somewhere deeper inside the Alliance. I never thought I'd go home again, see my family again, have a chance at anything again. And now . . ." He exhaled heavily. "If that Alliance officer had as much to do with it as you say, well, maybe someday I can look her in the eye and not have to hide how I feel."

ROGERO made sure to be on the freighter's command deck as the small convoy approached the jump point that led to Atalia. The six freighters lumbered along steadily, not far from each other but not in anything resembling the ordered formations that mobile forces units always adopted.

The three Alliance warships had fallen back, opening the distance between them and the freighters. They had never communicated with the freighters, and didn't seem likely to say good-bye. Rogero wondered whether he should send a message to the warships.

Bradamont came onto the command deck, her eyes going directly to the display where the three Alliance warships loomed nearby.

"Should we say something?" Rogero asked her. "Thank them for their assistance? Just say farewell?"

"No." Bradamont's voice sounded hollow. "You can't acknowledge that they did anything for you. It could get them in trouble."

"But everybody knows. It was obvious."

"Yes, everybody knows, but nobody is admitting that they know."

Rogero shrugged. "All right, but it sounds like how we did things in the Syndicate."

"I didn't need to hear that." She clearly wasn't taking the comment humorously.

He watched her, seeing the look in Bradamont's eyes as they prepared to leave Alliance space and leave behind Alliance warships, everything that Bradamont knew and held dear. Everything except him. And for him as much as anything she had given this up, official orders or not.

"Ready," the freighter's executive said.

"What about the other five?" Rogero asked.

"Yes. Ready to go. See those lights on the display? We've got our jump orders linked. When I go, we all go."

"Then go," Rogero said.

The stars vanished.

The endless gray of jump space filled the display.

Captain Bradamont left the bridge.

After a long minute, Rogero left, too. It would be four days in jump space before they reached Atalia. At least in jump space, everything traveled at the same speed, and they would reach the other star as swiftly as the fastest battle cruiser.

TWO days in jump, and Rogero was feeling uneasy. Uneasiness was normal in jump space. People didn't belong here, and the longer they stayed, the worse it felt. But that kind of discomfort usually took a bit longer than two days to be noticeable. This was something else.

He walked restlessly around the freighter, having to step over innumerable workers sitting in the passageways because there was not enough room elsewhere for them. The air had already gone a bit stale, life support not quite up to the task of handling so many people. It wouldn't become dangerous in the time they would have to live with it, but the smell would get worse, and headaches would become increasingly frequent.

Rogero found that his steps had brought him to the quarters occupied by Honore Bradamont. He frowned slightly as he realized that this was the source of his unease. Why? Since entering jump, Bradamont had stayed inside that small compartment, out of sight of the workers, not wanting to flaunt her presence before those who still saw her as the enemy. The two soldiers of Rogero's who were standing sentry outside Bradamont's door at this hour were alert. What, then, bothered him?

He walked up to the soldiers, who both came to full attention and saluted him. "How does everything look?" Rogero asked.

Syndicate soldiers were trained to not ask questions, to not volunteer information, to do what they were told and nothing more or less. Rogero's soldiers, like many of those in General Drakon's forces, had been given different training for the last few years. Observe. Think. Tell someone if something looks wrong.

So when he asked *how does everything look?* these soldiers knew that he meant it as a question to be answered.

The more veteran of the two chewed his lip for a moment. "We're being watched, Colonel, sir."

The other soldier nodded.

"By who? How often?"

"Pretty often, Colonel. It's a feeling. Someone is watching. Like on a battlefield, even when the armor sensors are saying there's nothing there, you can still tell there's a sight on you. They're staying low, though. So many workers go by all the time, they can just meld in with them."

The second soldier nodded again. "Especially when we're doing turnover, Colonel, relieving the shift before us or being relieved. Whoever it is pays close attention at those times."

"But you haven't seen anyone in particular?"

"No, sir. Just the feeling. The others who've been standing guard have mentioned it, too, Colonel."

Worrisome. Very worrisome. Veterans developed a feel for such things, sort of a new sense, or perhaps a very old sense brought to life again, one that had been mostly lost as humans developed tools.

No one person could be watching the soldiers that often. This was a group effort. Would someone try to get at Bradamont? The two sentries could stop one or two attackers, but what if there were many? What if an overwhelming number of workers came down this passageway, bent on revenge against the woman who represented the enemy and was within their reach?

Rogero studied the door. A freighter's internal door. Just a flimsy, lightweight panel that provided some privacy but little else. Like most living compartments on the freighter, this one couldn't even be locked.

She would be trapped in there.

But there were no better rooms, no more secure place on this ship, and he knew better than to suggest that she share his room. Bradamont would not agree under these conditions, and if, impossibly, she did agree, the blowback against him from everyone else on the freighter would be huge.

There must be something he could do. The vague sense of warning had grown stronger. *If I do not think of some extra measures to protect Honore Bradamont, she might not make it to Atalia. I must think of something, and I must do so quickly.*

CHAPTER FIFTEEN

TWO hours until the freighter left jump. Two hours until they reached Atalia. One hour until "dawn" as measured by the freighter's internal time. Colonel Rogero lay on his narrow bed in his very small quarters, staring up at the tangle of wiring and ducts that made up the overhead.

The sense that something was going to happen had been growing. Indefinable, perhaps only a new manifestation of the old jump-space nerves, but still it had kept him from sleeping much this night and brought him fully awake well before he needed to get up.

He sensed a trembling through the structure of the freighter before he could consciously feel it. The trembling grew with shocking suddenness, turning into an irregular beat of many feet in the passageway outside. Whoever they were, they were moving quickly and silently.

Rogero's feet were hitting the deck when he heard the sentries outside Bradamont's new quarters down this same passageway shout warnings and commands. He paused only for the barest fraction of a second, deciding between his sidearm or heavier armament and choosing the latter. He was reaching for the door when the shouts of the sentries were submerged in a roar of sound that erupted in the passageway as at least a hundred throats shouted hate.

As he opened the door, a crash sounded down the hall, the unmistakable sound of a grenade detonating nearby and only slightly muffled by having exploded inside some room off the passageway. Almost certainly, that room had been Bradamont's quarters. A small portion of Rogero's mind wondered where the mob had acquired a grenade, and resolved to find out. If one of his soldiers had lost or bartered away a grenade . . .

But that would be a priority for later.

Rogero came out of his stateroom, not wearing armor but his pulse rifle powering up. Every passageway on the freighter tended to have a lot of people in it, but right now this passageway was packed solid with the mob pushing toward Bradamont's quarters.

One of the uglier things about iron discipline was that when it cracked, it didn't simply cause minor disruptions. Any crack tended to be catastrophic. Which meant responses had to be immediate and overwhelming.

He would have had to react the same even if Bradamont had not been the target of this mob.

"*Comply!*" Rogero shouted over the tumult, then without waiting fired a shot into the worker immediately in front of him. The pulse rifle blew a hole completely through the worker and knocked down another in front of that man. "*Comply!*" Rogero yelled on the heels of the shot and fired again right after that.

This time three workers in the congested passageway dropped, Rogero pushing forward over their bodies. "*Comply!*"

A third shot, two more down, but the others finally grasping what was happening, workers reacting from habit and fear drilled into them, twisting to put their backs to the nearest bulkhead, raising their arms to place both hands on their heads, staring outward without speaking as Rogero bellowed the command a fourth time. "*Comply!*"

There was a small group before the door to Bradamont's quarters, trying to push their way inside past a door loose on its hinges but still somehow holding them back as if solidly braced from behind. Traces of smoke from the grenade explosion drifted past the edges of the door from inside. Caught up in their efforts, reacting more slowly to the sounds of the shots and the commands, some were still pushing when Rogero fired a fourth, fifth, and sixth time without pausing.

Silence fell then, except for a couple of wounded workers gasping in pain. Everyone else had their backs flattened against a bulkhead, hands locked on their heads in compliance.

The two soldiers who had been on guard were trying to struggle to their feet when Rogero reached them. He wasted a precious second looking them over, searching for evidence of whether they had resisted the mob or just given in. But uniforms were torn, bruises and scratches were evident, and one of the soldiers, face drawn with pain, cradled an arm broken in at least one place.

"We locked arms," the other soldier reported. "But we couldn't hold." She stood at attention now, almost trembling in anticipation of two more shots aimed at punishing her and her comrade for their failure.

But Rogero lowered his weapon. "You tried." The grenade detonation and the shots he had fired had set off alarms inside the freighter, the frantic tones stuttering warnings that no longer had any purpose. "There should be more soldiers here very soon. See that you are checked in the freighter's autodoc."

He turned to the broken door and carefully knocked in a special pattern. After a moment, the door finally gave way, falling inward to reveal a figure in battle armor standing amid the wreckage created by the grenade explosion in the small room. "Are you all right?" Rogero asked.

Bradamont nodded, unsealing the suit's faceplate to speak to him directly. "The armor took some damage from the grenade. I'm all right, though. With the help of the armor, I could hold that door for a while."

It had been the only possible solution. While all eyes had been on Bradamont as she shifted her belongings out of her old quarters and began walking to this one, while this passageway had been temporarily cleared of anyone else in the name of security for Bradamont's move, Rogero had quickly brought his own armor out of his quarters and slid it inside Bradamont's new living space. If the soldiers outside held long enough, and she had any extra warning, Bradamont would be able to get into that armor and hold off an attack until relief arrived. So he had hoped.

The alarms cut off as someone on the freighter's bridge shut them down, the silence now filling the passageway holding an ominous quality as Rogero turned to confront the workers and low-level supervisors lining the bulkheads, all of them trying their best to be motionless but more than one quivering with terror.

Executive Ito came running down the passageway, her face contorted with anger. "Who did this? Who led this? Talk, you miserable low forms of life!"

Rogero stopped her with one raised hand. "Get the names of everyone here. Organize a working party to get the bodies packed up." He looked down at the two still-living-but-wounded workers trying not to writhe in pain, both of them literally biting their lips to keep from moaning.

A few moments ago he would have killed them without hesitation. Now they were helpless. They might have information.

A half-dozen soldiers came dashing up, grim expressions taking in the scene. Lieutenant Foster saluted, his own face rigid. As immediate unit commander, he might also face the severest form of discipline for any failure of his soldiers to protect Bradamont.

But she was unharmed. *How would I have reacted if she had been badly hurt or killed? Hopefully even then I would have recognized that punishment would serve no purpose when men and women had done their best.*

Rogero jogged his head toward the two battered guards. "Your soldiers did their duty. See that they are looked after. Try to keep those two wounded workers alive. I want them able to talk."

"Yes, sir."

"Post half of your unit on guard here, four-hour shifts on and off, until Captain Bradamont leaves this ship."

"Yes, sir."

"Captain Bradamont, I recommend you remain in that armor until we can get you aboard a shuttle at Atalia."

"Yes, Colonel," Bradamont said, her own voice subdued but betraying no feelings. She looked outside, at the carnage wrought by the mob and by Rogero's suppression of it, and he wondered what she was thinking.

She was seeing the Syndicate way. Cowering workers against the walls and deadly force against disruptions. He had never liked it even when it was necessary to prevent worse things. *I know what Honore will think of it. What will she think of me?*

Rogero walked back to his room, the pulse rifle radiating heat in a glow that reflected back from the cowed workers lining the passageway. Behind him, Ito was savaging the workers as other senior supervisors showed up to verbally lash the rioters, tossing in occasional physical blows to emphasize their points. The workers took it passively, as they knew they must.

He had become used to such things. But now he was imagining seeing them through the eyes of Honore Bradamont, and the ugliness of it all was hard to bear. *We are changing things. We'll change this, too. It will take time, but the day will come when I will not have to face down rioting workers with a combat weapon.*

Close to two hours later, the freighter flashed back into normal space, the stars gazing down impassively on six ships full of humans who were finally accepting that they were free. Rogero, still depressed over the riot and his suppression of it, gazed morosely at those stars. *I don't want to do this anymore. But what else can I do? And if I don't, who takes my place? General Drakon says he needs me.*

The four light cruisers and six Hunter-Killers were still here. Far off, light-hours distant, the two heavy cruisers waited at the jump point for Kalixa.

A virtual window popped open near Rogero, the image of the commander of the light cruiser *Harrier* looking out at him. "Welcome back. We were taking bets on whether you would miss them."

"Miss who?" Rogero asked.

"Black Jack's fleet. They jumped for Varandal three days ago. You must have passed each other in jump space."

ROGERO used the special, secure comm equipment in the private compartment to send his report to Marphissa. "Kommodor, I have the pleasure to report that our mission was successful. We have over five thousand released prisoners on board, the vast majority from the Reserve Flotilla. In view of the strain on the freighters' life support, and in light of recent events aboard this ship, I urge that we off-load here at Atalia those who do not wish to go to Midway."

He provided a summary of events at Varandal, then described the riot a few hours ago. "I will keep Captain Bradamont safe, but the sooner she is transferred back to *Manticore*, the better. For the people, Rogero, out."

Marphissa's reply came back hours later. She didn't look pleased.

"Colonel Rogero, I was distressed to hear of the threat to our liaison officer. I agree with you that we must get her back aboard *Manticore*. I am leaving *Kraken* at the jump point to maintain our blockade of the path back to Indras but will be bringing *Manticore* to join you. I do not want to delay here off-loading hundreds of people, but I don't see any alternative. Even if there weren't a security issue, the life-support readings on those freighters are not good. We need to reduce the load on them. I'm sending the ships with you a new vector to follow toward an orbiting facility that can take on the workers we're going to be leaving behind. Have your soldiers on the freighters sort out who is leaving. We need that done before we get to the facility, so we can get the off loud completed as quickly as possible.

"I am grateful you are all back safely. For the people, Marphissa, out."

TRAVELING through space, Rogero decided, was like running in quicksand. You could put tremendous effort into it, but it still felt like you were running in place. Days after arriving at Atalia, he stood, disconsolate, outside the air lock, where a shuttle carrying Honore Bradamont had only just departed.

A bit of Bradamont remained with him, in a way. She had been forced to continue constantly wearing Rogero's battle armor, with the result that she and it had stunk pretty bad by the time she had finally shed it outside the air lock. There had been witnesses, they couldn't say much, but she had looked into his eyes, and the message there had been clear. Her feelings for him had not changed.

A large group approached, led by Sub-CEO Garadun, who smiled ruefully at Rogero. "I'm told the next ride is ours. You never promised we'd get to ride farther than Atalia."

Rogero waved one hand in front of his face as if shoving aside the odors that had seemingly grown strong enough to see as the freighter's overburdened life support kept up its losing battle. "I'd think you'd be glad to leave this."

"No, Donal, I want to see those aliens! I'm going to get to Darus, somehow, but look for me after that."

"I will." Rogero clasped Garadun's hand with real warmth. "At least you won't have to go back with us through Kalixa."

Garadun shook his head, glowering. "You see, Donal, that's one of the reasons why we continue to hate the Alliance. Before our flotilla was destroyed, the CEOs showed us images of what happened there. Of what the *Alliance* did at Kalixa."

"What?" Rogero gave Garadun a startled look. "Didn't anybody tell you what really happened, Pers?"

"What do you mean? The Alliance collapsed the hypernet gate. That's what killed Kalixa Star System."

"No. It wasn't the Alliance. It was the enigmas."

Garadun stared at Rogero wordlessly.

"We found out the enigmas could send a signal that traveled faster than light," Rogero explained, "a signal that could cause any hypernet gate to collapse and emit a huge burst of energy. All of the gates now have a special modification that prevents that from happening, but we didn't learn it until too late to save Kalixa."

Garadun finally found his voice. "Why did the enigmas destroy Kalixa instead of someplace closer to them?"

"Because," Rogero said, hearing his own voice grow hard, "they wanted us to blame the Alliance. They wanted the Syndicate Worlds and the Alliance to start collapsing hypernet gates in each other's star systems."

After a long moment, Sub-CEO Garadun looked away angrily. "Wipe each other out. They wanted us to wipe out each other. Let humanity kill itself, and they'd inherit the wreckage."

"Yes."

"And we almost did it. We almost did exactly what they wanted. The Reserve Flotilla had orders to collapse the hypernet gate at Varandal. Did you know that? In retaliation for what happened at Kalixa."

It was Rogero's turn to stare without words.

"We almost did it." Garadun shuddered, his face twisted with pain. "Dammit all. If we hadn't lost that fight . . . I need to tell people about this. They don't know. They think the Alliance destroyed Kalixa. Are you absolutely certain, Donal? There's no doubt of what you say?"

"No doubt at all. It's widely known because of the crash program to get the modifications installed on the hypernet gates." Rogero paused. "You should know what happened at Prime. The gate there collapsed as well, at a time when it would have destroyed not only Prime but also Black Jack's fleet. But it had the modification installed, and so did not collapse in the way that led to something like Kalixa."

Garadun shook his head, looking around. "There's Ito. Hey! And you, Jepsen. Did you hear what Colonel Rogero said? You're staying with him, so you two make sure everyone on this ship and the other freighters know the truth. I'll tell the ones who are going to be dropped off here. There are plenty of real reasons to hate the Alliance for what they did during the war, but none of those reasons approach the scale of what happened at Kalixa. Our people need to know who was really responsible."

"The enigmas tried to use the hate we felt for the Alliance," Rogero said, "and the hate the Alliance felt for us, to achieve their own goals."

"That's the problem with hate, isn't it?" Garadun said. "It's very easy for hate to hit the wrong targets. Yes, I know that. I always have. I couldn't change my feelings about the Alliance, but I could stay aware of the mistakes those feelings might cause me to make. Collapsing that gate at Varandal might have been the worst such mistake, and in that case I didn't realize it until now." The air lock cycled open. "Here's my ride. Thank you, Donal. I have a life again. I won't waste it."

"See you don't," Rogero advised, as Garadun entered the air lock, followed by other workers and junior supervisors who had chosen to leave the freighter at Atalia.

"I'll see you at Midway!" Ito called before the air-lock hatch sealed. "Can we talk?" she asked Rogero.

"Of course. Help me carry my armor back to my quarters."

Ito wrinkled her nose. "Even with this air, I can smell that. Better clean it out."

"I've done it plenty of times before after a long fight," Rogero said. "Have you discovered anything about that riot?"

"That's what I wanted to talk about," she said, falling into step beside him. "None of the workers knows who motivated it. Just the usual *somebody said something* and *everybody was doing it* nonsense." She snorted in derision. "Sheep."

"What about the wounded?"

"The wounded? Oh, you mean the two injured workers? One died."

Ito didn't sound concerned about that. "The other will be able to return to duty eventually if you don't want to execute her as a lesson to the others. Those two didn't know anything, either."

"It was planned," Rogero said. "Someone planned that and led it, and I very much doubt that whoever motivated that mob was anywhere near the forefront of the action. More likely they were a ways back from it, building an alibi."

"You're right. But anybody who knew who that was must have died when you put down the riot. I used the portable ground forces interrogation gear you guys brought. It's not great, but it's good enough. None of those workers were trained to handle interrogation."

"What about the grenade?" Rogero asked. "I was able to determine that it was stolen from our supplies, not delivered to someone by one of my soldiers. That theft took considerable skill, getting past the alarms set in that cargo area and leaving no trace of the intrusion. But there was only one grenade missing."

"You probably killed the one who got it from whoever stole it," Ito said. "He or she had to have been at the front of the mob to toss it through the door when they got it partway open. They only took one because if they had taken two, we might have found it during a search after the riot; and then we would know who was behind everything."

"Most likely," Rogero agreed. "Whoever planned this did a professional job. They need to be caught."

"And killed?"

"Probably. After they answer a few questions."

"So," Ito said, "tell me something. You killed all the snakes at Midway? What did the workers do without the snakes keeping them down? They must have rioted. Did you have to do a compliance action on the whole planet?"

Rogero's memory filled with images of the nearly hysterical crowds, which had celebrated the deaths of the snakes on Midway and the destruction of the Internal Security Service headquarters by General Drakon's soldiers. He had seen the trouble developing, he had known the celebration was growing more frenzied and would soon descend into riot. "No. I could tell things were going to get out of hand. But they didn't. General Drakon sent us out, but he sent us out to enlist the citizens in preventing the celebration from turning into a rampage of looting and destruction."

"Enlist them?" Ito asked. "You mean he drafted a lot of them to use for locking down the rest?"

"No. General Drakon talked to the citizens. He told them they needed to keep anyone from using their freedom to harm the rest of them. He told them any surviving snakes might try to convince them to riot and destroy things. He got the police on the streets, with our backup. He went out himself on the streets, and calmed everyone, got everyone to think about tomorrow, and what they needed to do to keep themselves and their families safe."

Ito was watching him with a baffled expression. "But he also threatened them." She made it a statement, not a question.

"No," Rogero said. "He and President Iceni told the people that they must act responsibly, and made it clear that anyone who didn't would be dealt with."

"That's a threat," Ito concluded. "How much unrest has there been since then?"

"Very little. Demonstrations, yes. President Iceni permits those as long as everyone behaves. It lets the people know they have a real voice."

They reached his quarters, and Ito left Rogero to the familiar but tedious job of cleaning out his armor. *I love you most dearly, Honore, but you stink remarkably after a few days in armor. I won't be telling you that to your face, though.*

I haven't thought much about those days right after the revolt when we killed the snakes at Midway. There's been too much else to keep me busy. But what would have happened if General Drakon and President Iceni had ordered Syndicate methods be used to suppress the citizens?

We would have been on constant garrison duty, fighting to keep a rebellious people from doing to us what we had done to the snakes.

We were given the leaders we needed, when we needed them. I must remain grateful for that, because Honore told me of many other star systems that lacked such leaders and have paid an awful price. I've heard about Taroa and some of the things that happened there. Was it coincidence that we had both Drakon and Iceni? I think not. Who or what do I thank for our good fortune?

Not the people. This was beyond our powers.

MARPHISSA watched Bradamont board *Manticore* and could not help but hug her in welcome. "You made it back."

Bradamont laughed, surprised by the gesture. She had dark circles of fatigue under her eyes and smelled like she had been buried for a few days and dug up. "I was wondering if I would make it back. I've been wearing battle armor nonstop for a while."

"No wonder," Marphissa said.

"No wonder what?"

"Nothing! I'm sure you want to clean up and rest. Don't worry about anything else. We'll get the one thousand three hundred twenty six Syndicate lovers dropped off and head back for the jump point. Life support on the freighters will gradually recover with the load on them reduced, and with any luck, we won't need you again on this trip."

"Don't jinx me," Bradamont cautioned. "Not everyone we're leaving is a Syndicate lover, Asima. Some just didn't want to go to Midway."

"Their mistake."

"Did Atalia give you much trouble about accepting them?"

Marphissa grinned. "I've been around President Iceni enough to know how to do these things. I didn't ask Atalia if they'd accept them. I told Atalia they were getting them. Atalia decided not to argue since I had so much more firepower than they do."

"Don't learn the wrong lessons, Asima."

Marphissa paused at Bradamont's stateroom before heading back to the bridge. "Let me tell you something, Honore. You're on *Manticore*. Keep your hatch locked as usual, but you're safe here."

Bradamont smiled wanly. "You warned me about the crew, remember?"

"That was before. You've been on board awhile. They know you. Then word got around about that riot. To them, *Manticore*'s Alliance officer, *their* Alliance officer, was almost killed by a bunch of louts from the Reserve Flotilla. They may not love you, but you belong to *Manticore*. That's what they're thinking. You'll be safe here," Marphissa repeated.

"I'll never understand sailors," Bradamont said.

"You understand them well enough. Welcome back, you Alliance monster."

"I'm glad to be back, you Syndic devil."

IT hadn't been easy waiting at Atalia. It wasn't easy transiting back through Kalixa. But Marphissa had reserved most of her worries for what might await them at Indras.

Why did I have to be right?

"Damned snakes," Kapitan Diaz spat.

There were now three light cruisers and five Hunter-Killers at Indras, and they were orbiting ten light-minutes from the jump exit to Kalixa, along the most direct route from there to the hypernet gate.

"Maybe we can bluff our way past them," Marphissa said. She was once again wearing the Syndicate CEO suit. *Don't sit too straight. Look bored. Act like you are the biggest thing in this star system and every surrounding star system.*

She reached for her comm control and schooled her voice again to an arrogant drawl. "This is CEO Manetas. Our mission at Atalia has, naturally, been successfully completed. We are returning to Prime with prisoners for special evaluation and interrogation. All ships are to remain clear of the path of my flotilla. Manetas, for the people, out."

"I'm praying again," Diaz told her after the transmission ended. "My parents taught me how to do that in secret."

"They did? I hope you learned well."

Their answer came much quicker than expected. "Kommodor, it is an eyes-only message, from the Syndicate flotilla ahead of us, for your private viewing."

Marphissa knew what everyone expected. She would go to her stateroom and view the message alone, a message that probably contained secret offers as lucrative as the Syndicate could come up with. That was what Syndicate bosses did. "I'll watch it here," she said. "Anything the Syndicate has to say to me is not private."

"Yes, Kommodor," the comm specialist said, betraying a pleasant sort of surprise. "On your display."

The man looking out at them was clearly a snake. A senior snake. Marphissa felt her blood growing cold just seeing him, despite knowing that his eyes could not actually see her. Such eyes, such a gaze, had been the last thing many of her friends and acquaintances had ever seen before being hauled off to a labor camp or simply disappearing without a trace.

"I am Sub-CEO Qui. I don't know who you really are, but I will find out. You have something the Syndicate Worlds needs. What we need is you. The Syndicate Worlds requires good CEO material. You have proven your abilities by the accumulation of a substantial flotilla of mobile forces, a flotilla that follows your orders.

"If you were of lesser talents, you would not receive this offer, which is fully backed and guaranteed by the government on Prime. If you accept Syndicate authority again, if you bring these mobile forces back under the command of Prime, you will immediately gain actual CEO rank, as well as full immunity for any actions that might have violated Syndicate law or regulations or procedures. Blanket immunity for any possible offense, as well as a leap into the highest ranks of the Syndicate Worlds.

"I hope you recognize the benefits of this very generous offer," Sub-CEO Qui continued, his eyes and smile equally cold. "You gain high rank and a certainty of safety, and the Syndicate Worlds gains a very talented CEO and a small but valuable flotilla of mobile forces units. You need not fear opposition from your subordinates or workers. We will provide you with a plan to get sufficient forces aboard each unit to subdue any resistance."

Qui's smile changed, gaining a terrible kind of promise. "Or, you could reject this offer. It would be an awful waste of your talent. We'll destroy every freighter with you before you can reach the gate, which means you will return to wherever your home is as a failure. You know the rewards that come to failures. And we will determine who you are, and where your family is, and we will hold them accountable for the crimes against the Syndicate Worlds you have surely committed, and they have surely conspired to assist.

"Far better to pursue the most profitable course. I'll await your reply on this channel. Qui, for the people, out."

The silence on the bridge when the message ended was close to absolute, broken only by the soft noises from the ship's automated systems and the breathing of the men and women around Marphissa.

She laughed, letting all the scorn she could manage go into the sound. "Does he think I am like him? Does he think I really am a Syndicate CEO? Is he so stupid as to think I would betray those who follow me, who have sworn to follow President Iceni, who fight for our freedom and the freedom of our families?"

"I think the answer to all of those things is yes," Kapitan Diaz replied.

Bradamont had been listening with disbelief painted large on her face. "He actually proposed that, thinking you would accept?"

"It's probably how he got to be a CEO. By accepting similar offers and selling out people who were depending upon him," Marphissa explained. "And he's a snake. He doesn't mean it. Every word was a lie. I would die along with everyone else in a command position, while the workers were shipped off to slave labor. He thinks my greed will override my common sense and cause me to ignore my experience with watching people being betrayed every time they were fools enough to believe the soothing words of a snake."

"Are you going to tell him that?" Diaz asked with a grin.

Marphissa almost said yes, then shook her head. "No. I want to buy time for us by making him think I am considering his offer. The closer we get to the gate before the Syndicate mobile forces start attacking, the better chance we have of getting some of the freighters through."

She looked around the bridge at the grim expressions her last words had brought to life. "We have to accept this. We outnumber them, but stopping them from hitting the freighters is going to be very difficult. We'll do our best."

"Those freighters are packed with workers," Diaz said. "Any hit at all will kill many."

"We will do our best! Let me send my reply to Sub-CEO Qui. Comm specialist, can you give me a digital background that makes it look like I am in my stateroom?"

"It is done, Kommodor," the comm specialist said. "Ready for your transmission."

Marphissa put on a wary expression this time before hitting the reply command. "Sub-CEO Qui, your offer is intriguing. I am carefully considering it. You understand that I must maneuver carefully to ensure none of my subordinates suspect they may be supplanted. I will give you my reply soon. Out."

She looked around. The Syndicate flotilla was ten light-minutes distant, so it was a bit over an hour and a half before any physical contact was possible. "I'm getting out of this CEO suit now," Marphissa announced. "If I'm going to fight, it will be in the uniform of Midway."

She was back on the bridge a few minutes later, in time to hear the operations specialist call out a warning. "The Syndicate flotilla is maneuvering."

Marphissa watched, waiting, as the vectors on the Syndicate mobile forces changed. "They're accelerating to intercept. I guess Sub-CEO Qui didn't like my answer."

"Forty minutes to contact on their current vector," Diaz noted. "He said he'd be going after the freighters, and even though snakes always lie, I think this time he told us what he was actually going to do."

The freighters were sitting ducks and would be all of the long transit from this jump exit to the hypernet gate. The light cruisers and HuKs the snakes had at their disposal couldn't defeat Marphissa's warships, but they could target the freighters and blow the large, clumsy ships apart one by one.

I've never done this. How can I save those freighters? Can I save those freighters?

CHAPTER SIXTEEN

MARPHISSA bit her lip as she thought. Defending against slashing attacks was going to be hard. "We need to keep close to the freighters. Right on top of them."

A gentle touch on her shoulder caused Marphissa to look up and over. Bradamont was there, looking at Marphissa and shaking her head in a barely perceptible way.

Marphissa looked at her display again, then stood up abruptly. "I'll be right back," she told Diaz, and left the bridge quickly once more.

As she had guessed, Bradamont was right behind. "Let's talk," Bradamont urged. "In your stateroom."

Marphissa walked to her stateroom, waited until Bradamont entered, then sealed the hatch. "What do you want? I don't know how to do this. I've done other operations. I have some experience. But convoy protection? The one time I did something like that, I was the most junior executive rank and not even on the bridge of my ship."

"I know what to do," Bradamont said.

"Please, *please*, do not give me a talk about how Black Jack saved a convoy at Grendel—"

"That was different. He was badly outnumbered. You have an advantage in numbers of warships here, and you can use that to get through to the hypernet gate without losing *any* freighters."

"If you know how to do it, then you should—"

"No. You have to command. Here's the key. You can't tether your defending warships too close to the freighters. That's a natural thing to do, but it's the worst thing you can do."

Marphissa sat down, staring at Bradamont. "Why?"

"Because you need to break up the firing runs by the attackers before they get so close to the freighters that you can't stop them. That means ranging out, hitting the attackers while they're trying to position for firing runs. Up, down, right, left, all directions. Keep hitting the attackers, and they won't have a chance to go after the freighters."

She could understand what Bradamont was saying, but her instincts rebelled against the tactics. "I'm sorry, but that doesn't make sense. If my warships are away from the freighters, the freighters will be exposed to attack. I can't put out a distant screen strong enough to stop incoming warships around the entire sphere surrounding the freighters."

"You don't have to! It's an active defense. Watch the movements of the attackers, get your warships out there, and when the attackers start to line up to hit the freighters, hit *them*."

Marphissa thought carefully, trying to drive away distractions and fears that hindered her focus. "How do I know where the attackers are going to go, so I can have my warships out in the right directions?"

"*That's* the easy part, Asima. The attackers have to go where your freighters are. If you can stop them from doing that, it doesn't matter where else they go in this star system." Bradamont knelt in front of her so that their heads were on a level. "You can do this. You're good. You listen to the movement of your ships, you feel where they should go and how to get them there. You do the same thing when watching other ships. A lot of ship drivers never figure that out and need automated systems to handle everything. Yes, you need more experience, but I've seen you handle this ship. You can do this."

"Am I as good as Black Jack?" Marphissa asked, standing up and taking a deep breath.

"Nobody is as good as Black Jack. But, someday, you might be," Bradamont said, standing as well to face her.

"I was kidding," Marphissa said.

"I'm not."

Marphissa stared again, stunned, studying Bradamont's eyes and face for any trace of humor or mockery. "Do you really believe that?"

"Yes. Now get back on the bridge and get this flotilla safely to the hypernet gate, Kommodor."

"Is this . . . some kind of . . . motivation?" Marphissa asked.

Bradamont gave her a puzzled look. "Yes. Though it's also true."

"How strange. I'm used to Syndicate-style motivation. *Don't screw this up or you will be shot.* That sort of thing."

Bradamont laughed. "Now you're kidding me."

"No. Really. I'm not." Marphissa took another long breath, pretending not to notice the consternation on Bradamont's face. "Stay on the bridge with me. If I'm missing something, if there's something I should be doing that I'm not, let me know."

"You don't need me," Bradamont said, "but I'll be there. Purely because I have more experience at this."

They were back on the bridge seconds later. Marphissa took her seat, feeling some confidence now that she had an idea of what to do. The worry and uncertainty from the watch specialists was almost palpable when she walked back onto the bridge, but as everyone picked up on their Kommodor's new attitude, the atmosphere lightened a bit.

Marphissa took another close look at the situation. The Syndicate flotilla was coming in from slightly below and to starboard of her flotilla. Her freighters were arranged in two columns of three, one above the other. Loosely arranged in columns, that is, since even automated systems couldn't seem to keep citizen-crewed freighters from wandering off station a bit like easily distracted packhorses. The warships were ranged in front of and to either side of the freighters.

Her hand went to her display, tentative at first, tracing paths to new positions for her warships well ahead of the freighters. As she filled in the picture, her self-assurance grew. Yes. *Manticore* and *Kraken* positioned along the direct intercept vector the Syndicate forces were on. The four light cruisers roving above and below the heavy cruisers, and slightly behind them. The six HuKs outside the light cruisers, to left and right, above and below, slightly behind them, ready to move in support of the light cruisers or the heavy cruisers. She resisted the urge to look back at Bradamont for approval. Everyone else would see that gesture, undermining their confidence in her. Instead, Marphissa made a show of tapping her comm control. "All units in the Recovery Flotilla, this is Kommodor Marphissa. Orders are on the way for new positions. Execute immediately upon receipt."

Diaz took his worried gaze from the Syndicate flotilla to the orders for *Manticore*, his eyebrows rising in surprise as he saw them. "Out there?"

"Yes," Marphissa said. "Out there. We're going to meet the Syndicate warships and kick them hard before they can get near the freighters."

"But—"

"Move it, Kapitan."

"Yes, Kommodor."

Manticore's main propulsion lit off, kicking her away from the freighters. All about her, the other warships from Midway surged into faster motion, altering vectors to pull ahead.

"Kommodor?" the comm specialist asked. "The executives commanding the freighters are all calling, asking to speak to you."

Marphissa waved an angry hand toward the specialist. "Tell them that I will prevent them from being damaged or destroyed as long as

I am not distracted by unneeded conversations and as long as they stay on their vectors for the gate. If they try to run, if they scatter, they will die."

"Yes, Kommodor. I will tell them."

It felt good to have others responding to her orders. It also felt . . . scary. They were doing what she said. If it didn't work, it would be her fault. *I suppose I could do the Syndicate thing and blame some of my subordinates, but I won't. Besides, that won't bring back the freighters if they have been destroyed.*

The distance to the Syndicate mobile forces had been down to eight light-minutes when Marphissa ordered her own warships into their new defensive formation. By the time her warships had reached their assigned positions relative to the freighters, the Syndicate flotilla was only three light-minutes away and coming on at a steady point one light speed, matching Marphissa's warships.

Three light-minutes at a combined closing speed of point two light would be covered in fifteen minutes.

Marphissa tapped her controls again. "All units in the Recovery Flotilla, this is Kommodor Marphissa. Our primary goal is to protect the freighters. That means forcing the Syndicate mobile forces to break off any attack runs, or, if they maintain attack runs, to disable or destroy those warships before they can get within range of the freighters. Once a Syndicate warship has been forced to break off an attack run, you are *not* to pursue it. Remain in position where you can intercept other Syndicate attacks. Pursuit is only authorized if a Syndicate warship manages to get past our defensive screen and is actually on a firing run against the freighters. If that happens, that Syndicate warship must be stopped. We have rescued our comrades from imprisonment. Now we must ensure that the snakes do not stop us from getting those comrades home. For the people! Marphissa, out."

The Syndicate flotilla, badly outnumbered as it was, continued heading straight for an intercept with the freighters, the smooth curve of its vector running straight through the center of the defensive shield set up by Marphissa. The Syndicate ships were in a simple, standard formation, a rectangle with the three light cruisers in the center and the HuKs ranged in front of them. On the display, it looked a bit like a battering ram aimed at the shield of Midway warships. "Is he going to try to blow right through us?" she wondered.

"It's been tried," Bradamont commented. "If he did, how much would make it through?"

"If I collapse my defensive shield around his vector and hit him with everything? Not much. But if all he cares about is hitting the freighters, I'm guessing one or two HuKs and one of the light cruisers would get past us unless we scored a lot of lucky hits on him." Marphissa leaned forward, thinking. "He's a snake. They don't worry about how many citizens die. But they do worry about equipment. Ramming through our warships would mean losing a minimum of two-thirds of his force, assuming we didn't manage to catch and wipe out the survivors after they had managed to hit the freighters. That's the big question. How badly does he want to hurt those freighters?"

"We don't know his orders," Kapitan Diaz pointed out.

"But he's a snake. He's in command of the flotilla, meaning he is responding to orders from the senior snake in this star system. What would that senior snake want?"

Diaz made a derisory noise. "He's a Syndicate CEO, right? So he wants optimum results at minimum or no cost."

Marphissa nodded. "He's not going to want to take losses doing this, or at least he'll want to keep those losses to a minimum. This isn't a war engagement to them. It's an internal security action where our losses don't matter, but they want to keep theirs down."

"Why is he holding that course, then? We'll shrink our defensive shield down to hit him with everything when he comes through it. He'll take heavy losses and not manage to hit the freighters hard."

"Ah!" Marphissa banged her own fist against her forehead. "That's what he's doing! His goal is to get through to the freighters!"

"I thought I said that," Diaz complained.

"He wants me to concentrate my screening forces! And I'm going to make him think I'm doing that!" Her hands moved across her display, painting new tracks for her ships, fixing that as stage one of a maneuver, then altering the tracks dramatically for stage two. *I have to time this right. He needs to think I'm falling for it.* "All warships in the Recovery Flotilla, new maneuvering orders are attached. Execute orders at time one seven. Marphissa, out."

Diaz nodded as he viewed the attachment, then frowned. But he had been trained in the Syndicate system, so he entered the commands into *Manticore*'s maneuvering systems without asking further questions.

At time one seven, thrusters fired on the cruisers and HuKs of the Midway force, pitching them onto converging courses that would dramatically shrink the size of the defensive shield and allow concentrated fire against the oncoming Syndicate flotilla. *What if I'm wrong?* Marphissa worried. *If I guessed wrong, what happens next will let him get through with a lot more of his mobile forces intact. But I must be right. Sub-CEO Qui may or may not be worried about losses, but he is worried about fulfilling his orders, and he needs his ships intact to do that.*

"Five minutes to contact," the operations specialist announced.

"All units," Marphissa sent, "engage any Syndicate warship that comes within range. Keep any of them from getting on vectors that intercept the freighters."

"They're already in those vectors," Diaz pointed out.

"Not for long," Marphissa replied with considerably more confidence than she felt inside.

At two minutes before contact, the second stage of her plan cut in. Thrusters fired again, pitching ships up and outward from the line the Syndicate flotilla would follow to reach the freighters. Even the two heavy cruisers swayed out from a direct intercept of the oncoming Syndicate forces.

Diaz, clearly nerving himself to question her orders, suddenly stared at his display. "What are they doing?"

"What I knew they would do!" Marphissa announced trium-
phantly.

The Syndicate formation had broken, the individual warships flow-
ering outward in a spreading pattern that would pass above, below,
and on all sides of the vector they had been following.

"If we had concentrated around the vector line—" Diaz began.

"They would have passed outward of us on every side! That was
Sub-CEO Qui's plan, to trick us into a compact formation that he
would bypass by suddenly spreading out his ships. Now, Kapitan, get
one of those light cruisers for me!"

Manticore's new vector was swinging up and to port, toward the
new vector from a Syndicate light cruiser that had bent his vector forty
degrees upward to pass over the Midway forces.

Marphissa's hands flew across her display, ensuring that every Syndicate warship had at least one Midway warship slewing outward to
intercept it before it could get past the defensive shield.

Manticore was heading for a light cruiser, *Kraken* had targeted another, and three of Marphissa's light cruisers, *Harrier*, *Kite*, and *Eagle*,
were swooping down and to the right after the third Syndicate light
cruiser. Light cruiser *Falcon* had a Syndicate HuK in its sights, while
the six HuKs of Marphissa's forces were accelerating onto vectors
aimed at the remaining three Syndicate HuKs. The single, rapidly approaching time to contact had dissolved into a dozen different estimates of when different parts of the opposing forces would come
within weapons range of each other.

But those estimates began shifting wildly as the Syndicate warships realized that their ploy had failed, and they were facing superior
numbers of defenders at every point on the approach to the freighters.
Syndicate light cruisers and HuKs bent their vectors even farther,
spreading wider and fanning outward to all sides, as they tried to
avoid contact with the Midway warships.

The light cruiser *Manticore* was aiming for twisted to starboard
and out, then swung port and in, climbing and turning in a vast cork-

screw as it attempted to get past the defending heavy cruiser. Diaz, his face tense with concentration, matched the maneuvers, trying to ensure he would remain on an intercept and not tear past the attacker and leave the light cruiser with a clear path to the freighters.

All around the vector along which the freighters would be coming, similar moves and countermoves were taking place as warships moving at point one light speed, or thirty thousand kilometers a second, twisted through arcs and turns whose width would have been incredibly broad measured against the surface of a planet. The distance required to change direction when moving at such velocities was huge in space as well, but also tiny compared to the size of the enormous, literally limitless-in-all-directions, battlefield on which the warships were engaging each other.

A Syndicate HuK being blocked by two Midway HuKs darted toward what looked like a gap between them, getting past one defender but finding itself unable to avoid the second. Hell lances shot between the two HuKs, hammering at the weak shields and nearly nonexistent armor of the Hunter-Killers, the Syndicate HuK breaking back, then diving away to avoid the second Midway HuK as it stormed into the engagement.

The light cruiser trying to evade past *Manticore* inadvertently swung for a moment into the missile engagement envelope of *Kraken*. The automated fire control systems on *Kraken* immediately pumped out two missiles, doubtless startling *Kraken*'s crew almost as much as it did the light cruiser. As *Kraken* continued swinging far to port to block the light cruiser she was pursuing, her missiles tore after the light cruiser being chased by *Manticore*. Unable to cope with both threats and continue trying to reach the freighters, that light cruiser rolled all the way over and began accelerating away for all he was worth while the missiles thundered in single-minded pursuit.

The single Syndicate HuK trying to get past light cruiser *Falcon* tried to dart under her, but *Falcon* had anticipated the maneuver and slammed repeated hell lances into the HuK. The Syndicate warship staggered away, accelerating frantically, holes pitting him where hell lances had punched completely through hull, equipment, and any crew members unfortunate enough to be in the way before the only-slightly-weakened particle beams shot out the opposite side.

The other Syndicate warships pulled away, taking up positions where they hovered relative to the defenders, unable to get through this time but clearly preparing to try again.

The entire bridge team on *Manticore* gave the impression of sighing with relief as it became apparent the first assault by the Syndicate warships had been deflected.

"Don't relax," Kapitan Diaz ordered his crew. "We stopped them, but they'll be back."

Marphissa, taking in the sheer volume of space involved in her defensive effort, shook her head. The light cruiser being chased by *Kraken*'s missiles had managed to outrun them and was now coming back, while the damaged HuK had slowed its retreat and was angling back toward his comrades. Syndicate warships were ranged around the forward portion of the freighters' track and out to all sides, with great gaps between them. None of them had shifted position farther back than about even with the freighters, wanting to avoid stern chases as they made firing runs. That left a defensive perimeter in the shape of half of an elongated sphere, the long axis running forward of the freighters.

"You were right," Marphissa told Bradamont. "They've spread out in an attempt to make me spread out my own ships. If I tried to defend every point in a region that size, it would be hopeless. Only by focusing on the attackers and stopping them at each specific point where they try to penetrate the defenses can I make this work."

"You'd still have a lot of problems if you didn't have the superiority in numbers that you do," Bradamont pointed out. She must have noticed Kapitan Diaz looking speculatively at her and Marphissa, because Bradamont added something else. "I discussed the theory of this type of operation with your Kommodor, Kapitan Diaz. *She* is commanding your defense."

Marphissa took a moment to glance at Bradamont. "What do you think Sub-CEO Qui will try next? Just more of the same?"

"Probably plenty of more of the same," Bradamont said. "Individual ships trying to get to the freighters if they think they see an opening, and coordinated attempts to break through at multiple points. But you also need to look for him deliberately sacrificing some of his ships by putting them onto vectors that lure a lot of your ships into lunging for them to get in on the kill. If Qui does it right, that could leave big gaps in your defenses that his remaining ships could charge through."

Marphissa shook her head again. "No. That wouldn't work. I've assigned targets to each of my ships now. They're not going to go after someone else unless I tell them to."

"Huh?" Bradamont's look of puzzlement cleared. "Oh. I forgot. You're Syndics."

"What did you say?" Normally, Marphissa probably would have enjoyed knowing that Bradamont had forgotten for a moment at least that she and her comrades had been part of the Syndicate not all that long ago. But a statement that she and they still *were* Syndicate was another matter.

The heat in her response caused Bradamont to flush. "I'm sorry. I didn't mean it that way. I was thinking about what would work against an Alliance force defending those freighters. But you've been trained differently."

Differently. That was a nice way of describing a system in which failure to obey in all ways meant extremely serious consequences. But . . . "It's nice to hear one way in which we're superior to Black Jack's fleet," Marphissa said.

"I guess in this context you are," Bradamont admitted.

"Kommodor," Diaz said cautiously, "I believe that the Alliance Kapitan may be right in her suggestion."

"You do?" Marphissa felt an alarming impulse to slap Diaz down for expressing an opinion contrary to hers. *When did I start getting angry at people who didn't agree with me? When did listening become harder?* "You do?" she repeated in a manner more questioning and less intimidating.

"Sub-CEO Qui is a snake," Diaz explained. "Snakes always think citizens will do things they are not supposed to do. They always think we're going to do something wrong. And Qui is a sub-CEO. You know what Syndicate CEOs and sub-CEOs are like. They think if they're not standing right behind you and making sure you do just what they say, you'll screw up and do what you're not supposed to. It doesn't matter how many times they see workers do things right. They still think that."

"Not all CEOs and sub-CEOs are like that," Marphissa corrected. "Look at President Iceni. But, otherwise, you have a point. Qui may think that would work, especially since he will assume our ships are controlled by recently promoted executives and workers."

"They are," Diaz pointed out. "A lot of them, anyway."

And, maybe, Diaz was right that not all of those new commanders would adhere to strict Syndicate discipline, lacking enough experience with higher rank under that system. Two of the Midway Hunter-Killers had commanders who had been vaulted up in rank even more rapidly than Marphissa had. "Thank you for bringing that up," she said. "Both of you."

After another moment's thought, she tapped her comms again. "All warships in the Recovery Flotilla, you are to remain focused on the Syndicate warships you have been assigned as targets. You are not to attempt to engage or pursue any other Syndicate warship unless you receive orders from me to do so. I am confident that if you continue to perform as well as you have so far, we will defeat the Syndicate."

She slumped back, keeping her eyes locked on her display. *Why am I so tired? I feel like we've been fighting for hours.*

Stars in the heavens. We have been.

As the Syndicate light cruisers and HuKs swung restlessly around the protective screen of Midway warships, Marphissa checked the path of the freighters, plodding along en route to the gate, where lay safety.

The transit to the gate would take another forty-one hours.

She stared at the time, disbelieving, then despairing for a moment. All they had to do was keep doing for another forty-one hours what they had been doing for the last few hours, each warship constantly alert to any motion by the Syndicate warship it was targeted on, and Marphissa watching every warship to ensure that none of the Syndicate warships threatened to make it through the defenders and none of the defenders wavered in their responsibilities. *Yeah, that's all we have to do. For another forty-one hours straight.* Marphissa clenched her teeth, breathed in through them in a hiss, then spoke to the senior watch specialist on the bridge. "Contact the ship's doctor. We need to have a good supply of up patches on the bridge."

"Yes, Kommodor," the specialist replied, followed a few seconds later by a question. "The doctor wants to know how many would be a good supply."

"Enough to keep me awake and functioning for the next forty-one hours."

"Kommodor, the doctor says—"

"*I know what the regulations say!* Get those damned patches onto the bridge!"

"Yes, Kommodor," the senior watch specialist said warily several seconds later.

Bradamont went to one knee beside Marphissa's seat, her voice a low murmur. "What do the regulations say?"

"They say," Marphissa growled in reply, "that use of up patches for any period in excess of thirty-six hours must be authorized by the senior commander. That's me."

"Will you be safe? I can take over for a while if you need to rest."

Marphissa shook her head, her eyes not leaving her display. "You said it, Honore, and you were right. They won't let you command them now that they know what you are. I have to do this."

"Then make sure there are enough patches for both of us."

"Three of us," Diaz said.

Marphissa contemplated ordering either or both of them to take rest breaks, then changed her mind. *If they can't do it, I can't do it. So we three will do it.* "Make certain that the watch specialists and other crew members cycle through their watches and get rest," she ordered Diaz.

"We'll have to go modified on-watch/off-watch to make that work," Diaz said. "Eight hours on, four hours off for the duration, with individual shifts staggered. We don't have enough specialists on board to work the ship at combat status around the clock except by doing that."

Damned Syndicate economizing on crew sizes. *Don't worry,* they would say. *If anything breaks, it will be fixed the next time you're at a dockyard. Cold comfort when you're fighting a battle!* "I understand. I've been through that. We have to keep as close to peak combat capability as possible for the next forty-one hours because you can be sure that the Syndicate flotilla will not give us any rest breaks."

"Incoming message from Colonel Rogero," the comm specialist advised.

Any message was a distraction she didn't need, but she couldn't blow off Rogero. "Yes, Colonel?"

Rogero was on the bridge of the freighter carrying him, wearing his armor. "Kommodor, I wanted to advise you that you need have no fear of any of the freighters acting contrary to your orders. I have soldiers posted on the bridges of each freighter. I'll keep at least one soldier there on each ship as long as we're still in Indras, to ensure that none of your orders are misinterpreted, misheard, or misunderstood."

She could read between the lines on that one. At least one of the freighter executives had thought to bolt or was wavering, only to be brought up short by armed soldiers determined to enforce Marphissa's orders. "Thank you, Colonel. That does relieve a concern of mine."

Rogero smiled grimly. "I won't bother you again unless it is absolutely necessary, Kommodor. For the people. Out."

"Any problems?" Diaz asked.

"No," Marphissa replied. "Just some reinforcement for the spines of the freighter executives."

"Oh. You know," Diaz added, "they're not military. The freighter executives and crews, I mean. No weapons, no defenses, they're just sitting ducks. That can't be easy."

"Do you think what we're doing is easy?"

He flinched at her tone of voice. "No, Kommodor."

But she thought about it, thought about all of the men and women on those freighters, most of them unable to even see a display to know what was going on, with no means of defense, and nothing they could do but sit and wait to see if hell lances would punch holes in the ships carrying them, as well as holes in the people on those ships.

At least the warships carried what were in theory enough escape pods to carry their crews to safety if the ship was too badly damaged to save. Not their entire crews, of course, because the Syndicate had carefully calculated what percentage of damage on average would render a ship helpless and what percentage of crew members on average would be killed when that damage was sustained, then budgeted for just enough escape pods to save the average surviving percentage of the crew. It was all very scientific, including the calculations that offering escape to the surviving crew members cost less than what would be required to conscript, transport, and train new crew members to replace them.

But for all that, the crews of the warships were better off than those on the freighters. The only escape pod on each of the freighters was designed to handle the crew and perhaps a few passengers. "You are right," she commented to Kapitan Diaz, "it cannot be easy on those freighters."

"It's not easy on you, either, is it?" he asked.

"No," Marphissa admitted. "There's a comfort in having someone higher in authority to turn to, having someone else who must make the decisions. Having been frustrated all of my time in the mobile forces by superiors who handled that role badly, I now have the freedom to make the decisions, to make the mistakes, all on my own. Hold on."

The Syndicate warships had all swung in again simultaneously, veering onto vectors aiming for the freighters. Marphissa watched the entire situation with all of her concentration, trying to spot any place where any of her warships were being outmaneuvered by the Syndicate attackers. She was barely aware of Diaz maneuvering *Manticore* to engage the light cruiser that was *Manticore*'s designated target, but Marphissa was fully alert to *Manticore*'s track on her display, alert to any indication that Diaz might let the light cruiser get past him. She took in every one of her ships' maneuvers that way, hoping that neither she nor one of her ship commanders would miss something.

One by one, the Syndicate warships, facing intercepts by superior firepower, broke off their runs against the freighters. They went back to positions hovering in front of and to all sides of the Midway Flotilla, roaming restlessly like wolves seeking openings to get at sheep guarded by alert watchdogs.

Over the next several hours, the Syndicate warships tried again and again at irregular intervals, sometimes all at once, other times in staggered rushes, and many times only one or two ships testing the defenders. "Sub-CEO Qui is trying to wear you down," Bradamont said. "He's hoping that if he keeps the pressure on, sooner or later, you or one of your ship commanders will get tired enough to make a serious mistake."

"I can do this longer than he can," Marphissa retorted. The up patch on her arm was trickling drugs that kept her alert into her body. There would be a price to pay for that as time went on, but, for now, she felt fine.

As the hours and the Syndicate probing attacks went on and on, the Syndicate warships spread wider around the Midway ships, so that eventually they completely surrounded Marphissa's warships and freighters. The Midway warships were now defending an elongated bubble stretching along the vector that the freighters were traveling to the hypernet gate. In space, any ship could build up velocity if given time. Freighters usually didn't move too fast, because accelerating and braking cost fuel cells, and transport companies liked to minimize costs, but this time Marphissa had told them to get up to point one light speed and hold it there.

It would have been nice to get the freighters going even faster, but she had to worry about their using up too much of their fuel cells. For that matter, the frequent attacks and counterattacks under way had been a serious drain on the fuel cells of her warships. *The Syndicate warships have to be using up their fuel cells as well. How close to maximum were they when this started?*

Sixteen hours into the running battle, a Syndicate light cruiser and two HuKs lunged toward the freighters along vectors that invited interception by multiple defending warships. Sub-CEO Qui was finally trying the trick that Bradamont had warned of.

"All units, maintain focus on your designated target. Do not attempt intercepts of any other Syndicate warships unless I order it."

The light cruiser and HuKs held their approaches until the Midway warships targeting them were nearly within weapons range, then slewed around as fast as they could turn and darted out of range.

At twenty-five hours after the fight had started, every Syndicate warship again attacked at once. Two of Marphissa's ships, the light cruiser *Harrier* and the HuK *Vanguard*, reacted slowly this time. The other Midway HuK, *Scout*, watching that particular Syndicate HuK tore after its target so ferociously that the Syndicate vessel broke off.

But the Syndicate HuK that should have been stopped by *Harrier* kept coming.

Marphissa's eyes flew across her display, too little time available to run intercept calculations, her instincts feeling the next right move in the second she had to decide. "*Kite*, alter course to intercept new target. Maximum acceleration authorized."

Had she chosen right? No one was close to the Syndicate HuK, but the light cruiser *Kite* had the best chance. Kite's *commander will have to push her past the red lines on hull stress to manage an intercept. I might lose* Kite *to hull breakup and have that Syndicate HuK get through anyway.*

Kite was located above and about even with the freighters. The Syndicate HuK was climbing in from partly below and behind the two columns of freighters. If not for the velocity of the freighters themselves, forcing the Syndicate HuK onto a longer approach to catch up, there would have been no chance of stopping the attack at all.

A single tap by Marphissa produced detailed status information on *Kite* from the light cruiser's data feed. Her thrusters firing, *Kite* was angling over and down, her main propulsion lighting off at maximum, hull-stress readings climbing.

An alert appeared next to *Kite*'s symbol on Marphissa's display. *Excessive hull stress imminent. Reduce acceleration.*

She negated the warning, only to have it pop up again. *Action required.*

Marphissa punched the negate command this time. It appeared once more. "I thought we killed this function in the software," she complained.

Diaz motioned to the senior watch specialist, who went to work on that.

The vector for the Syndicate HuK formed a flattened curve aiming to pass between the top and bottom columns of freighters. The arc of *Kite*'s vector was swinging over, sweeping steadily toward an intersection with that of the Syndicate HuK's projected path.

Another alert appeared over *Kite*'s symbol, this one blinking in red. *Excessive hull stress. Reduce acceleration immediately.*

Bradamont had knelt by Marphissa's seat again. "Can *Kite* do this?"

"It's up to her commander," Marphissa replied without looking away from her display. "Only he can judge whether *Kite*'s hull can take it."

Excessive hull stress. Structural failure imminent. Reduce acceleration immediately.

The point where *Kite*'s vector crossed that of the Syndicate HuK had crept just ahead of where the HuK would catch up with the freighters. The HuK was also accelerating for all it was worth, trying to steal the march on *Kite*, but wasn't able to equal a light cruiser's maximum effort. *That's enough, damn you!* Marphissa thought, reaching for her comm controls.

But before she could touch them *Kite*'s data feed changed. "He's throttled back a little."

Had it been enough? The warnings continued to blink their crimson message, and now *Kite*'s data feed rippled as damage reports came in. "Asima," Bradamont cautioned, sounding horrified. "If any of those stress points completely blow, that ship will disintegrate."

This time, Marphissa reached for her override. All ships designed to Syndicate standards contained overrides that allowed a flotilla commander to take over control of that ship directly. She had once vowed that she would never do such a thing.

But it might already be too late.

CHAPTER SEVENTEEN

BRADAMONT'S gasp halted Marphissa's motion.

Kite had throttled back again, this time significantly. The damage to her structure was still there, but the red-line warnings of hull stress were sliding downward toward safer territory.

Kite whipped past the stern quarter of the last freighter in the upper column and bore down on the lone Syndicate HuK, pounding it with hell lances and the metal ball bearings known as grapeshot that became incredibly dangerous projectiles when they struck something at thousands of kilometers per second.

The Syndicate HuK, which had been pushing his own acceleration to the maximum, took those blows on a hull already under the most stress it could handle.

The HuK exploded into fragments, some large, some small, fountaining outward and forward along the vector the warship had still been accelerating upon when the vessel came apart. In an instant, the track of a single oncoming warship turned into hundreds of pieces of wreckage, racing toward the freighters as if the HuK's remnants were still trying to get in a blow even after the warship's destruction.

But because the HuK had been aiming to pass between the upper and lower lines of freighters, most of the debris went through that open area as well, passing onward harmlessly.

Some fragments did impact the last freighters, bringing to life new warnings on Marphissa's display as the damage reports flowed in automatically. The thing she feared most to see, a major hull breach on one of the freighters, did not appear in the first wave of damage reports. A scattering of new reports came in, minor hull damage and some minor systems damage, then the wave of wreckage was past.

Kite was swinging back up and around in a vast parabola that was not nearly as stressful on her hull as the previous maneuvers had been. "Target destroyed," *Kite* reported rather smugly. "Reverting to previous assigned target."

Bradamont clapped Marphissa on the shoulder. "Only sixteen more hours to go."

"Is that all?" Marphissa got control of her voice, then called *Kite*. "Very good job. Let's all ensure no one else gets through."

She shook her head, gazing at *Kite*'s damage status. "She's going to be limited in maneuvers until we can get her into a dockyard. And she burned a lot of fuel doing that. Only sixteen hours, you said?"

"Yes," Bradamont replied. "Are you good?"

"I'm great." *At lying.* Her heart pumping from stress that had burned through drugs quicker than usual, Marphissa checked the status of her up patch, pulled it off, and slapped on another.

The next six hours were a nightmare of repeated lunges by the Syndicate ships and parries by Marphissa's warships. Fire was actually exchanged again twice; once when *Manticore* fired missiles at the Syndicate light cruiser that was her target, causing the light cruiser to flee, and once when two Midway HuKs maneuvered a Syndicate HuK into a sandwich, where they could get in a few hits before the Syndicate HuK twisted away.

After a pause, the attacks resumed. Lunge. Intercept. Reposition. Attack. Defend. Re-form. Despite the drugs in her, Marphissa felt the strain of nearly constant concentration on the movements of multiple ships as two, then three more hours went by inconclusively.

An entire hour passed without more attempted attacks, the Syndicate warships positioned all around the Midway Flotilla continuing to stalk their prey but making no moves to strike.

"What's he doing?" Marphissa asked Bradamont, shocked to hear how her voice cracked when she spoke.

A watch specialist approached Marphissa, Bradamont, and Diaz with a ration bar and water for each of them. Marphissa barely looked at him, not able to risk taking her focus from her display, but nodded her thanks and tried briefly to remember how many times the watch specialists had been relieved and replaced while she, Diaz, and Marphissa had remained on duty.

She popped open the gray ration-bar wrapper with the big, block letters that shouted "Fresh! Tasty! Nutritious!" as if font size could somehow make the claims reflect the reality of a ration bar. Marphissa chewed the ration bar mechanically, discovering that probably thanks to the up patches, she couldn't sense the usual bitter aftertaste, or the usual moldy, musty flavor that was actually preferable to the aftertaste.

Bradamont finished swallowing a bite before answering, her own voice hoarse. "We always wondered if these Syndic ration bars tasted any better when they were less stale. Now I know that they don't. I don't know what Sub-CEO Qui is doing. But he's got to be getting desperate. You are less than five hours' travel time from the hypernet gate. If he's going to stop you or hurt you, he has to do it within that time."

Marphissa nodded again. "If we can use the hypernet gate," she whispered, putting into words what they both feared.

"He's trying awfully hard to hammer us," Bradamont whispered back hoarsely. "If Qui knew we couldn't leave via the hypernet, he would know he had a lot more time to wear us down."

It was odd how, even under the stress of such a long, running fight and with everything except her mental clarity impacted by the up patches, Marphissa could still feel a sense of pleasure at hearing Brad-amont use the words "we" and "us." "I think," Marphissa said, "that he is trying to lull us. He knows how worn-out everybody on these ships is. He might be assuming that giving us an hour or two of inac-tivity might make us slack off."

"Or he could be resting his own crews," Bradamont pointed out.

Marphissa almost choked on another bite of ration bar, swallowed it painfully, then gasped a brief laugh. "He's a snake. Sub-CEO Qui is a snake. He won't let them rest."

Kapitan Diaz, slumped in his own seat, nodded in agreement. "You'll get a rest when the job is done," he quoted. "Unless you have to do it over again."

"No work breaks until morale improves!" Marphissa added. "No, Honore, I guarantee you that Sub-CEO Qui is not giving his crews a rest. So far they have failed. *He*, their leader, has not failed," she added sarcastically. "They have. That's the Syndicate way. He is riding them hard, making them work harder, telling them that unless they suc-ceed, they will be punished for their failure."

"But he'll be punished, too," Diaz said, "especially once the Syndi-cate learns who we are and that we brought those Reserve Flotilla survivors back with us."

"Right," Marphissa agreed, "because it can't be the fault of the CEO who sent Sub-CEO Qui on this mission, so it has to be Qui's fault."

"There are times," Bradamont said, "when the Alliance fleet works the same way."

"That's probably why you couldn't beat the Syndicate until Black Jack came back," Diaz said. "That and because we're such tough bas-tards." He laughed.

"Check your up meds, Kapitan," Marphissa ordered him. She drank all of her water, wondering just how much more uncomfortable she would get in the hours remaining, then hit her comm controls. "All units. It is likely that Sub-CEO Qui, the snake commander, is trying to lure us into losing alertness by conducting no actions for an extended period. Remain prepared." What sort of motivation would someone like Bradamont give? Not the standard Syndicate *fail and you will regret it.* "You have all done an exceptional job so far. A few more hours, and we will have won. For the people, Marphissa, out."

Another hour passed. Marphissa felt a growing sense of worry battling with the bodily fatigue the up patches couldn't completely banish. *Maybe Qui has learned that we can't use the hypernet gate. Maybe he's waiting until we get to the gate and realize we can't escape that way. He'll have a lot more time to wear us down then, and a lot more time to wait for reinforcements, while I try to keep defending these freighters using ships with worn-out crews and fuel-cell levels that are already lower than I'm comfortable with. Where the hell would I jump to? We'll never make it back to the jump point for Kalixa in one piece.*

"Two hours left," Diaz mumbled, then blinked, sat straighter, and slapped on another up patch.

The nest of vectors for the Syndicate warships, which had been unchanging for hours, suddenly altered.

"They're coming again!" Marphissa snapped. "This may be their last shot. They're going to push these firing runs. Everyone, don't let them through!"

The surviving Syndicate warships, three light cruisers and four Hunter-Killers, were coming in hard and fast. Marphissa watched them, feeling a growing, bleak certainty that this time the Syndicate warships would not avoid action no matter the odds. If they did not damage or destroy those freighters this time, they might not get another chance.

The light cruiser that was *Manticore*'s target had spun to one side and climbed, then dove, to confuse *Manticore*'s intercept. But Diaz kept *Manticore* glued on the light cruiser's vector, his face gray with fatigue but his eyes sharp. "All weapons," he ordered in a voice that came out in a croak. "Engage."

Two missiles leaped from *Manticore* as the heavy cruiser raced to an intercept that went past in less time than the blink of an eye, hell lances and grapeshot lashing out on the heels of the missiles. All around the loose perimeter of defenders, other warships were closing to contact, weapons pummeling each other.

Marphissa could only wait to see the outcomes of engagements that took place far too rapidly for human senses to register.

The light cruiser targeted by *Manticore* had tried another last-second evasive maneuver, but *Manticore*'s missiles had both slammed home, inflicting massive damage amidships that had been joined by numerous hits from hell lances and grapeshot that had riddled the light cruiser's bow. All weapons and many other systems out of commission, thrown off of his intended course by the missile impacts, the Syndicate light cruiser spun away helplessly.

Behind and below the freighters, light cruisers *Harrier*, *Kite*, and *Eagle* hit another Syndicate light cruiser in successive firing passes within a few seconds of each other. In their wake, an expanding ball of dustlike debris marked all that was left of the Syndicate warship after its power core had overloaded under the blows.

One of the Syndicate HuKs also died as light cruiser *Falcon* caught it with a perfect barrage that tore apart the small, lightly armored warship.

The light cruiser targeted by *Kraken*, though, was coming up from almost dead astern, his approach prolonged by the stern chase, and saw the other two light cruisers destroyed. He broke off from his firing run, climbing above the formation, out of range of *Kraken*'s weapons.

The three surviving Syndicate HuKs, all bearing wounds from clashes with Midway HuKs, also had second thoughts, tearing away to right, left, and below-ahead of the Midway formation.

Marphissa inhaled deeply, wondering how long it had been since she had breathed. "I wonder if we got Qui."

"He might have been on one of those light cruisers we destroyed," Diaz said. "Or he might have been the one who decided to save his own skin."

"He is a snake," Marphissa agreed. She rubbed her eyes and refocused on her display. "They could still get us." Moving carefully, she touched her comm controls. "All units, this is Kommodor Marphissa. Very well done. But we cannot relax yet. It is another forty-five minutes until we reach the gate. I am redistributing assigned targets. Make sure anyone who attacks again does not survive."

She assigned the sole remaining Syndicate light cruiser as a target for both *Manticore* and *Kraken*, then distributed her light cruisers and HuKs to watch the three remaining Syndicate HuKs. *Are we safe? They shouldn't be able to make it to the freighters now. But I can't relax, can't assume they won't try again out of desperation. Can't relax. Don't dare relax. Not yet.*

"Kommodor?"

Marphissa blinked at the senior watch specialist who had called to her, trying to reorient thoughts that had been locked obsessively on the Syndicate flotilla. "What is it?"

"Kommodor, our hypernet key indicates that Midway's gate is accessible."

"It's . . ." Marphissa looked away from the Syndicate warships, seeing the hypernet gate looming massive and near.

"We're here," Diaz said, his voice disbelieving. "We're at the gate."

"When can we leave?" Marphissa asked. "Is the destination entered?"

"We can leave at your command, Kommodor. Midway is entered as the destination."

She took another look at the Syndicate warships, which had begun to fall back, increasing the distance between them and the Midway Flotilla. Her own warships were still ranging out from the freighters, but were within the radius that could be set for the hypernet key. "Go. Now. All ships."

There was no jolt to the nervous system as in entering jump space, but even if there had been, Marphissa doubted whether she would have been able to feel it. She stared at her display, where the Syndicate warships and the Indras Star System had vanished along with everything else.

Manticore and all the other ships of the Recovery Flotilla, all the warships and every one of the freighters, were nowhere, safe in the hypernet.

She heard a strange noise and turned to look, seeing that the watch specialists were all applauding. Why? They were looking at her. Why?

Bradamont was hauling Marphissa to her feet, though once she was up Bradamont had to lean on Marphissa as much as Marphissa leaned on her. "I told you that you could do it," Bradamont said, her voice seeming to come through a few layers of gauze.

Marphissa managed to stand straight and look at the watch specialists. "I could not have done it without you," she said. "We did this . . . I am going to rest now. You, too, Kapitan Diaz."

"Yes, Kommodor. Senior Watch Specialist Lehmann, you are to . . . call Leytenant Pillai . . . to assume command of the bridge. Return the crew to . . . standard ship's routine." Diaz staggered upright, grinning foolishly at his success in saying the orders coherently.

They walked off the bridge. Marphissa wondered if the ship's gravity was having problems. As she walked, the deck seemed to be going up and down under her feet like the deck of a ship on a planet's sea. She reached her stateroom and realized that Bradamont had dropped off along the way at her own stateroom.

Marphissa entered, sealed the hatch, and locked it out of habit, fell into the bunk, grabbed the crash patch the ship's doctor had laid out there almost two days earlier, slapped it on, then lay back, wide-open eyes staring at the overhead. Until the crash patch counteracted the drugs in the up patch, she wouldn't be able to sleep.

She didn't remember when that happened, didn't remember dropping into the deep sleep of utter exhaustion. But at some point dreams intruded, dreams of Syndicate warships conducting firing runs, getting past her defenses, blowing apart freighters. And she was asleep on the bridge, passed out, unable to wake up even though she was bending every effort—

Marphissa jolted awake, her eyes open, staring into the darkened stateroom. *I'm not on the bridge.* She fumbled for her display. *We're in the hypernet.*

Tense nerves collapsed with relief, and sleep overcame her again.

HE had been awake the entire fight, making sure the freighter executives didn't do anything they shouldn't, and had now slept for what felt like almost as long a time. Instincts honed by a life of combat had recovered enough that Rogero came awake instantly at the soft knock on his door, one hand already closing about his sidearm. "Who?"

"Seki Ito." The door opened, revealing Executive Ito with her open hands held out from her sides. "No danger. I just thought you might like some company."

"Company?" That could mean a lot of different things.

Ito's smile in response to his question made it obvious what company meant in this case. "I bet it's been a while for both of us. No strings. Unless you want that."

It had been a while, and having Bradamont on the same ship but being unable to even touch her had not made things any easier. Nor was it unheard of for single (or married) personnel far from home to temporarily step outside of partnership commitments.

But as nice as Ito looked at the moment, and as much as he knew he would enjoy her "company," Rogero did not want to cheat on his commitment to Bradamont. "Thanks, but . . ." He tried to leave it at that.

Ito gave him an inviting look. "Are you sure? With Pers Garadun gone, I could use another patron."

Ouch. Maybe this is more about Ito's chances of getting a mobile forces command at Midway than it is about me. Perhaps I'm not that desirable after all. Fortunately, I'm old enough not to be devastated by that. "I can already recommend you for assignments, but General Drakon has strict rules about seniors sleeping with subordinates."

This time Ito raised both eyebrows at him skeptically. "There have always been strict rules against it everywhere in Syndicate space, and it happens all the time everywhere in Syndicate space."

"Yes, but General Drakon actually enforces those rules."

"That's boring. Well . . . if you're certain you're not lonely . . ." Ito changed her posture only slightly, but suddenly her body looked a lot more alluring to the male eye.

How do women do that? Rogero wondered. "No. Nothing personal."

Ito sighed theatrically, spreading her hands in the ancient gesture meaning what-can-I-do?

"Ito?"

"Yes?" She smiled.

"I heard Pers Garadun tell you and Executive Jepsen to tell everyone about what really happened at Kalixa, but Jepsen told me when I saw him that you had directed him not to, that you would take care of it alone."

"That's right," Ito agreed.

"I told Jepsen to go ahead and tell everyone while we were transiting through Indras. There was no need for you to be the only one responsible. I wanted you to know that Jepsen didn't disregard your instructions."

"Oh. All right. If that's what you want." She gave him one more questioning look. "If that is *all* you want?"

"Yes."

She left, closing the door behind her.

Exhaling in relief, Rogero lay back and looked upward, feeling ridiculously proud of himself for having resisted temptation. *It is a triumph I will have to keep to myself, of course. Honore Bradamont is unlikely to be as impressed by my achievement. Though if I had given*

in to temptation and she had ever learned of it, the consequences would
no doubt have been apocalyptic.

GWEN Iceni was awakened by the urgent pulsing of the comm panel next to her bed. She had a weapon in her hand and was scanning her darkened bedroom before waking up enough to realize that it wasn't a warning of intrusion. "Iceni. What is it?"

"They're back, Madam President!" the command center supervisor announced. "The Recovery Flotilla. They have arrived at the hypernet gate, and Kommodor Marphissa has sent a message saying they accomplished their mission. She is sending a more detailed report."

A weight she had not been aware of carrying dropped from Iceni. "All of them? All of the ships we sent came back?"

"Yes, Madam President. They are all here."

"I'll see the detailed report in the morning. If Kommodor Marphissa hasn't already begun doing so, tell her to bring the ships of the Recovery Flotilla to this planet and place them in orbit."

There were plenty of weights left on her, and those Reserve Flotilla survivors would have to be screened to ensure they could each be trusted, but thousands of new, trained crew members for her warships would make every other concern a lot easier to bear.

Everything had worked out.

Something was bound to go wrong very soon.

ICENI ran one hand lightly over the display before her, causing virtual sheets of debriefing papers to ruffle past like the pages of a real book. "These supervisors and specialists from the Reserve Flotilla are a real gift."

Togo caught the reserve in her voice, but then anyone could have. "You are concerned, Madam President?"

"I am concerned when things seem to be too good to be true." She pressed one fist against her mouth as she thought. "We need to screen these people very carefully. I want to be sure they are who they say they are, I want to be sure they feel no allegiance toward the Syndicate, and I want to be sure they can be trusted to make up the majority of the crews of two extremely powerful warships."

"This can be done," Togo said. "But it will take time. That level of review will require use of facilities with limited capacities and use of skilled interrogation personnel who are in limited numbers."

"Take the time." Iceni glanced at her calendar. "How are the elections going?"

"There have been no reported problems. Many citizens are voting, believing your assurances that these elections will actually count their votes to decide the victors. A few troublesome candidates may win their posts, but we can easily manipulate the reported vote totals to ensure they lose."

"Do we want to do that?" Iceni asked. "I've been thinking. If these people gain power, no matter how little we actually give them, they'll also gain responsibility. They'll either do their jobs well, in which case they may be worth listening to, or they'll fail, in which case their troublesome aspects can be used to justify their losses in subsequent elections. But we may not have to manipulate the vote totals if we hold these candidates' feet to the fire when it comes to their actual performance."

Togo did not reply at first, undecipherable thoughts moving behind his eyes. "You would treat them as another class of workers?"

"Why not?" Iceni demanded. Malin had given her the idea in one of his covert communications, or suggested it anyway, and she had found the concept growing on her. "They are workers. They are working for me and for whoever voted for them. If they don't keep me happy, if they don't keep those who voted for them happy, then they will be held accountable. That's how even an extremely limited democracy is supposed to work. In theory, anyway."

"Madam President, what if they keep the people who voted for them happy but make you unhappy?"

Iceni smiled. "That would be a dilemma, wouldn't it? But as someone whose judgment I respect remarked to me, the most difficult subordinates can be the most valuable. They make you take a second look at things you might take for granted, and they may see things you do not."

Togo, who rarely caused a ripple in the smoothness of her routine, hesitated before replying. "There are risks," he finally said.

"Of course there are. I still have the option of playing with vote totals if necessary, don't I?"

"Yes, Madam President."

"These elected positions have very limited power. Let's see what the people do with that. The Syndicate system is based on the assumption that the people cannot be trusted and have to be led like sheep. Is that true? I want to know. Which requires giving them some freedom in this matter, so I can see how they do."

"Yes, Madam President." If Togo still had reservations, he kept them to himself.

THE official certification of winners in elections had been held on Syndicate planets as long as Iceni could remember, elaborate affairs in which the preselected victors were congratulated in their preordained victories and sent forth with lofty calls to serve the people. The fact that those calls were as phony as the rest of the ceremony had always made it necessary to order supervisors to bring in large crowds of workers and their families to applaud when mandatory and otherwise simply act as props in the entire charade.

Iceni could feel the difference this time, and not simply because the event planners had been extraordinarily upset at not knowing who the winners would be well in advance while planning the ceremony. They seemed to take it as a personal insult that their planning would be dependent on who actually got the most votes. She had finally sacked half of the planning supervisors to shut them up, discovering afterward that the efficiency of the process appeared to have improved dramatically.

There hadn't been any need to order in crowds for the occasion this time, either. They were here, they were there in all cities, in numbers and with enthusiasm that was very sobering.

"We've unleashed a monster," Drakon observed. They were standing side by side on the stage from which the victors would be certified, their images being broadcast throughout the star system.

"A very large and demanding monster," Iceni said. "But it was always there. The Syndicate just kept it suppressed. Unless we were willing to act as the Syndicate does, as the snakes do, we had to deal with that energy somehow. I am concerned about keeping it under control, though."

"That may be very difficult," Drakon agreed. "I've done some more exploration of my soldiers' attitudes, and it confirms the suspicions I passed on to you earlier. If I gave them orders to fire on citizens, discipline might crack."

Iceni nodded, smiling toward the crowds as if she and Drakon were engaging in small talk. Their lip movements were blurred by security fields, of course, ensuring that no one could read words off them and know what was really being said. "If your ground forces are no longer reliable, the local ground forces can't be counted on for internal security missions at all."

"I thought that you would be more upset by the news."

Her smile held an edge of self-mockery. "I can be as hypocritical as anyone, but not on this issue. I've known since we took over that the workers and officers on our warships would refuse to participate in bombardments of citizens. They wouldn't even cooperate in a threat to do so. Your soldiers were always our only means of enforcing control of the citizens."

Drakon smiled, too. "We're riding a tiger."

"Exactly. Try not to get thrown."

"You won't throw me." He made it a statement, not a question. "But the tiger might."

"It will if we don't keep it fed by measures like these elections. And they were clean elections," Iceni said. "Mostly. Isn't that a strange thing? We kept our words to the citizens."

"Mostly," Drakon agreed. "They're going to want more, though."

"We'll feed them slowly," Iceni said. "It will be difficult, but I like that. I'm tired of easy solutions."

"Like ordering executions of anyone who gives us trouble?"

"Like that. I'm not a Syndicate CEO anymore." *I can almost believe that when I say it. Almost believe that I never did anything on my climb to the top that can't be forgotten now. But I left victims behind me. We all did.*

The official results were released to the media, appearing everywhere simultaneously. Cheers erupted. Iceni and Drakon waved, generating more cheers, then, after a few minutes, left the stage. "Even the ones who lost were applauding," Iceni commented.

"If they believe the game isn't rigged, they also believe that next time they might win," Drakon pointed out.

"Buy-in. Yes. We need that. It's something the Syndicate never appreciated the need for among citizens even though they obsessed about it among top-rank CEOs." They walked to the two impressive vehicles awaiting them. "Would you ride with me?" Iceni asked.

He gave her a surprised look, then nodded. After passing orders to his own vehicle to follow, Drakon joined her in the spacious back of the Class One VIP Limo. "I've seen a lot of tanks that had less armor than these Class One Limos," he said, sitting down opposite Iceni.

She smiled crookedly and rapped the virtual window next to her. It looked real, exactly as if a broad, clear view of the outside were visible through glass. In fact, it just overlay the same heavy armor as everywhere else on the vehicle. "Have you ever thought of these limos as metaphors for our lives?" Iceni asked. "Outwardly, you see one thing, something that appears transparent in many places. But, inside, things are very different than they appear."

"Your staff and my staff didn't appear to be thrilled at us riding alone together," Drakon replied. "I'm pretty sure that reflected their inner feelings."

She laughed. "They want to protect us. At least, I hope that's their motivation. In an odd way, they control *us*."

"Yeah," Drakon agreed, leaning back against a cushion that molded itself to his back so swiftly and smoothly that it was scarcely noticeable. "They set our schedules, they can filter the information we see, they can make decisions in our names that we might not ever hear about. It worries me when I let myself think about it."

Iceni nodded, then looked sidelong at him. "I wanted to thank you again for not even hesitating on handing *Pele* over to me. There's a fair amount of damage to be fixed, but she'll be operational before *Midway* is. That will go a long way toward making us secure." She blew out an exasperated breath, then leaned toward him. "Damn you, Artur Drakon, tell me the truth. Why aren't you worried about my controlling that amount of firepower relative to yours? Why aren't you worried about me throwing you off the tiger?"

He searched her eyes for a moment, then leaned forward as well, so they were as close as the size of the limo allowed. "Because I know that if you wanted to kill me, Gwen, you would have succeeded in that already."

"How sweet," she said with a laugh. "Maybe I'm just planning on making you into a nice, controllable subordinate."

"Hah! You know that I'll never be anyone's lapdog."

"Then why do you . . . ?" She searched for the right word.

"Why do I trust you?" He laughed this time. "I said it. I trust you, Gwen. You'd stick a knife in me if I betrayed you, and you'd make sure it hit a vital spot. But if I play straight with you, I don't think you'll betray me." Drakon shrugged. "So I guess I'm stupid."

"No." *Don't say it. Don't say it.* "You're a good judge of character.

And I am lucky to have you as a . . . as a . . . partner." *Why did you say it? Fool! You've given him leverage to use against you!*

Oh, shut up! I am so tired of the games and the schemes and the daggers in the night!

Drakon looked back at her with genuine surprise. "Thank you. That probably sounds like a dumb thing to say, but I don't know what someone in my position is supposed to say when someone in your position says something like that."

"Thank you is acceptable." Gwen smiled, the expression vanishing as she suddenly became aware of a strong and alarming urge to lean in farther and kiss Artur Drakon. She sat back quickly, putting distance between them.

"Is something wrong?" Drakon asked.

"No. Nothing. I'm fine." *Talk about something. Anything.* "I've been trying to decide who should command *Pele*. I think I'll transfer Kontos over to her and promote him to full Kapitan."

Drakon sat back as well, plainly disconcerted by her quick changes in attitude and topic. "Umm . . . that's your call. Kontos is unquestionably loyal. He's had a pretty meteoric rise, though. Can he handle being commanding officer of a battle cruiser?"

"Now that they're back, I posed the question to Kommodor Marphissa, and she discussed it with Captain Bradamont. They both think he can if there is sufficient experienced depth in the other officers on the battle cruiser."

"Who ends up with the battleship?"

"I don't know. I'm going through the survivors from the Reserve Flotilla, trying to narrow it down. Did you ever meet Sub-CEO Freo Mercia? She was second-in-command of a battleship in the Reserve Flotilla."

"Not that I recall. Do you know her?"

"In passing," Iceni said. "She impressed me during that brief encounter. If the reports we have from the other survivors of her ship are accurate, she assumed command after the commander of her battleship was incapacitated and did an excellent job of fighting the ship until it was hopeless, then getting as many of her surviving crew off as possible."

"Incapacitated?" Drakon asked.

Iceni twisted her mouth. "Shot by the senior snake on board when he appeared to be wavering in his duties. Freo Mercia then shot the snake, ordered her crew to finish off the rest, and continued the battle with the Alliance until her battleship was too badly damaged to fight."

"She sounds like a very good choice," Drakon agreed.

"You deserve the chance to evaluate her, given the power we're thinking about placing under her control. I'll send her to you for a personal interview. We've been bringing the Reserve Flotilla survivors down to the surface since Kommodor Marphissa escorted the freighters into orbit. I understand that Colonel Rogero made it back to you safely?"

"He and Captain Bradamont," Drakon said. "What do you think about that riot on the freighter?"

"It could be explained by resentment of an Alliance officer," Iceni said slowly, "but . . ."

"Yeah. But. Colonel Rogero recommended careful screening of everyone on those freighters, which you are already doing."

The vehicle slowed to a gentle stop. "Here we are," Iceni said. "You can return to the safety of your staff, and I can reassure mine that I remain intact despite being alone with you."

"Gwen . . ."

"Yes?"

Drakon shook his head. "Nothing."

He left her wondering what he had almost said.

"WHY did she invite us to this?" Morgan asked darkly.

"To emphasize that General Drakon is co-ruler of this star system," Malin replied in his most patronizing voice.

"He's not co-ruler of the mobile forces," Morgan shot back. "Is this supposed to make us think he has any authority over them? A play act to make the General feel appreciated when it doesn't actually mean a damned thing?"

"That's not what President Iceni intends."

"And just how do you *know* what President Iceni intends?" Morgan demanded, her eyes smoldering with suspicion.

Malin gave her back the look of an innocent man trying to understand the charges against him. "I listen. I have sources, and I listen. If you did the same, you would know why President Iceni is rushing the acceptance of this group of former supervisors so they can be sent out to the battle cruiser to help get it fully operational as soon as possible."

"You listen?" Morgan smiled at Malin with such vast insincerity that Drakon almost laughed but caught himself in time. "I listen, too. I hear lots of things. Among them is that some of Iceni's sources in the Syndicate sent a message on that last freighter that passed through this star system. A message saying that another attack by the Syndicate against us is being prepped right now. Do you want to know what I hear about you?"

"If it was anything you had proof of, you would have brought it to the General already," Malin replied coldly.

"Behave yourselves in there," Drakon told them both. "I don't want the President to see my staff acting like a couple of quarreling kids."

"Yes, sir," Morgan replied, her expression perfectly serious. "But he started it." She broke into a sharp laugh.

They entered the moderately sized auditorium selected for the ceremony. President Iceni, trailed by her bodyguard/assistant Togo, was just coming in from another door. In front of them all, three rows of former Syndicate supervisors who had once been executives and sub-CEOs of varying ranks stood at attention in their new uniforms as Leytenants and Kapitan-Leytenants.

Colonel Rogero also awaited them, saluting at the sight of Drakon.

Iceni came to a stop near Rogero. "It is only fitting that the man who played such a large role in the rescue of these personnel from an Alliance prison camp should be present as they join our forces," she said.

Drakon, who had been told by Rogero of his invitation, returned the salute and nodded to Iceni. "The Kommodor couldn't be here?"

"The Kommodor is with her flotilla," Iceni said. "We have reports that another Syndicate attack could come at any time."

"Really?" Drakon looked back at Morgan and Malin to subtly acknowledge the accuracy of their information, catching Morgan looking flatly toward Rogero as if waiting for a single betraying gesture.

As he looked back toward the rows of new officers, Drakon spotted one who seemed barely able to contain her happiness. He recognized her from the reports Rogero had provided. Former Executive Ito. She caught Rogero's eye and smiled very quickly before returning her expression to a militarily correct rigidity.

Iceni gave a speech. Drakon felt his attention wandering, his eyes scanning the new officers, wondering what had led them to choose the risks of fighting for Midway over returning to Syndicate-controlled space. They had all been screened to ensure they would be loyal to him and Iceni, but Drakon had long since learned never to take such things for granted.

As Iceni finished, the new officers saluted her, and chorused "for the people!"

The ranks broke, the officers talking excitedly among themselves. Iceni turned to speak to Togo.

Newly appointed Kapitan-Leytenant Ito strode toward Rogero, openly smiling, then veered toward Drakon. She saluted him proudly. Drakon returned the gesture, aware that Malin had taken a couple of steps closer to him, as if prepared to make some remark.

Ito took another step toward Drakon, still smiling, right hand raised slightly and held out. "General," she began, "may I presume to ask—"

Malin's moves were so fast they blurred. One moment he was standing to the side of Ito and Drakon, the next he had his right hand locked on Ito's right wrist. Malin's left hand grasped his sidearm, the barrel of which was resting on Ito's temple.

CHAPTER EIGHTEEN

NO one moved for several seconds, though Togo seemed to have teleported to a position between Iceni and Malin, one hand concealed under his jacket.

Finally, Iceni spoke, her voice angry. "Another one of your officers has drawn a weapon in my presence, General. What is the meaning of this?"

"Colonel Malin?" Drakon asked, making sure that his voice carried the promise that Malin's explanation had better be a good one.

"She's a snake," Malin said, his own voice as calm as if he were giving a routine briefing. "Check the palm of her right hand. Carefully, without touching it."

Ito's hand twitched, and muscles stood out on her arm as she tried to move it, but Malin's iron grip held the hand motionless.

Iceni gestured to Togo. "Do it."

Togo, betraying no sign of what he felt about Malin's actions, walked forward and scanned Ito's exposed palm with an instrument that appeared in his left hand, then bent slightly to study it closely. "Poison," he announced. "Contact poison, absorbed through the skin."

"How can she have it on her palm?" Rogero demanded, looking shocked.

"There is a very thin protective surface." Togo produced a knife, using the blade to gently pry at the edge of Ito's palm. The knife slid and pulled away, taking what looked like a translucent layer of skin with it. "Whoever she touched with this palm would have died within a short time of sudden, catastrophic heart failure."

Drakon looked at Ito's right hand, held rigidly by Malin so that it still extended toward him. "How did you know?" he asked Malin.

Malin hadn't moved at all, his weapon still rigid against Ito's skull. "I have been tracking snakes for a long time, General, as you ordered me to, with particular emphasis on finding covert snake agents among the ground forces and the mobile forces. Executive Ito came to my attention before the Reserve Flotilla left here because a higher-than-usual number of supervisory personnel on her ship had been pulled in for questioning or outright arrest by the snakes. My investigations determined Ito herself had made some statements criticizing the Syndicate government. However, Ito was never called in by the snakes."

"Bait," Morgan said, her voice dripping with loathing.

Drakon nodded, knowing he was glaring at Ito now, too. Someone who had presented themselves as a sympathetic ear to draw out treasonous statements from others, then turn them in to the snakes.

"Hold on!" Rogero protested. "Colonel Malin, I was told by Sub-CEO Pers Garadun, whose account was backed by others, that Ito shot the senior snake on her ship before he could reach the escape pod leaving it!"

Malin's pistol didn't waver. "Of course she did," he said. "Who would she have been reporting to on that ship? Who could have betrayed her as a snake herself inside the Alliance prison camp? The snake knew what would happen at the hands of the crew unless he had something to trade them that might buy his own life. Ito knew that what he had to offer was her identity. The only way she could be sure of surviving, of hiding what she was, meant killing that snake. So she silenced him, and she made sure that your friend saw it so everybody would believe she hated the snakes even more than they did."

One of the new leytenants took a step forward, his horrified gaze fixed on Ito. "She fingered two other officers in the Alliance prison camp. Ito told us they were covert snakes. They both swore they weren't snakes, but Ito showed us strong evidence. We found them guilty. We . . . we executed them. I can't . . . no. No."

Ito finally found her voice. "I have no idea how that came onto my hand. I've been set up. I—"

"Shut up," Malin advised her casually, emphasizing the words with a little extra pressure on the weapon jammed against her skull. "Colonel Rogero, when the mob attacked Captain Bradamont on the freighter, who was the first supervisor on the scene?"

"Executive Ito," Rogero said, his voice gone flat.

"Closest to the event, the first to get there. The first to see who was still alive. Just as if she had set the leaders of the mob into motion and was standing by to see how well the plan worked. Who interrogated the workers for information about who instigated the mob attack?"

"Executive Ito," Rogero said, looking ill. "She said one of the wounded ones died before he could say anything."

"I don't doubt that," Malin said. "But, Colonel, you know to be suspicious when people who may know something you need to know conveniently die before they can tell you anything."

"Yes, I do." Rogero gazed at Ito with dawning anger. "Garadun told you and Jepsen to tell everyone on the freighters about Kalixa, that the Alliance hadn't committed that atrocity. You told Jepsen not to, that you would do it. But you never would have, would you?"

Ito said nothing.

"You were going to kill General Drakon first," Malin said conversationally to Ito. "At a gathering with many mobile forces personnel and President Iceni. Suspicion would have fallen on the President, wouldn't it? And when you subsequently found a way to murder

President Iceni, it would look like the ground forces had retaliated for the murder of General Drakon. The entire star system would have collapsed into civil war, making the survivors easy pickings for the Syndicate. And you would have been a Hero of the Syndicate. Am I right, Executive Ito?"

"Executive Ito," Iceni said in an icy voice, "seems to have lost her voice."

"We'll see how much she says under interrogation," Drakon said.

"No." Ito's voice had changed, had become as devoid of emotion as her expression now was. The habitual cheerfulness, the camaraderie, were gone, replaced by an awful blankness. "Do you think I want to die the way you'll kill me? Slowly, screaming for mercy from the likes of you? I will not be the last. I will not betray the Syndicate. I'll see you all in hell."

"Togo!" Iceni cried, a dawning awareness in her eyes as she gestured toward Ito. "Stop—!"

Ito stiffened, then went limp, falling lifeless to the floor. Malin let her drop, gazing down at her without feeling.

Togo halted his lunge toward Ito, instead going to one knee next to her and running a scanner over the body. "Dead. I cannot tell what did it."

"A suicide device?" Iceni asked. "But she was screened. The Alliance must have screened her, too, when they took her prisoner."

Malin had slowly knelt on the other side of Ito's body, his eyes on it. "A suicide device that cannot be detected by screens. We need to find out what it was."

"That's not all we need to find out," Morgan said sharply. "General, we need to talk."

Iceni spread her hands slightly. "Feel free." Despite her calm tone, she was almost shaking as she looked at Togo. "I'll make sure the body gets fully autopsied. And I will learn how that woman got through screening that should have spotted what she was. Don't shake anyone's hand, General."

"Don't worry," Drakon said. "I think I'm going to wear gloves for a while."

He led the way out, followed by Morgan, Rogero, and Malin. The now-stunned newly appointed officers stood around silently, doubtless wondering what would happen to them if the usual guilt by association they were used to in the Syndicate system was employed here as well.

Once in a nearby secure room, Morgan spun to face Rogero. "I think someone has some questions to answer."

Drakon held up an admonishing hand. "What questions?"

"Who brought that snake here? Who missed obvious clues as to what she was? Who was so besotted with an Alliance officer that he failed to personally interrogate the workers who took part in the riot on that freighter?"

Rogero's face had darkened, but his voice stayed controlled. "Ito fooled people she lived with for years."

"What about the interrogation, Colonel Rogero?" Morgan demanded.

"To that, I am guilty," Rogero said evenly. "I was too rattled by the attempted killing to focus on my job and improperly delegated something that I should have done myself."

"Was that because Bradamont was the target?" Drakon asked.

"Yes, sir. It was. I let personal considerations distract me from my duty. I will add something that was not discussed out there. After Bradamont left the ship, while we were in jump, Ito attempted to develop an intimate relationship with me."

"Attempted?" Drakon asked. "You turned her down?"

"Yes, sir."

"You got that right, at least. Anything else?"

"No, sir."

"All right. We'll discuss the matter later. Colonel Morgan, was there anything else on your part?"

Stymied by Rogero's blunt admission of failure, Morgan was glowering at him. "General, this kind of failure—"

"Will be further discussed with Colonel Rogero by me—in private."

"Sir, you can't let him get away with this because of his personal relationship—"

"Colonel Morgan, that is all," Drakon said, his voice rising in volume and dropping in pitch. "I don't require my officers to be perfect. I will carefully evaluate the mistakes made by Colonel Rogero and make my own determination as to the proper response, but I will also keep in mind that we are all capable of mistakes."

"Not me, General," Morgan insisted.

"Not you?" Malin's eyes on Morgan were flat and hard. "You might be surprised to learn about some of the mistakes you've made."

"If you know something—" Morgan began furiously, grabbing Malin's wrist much as he had grabbed Ito's earlier.

"That's enough!" Drakon said.

Stricken by the tone of Drakon's voice, Morgan dropped her grasp on Malin, came to stiff attention, and saluted. "Yes, sir. By your leave, sir." Turning, she pulled open the door and stormed out.

"I didn't think she disliked me that much," Rogero said.

"She dislikes everyone," Malin replied. "But this isn't your fault. Colonel Morgan is angry because I caught Ito, not her. She was flat-footed and unprepared when Ito almost killed General Drakon because she was watching you, Colonel Rogero, and me, not Ito."

"Bran," Drakon said with some heat, "I am enormously grateful for your work, but there's no need to bait Morgan about it."

"Anything I said would be considered baiting by her, sir. I guarantee you that she feels enraged at having failed to spot a danger to you before I did. Morgan cannot accept that I succeeded where she did not."

"You'd *both* better keep it professional, understand?" Drakon said, wondering if the rivalry had reached the point where he would have to break up the pair despite their usefulness, and their apparent loyalty, to him.

"It is a shame," Rogero commented in a neutral voice, "that Ito died before she could lead us to the other covert snakes hidden in this star system."

Malin shook his head. "I am beginning to strongly suspect that there are no other covert snakes in this star system."

"No other snakes?" Drakon demanded. "Then who has been behind the attacks, the spying, and the other things we've experienced?"

"I am still trying to learn that, General. And we certainly can't rule out more snakes among the survivors of the Reserve Flotilla. But what I have found is that often the way the things we have experienced have been done is contrary to snake procedures, except when something is done so clumsily it is certain to be detected. And then the snake procedures are followed to the letter."

"By someone who wants us to think they're a snake?" Rogero asked.

"Yes." Malin looked at Drakon. "No, I don't suspect Morgan in all of it. There are probably multiple players in this game, which has confused the tracks no end. For example, I know that Morgan would not target you. Nor have I seen any sign that she is targeting Captain Bradamont. But someone is trying to conduct preattack surveillance on Bradamont, and the last assassination attempt on you was dead serious."

Rogero turned on Malin. "Why haven't I been told?"

"Because I don't have anything that adds up to certainty of another attack or the identity of whoever is behind it," Malin explained. "And, Captain Bradamont is being appropriately careful of her personal safety."

"Yes," Rogero agreed reluctantly. "The mob attack on the freighter drove home to her that even in a supposedly safe environment, she can be in danger."

"Who is targeting me, then?" Drakon asked. "That assassination attempt by those People's Word fanatics had snake fingerprints on it, didn't it?"

"I'm not sure of that, sir," Malin explained. "We were meant to think that, but I have been considering the matter." He walked to one wall, where an illustration of the star system hung, providing both decoration and useful prop. Malin pointed to the image of the planet they were on. "That attack on you, and the subsequent security actions, effectively wiped out The People's Word organization. The leaders were killed or forced to resign, the most fervent believers died in the attack, and most of the members scattered to less radical organizations. The entire agenda of The People's Word was discredited for the citizens by its involvement in the attack on you. If you were a snake, and you wished this star system to be politically destabilized, wouldn't you want something like The People's Word to be strengthened rather than eliminated? To grow stronger and challenge the authority of both you and President Iceni?"

Drakon came up beside Malin, narrowing his eyes as he thought, his gaze on the image of the planet. "That's a really good point. Those People's Word types were already causing some disruption in the planned elections. Getting rid of them benefited me and President Iceni." He looked over at Malin. "Though getting rid of them could have also involved my death. Are you implying that the President was behind that whole thing?"

"No, sir. I am certain she was not," Malin said forcefully. "But that does not rule out someone in her camp."

"Or someone who wants you to think she was behind it," Rogero suggested.

"Or someone who wants her to think you are trying to frame her," Malin added.

Drakon's laugh was no more than a bitter snort. "I get it. We've still got no idea. But if you're concluding that whoever is behind all of this is not a snake, no matter which particular incident we're talking about, then President Iceni needs to be told. I'll do that. Colonel Rogero, you get with Captain Bradamont and make sure she understands that someone is still after her. She might want to know about Ito, too."

"And me, General?" Malin asked.

"Just try to avoid Morgan for a while."

GWEN Iceni offered Drakon a seat before her desk, her hand in the midst of indicating the seat twisting for a moment into a sign whose meaning she hoped he would recognize.

Someone may be listening.

They were in her office, the most secure place under Iceni's personal authority, but some instinct warned her that even here speaking freely could be dangerous. She hadn't felt that way before, but it had been growing on her. Was it justifiable caution or real paranoia?

Drakon sat down, his eyes on her, his first words indicating that he had seen and recognized the hand sign. "I know there are a lot of things we shouldn't talk about," he began in a conversational tone, "because we can't trust anyone."

"No," Iceni agreed. "We can't trust anyone."

"But there are some people I distrust a lot less than others." He looked toward the virtual window behind Iceni's desk, a window currently set to show a beach on the planet, the waves rushing up the sand and back again into the ocean in an endless rhythm. "Didn't that used to show the city?"

"I changed it," Iceni said. "Sometimes I find myself liking things that I never expected to."

He looked back at her, watching Iceni for a moment before speaking again. *If only I could know what you were really thinking, Artur Drakon.*

"I'm here to let you know," Drakon said, "that even though I've been the target of the last two assassination attempts, there are reasons to believe you are also still being targeted."

Instead of any fear, Iceni felt a sense of weariness filling her. "Of course. Does it ever end?"

"Beats the hell out of me. I also don't know who is doing the targeting, but my staff believes that more than one party is involved, with more than one set of goals."

"Interesting." *Malin already passed me that information this morning. I wondered what he would tell Drakon, but I'm no longer surprised that Drakon shared the information with me. I wish I knew exactly why he was doing it.* "Who besides the snakes?"

His hand made a negating sign. "I don't know."

Not snakes? Malin had passed the same conclusion to her. But that had been before Ito had tried to kill Drakon, and Ito had snake all over her. "You once apologized to me for not sharing information. Now I must . . . apologize . . . to you." That word *was* very hard to get out. "My people were supposed to have screened out any threats. Instead, I let an assassin get within reach of you."

How had Togo been so careless? She had grown to count on his ruthless efficiency. She had grown to count on it too much.

But why had Malin said nothing to her about his suspicions regarding Ito? Why make such a public demonstration of Togo's failure and his own effectiveness?

Or perhaps that had been the point of the whole display.

"We need to talk again later," Iceni said. "There are some things I need to check on."

"All right." Drakon stood up. "Gwen . . . stay safe."

"Don't get all sentimental on me, General," she chided him. "You might make me wonder what you're up to."

"I wish the hell I knew."

HE had barely left Iceni's secure office when his comm unit buzzed urgently. Very urgently. "I need to see you in your office right away, General," Morgan said.

"What's it about?"

"A threat to you. A threat right next to you."

"Morgan, this had better be—"

"You wanted evidence. I have it."

He paused. "All right. I'm on my way."

His thoughts on the short trip to his headquarters were a tumbled mess. Did Morgan really have conclusive evidence against Malin? Or had she finally gone too far down a road that had threatened her for a long time? *I wish I knew more about the medical waiver she got after that mission messed her up. It couldn't have been patronage pulling strings for her, so there must have been solid grounds for declaring her stable enough for service. But more than once I've wondered, especially lately.*

Morgan was waiting as he entered his office.

Consumed by thoughts, he hadn't realized that Malin had fallen in behind him, oblivious to events. His first notification of that was when Malin began speaking as the door closed, his tone as normal as if everything was routine. "General, I—"

"I finally found you out!" Morgan yelled. "I know what you are!"

To Drakon's astonishment, Malin's weapon was out in an eyeblink, the barrel leveled at Morgan's head, Malin's face drawn and rigid.

Morgan had been surprised as well, but only for an instant. She had shifted her posture, her lips drawn back in a frightening smile, hands posed for the sort of strikes that had killed before and would surely do so now if she attacked Malin.

"Stand down, both of you!" Drakon shouted.

Malin didn't seem to hear Drakon, his eyes fixed on Morgan, his expression rigid, his weapon aimed directly at her face.

Morgan looked back at Malin, scorn and anger radiating from her, ready to leap into attack.

"Colonel Malin," Drakon said again, this time in a more controlled voice but putting all of his command authority behind it, "lower your weapon. Colonel Morgan, don't attack when Malin drops his weapon, or I swear I'll shoot you myself. Now, both of you follow orders and follow them now or both of you will regret the days you were born."

Malin took a long, deep breath, blinking as if coming out of a daze, and took one step back, the hand holding his sidearm lowering as if it had been forgotten.

Morgan's eyes twitched toward Drakon, judging the ferocity in his gaze. She slowly dropped her hands to her sides and also stepped back.

"If this ever happens again," Drakon said in a voice that didn't sound like his own, "you are both gone from here. Do you understand? Out of this headquarters, off this planet, out of this star system, and out of anywhere within a hundred light-years of here. Is that clear?"

"Yes, sir," Malin said, his voice now calm and composed.

"Yes, General Drakon," Morgan said.

"The Syndicate is preparing another attack on this star system. It could come at any time. We need to be getting ready for that, focused on that, and not on internal rivalries and behavior so out-of-control that I don't know why I'm giving you two a chance. But there will not be another. Now get out of here before I order you both to be arrested, and don't come within a hundred meters of each other for the next two days."

Morgan shook her head. "General, I came here for a reason. A very important reason." She turned a once-more-contemptuous look on Malin. "Colonel Malin has some questions to answer, and once you read this," she added, holding up a data coin, "you'll want to ask them."

"Questions about what?" Drakon asked, not ready to give in at all to Morgan.

"DNA," Morgan said. "Colonel Malin's actual DNA," she continued with the cadence of a judge pronouncing sentence on a condemned prisoner, "which I recently acquired by using a sampler in my hand when I grabbed his wrist, does not match the DNA reference contained in the official service file of Colonel Bran Malin. Does it?" she challenged Malin.

"That's all?" Malin asked. "The DNA doesn't match?"

"That's enough," Morgan snarled. "You're a phony, someone else claiming to be Bran Malin."

Drakon held out his hand. "Give me the coin. Morgan, if you've manufactured false evidence—"

"You can get another DNA sample from him right now, General, and check it against the official record."

Taking the coin that Morgan smugly offered, Drakon looked at Malin. "Bran? Do you have anything to say?"

"Yes, sir. I will answer every question to your satisfaction, but"—he gestured toward Morgan—"I request in the strongest terms that Colonel Morgan not be here when I do."

"Why?"

"You will understand once I have answered your questions, sir."

Morgan spoke up again, shooting her words at Malin. "You have no right to demand any terms, Colonel Malin, or whoever the hell you are."

"Quiet." Drakon stood looking at the two colonels in the total silence that fell after his single word of command. He studied Morgan and Malin, recalling what he had asked of each of them in the past, remembering what they had done for him. What did he owe each of them now? "Colonel Morgan, if your information is on this data coin, then you need not be present when I look at it. Therefore, I will grant Colonel Malin's request. If I am not fully satisfied with his answers, I will be able to bring you in afterward."

Morgan scowled, but bit off whatever she had been planning to say, and instead turned her gaze on Malin. "You can't lie your way out of this one. You wouldn't have had to if you'd had the guts to kill me before I told the General, but you've always been a worm. I know General Drakon can handle you if you try anything, and I know what he'll do to you once he sees that evidence. Have a nice trip to hell."

Malin looked steadily back at Morgan. "I'll keep a place there free for you. A nice warm spot."

Drakon held out his hand again. "Your sidearm, Colonel Malin."

Shifting his grip on the weapon slowly so that he could no longer fire it, Malin offered the sidearm to Drakon.

Drakon placed Malin's sidearm on the desk, close at hand. "You may go, Colonel Morgan. Since Colonel Malin desires privacy, please return to your quarters while I speak with him."

Morgan bared her teeth in a vicious grin and saluted. "Yes, sir."

She left, deliberately turning her back on Malin and walking slowly as if flaunting her vulnerability to him during those moments.

The door sealed again. Malin waited, watching the security lights above the door shift from red to green to indicate that no surveillance devices could penetrate the room, then he faced General Drakon. "You should look at what Colonel Morgan gave you, sir."

Drakon pointed to a chair before his desk. "Sit down." He wasn't being courteous with the command, and Malin knew it. Sitting down would handicap Malin if he tried to attack Drakon or flee, that chair was the focus of more than one concealed weapon, and the chair contained a variety of sensors for determining whether someone was lying or telling the truth as they knew it.

As Malin took his seat, Drakon fed the data coin into his desk unit. Twin images of standardized DNA profiles appeared, one from Colonel Bran Malin's service record and the other from what was identified as a sample from the Bran Malin sitting before Drakon.

A segment of the DNA profiles was highlighted in red. Negative match. "You said you'd answer my questions," Drakon began. "Do you know what this shows?"

"Yes, sir," Malin said.

Drakon frowned at Malin, wondering why Malin sounded relieved. "And that is?"

"The mitochondrial DNA does not match."

Drakon flicked a glance at his screen. "That's right."

"The DNA sample in my official record was falsified." Malin slowly held up one arm, moving with care to avoid any appearance of threatening Drakon. "The DNA on my embedded personal data chip is accurate. Any variation there from my actual DNA would have been spotted long ago."

"You falsified your DNA in your official record? Why?"

Malin sighed, looking unhappy. "I had to. Otherwise, a connection might have been spotted during routine genetic screening using official records."

"A connection? To what?" Had Malin been a spy for the Alliance all this time? Or somehow linked to the enigmas? Or, impossible as it seemed, the snakes?

"Mitochondrial DNA, General," Malin said. "It identifies the mother of any individual."

"You wanted to hide who your mother was?" Drakon shook his head, baffled. "Your mother was a Syndicate medical executive. Even the snakes never claimed there was anything in her record that would bring suspicion on her. She died, what, eight years ago?"

"Yes, sir," Malin said, his voice growing thin with stress. "Medical Executive Flora Malin died eight years ago, of complications from exposure during Syndicate research assignments. She gave birth to me. She raised me. But she was not my biological mother."

"Hell, lots of people have tangled family histories. There was a war on for a century! Why hide who your biological mother was? Was she a snake?"

"No, sir." Malin pointed to Drakon's display. "Run a comparison check on the actual sample, General, the one Colonel Morgan pulled from me. You will find a match for the mitochondrial DNA."

"Your biological mother is on this planet?"

"You can limit the search to headquarters personnel, General." Malin looked as if his face had drained of blood now, but his voice stayed calm.

The sensors in the chair said there was no deception in Malin. Frowning in puzzlement, trying to guess which of the soldiers assigned to his headquarters could possibly be Malin's biological mother, Drakon ran the search.

The answer popped up almost instantly. A perfect match.

Drakon stared at the answer. He could read the words, but the meaning kept slipping away from him. They couldn't possibly be saying what his eyes kept seeing.

Colonel Malin's voice sounded as if it were coming from somewhere very far away. "As I am certain the DNA match confirms, my biological mother is Colonel Roh Morgan."

CHAPTER NINETEEN

"WHEN Morgan said she knew my secret, I thought that meant she had discovered not just the DNA discrepancy, but also our true relationship," Malin explained in that same unnaturally calm voice. "I admit that I did not react properly."

Drakon had been standing up until now, but he abruptly sat down, staring at Malin. "How? You're almost the same age as— That mission."

"Yes, sir," Malin said. Now that the secret was out he spoke quickly. "The mission. When Colonel Morgan was barely eighteen, a line worker in the commandos, she volunteered for a suicide mission aimed at learning more about the enigma race. She and the other volunteers were frozen into survival sleep. Twenty years after the mission began, it was canceled. Only Morgan and one other of the commandos were recovered."

"I knew that," Drakon said. "Though it's easy to forget that Morgan is about twenty years older than her apparent age. Twenty years chronologically, because she didn't age while frozen. But how—?"

"My mother was one of the medical executives assigned to prep the commando volunteers for survival sleep," Malin explained. "While she was prepping Morgan, she discovered that Morgan, barely eighteen years old, was pregnant, so recently that Morgan herself was certainly unaware of the fact."

"A last-minute fling before going off to die," Drakon guessed.

"Most likely, sir. Regulations called for the embryo to be destroyed under those circumstances. Medical Executive Flora Malin was unable to conceive on her own because of physical damage sustained during some of the same research projects that ultimately killed her. Deeply feeling the loss of her husband in the war, she saw the discovery of that embryo as a gift. Instead of destroying it, Flora Malin secretly preserved it and, a little while later, had it implanted. In time, I was born to her." Malin closed his eyes, then opened them to look intently at Drakon. "I didn't know. I hadn't a clue, not until I was about to join the Syndicate forces and leave home. Then my mother confided the truth to me because I needed to know that there would be inconsistencies between my official DNA and who I really was. With her position inside the medical service, Flora Malin had covered that up, but now I would have to do it unless I chose to openly acknowledge my biological mother."

Drakon sat back, not able to speak for a few seconds. "And Morgan had come back."

"Right about that time, yes, sir. That's why the deception was necessary. My mother Flora, as one of those involved in the initial mission, was called in to assist in reviving Morgan." Malin's mouth twisted in a wry smile. "She felt guilty. Guilty about what had been done to Morgan, about having Morgan's child. She did what she could to help Morgan."

The long-standing mystery finally explained itself. "Morgan got cleared for active duty and later for promotion to officer rank even though her psych evals were borderline, and she lacked any known patrons to pull strings for her. Your mother was in the medical service. *She* pulled the strings that got Morgan that medical waiver."

"Yes, sir. Though that would have meant little if you had not subsequently given Morgan a chance despite her psych evals." Malin looked down. "It took a while after I joined the ground forces to find out where Morgan was. I was torn about whether to see her. My mother, Flora, warned me that I might regret doing so, but as she lay dying, she urged me to finally follow my heart. I did so, arranging a transfer to your command, where Morgan was also serving."

A single, sharp, mocking laugh came from Malin. "And so I came to meet my true mother."

"And you found Morgan."

"I found Morgan," Malin agreed.

Drakon eyed Malin as he dredged up memories. "Morgan disliked you from the moment you first met."

"I've wondered if she sensed something even at that first moment," Malin said.

"And before long you returned the dislike."

"She is Morgan, sir."

"And your mother." Drakon's fist hit the desk. "That incident on the orbital platform. You *weren't* trying to kill her. You really were just trying to save Morgan. Trying to save . . ."

"My mother."

Drakon stared at Malin again, more memories coming to life. "You've stayed at this command to protect your mother? All those times . . . Malin, she's *Morgan!*"

"*I know.*" Malin sounded as if someone was choking him.

"And she has no idea?"

"Not consciously, no, sir. I'm certain that at some subconscious level she knows, though."

"I'd say it's pretty damned certain she knows even if she's not consciously aware of it!" Drakon exploded. "Morgan usually goes after people with fiery efficiency, but she *hates* you. Why the hell have you stayed around her? Why do you feel an obligation to protect her?"

Malin looked down, clasping his hands so tightly together that muscles, veins, and bones stood out clearly. "My mother, Flora, is not the only one who feels guilty."

No deception noted, Drakon's equipment advised.

Malin looked up again, relaxing. "And as I got to know you and her better, sir, I felt an obligation to protect you from her."

No deception noted.

"Does the fact that she's your biological mother also play a role? Do you feel an obligation to her because of that?"

This time there was a pause before Malin answered. "Yes, sir. I am aware that it makes no sense, but . . . yes."

No deception noted.

Drakon looked back at Malin, wondering what to do. The offense of fraudulently altering official records was a real one and a serious offense at that. But the reasons Malin had for such deception were understandable. *If my mother were Morgan, that's the least I would have done to hide the relationship.*

Morgan was Malin's mother. It explained some things. Certain similarities that had nagged at Drakon, only to be dismissed as coincidental.

How far had this particular apple named Malin fallen from the tree that was Morgan? Drakon had thought those two worked as checks on each other, but if Malin felt obligations toward Morgan, how far did those obligations go? He had thought he understood the dynamics between Malin and Morgan, but now Drakon wondered. *I wasn't aware of something this huge between them. What else don't I know? Are there other things going on behind the screen of what I used to think was reality between those two?*

Colonel Malin finally cleared his throat to break the lingering silence. "Sir, in respect to protecting you from Morgan, that is why I came to your office. There is something you need to know about her."

Drakon pressed both hands against his face, letting the pressure soothe his racing mind. "I can't wait to hear it, and I'm sure you've got solid evidence. At least I can be sure it's not about her being someone else's mother."

The silence stretched out again until Drakon dropped his hands and glared at Malin. "What is it?"

"You already said it, General." Malin gestured in the direction of Morgan's quarters. "Colonel Roh Morgan has not yet had another child, but I have learned that she is pregnant."

Oh, that's great! Who the hell— Drakon suddenly felt very cold. "Morgan is pregnant."

"Yes, sir." Malin visibly braced himself before speaking again. "You are the father. That is why she seduced you on Taroa."

The memories this time were of Morgan smiling the morning after on Taroa. *"Do you mind telling me what you hoped to accomplish?"* Drakon had demanded.

And Morgan had replied, *"I think it was pretty obvious what I was trying to accomplish last night. And I succeeded."*

He hadn't realized what she meant, hadn't even considered such a possibility. Not from Morgan. "Why?" Drakon finally managed to say.

Malin shrugged, much of his old composure back. "We can safely assume Morgan was not motivated by tender emotions or the desire for motherhood. And for all her . . . uniqueness . . . Morgan can also be exceptionally desirable to men. She could have gotten pregnant by anyone if a child were what she wanted. But she wanted *your* child, General."

Morgan, the mother of his child. The old beliefs said that when you did something that you knew was wrong, you sooner or later paid a heavy price. He had never believed the price could be this high.

Drakon looked at Malin with new understanding. "That's why you were so angry with her, why you actually drew a weapon on her. It wasn't just fear that she had learned your real relationship. You knew she'd gotten pregnant by me. The woman who instinctively rejects you has another child."

"It's not about me," Malin denied. The sensors in his chair wavered in their assessments, finally rendering a measured judgment. *Probably not deceptive.*

Or self-deceptive, Drakon thought.

"She has a use for that child," Malin said. "You know her. Morgan wanted that child, by you, for a reason. I do not know that reason. But—"

"No child of mine is going to be raised by Roh Morgan!" Drakon stood up, breathing heavily, trying to control an urge to dash to Morgan's quarters and—

And what?

"General," Malin said, the urgency in his tone penetrating Drakon's tangled thoughts. "Morgan must not know about me. I do not know how she would react."

Drakon found himself laughing harshly. "Morgan? I think it's safe to say that she wouldn't give you a teary-eyed embrace and coo endearments to her long-lost baby boy. Especially since you're biologically almost a year older than her." He paused, trying to think. "No. I won't tell her. How do you know she won't run a match on that DNA?"

Malin shrugged. "Probably for the same instinctive reason she hates me. Morgan will shy away from running that check because part of her realizes she won't like the answer. But if she does, I have taps in all systems that would notify me of the check, and of who ran it. If I am warned of that . . . I will take steps to protect myself."

"Why didn't you ever tell me this?" Drakon said.

"Sir, do you really need to ask me that?" Malin shook his head. "I was tempted at times, but I could never bring myself to tell you."

No deception noted.

What isn't *Malin telling me? What statements aren't being made because they would show deception? Malin is an expert at beating interrogation systems. That's why he's one of my best interrogators. He knows all the tricks someone else might use.*

Gwen warned me. Watch out for those beneath you. I thought I knew everything important about Morgan and Malin, and the biggest thing of all was a total surprise to me.

But I have to deal with Morgan now. "Colonel Malin, I need to know that I can trust you."

"I will not betray your interests," Malin said.

No deception noted.

But what exactly did that mean?

Drakon tossed Malin's sidearm back to him. "That's all for now. I'm going to see Morgan. It's probably best that you *not* accompany me."

MORGAN, sitting at ease with one arm draped over the back of a chair, smiled as Drakon entered her quarters. "Is he dead?" she asked. "Was it quick or slow?"

Drakon came to a halt just out of reach of her. "Colonel Malin is alive. He offered an adequate explanation of the circumstances."

Morgan froze for a moment, then her expression shifted as she studied Drakon. "You kept him alive for a reason."

"Yes, I did." *Leave it at that and keep Morgan wondering.* "Now there's something you and I have to discuss."

She feigned distress. "Did the little weasel accuse me of something?"

"At what point were you going to inform me that you were pregnant?"

It was rare to see Morgan off-balance, but it only lasted for a fraction of a second. Then she laughed as if genuinely amused. "He found out? The man has more talent than I thought. And, of course, he told you."

"Answer my question, Colonel Morgan."

"Is that any way to talk to the mother of your child?" she teased, then automatically jerked into a defensive posture as Drakon's expression changed. "I would have told you at the right time."

"How long did you think you could hide something like that?"

Morgan smiled. "A very long time." She patted her flat stomach. "There's nothing here to concern you. I had the embryo removed and implanted in a surrogate."

Drakon hesitated, thrown off by her admission. "You think I can't find that surrogate?"

"I think, General," Morgan said with soft menace, "that certain safeguards are in place, and if anyone or anything gets too close to that surrogate, then she and the baby will die." The smile came back. "I covered all of the contingencies. That's what you taught me. If you arrest me, confine me, something might happen. Maybe not. You don't know. Kill me, and something *will* happen. A horrible thing to have on your conscience."

"Why did you want that child?" Drakon demanded.

Morgan looked steadily back at him, her expression admiring now. "You don't get it? Really? But that was always one of your flaws. You don't have many. You're an amazing man and an amazing commander. But you never seem able to realize just who and what you are. You accept limits that you don't need to live with."

"But *you* know what I am?" Drakon asked.

"Oh, yes." Morgan stood up, her eyes bright with emotion. "You showed me, you taught me. I know you, and I know what I am. Know the enemy and know yourself, and you'll always win. That's one of your lessons."

"I didn't originate that. It's ancient advice."

"But you understand it. And you made sure I understood it." Morgan nodded, her smile triumphant. "You taught me many things. The wise commander makes the proper preparations and takes the proper actions to ensure that eventually her goal is achieved."

"And what goal is that?" Drakon said in a voice gone quiet but dangerous.

"*Our* child, General Drakon. A child with your abilities and mine. Able to do anything she turns her mind to, and with the will to choose to do those things." She shook her head, Morgan's smile now that of someone sharing her victory with Drakon. "I owe you so much, and this is how I am repaying you, with a child who combines the best of us both."

"I didn't ask for that," Drakon said. "What do you think this child is going to do? Take over this star system?"

Morgan laughed. "One star system? That's only the start. She will be a leader who will build an empire on the ashes of the Syndicate Worlds. And perhaps an empire whose reach stretches much farther than that. Do you think even Black Jack can withstand our daughter after she has been brought up to fulfill her destiny?"

"Our . . . daughter." Drakon knew he was looking at Morgan with disbelief, but he couldn't seem to react, couldn't do anything but listen.

"She'll be unstoppable," Morgan said in a whisper that filled the room. "Humanity will be united. Under her rule."

The spell finally broke under the pressure of the visions of renewed wide-scale war that Morgan's words evoked, a war worse and more widespread than even the century of the Syndicate/Alliance conflict. "I will have a say in the destiny of any child of mine," Drakon insisted. *Borderline stable? Damn the psychs and damn their useless evaluations. Damn Malin's surrogate mother for arranging that psych waiver out of guilt. Morgan's loyalty to me has gotten mixed up with delusions and dreams of grandeur to create a monster. With my unwitting help.*

"Whatever say you have will be up to me," Morgan said. "She has to be strong. I'll be sure she is."

"I'll find her. No matter what you do."

Morgan paused, her expression very serious now. "What I do? General, you should stop worrying about what I'll do. Everything I do is for you. If you want to worry, don't worry about me, or about the citizens playing at being free, or about the Syndicate launching another attack. Start worrying about what our daughter will do."

Drakon stood looking at her, realizing just how helpless he was at the moment, one thought intruding louder than the rest. *How the hell am I going to tell Gwen Iceni about this? And what is she going to do when she finds out?*